WORKHOUSE GIRL'S CHRISTMAS DREAM

VICTORIAN ROMANCE

ROSIE SWAN

PUREREAD.COM

CONTENTS

Dear reader, get ready for another great story… … 1

Part I
CHRISTMAS STORMS
1. The Curtain Falls … 5
2. Dire Straits … 26
3. The Tyrant … 41
4. Unwanted Visitor … 59
5. Trouble for Sure … 78

Part II
INTO THE ABYSS
6. Endless Desolation … 105
7. Unfit for a Lady … 133
8. Perilous Times … 158
9. No Way Out … 181
10. The Escape Route … 199

Part III
COMING HOME FOR CHRISTMAS
11. Just Reward … 223
12. Is This Home? … 240
13. Taste of Victory … 262
14. Rest for the Weary … 281

Epilogue … 292

Love Victorian Romance? … 303
Our Gift To You … 305

DEAR READER, GET READY FOR ANOTHER GREAT STORY...

A VICTORIAN ROMANCE

A cruel Christmas tragedy.

A soldier saved by the actions of a little girl.

One woman's determined journey from helpless rags to the rich arms of love...

Turn the page and let's begin

PART I
CHRISTMAS STORMS

THE CURTAIN FALLS

C*hristmas Day, Walsall County, England.*

The storm that had been threatening for days reached the mining village of Walsall when least expected. Its violence was particularly felt in the old farmhouse that stood next to the village crossroads early in the morning on Christmas Day. A clap of thunder as loud as a blast from the dynamite used in the coal miles rumbled across the house, shaking its very foundations. A bolt of lightning sliced through the sky and struck a tree out in the yard, which immediately burst into flames. It seemed as if nature itself were sending out an ominous sign to the inhabitants of the old farmhouse that morning.

The flaming tree frightened the little girl whose face was pressed to the window as she watched nature in all her glory. She jumped back and crouched under the window sill like a scared rabbit, her eyes wide and filled with terror. In her whole life she'd never seen something as fascinating or as frightening as lightning striking a tree and causing it to burst into flames. That was the tree that she and her parents liked to sit under in the summer, sipping lemonade and watching as the villagers went past. Once in a while villagers would stop and be offered a glass of lemonade to refresh their thirsty throats. Now there would be no more reposing under the tree, and smoke from the burning tree filled the house, causing the child to choke.

For many years to come, eleven-year-old Amanda Jane Wood would always associate Christmas Day with terrible storms, fire, smoke and fear. First, fear of the terrible storm that was raging outside and then also the dark shadow of death that hovered in the three-roomed farmhouse. She coughed and tried to cover her face but in vain; the smoke was thick in the small living room.

Rain blew into the house through one of the cracked windows, soaking the child as she cowered under the windowsill. She rushed out of the living room and went to find her mother who was in her bedchamber. Mandy knew that when her parents' door was closed she wasn't supposed to open it without knocking first. And even then, she had to wait until she was bid to enter, so she stood there with her small hand raised as she prepared to knock. The storm made it impossible for her to hear whatever was going on and she knocked softly then waited.

Mrs. Edna Wood had just finished giving her husband a bed bath and dressing him in his best clothes as a way of preparing him for what was to come. Husband and wife both knew that this day wasn't going to end happily as most Christmas Days in the past had. That was the reason the twenty-nine-year-old man had held onto his wife's hand for a long while. The storm raged on outside, but in this small cosy room two souls were bidding farewell to each other, even though neither wanted to let go.

"Promise me that you'll always take care of Mandy," he whispered, his voice raspy even as his chest heaved. He was struggling to breathe, and she wished he would reserve his strength because talking was taking its toll on him. His once-ruddy skin was now sallow, and she could see the veins on his scrawny hands. Her once-virile man, the champion of her heart, was now nothing but skin and bones. Her heart was breaking, but she put on a brave smile. "And promise me that you'll also take good care of yourself."

"I promise," her voice was also a whisper as she fought back her tears. She had wept in private for many days, and this wasn't the time to do it openly. She had to be strong even though all she wanted to do was raise her head and scream, and ask why this was happening to her happy family. Why did death have to come to one so young when there were many old people in the village, she asked silently, then repented for her wicked thoughts. God was the giver of life and He chose who to preserve and who to take away. It wasn't up to her to decide because she was just a mere human being. But it hurt to know that this was the last time she was going to be with this man who held her heart.

"And always tell her that I love her so much but I have to leave. It's time for me to go, even though I wish I could stay with her, with you, my darling." And his shaking hand brought her palm to his cracked lips where he placed a soft kiss. His face was lined with the fatigue that comes to one who has been ailing for a while and whose body is giving up the fight. "It was so good with you, Edna," he whispered as he let her hand drop, his own too weak to continue holding it, and he closed his eyes. He opened his eyes briefly and smiled, "If I had to do it again, I would choose you over every other woman in the world. I would love you and be with you; always remember that."

The woman nodded, and when he fell asleep, she gazed at the face of the man she had loved for nearly twelve years, and tears coursed down her cheek. Why was death so cruel? And what would happen to her and Mandy when her beloved was gone?

She wiped her eyes because she didn't want Mandy to see her tears and rose up to go and empty the small basin. That's when she met with Mandy at the door of the bedchamber and the child looked terrified.

"Mandy, what's frightened you like this?" She looked toward the living room which was filled with smoke. "And why is there so much smoke in the house? Have you been burning things again?" Her voice was unusually harsh; then she toned it down. "Mandy you know that I've always told you to be careful with fire."

"Mama, the tree in the yard is burning and then the rain is pouring into the living room," Amanda was shivering but whether from the cold or fear or both wasn't clear. "The lightning struck the tree and it started burning."

"I'll fix the window later," Edna wiped the sweat off her forehead with the corner of her sleeve.

"How is Papa? May I go in and see him now? He promised that he would tell me the Christmas story today, Mama."

Edna gave her daughter a sad smile, "Not now, Mandy," she whispered. "Papa is tired and resting." She was normally a strong woman but taking care of her sick husband for the past one month had taken its toll on her. Slender and of average height, her blue eyes were troubled as they settled on her only child. She didn't want to frighten Mandy, but things weren't looking good for them, and their future was uncertain. She knew that Mr. Wood wasn't going to make it to the evening, and she didn't want to imagine what would happen to them after today. He had been her rock from the moment they had met and she felt like she was falling with no one to hold her.

"Mama today is Christmas Day and Mrs. Fount said we should celebrate it at her house with them. Will we be going there later, and will Papa come with us?" Mandy asked as she followed her mother into the third room of the house which served as both kitchen and Mandy's bedroom. Her mother had partitioned the room with a curtain to separate the child's sleeping area from the side they prepared meals on.

"Indeed it's Christmas Day," Mrs. Wood responded absentmindedly as she stroked the fire in the grate. There was a pot of chicken bones on it from their dinner last evening. She was preparing some broth to feed her husband, even though he'd told her that he wasn't hungry any more.

Mandy looked around the kitchen and frowned slightly, wondering why her mother wasn't preparing the delicious pies that she always did when they were visiting their neighbours. In the past all the families in the village celebrated Christmas together and gathered at the home of anyone who chose to be the host for that particular year. This time it was Mrs. Fount who lived on the west side of them and whose house was much bigger than everyone else's in the village. Her husband was the village constable, and her two daughters Gillian and Alison, who were ten and eight respectively, were Mandy's best friends.

Christmas was always such a fun-filled and happy season, but Mandy had the strange feeling that it wasn't going to be like that this year.

"Ma?" Mandy saw the sadness on her mother's face.

"Yes my love?"

"You haven't baked anything to take to Mrs. Fount's house. Will we not have Christmas this year?"

Mrs. Wood sighed as she turned to her daughter. Now was the time for the truth which couldn't be hidden any longer.

"Mandy, you'll soon be twelve and are growing up, and I don't want to hide anything from you any longer."

Mandy felt fear but looked at her mother with wide eyes, hazel like her father's.

"You know that your father has been very ill this past one month and we were hoping he would get better. Sadly, that hasn't been the case, so all the money we had has been used up in getting him medicines. There's nothing left for me to buy even half a pound of ham to make pies, and we have no flour in the bin," She smiled and pulled Mandy close. "But I promise you that next year things will be better."

"So Papa will get better and then we'll have a good Christmas next year, Ma?"

"Oh Mandy," Edna had prayed for that miracle from the moment her husband had noticed the blood in his sputum when he coughed. That had been two months ago and she had done all she could, using all the traditional remedies she remembered her mother teaching her. From warm milk laced with honey, to boiled roots, there was nothing she hadn't tried. But the cough had only gotten worse and finally they had to accept the truth.

Mandy and her mother held each other for a while listening as the storm began to abate. As the storm died down, a heavy bout of coughing from the bedchamber made her mother immediately release her. She ran out of the kitchen.

Mandy wanted to follow her, but something held her back. She hated seeing her father suffering and especially when he tried to pretend he wasn't in pain. Her mother had told her that she shouldn't tire him by asking too many questions. She also didn't want to go back to the living room which was chilly and full of smoke. Her stomach rumbled with hunger and she wished her mother would serve her some of the broth that was bubbling merrily on the fire.

Mama would take care of things once she was done taking care of Papa, the child thought as she moved behind the curtain to her small cot. She climbed on it and curled up, feeling the warmth from her frayed blanket. Papa had promised to buy her a nice woollen one once he got better and she smiled at the thought.

Mandy never complained even when she went without a lot of the things that Jill and Ally possessed. She always believed that one day her father would buy her everything her heart desired, and so her life was filled with childish contentment.

Jill and Ally had a large bedroom in which they slept but Mandy loved her spot here in the kitchen. She always lay on her small bed and watched her mother cooking, most times falling asleep because of the warmth from the fire and having to be woken up to eat.

Her eyes felt heavy even as she listened to the murmuring voices in the other room. Her parents were probably talking about what to do for Christmas and she smiled as she closed her eyes. The little girl was soon asleep, unaware that life was about to change for them forever.

It was the wailing that roused Mandy from her deep sleep. At first she thought it was part of the dream she'd been having. But then she became aware of footsteps coming and going in the kitchen which had earlier been empty. And she could smell something besides the chicken broth that had been boiling on the fire. Pie and freshly baked bread!

The little girl's stomach growled again and she pushed the curtain aside and got off her narrow cot, wondering if her mother had been fibbing before. A smile broke out on her face as she saw the small kitchen table. It was loaded with many covered dishes emitting delicious aromas. Yes,

Christmas Day was going to be a celebration and it was being held at their house.

"I must be dreaming," the child thought because just before she'd fallen asleep there had been nothing in the kitchen. Yet now the small table was groaning under the weight of all the dishes placed upon it. No one seemed to have noticed her yet so she reached out a hand to pick up a pie from the tray nearest to her bed. Mama wouldn't mind and besides, she was so hungry. She'd just taken the first bite out of the fruit pie when the loud wail came again and the small sweet pastry dropped from her hand to the floor.

"Mama," Mandy cried out, recognizing the wailing voice and rushing out of the kitchen, brushing past neighbours who moved out of the way for her. Her mother was in her bedchamber and Mrs. Fount and Mrs. Wiser another neighbour were seated on the bed on either side of her mother.

Mandy frowned because this room was her parents' private domain and she couldn't recall any time that neighbours had been allowed inside. And yet here they were and she couldn't see any signs of her father who was supposed to be in the bed that her mother and the neighbours were sitting on.

"Ma?" Mandy stood at the doorway, too scared to go into her parents' bedchamber. That her mother was crying and wailing clearly meant that something bad had happened.

The only other time she'd seen her mother this upset was years ago when she was about four and her grandmother and grandfather had died just days apart from each other. And on that day Mandy had seen her father wrapping his arms around her mother and comforting her. But if something bad had happened, where was her father to comfort her mother again?

"Oh, Mandy," her mother caught sight of her and held her arms out. Mandy ran to her mother and fell into her arms. "Oh, Mandy," she repeated, tears clogging her throat.

Mandy suddenly got the feeling that she was never going to see her father again. At eleven years of age the young girl knew about death after losing both sets of grandparents when she was of an age of reasoning. And also, they lived in a mining village where they had one or two funerals a week. Though she was still too young to comprehend the effects of coal mining on the lives of the miners, she knew that people who worked in the mines were always dying; then they were buried and their families mourned.

When her grandparents had died, she and her mother had been comforted by her father. But he wasn't here now, and she'd never once thought that she would be one of those children in the village who lost their fathers. A few of her friends had buried their fathers, but Mandy always thought that such a misfortune was far from her. Now a red cord would be stuck to the front of their door, signifying that the angel of death had visited them, as her father liked to say.

"Papa?" She asked softly and her mother heard her. This had to be a bad dream and she willed herself to wake up.

"Mandy, we have to be strong. Your father has gone and left us," Mrs. Wood broke into sobbing even as her arms tightened around her daughter. "What will I do now without you, Anthony," the woman wailed.

"We're here for you and your daughter," Mrs. Fount put her arms around Mandy and her mother. "My family will help in every way that we can," she made the promise, which Mandy was to remember at a later date.

"Death comes to all of us at one time or other," Mrs. Wiser said, confirming Mandy's fears. Her father was dead and she knew that he would soon be put in a hole in the ground like all the other dead people she'd seen; they would cover him with earth and she would never see him again.

Then Mandy felt something rising within her, from her stomach it moved to her chest then throat and forced its way out of her in a wail that many would later say had sent chills down their backs.

"No," she struggled to get free of her mother's arms. Mrs. Fount's arms dropped but her mother's held fast. She wanted to be set free so she could go and meet her father at the end of the bridge where she liked to wait for him as he returned from the mines which were about two miles from the village. What her childish mind refused to accept was that the coal mines had claimed yet another victim, and this time it was her father. Anthony Wood, loving husband and beloved father was no more.

"Pa is coming back," the child wailed. "Let me alone so I can go and wait for him at the bridge," she struggled to get free but her mother's arms only tightened around her small body.

"Mandy, you have to be strong," Mrs. Wiser said. "Your mama needs you right now. Stop that nonsense at once and accept what has happened. Denying it won't make your father come back."

But the child ignored the woman's harsh rebuke and continued to struggle in her mother's arms. Finally Mrs. Wood's hands were too weak and tired to continue holding the struggling child and she let go. Mandy rushed out of the room, ignoring calls from the neighbours who seemed to be everywhere. Their small house was filled with people, but she brushed them all aside when they tried to reach for her. She raced through the small living room where she saw Mr. Fount, the police constable who also acted as coroner whenever anyone died, and she also saw Reverend Jones, the vicar of their parish along with a few other male neighbours. They were standing around talking, but she didn't wait to hear what they had to say.

"Mandy," another voice called out as she tore out of the house through the front door, noticing the red cord hanging from the door. Her eyes were fixed on the road. It had stopped raining and the sun was even trying to break through the thick clouds. Mandy's focus was on getting to the bridge where she would wait for her father and skip beside him all the way home. Usually he left a little bit of whatever her mother had packed for his lunch and gave it to her as a present for waiting for him.

Come rain or sunshine, the child never missed a day waiting for her father at the bridge, unless she was sick and in bed.

There were few people on the road on account of the heavy storm that had passed. And also, it was early afternoon on Christmas Day and most folks were at home taking long lunches or early dinners. But none of Mandy's friends whose fathers also worked in the mines were outside as usual. That didn't even occur to her as she ran on, even though she soon found herself alone on the road.

Usually all the children of Walsall Village whose fathers worked in the coal mines would race each other to Old Walsall Bridge and play there among the rocks until the men arrived. Then each child would walk or dance back home with their father.

Today, however, it didn't occur to Mandy that the road leading to the bridge was empty. Her grief shrouded her in a world of her own, pushing her back into the past and she didn't even remember that it was Christmas Day and the mines were shut down until after the holidays. All she wanted was her father.

Mandy got to the bridge, crossed it and sat down on one of the many little rocks that someone had once called the waiting station. One or two people passed by, giving her odd looks but the child's eyes were fixed on the path that her father usually took from the mines.

"Not my Pa," Mandy muttered as a man hurried toward the bridge and crossed it to the other side. "Not my Pa," she said of yet another, getting into the game she and her friends usually played as they waited. The game would go on until one of the children spotted his or her father. Thereafter, the lucky child would jump up and shout,

"My Pa is here, no more delays, no more waiting," and the others would giggle and continue with the game until the last man had returned. Sometimes when there was an explosion or a cave in at the mines, the children and their mothers would huddle together at the 'waiting station', each praying that their father and husband wasn't the latest victim to be claimed by the mines.

"Mandy," the soft voice broke through the child's continuous muttering and she looked up to find her mother crossing the bridge.

"Ma," she said, "I've been waiting for my Pa, but he isn't here yet. And I haven't seen the other men returning. Are they still working in the mines?" Mandy's eyes returned to the path leading to the mines.

"Oh Mandy," her mother walked slowly towards her. Mandy noted that she looked very tired and her eyes were red. Mrs. Wood had suffered five miscarriages, and when she'd given up hope of ever having a child, Mandy had been conceived.

It was clear to all that the little girl was the apple of her parents' eyes, but rather than become pampered and spoiled, she had such a sweet nature that everyone in the village liked her. The traders and store owners always had little treats for her whenever her parents sent her to get groceries.

"Mandy, today is Christmas Day and the mines are closed for the holidays," her mother reminded gently. She sat down on the same rock as her daughter and stretched out her shawl to cover them both.

Mandy raised stricken eyes to her mother. "Then where is my Pa?"

"Oh, Mandy," Mrs. Wood pulled her daughter close. "It's so cold out here and I need to get you home where it's warm. Besides, we have visitors and shouldn't leave them alone or they will think that we're being very poor hosts."

"But Pa…"

"Mandy!" Her mother's voice was gentle but firm. "For the past one month your father never went to the mines and you know the reason why, don't you? Remember that you haven't been out here to the bridge in all that time," Mrs. Wood raised her daughter's chin. "Your Pa was very sick and he was hurting terribly. You even saw that sometimes he would cough out blood and then wasn't able to breathe properly. He wanted to stay with us but the pain was too much for him to bear," Mrs. Wood's voice broke on a sob. "He begged me to let him go even when I didn't want to, and told me to tell you that he loves you so much and will be watching over you from heaven."

"But he didn't ask me before he left," Mandy cried out. "Why didn't he ask me? I wouldn't have let him go."

"Mandy, your father didn't want you to be sad so he didn't ask you."

"Ma, but why did he leave us? Didn't he love us anymore?" Mandy began to sob. "Why did he find it so easy to leave us?"

"Mandy, he didn't find it easy to leave us because he held on for as long as he could," Mrs. Wood said. Her husband, like many other miners before him, had suffered from black lung disease, which had only worsened as the days went by. "Your Pa loved us both so much but the pain became unbearable, and I let him rest," Mrs. Wood sobbed. The two held each other close and wept together for a long while.

They sat there at the 'waiting station' until the village lamplighter passed over the bridge, his ladder in his hand, on his way to light the gas streetlights.

"We have to get back home," Mandy heard her mother saying as if from a distance. "It's getting dark and we don't want to be out here until late." She rose to her feet and pulled Mandy up. Mother and daughter walked back home hand in hand, stopping every few steps to receive condolence messages from their neighbours.

And everyone had nice things to say about her father. Mandy heard them praising her father and saying that he was a good man who would be greatly missed. She wanted to shout and tell people not to talk about her father as if he wasn't there. Then she remembered that he was gone and actually wasn't there and fresh tears filled her eyes.

She would miss her Pa so much, and it was true: he'd been a very good man. Young as she was, Mandy understood what love was because she'd seen and experienced it in her home. And her father never stopped telling her and her mother that he loved them with his whole heart. Though they didn't have much, no one in need was ever turned away from their door.

"Even if there's nothing to eat in the house, make sure that everyone who comes to our door gets at least a simple glass of water," were her father's words to her so many times.

Mandy never understood why her father was so generous, sometimes causing her mother to complain that he was too kind. But Mr. Wood would simply laugh, ruffle Mandy's hair and kiss his wife's cheek.

"The Apostle Paul tells us to always open our homes to strangers for who knows, we may one day even welcome an angel into our humble abode," he would say. "And always remember that…"

"Angels are messengers who bring blessings from God to His people," Mandy and her mother would finish his sentence and they would all laugh.

It was because of her father's example that Mandy had learned to share everything she had with her friends. But sometimes they weren't as giving as she was, and she would then get upset and complain to her father.

"Mandy, don't always expect to be repaid for your kindness and generosity," he'd once told her when Jill and Ally refused to share their pastries with her. She had complained to him that her friends were very mean and yet she always shared everything with them. "Just do good, and one day it will find you when you need it most. God always rewards generosity even if it isn't immediately. What you hand out to someone through the front door returns to you through the back door."

Mrs. Wood paused at their small gate and Mandy looked up to see that someone had already lit the lanterns in the house and even placed two on the small porch. Their house was brighter than usual and she could see the red cord hanging on the open door. She wanted to rush up and tear it down.

Their small living room was filled with people and as soon as Mandy and her mother entered the house, the mourners parted to let them through. And that was when Mandy saw her father lying on the bier, covered up to his neck with a white sheet. He looked so peaceful and it was as if his lips were about to burst into a smile like they always did. Her Pa was such a happy man and she couldn't remember ever seeing him sad.

There was silence in the house as everyone watched to see what the child would do. They had seen her running out before and were worried that she wasn't in a very good frame of mind.

Mandy approached the bier, "My Pa looks like he's sleeping," she spoke to no one in particular. Mr. Anthony Wood looked peaceful in death, just as he had in life. "I wish he would open his eyes and wake up," she murmured.

She stood beside the bier for a long time, not feeling afraid of the dead body as was her usual practice. Even when a neighbour died and her parents took her to pay their respects to the family, Mandy would never get close to the bier.

Yet now she drew close without any fear, putting out a hand to touch her father's cold face. "Pa is cold," Mandy said, adjusting the bed sheet. A sob broke out among the mourners but Mandy ignored it. "I wish he was still here with us," she said sadly.

Then she turned to find her mother watching her. So she walked to where she was and put her arms around her.

"Ma, please don't ever go away like Pa and leave me alone."

Mrs. Wood choked up, "Oh, Mandy!"

"Now what will we do without my Pa," the child asked in a soft voice, sounding very lost.

DIRE STRAITS

Mandy stared out of the train coach window, watching as people, animals, trees and buildings seemed to race backward in the opposite direction from which they were travelling. This was by no means her first train journey, and her mother had told her that it wasn't going to be a long one.

In the past, her father had taken her and her mother on the train to London. The journey had taken them a whole night and they had been in a sleeper coach, unlike this one which looked like a moving room filled with hard seats.

"We're going to London to see the Queen," her father had laughingly told her. Of course, they hadn't ever seen the Queen but it had been a very memorable trip for the little girl. And seeing how much she had enjoyed herself even though their quarters were very basic at an out-of-town inn, her father had promised that on her twelfth birthday they would go on another trip to London. But sadly that wasn't ever going to happen.

It had been two months since her father's death and life had become very hard for them. Mandy hadn't understood why almost overnight all her friends seemed to shun her. Well, she no longer went to the bridge with them because she had no father to receive. But she also had no playmates either. Jill and Ally no longer came to their house, and the one time she'd gone over to their house, Mrs. Fount had told her that they weren't at home, even though she had seen them peeping at her through the window of their bedroom.

When she'd gone home disappointed and a little angry, she'd told her mother what had happened. And her mother had cried and told her to stop going to play. So Mandy learned to play alone in the house, avoiding her mother's bedchamber because going there made her think of her father whom she would never see again. She'd seen her mother packing up her father's clothes, weeping and looking so broken but didn't bother asking where she was taking them.

Then a few days later Mandy had watched as her mother sold nearly everything they had of value, retaining only an old wooden trunk in which they stored all their belongings. She had used some of that money to pay rent on the house and also buy food for them.

The first few days after her father's death hadn't been so difficult because their neighbours had brought them food and anything else they needed. But gradually this all came to an end and her mother had to look for other ways of finding food for them to eat.

It was also around that same time that Mandy noticed that the neighbours and especially the women, were acting very cold toward her mother. Mrs. Fount and Mrs. Wiser who had always been her mother's best friends had even stopped coming around to their house. It had puzzled the little girl because she remembered Mrs. Fount saying they would always be there for Mandy and her mother. Much as she'd wanted to ask her mother what was going on and why her friends no longer came to their house or invited them over to theirs, the child had held her peace. Many things easily upset her mother and she had even stopped smiling like she used to before. Their once cheerful and laughter-filled house had become as silent as a graveyard! Mandy sighed as she cast a quick look at her mother, who was leaning back on the stiff wooden bench, her eyes closed as if she were asleep. But Mandy knew that she was awake and didn't want to be disturbed.

"My poor Mama!" the little girl thought. Her mother's once-smooth face was now lined with grooves, making her look so much older than before. Mandy had also noticed that her thick dark hair was greying at the temples.

Then just two days ago, her mother had informed her that they were leaving Walsall Village and moving to Birmingham to a small borough just a few miles from the city itself.

"But why," Mandy had asked tearfully, knowing that she wasn't going to get an answer from her mother, at least not one that would make sense to her. "All my friends are here and I don't want to go."

"Mandy, we're no longer welcome here like it was before when your father was alive," Mrs. Wood had said with tears in her eyes. "Now the neighbours look at us as if we're here to make trouble. Besides, with your father now gone I had to look for work so we can earn our living. I answered an advertisement in the newspaper and found a position in Birmingham. You'll soon make new friends so cheer up. You wouldn't want us to stay here and starve or have no money to pay our rent now, would you?"

Mandy shook her head. She couldn't understand why the neighbours who had promised to help them had now turned their backs on them. But her mother had made up her mind and there was no changing it so they had to leave.

No one escorted them to the station to see them off and Mandy thought that it was because they were taking the early morning train. It was dark when Old Farmer Giles had come with his cart to take them to the station. Their luggage was comprised only of the wooden trunk and a small carpet bag. At the station, the elderly man had looked at them with so much pity in his eyes. "Folks are wicked," he'd whispered, shaking his head. "May God go with you," and tipping his old straw hat at them, he'd gotten back on his cart and driven away, not once looking back.

"We're nearly there," Mandy heard her mother saying, and she was glad that the journey was almost coming to an end. Though the coach wasn't crowded because it was Sunday and this was the early morning train, it was filled with the smell of tobacco and stale beer. One or two drunkards lay on the uncomfortable benches, snoring as if they didn't have a care in the world. Two women sat behind Mandy and her mother. They were talking and laughing loudly and one kept tossing peanuts into her mouth. Her chewing was loud and Mandy wanted to point out to her that it was bad manners and lack of etiquette to speak when one's mouth was full of food. That's what her Pa had taught her. And she nearly did but caught her mother's eye.

So she turned her face back to the window and then pressed her face to the glass. She wanted to ask her mother if this was another London for she could see very many buildings, some tall and with smoke pouring from large chimneys. But the journey had been too short for them to have reached London.

"Birmingham Station next," a portly man shouted from one end of the coach.

"We're here now," Mrs. Wood waited for the train to come to a complete stop before she stood, taking the carpetbag from the overhead carrier in one hand and Mandy's hand in the other.

Once their trunk was offloaded with other luggage from the caboose, the two of them watched as the train chugged its way out of the station, headed for towns beyond Birmingham. Mandy heard her mother sigh, a sad sound that caused her heart to ache for her remaining parent. She knew that her mother missed her father very much because she'd heard her weeping in her bedchamber almost every night. And sometimes she would wake up in the middle of the night only to find her mother walking around the house as if she was unable to sleep.

Death, the child thought, was a really terrible thing and she prayed that it would stay far away from them for many years to come.

A porter hurried over to them with a baggage cart and stopped in front of their trunk. "Ma'am, do you need that carried for you?"

"Yes, please," Mrs. Wood said. "If you would be so kind as to show me where I can get transport to Weatherly Estate, I would be most grateful." Mandy was surprised when the porter seemed taken aback at her mother's words. His face creased in a frown. "Is there a problem," her mother asked.

"Are you sure that's where you want to go, Ma'am?"

"Yes," her mother's tone was firm, exchanging a swift look with Mandy. "I'm taking up a position on the Weatherly Estate as the new cook and housekeeper," she said. "Mr. Weatherly himself sent for me, so if you would be so kind, I'd be most obliged."

"Good luck to you then," the man said under his breath but they both heard him. He loaded the trunk onto the cart. "Little lady," he smiled at Mandy, "Would you like to ride on the cart with the trunk?"

"Ma, please may I?" Mandy asked excitedly.

"Sure, go ahead," Mrs. Wood hoisted her daughter onto the trunk told her to hold fast so she wouldn't fall and then followed the porter out of the station. Being early morning, there didn't seem to be many carts for hire around. The porter told them that most cart drivers first go to church on Sunday before coming to meet the train that arrived at nine. But he found them an old cart, helped the driver to load their trunk onto it and Mandy noticed that, unlike many others, this one was being pulled by an ox and not a horse.

There were a few bales of hay on the back and Mandy bounced on them, her curious eyes taking in everything around her. Her mother sat at the front with the driver. They travelled for about two miles on a puddle-riddled road. From time to time, the ox would meander and cause the cart's wheels to hit one of the puddles, causing Mandy to jump. She laughed, finding it all a game.

Finally the driver stopped before a large cast iron gate. Mandy peered over the cart to catch sight of her new home. She saw a large house in the distance, about fifty yards or so from the gate. The child was stunned into disbelief.

"Is this our new home, Mama?" Mandy stared with horror at the ugly-looking house. She saw the disappointment on her mother's face.

"This is it, Ma'am," the cart driver said. "Mr. Weatherly lives here by himself though it wasn't always this way." The man shook his head. "This used to be one of the most beautiful houses in this county, but as you can see…" he shook his head again.

The Weatherly Manor, Mandy noted, was a two-storeyed frame house with a balcony running all around the upstairs part of the house. Even from this distance Mandy could see someone standing on the balcony. It was a man, and he was looking at them.

Untrimmed shrubs and a tall hedge obscured the ground floor from their sight but Mandy was sure it looked as dismal as the upstairs. Some of the windows looked broken and had boards nailed to them while the roof also looked like it was falling apart. Paint was peeling from the walls of the part of the house that she could see. Never had she seen such a terrible house. Even their old farmhouse back in Walsall had always looked so pretty because Pa would paint it twice a year.

"Ma, I'm scared," Mandy shivered, feeling the man's fixed gaze. What kind of a person lived in a house that looked like it shouldn't even be standing? "Will we be living in that house with that man?"

"No," her mother laughed, "Mr. Weatherly said there is a cottage for our use on the estate. He'll show it to us."

Mandy could see that her mother was trying to be brave though she looked shaken at the state of the house and its environs. Even the fence was overgrown and Mandy thought she saw something scurrying in the undergrowth.

"Please could you take us up to the manor," Mandy heard her mother asking the cart driver. "I can't carry this trunk down the driveway alone and Mandy is too small to help."

"Mr. Weatherly never opens this gate and he doesn't take too kindly to folks setting foot in his compound. So this is as far as I can go, I'm sorry about that," he finished when he saw their crestfallen faces.

"Please Sir, I can't carry this trunk alone and besides, Mr. Weatherly surely won't be annoyed if you take us up to the house because I'm going to be working for him."

But the cart driver refused to move forward. "Go and ask the man for his permission first. If he says I can open the gate and drive my cart through to the house then I'll do so very willingly."

Mandy saw her mother's swift nod. "Stay here with this kind gentleman," she was told, "And I'll be back as soon as I can."

Mandy and the cart driver watched as her mother slipped through a small gate on the side of the larger one. She waved at them as she started down the driveway and then for a brief moment she went out of sight as the hedge obscured her from sight. Mandy wanted to jump down and rush in to find her mother, but then she appeared again.

The man was still standing on the balcony. As soon as her mother got close, he began to make gestures with his hands and then it seemed as if the tossed something down at her. Mrs. Wood bent down and picked it up then started walking back towards the gate.

"What was all that about," the cart driver asked Mrs. Wood as soon as she returned.

"Mr. Weatherly says to use the path on the other side of the fence," she pointed and the driver bent forward to see better. "He says the path is usable and we shouldn't open the gate because shutting it is a problem and I can see why." Mandy noticed that small plants had grown in the cracked surface around the gate. Yes, opening it would require strength and much effort, and she doubted that her mother or even the cart driver could do it.

"Where are we going?" the cart driver asked.

"To the cottage at the edge of the woods. Mr. Weatherly says it's at the end of the fence which was torn down."

"Well, that's better than going through those gates," the cart driver shuddered. He had to tug hard at the reins because his ox was busy feeding on the overgrowth. The path was narrow, and as he drove the ox down it toward the place where the fence ended, Mandy tried to peep through the thick shrubs to see if she could spot anything. Apart from brief glimpses of the ugly house, all she saw were trees and more shrubs.

They seemed to have been driving forever when they eventually got to a small clearing, and there the fence ended. Mandy looked back and saw the house in the distance, nearly a quarter mile away. There was a little cottage at the edge of the woods. It looked so forlorn, as if it was about to fall over since it leaned on one side. And there was a smaller sod building a few feet away from the cottage, which she guessed to be the outhouse.

As Mandy glanced at their new home, a flutter of apprehension ran up her spine. The cottage looked haunted.

"Is this where you and this little one will be staying?" The cart driver's tone conveyed his shock.

"This seems to be the only cottage at the edge of the fence and next to the woods," Mrs. Wood said, trying to look excited but failing miserably. She couldn't believe that she'd been enticed by promises of fitting and comfortable quarters, only to find a dilapidated cottage waiting for them.

"Ma, I'm scared."

"My love, remember what your Pa used to say," Mrs. Wood turned to Mandy. "That God is always there to protect us when we call on Him. Think about one of the Bible verses Pa used to read to us, one that tells us that we should never be afraid because God is watching over us."

Mandy sniffled and wiped her nose with the edge of her cardigan sleeve. She scrunched her little face then smiled. "God is our refuge and strength," she said triumphantly.

"That's my girl. Yes, God is a very present help in time of trouble. We shall not fear anything, so smile for your mother."

Mandy beamed at her mother and they got down from the cart.

"You're either very brave or mad, or very stupid," the cart driver brought down their trunk and dumped it close to the door. The cottage had only one entrance. "My wife would have my neck if she knew that I brought you to this terrible place and didn't check to see if the cottage is safe or not. If you need a place to stay there's a small room on our farm, which isn't too far from here," the man held out his hand. "This hut isn't fit for people to live in, and even animals will run away if offered such accommodation."

Mandy saw her mother place a coin in the man's palm and he chuckled, pocketing the money.

"Thank you for the money but I was asking for the key. Though there isn't much I can do for you under the circumstances, I can at least make sure that there are no harmful creatures lurking inside the house and waiting to attack you. If you can look around for some dry twigs I can at least start a fire inside to warm the place up."

"Thank you," there was a catch in Mrs. Wood's voice. She cleared her throat. "You're very kind."

"Stay out here with the little one until I'm sure that it's safe for you to enter the house, if one can be so brave as to call it such."

As the man was walking inside the house, Mandy bent to pick up a few twigs which, though wet from the morning dew, were nevertheless dry enough to light a fire with. She wondered where the man would get matches from.

It took the man a few minutes to make sure that the two-roomed cottage was safe enough for Mandy and her mother to enter. Then he reached into his pocket and produced a box of lucifers, then gathered the twigs Mandy had collected and lit a fire in the small grate. Once the fire was blazing away, he allowed Mandy and her mother to enter the cottage.

Surprisingly, the inside was dry, and the window, which the cart driver had opened, seemed to be strong, as was the door. There was an old chair which stood on three legs and a rickety table at the centre of the room.

"There's even a metal bed inside the second room," the man said, "But like this chair and table, it might not support both of you. And it doesn't have a mattress. But don't worry, I'll return tomorrow to repair the furniture for you and maybe bring you a few more bits and pieces to make this place seem like home. For now, you'll have to make do with sleeping on hay until I can bring you a mattress also."

"That won't be necessary," Mandy heard her mother saying. "We're used to making do with the little that we have. Mandy and I will be all right."

"Be that as it may, we're good folks out here in this county, and even if you don't want anything for your own comfort, at least think about the child." And the man went out and brought in two bales of hay from his cart. "Those should do for now though they won't last long."

Mandy waited for the cart driver, who finally told them that his name was Stiles, to leave; then she turned to her mother.

"Ma, Mr. Stiles is a kind man and generous too, for saying he will bring us some things."

"Mandy there are many things you need to learn in life and one of those is that accepting free gifts from people can lead to all kinds of trouble."

"But Ma, Papa used to give people things all the time, and they never paid him. He always said that we should give without expecting anything in return. Maybe that's what Mr. Stiles is doing."

Mrs. Wood's lips tightened. "One day when you're older you'll understand."

Mandy didn't take her mother's words seriously because she felt that, like her father had once told her, the goodness they had showed others was now being repaid because they needed it.

THE TYRANT

❄

Twenty-one-year-old Cecil Miller crawled on his belly, then straightened up and darted behind a tree. His heart thundered in his ears as he heard his pursuers searching for him.

He was exhausted and had realized that he was on dangerous ground the moment he'd confronted his adversary. The man who his grandfather had trusted and left to run his estate had turned around after the old man's death, deceived Cecil's mother and robbed the young man of his inheritance.

And Cecil had no idea where his mother was or if she was even still alive. He'd returned home expecting a warm welcome, only to find that things had changed in the four years he'd been away serving his country overseas as a soldier.

This had been his home from when he was three years old, and his mother brought him here. His father, a sailor, had passed away at sea when the merchant ship he sailed on sank off the coast of Africa as they were returning home from the Far East. Cecil could barely remember his father because the man was always gone from home, so he didn't miss him in his years of growing up because his grandfather had always been there for him. He couldn't even remember what the man looked like and his mother had no paintings to show him. Sometimes Cecil felt as if his father had never even existed.

Sadly, Roger Miller had never been accepted by his father-in-law, who'd considered him nothing but a gold digger and quite beneath his only child and daughter. Grandpa Sinclair had given them a home and Cecil had always believed that he would live here forever. But now he was on the run and the home no longer belonged to him.

Cecil knew that, if his pursuers caught up with him, they wouldn't hesitate to finish the work they'd started. Mr. Weatherly had made it clear that he was to be beaten up until he could no longer walk. Cecil had received quite a beating at the hands of the two goons who worked for his supposed stepfather. He'd just managed to escape because of his youth and agility and the men were both plump, clearly from imbibing too much on alcohol and feasting on rich foods. Cecil also thanked the strict exercise regime he and his fellow officers in the army were exposed to. With many reforms being done in the British Army, ensuring that all soldiers were fit for service was one of the top priorities.

Cecil realized that so far he'd outwitted his pursuers because he was a very fast runner. But his whole body, and especially his left side, ached terribly. He suspected that the men had bruised, if not broken a couple of his ribs. He wasn't going to go down without a fight, so he pushed himself away from the tree and stumbled through the thick woods, trying to put as much distance as he could between him and his enemies. If he could only find his way back to the main highway, he was sure he would be safe. The men wouldn't dare attack him in the sight of so many people.

Cecil took a painful breath and looked around him to see if he could get his bearings. Then he smiled because he recognized a few landmarks like an old oak tree that had been struck by lightning three times. When he was a small boy he used to spend hours playing in these woods even though his mother would try to stop him. His grandfather, mindful of all his tenants on the estate and the employees at the manor had ensured that there were many usable paths through the woods.

"You never know when you may require to make a hasty exit either while escaping from foes or even any other danger. The paths must always be cleared and ready to be used."

But as he went deeper into the woods, it became clear to Cecil that in the four years since his grandfather's death and his own absence from the estate, so much had fallen to ruin. Decay had started with the manor itself, then moved to the stables, which were now empty, whereas once they had held over twenty prize horses, and then the tenants' houses. Even the sawmill that had been his grandfather's pride and joy was shut up, and the wooden buildings were falling apart. The lumber yard was empty, and it looked like no one had worked there for ages.

"Oh, Grandpa!" the young man paused to wipe the sweat off his brow. His clothes weren't intended for such strenuous endeavours. Dressed in a suit and a new shirt to impress his mother, he'd nearly lost his coat and wallet to the goons. Thankfully the coat had deep inner pockets and he felt to see if his wallet was still on his person. It was, and he breathed a sigh of relief. All his wages for the past few months were in his wallet, and he needed the money if he was to return to safety. "Grandpa, it's a good thing you're not here to see what devastation has been wrought by those you entrusted with your life's work. The estate is in ruins, and Mama is missing."

Cecil's great grandfather had expanded this estate with money from the sawmill that he'd built. This land had thousands of trees and the timber business had been lucrative. The Sinclair Sawmill had been well managed and run by his grandfather who, having no sons, had always told Cecil that he was his heir. Being too young to understand much of the business dealings that went on at the sawmill and even on the estate itself, Cecil would just laugh. To safeguard his grandson's inheritance, Grandpa Sinclair had employed Mr. Weatherly to run things. And under Grandpa Sinclair's keen and watchful eye, things had been smooth and the tenants had prospered. But that was no longer the case.

Right now all Cecil could see around him was destruction and despair. It was clear that after his grandfather's death the manager had mismanaged and squandered everything and even let the estate and all buildings on it fall into disrepair. From what Cecil had seen of the manor that had once been his grandmother's pride and joy, all the precious sculptures, paintings and furnishings she had so lovingly collected over the years were gone, no doubt sold off by the usurper now occupying the manor.

Not only was Cecil disappointed in his legacy but as he stumbled through the thick shrubbery he felt deep apprehension especially when he thought about his mother. Had loneliness and despair driven her into the arms of one who would end up destroying her? If she wasn't dead, then where was she right now? That wicked man had laughed in Cecil's face when he insisted on being told where his mother was.

"She's in a place that keeps her away from causing any more trouble in this world," were the words thrown at him in mocking tones. "You should never have come here, boy," the man had said scornfully. "Because your own temper and foolishness will lead to your destruction. And as you know, since you're educated, no man can ever be faulted for defending himself and his property

from any intruders. You're an intruder in my home and I feel threatened and frightened," said the man who looked anything but fearful. And that was when the two men in Mr. Weatherly's employ had set upon Cecil and beaten him to within an inch of his life.

Darkness seemed to suddenly come over him and he stopped moving. His chest felt like it was on fire and about to explode. He could feel consciousness slipping away from him but he forged on. At least he could no longer hear his pursuers and prayed that they had given up pursuit. They looked like lazy sloths and he hoped they would return to tell their master that they had accomplished the task given to them.

And not for the first time, Cecil thanked the Lord that the hounds his grandfather had kept on the estate were no more. Or else his pursuers would have caught up with him hours ago. He'd led them a merry dance around the woods he knew very well. He ought to have known that Mr. Weatherly wasn't a good person when even the cats in the manor never went anywhere near him. His grandfather used to say that one could tell the character of a man by the way animals responded to him. Right now there were no cats at the manor, probably having run away to other homes or into the wilds.

The large dogs were gone too. Those eight dogs had been his grandfather's pride and joy and especially during hunting season. Cecil remembered joining the hunters in the summer when he turned seventeen and before he'd left to join the army. For the first time, against his mother's wishes, his grandfather had gifted him with his own rifle and two pistols.

"I don't want my son learning how to kill anything," his mother had protested on his birthday as he was rejoicing over his gifts.

"Rachel, will you stop trying to mollycoddle the lad," his grandfather had scolded her. "Cecil is no longer a little boy to be tied to your aprons and hidden under them. He's a fine young man, and just so you know, I've already purchased a commission for him in the army. He's going in as a Lieutenant so, my dear daughter, your son killing rabbits and foxes will soon be the least of your worries. In a few months' time Cecil will be hunting down Britain's enemies and killing them off."

"No," his mother had cried out in horror. "Papa, you can't do that to my son. He's all I've got. I won't allow my son to become a bloodthirsty soldier and murder people."

"Stop being such a hypocrite, Rachel, and a selfish woman. You sleep safely and soundly in your bed, knowing that Britain is not at war with anyone. And you know that the reason for that safety is because someone's son is out there serving this country as a soldier and keeping our borders and waters safe. It's time for this young man to take his place alongside others like him and keep this great country safe. I served with pride and, when my time was up, I returned home and built this estate after your grandfather. Your grandfather and his father before him all served this great nation as soldiers in the Royal British Army or sailors in Her Majesty's Royal Navy. For as long as the Sinclair *name stands, there will always be a soldier or a sailor in the family."*

"But Cecil is not a Sinclair," she protested.

"More's the pity, but he's my heir and so he's a Sinclair by association if you want to put it that way."

Cecil wanted to please his grandfather but he could see that joining the army would break his mother's heart. So he decided that he wasn't going to take up the army commission. But then Grandpa Sinclair had suddenly died, and just weeks later his mother had announced that she was getting married again. And to the estate manager, no less! That's what had pushed Cecil into honouring his grandfather's wishes. He'd left home just two weeks after his mother's wedding to Mr. Weatherly, and stayed away for four years.

"Oh, Ma!" he fell to his knees, too tired and in pain to go much further. He crawled under a thicket and lay on his back, tears running down the sides of his face. "Lord, if this is it for me please let my death be swift and painless," he prayed as he closed his eyes and let the darkness overcome him.

❄

"I don't like it when you go deep into the woods to play," Mandy's mother told her. "There are all sorts of dangers lurking in the woods."

"Ma," the girl gave her mother a patient look. "You know that I don't just go out there to play but also to gather firewood. Sometimes I even bring back berries and even a fowl or hare for our dinner."

"That's what I'm afraid of, Mandy. You steal from the traps laid by people you don't know. What if one day one of those people catches you and harms you? It would break my heart if I lost you or something even worse happened."

Mandy knew that her mother was right to be scared, but she was very careful. It had taken her a while before she started stealing from people's traps. She'd studied those who hunted in the woods, hiding in the thickets to watch them for hours as they went about their business. Luckily none of them had dogs that might have spotted her, because it was clear they were poachers and not there to hunt legally.

But she didn't want her mother to become so fearful that she had to lock her up inside the cottage as she went to work at the manor. She hadn't started off being left alone by her mother to her own devices like it was now. In the first week they'd arrived, Mandy had accompanied her mother to the manor when she reported for work.

Mrs. Wood had found out that she was the only servant working at the manor, the others being long gone. And she was expected to clean all the six bedchambers upstairs and the two that were on the ground floor, the two parlours and large living room that looked like a ballroom to Mandy. During their one and only visit to London her father had taken them to Windsor Castle because his distant relative was one of the footmen there. That rare favour had been granted because the Queen and her family weren't in residence then. Mandy's eyes had glowed when she saw one of the ballrooms, and her father had told her that balls were frequently held there.

"If you work hard in your studies, who knows, you may one day become a lady-in-waiting and dance in these very halls," her father had said. *"Or a governess and teach the queen's or other noblemen's children."*

Seeing the large living room in Weatherly Manor had reminded her of the ballroom in London.

The moment Mandy had set eyes on her mother's employer she'd disliked him on sight. He had beady and shifty eyes and never quite looked at anyone. Mandy recalled her father telling her that only those with something to hide never looked at people right in the eye.

And the manor was dark in spite of the many windows because many of them were boarded up with timber sheets. Mr. Weatherly, her mother told her, also didn't like sunlight, and so the few windows with glass had thick drapes over them, which were never opened.

For the first two days, Mandy had helped her mother since Mr. Weatherly had left for somewhere. But then on the third day she'd had a run-in with the scary Mr.

Weatherly. It happened when she was cleaning the smaller parlour, which seemed to be the man's favourite room for repose. It had shelves full of books that Mandy longed to read, but she was forbidden by her mother from touching them, and the fire was never supposed to go out in the parlour.

Mr. Weatherly had come in with some woman as she was wiping the floor and hadn't immediately spotted her because she was crouched behind one of the large couches and stayed silent.

She could hear the woman giggling from time to time and wondered what they were doing. Mandy would have stayed hidden the whole day if need be but for a mouse that chose to run over her leg. Mandy screamed and jumped out of her hiding place, startling Mr. Weatherly and his companion.

"What are you doing in here, you insolent child?" He screamed at her, shielding his companion from her view but Mandy had already seen her. Mandy knew that Mrs. Burns was the wife of one of the tenants on the estate because she'd met the woman and her husband just the previous day, and it was odd for her to be here alone with Mr. Weatherly. "Little girl, I asked you what you're doing in this room."

"Nothing," Mandy cast her eyes down, trembling from head to toe. She was shaking from her ordeal with the mouse and also at being caught.

"Why were you hiding behind the couch if you're doing nothing here?" Mr. Weatherly approached her and she shrank back, making sure the couch was between them. "Are you here to spy on me so you can go and gossip with the other good-for-nothing people on the estate, or are you here to steal from me?"

"What's going on here," Mrs. Wood walked into the parlour and Mandy was never happier to see her mother. "I heard raised voices," she nodded at Mrs. Burns who turned pale.

"This child was lurking about and looks very suspicious. She must be the child of one of those tenants and has come here to spy on me and also to steal from the house. I'll have her whipped as a deterrent to other vagabonds like her."

"No, Mr. Weatherly, this is my daughter, Amanda. And she's not here to spy or steal but has been helping me with my duties in the manor."

Mr. Weatherly turned angrily to Mrs. Wood. "If you feel that the work here is too much for you, then you should leave at once. I didn't hire you so you can also bring all sorts of vagabonds into my house. I caught this girl hiding behind the couch. You call hiding behind a couch helping you clean?" He glared at mother and daughter, who were both shaking. "I don't ever want to see this vagrant in my house again, or I'll whip her sound and send for the police constable. And if you want to retain your position, you'll do as I say; is that clear?"

"Yes, Mr. Weatherly. I'm sorry, Sir, and it won't happen again."

And that was the last time Mandy had set foot in the manor. So now she stayed in the cottage when her mother went to work. Or else she went to sit with some of the elderly tenants. They usually nodded off to sleep after a short while, and she got so easily bored. When she was bored, she then ventured into the woods to play.

For some reason she wasn't afraid of being alone out in the woods. Back in Walsall she and her friends used to play in the woods a lot. Her father had told her that most animals only attacked when hungry or startled. So she was always careful not to startle any animals in the undergrowth. And she always carried a large stick to tap at any shrubs to make sure its residents left.

"Mandy, promise me that you won't go into the woods. If you feel like you don't want to be alone then go and sit with Mrs. Shaw, and when I finish my duties, I'll come by to get you."

"I'll play at the door," the child said, not wanting to lie to her mother. But Mrs. Shaw liked to ask too many questions that made Mandy uncomfortable, so she avoided the woman. She also knew that one of the traps laid by the poachers had probably caught something. They never came on Wednesdays so it was her day to reap where they had sowed. She had a desire for some hare meat after eating the scanty and tasteless leftovers her mother had brought back from the manor for days now. And Mrs. Wood had to hide whatever she carried under her garments so Mr. Weatherly wouldn't see them even if it was waste to be thrown away.

"All right then, I'm going up to the manor. If you won't go to sit with Mrs. Shaw, then stay inside the house and lock the door and don't open it for anyone unless it's me."

"Yes, Mama," Mandy walked her mother to the door. Mrs. Wood bent down and kissed her daughter on the forehead.

"Be a good girl and I'll bring back some pie for you, because today is the day that I bake."

Mandy merely smiled and nodded even though she knew that the chances of any pie trickling down to her were next to none. She knew that her mother was very unhappy working for Mr. Weatherly because he was so stingy, but since they had nowhere else to go, she had to persevere.

When they first came here, Mandy had wandered around the estate in search of other children to play with but found none. There were very few tenants left on the estate, and these were all very old according to the girl. Their children were all grown up and gone away in search of better work.

And in her wanderings around the estate she'd once eavesdropped in on two elderly women, getting curious when she heard her mother's name mentioned.

"Poor Mrs. Wood, she has no idea of the kind of man that Mr. Weatherly is," one of the women said.

"I know that he overworks her and then underpays her grossly. The last cook and housekeeper left because of that. And do you know that the stingy man has his pantry in his bedchamber?"

The two women laughed, "I thought Mrs. Andrews was exaggerating when she told us the story; so it's true?"

The second woman nodded. "That is so he can be sure that no food is left over for the servant to carry home."

"What a mean and miserly man," the first woman had said. "I miss Mr. Sinclair and how kind and generous he was to all of us. He would give us gifts for Christmas and treated us with dignity even while collecting rents from us. The man was a saint, making sure that no one lacked anything. Sadly, after his death, all the young people moved off the estate and to the cities or other estates, leaving us old people who can barely work. And the man still demands high rents from us. Where are we supposed to get the money when the land has refused to yield its best for us? We barely grow enough for ourselves, how then does the man want us to keep supporting the manor when he doesn't even provide us with seed like Mr. Sinclair used to?"

"I always dread the times he comes around because he's always sure to evict someone for non-payment of rent. Now our men have become poachers so they can sell the animals so we can eat."

"What kind of life is this? If we were still young, I would urge my husband to leave this forsaken place."

And now even as Mandy sat outside on the small bench her mother had erected a few days ago, she wondered, like those two elderly women, what kind of life this one would be for them. It was clear Mr. Weatherly gave her mother very little money even though she worked very hard.

While her father had been alive, he'd promised that she would be very well educated because the world was changing. Women were now doing more than just being wives and bringing children up. Mandy had always thought that she would be a teacher one day.

Her father had paid Miss Lander, who was Gillian and Alison Fount's governess to tutor Mandy too. Being an eager learner, and also because she wanted her father to be proud of her, Mandy had studied diligently and excelled, surpassing all her peers. She could read and write very well because Miss Lander had been a good teacher, and she missed her. Her desire had been to one day go to one of the girls' boarding schools that had recently come into being and her father had promised that he would make it happen for her. His dream for her was that she would succeed and get a good education, ending up as a very qualified teacher.

But with his death and their moving to this isolated estate it seemed as if she would never accomplish any of her dreams.

The child played alone for a while until boredom got the better of her. She locked the door securely and hid the key under a rock like her mother had taught her to do. She would go to the woods and check on one or two traps then return. Her mother would never know that she'd not stayed at home. But even if her mother found her gone, she hoped to return with some eggs or a small animal or fowl to appease her parent. Even though Mama would always scold her for going out into the woods, she always enjoyed the meat or fowl that Mandy prepared after raiding the traps.

Picking up a stick as she always did, Mandy set out for the woods. It comforted her to have the stick with her even though she hoped to never use it as a weapon to defend herself.

"Thy rod and Thy staff, they comfort me," she recited the verse from the twenty-third Psalm which had been one of her father's favourite Bible verses. Then she giggled as she held up her own 'staff' waving it in the air. This was just a small stick, not a shepherd's rod that was big and heavy. But it was hers, and she felt safe carrying it.

One of the traps yielded a guinea fowl and she wrung its neck quickly like she'd seen her mother doing to chickens. Once she had wrapped it up in leaves, she tucked her prize under her armpit and started for home, using a different route. She wasn't very far from the cottage when something stopped her cold. She heard what sounded like a groan and it was coming from under one of the thick shrubs. Heart pounding, she held her package more securely and then used her stick to tap on the leaves.

"Go away so we don't have to fight," she said as she usually did when she didn't want to meet any animals. But the groan came again and she decided to part the leaves. The little girl was shocked to find that it was a man lying under the bushes. He was on his back and his eyes were closed.

UNWANTED VISITOR

❄

"Mister," Mandy prodded the man's hand with her stick. He moved his hand and she thought with relief that at least he wasn't dead. But she could see the blood on his clothes and his face. There were deep cuts on his face and one on his temple was still bleeding. "Mister," Mandy prodded again. "Are you awake?"

A groan was the only response she got and she drew closer, seeing that the man posed no immediate danger to her. In her innocence Mandy didn't stop to think about what would happen if the man turned out to be dangerous. All she could remember was the story from the Bible that her father had once read to her about the Good Samaritan. She couldn't very well leave this man out here now that she'd found him. What if he died or an animal attacked him as he lay unconscious?

"Mister," she said impatiently, "If you want me to help you, then you have to open your eyes. Please open your eyes so I can bring you home and help you."

Cecil heard the soft voice as if coming from a long way off. He pried his eyes open with difficulty and looked into the most startling hazel eyes that he'd ever seen. Honesty, innocence, curiosity and a little wariness were what he saw in the child's eyes and smiled. Then he closed his eyes again, feeling very tired.

"No, you can't do that," Mandy shook the man's shoulder. "Wake up so I can take you home. I'm too small to carry you all by myself so Mister, open your eyes and stand up."

"I have heard you. Little Girl," Cecil murmured. "All right, I'm standing up," and he groaned as he rolled to his side then to his stomach. Getting on his knees, he crawled from under the shrub then lay flat on his stomach again across the path, feeling too weak to do anything else. He couldn't believe that of all people on earth, it had to be a child that had rescued him. Where had this little girl come from?

"Mister…"

"I know I have to get up so you can help me home, but please give me a moment to catch my breath," he gasped.

"Your head is still bleeding and I don't want you to die," Mandy's lower lip trembled. "Please Mister, try to get up so I can bring you home and wash your wounds. Mama has some salve which will make you feel better. She always puts it on my wounds whenever I get hurt. Wake up now."

Cecil smiled as he listened to the little girl. Someone had brought up this child very well. She seemed like a determined little thing, and he didn't want to disappoint her. So, he forced himself back to his knees, then rose to his feet, swaying like one who had imbibed too freely in the fruit of the vine.

"Lean on me," the little girl said, moving close to his left side. Her hand accidentally brushed against his ribs and he hissed in pain. "Your stomach is hurt," she looked like she was about to cry. "I'm sorry."

"Child, it's not your fault but those who set upon me."

"Come then," Mandy moved to his other side. "Are you also hurt on this side?" He shook his head. "Lean on me."

"If I should lean on you then we'll both end up on the ground and you'll be hurt. Besides, I can see that in your hands you have dinner. We don't want that to be ruined now, do we?"

Mandy scoffed at him, "I'm stronger than you think. When my Pa was sick and Ma wasn't at home, I used to help him to get up and about. Lean on me, I'm strong and can hold you."

With her package under her right armpit, Mandy supported Cecil with her left. And much to his surprise the child was able to support him, though he tried not to lean too much of his weight on her. After all, she was a child and came up to just slightly above his waist.

"Here, hold my stick and use it too," Mandy let him have the stick. They walked in silence for a short while and came to a clearing where he saw a cottage.

"What's your name, for I can't continue calling you little girl?" he asked as they stepped into the small clearing.

"Amanda, but Mama calls me Mandy. Papa used to also."

"And is this where you live?" Cecil looked at the cottage in dismay. It looked like it was about to topple over. Were he stronger he might have offered to do some repairs but he felt as weak as a little baby.

"Uh huh!" She nodded, sounding breathless. She led him to the small bench on the side of the cottage. "Sit on this bench for a little while but be careful not to lean too hard on it. Mama isn't the best of carpenters, and she was the one who fashioned it. The cart driver, Mr. Stiles, who brought us here from the railway station wanted to come by and help, but Mama wouldn't let him. If my Pa were here, he would have made a better and stronger bench. Sit," she ordered, and Cecil was glad to get off his feet. He pulled his coat around him, patted it to feel for his wallet and found it intact. No one had robbed him while he lay unconscious under the bushes, though he didn't know how long he'd been there.

"What day is today?" He asked.

"It's Wednesday, and I know that because Mama told me, and she bakes pies today."

As he watched Mandy reach under a rock for the key, he remembered that this cottage used to belong to an eccentric old woman in his grandfather's day. Everyone feared her and said she was a witch. But for some reason, Cecil never felt threatened by her, and he liked visiting her whenever he got tired of being in the manor. She used to bake the best ginger bread and did it over the stones in her grate. He had also discovered that his grandfather would visit the old woman from time to time and drink chicken broth with her. He'd let her live in this cottage rent free. But the summer he turned seventeen, the woman died and was buried somewhere in the woods. Yet this cottage still stood.

"Where is your Pa?" He asked Mandy when she placed her package at his feet, opened the door and entered inside. He waited for her to return and answer his question.

Mandy emerged with hot water in a pitcher and a small bowl. She looked really sad as she crouched close to him and unwrapped the package. That's when he saw that it was a dead guinea fowl.

"My Pa died, and then we had to come here because Mama came to work for Mr. Weatherly," the scowl on her face told Cecil that she didn't like the man. "He's a mean old bat," Mandy blurted out then covered her mouth with her small hand. "I'm sorry for saying that. Pa told me that only unkind people say mean things about other people."

Cecil wanted to agree with the child that indeed Mr. Weatherly was a mean old bat but she looked distressed at her words.

"So, you live here with your Mama, and she works at the big house?"

"Yes." As Cecil watched, Mandy put the fowl into the small bowl and then poured the hot water over it. She quickly removed the feathers. "I have to do this quickly and prepare it; otherwise, it will go bad and then we can't eat it," she told him. "When I'm done I'll bring you some water to drink and then bathe your bruises and put salve on them."

Cecil chuckled softly, wondering how a small girl could do so much. Mandy was a really precious child and he lauded her parents for her good upbringing. She was small and yet behaved like an adult. "Mandy, how old are you?"

"Eleven years old," she said proudly then her face fell once again. "If my Pa was here he would have taken me to school next year when I turn twelve. Pa told me that he would take me to London to see the Queen on my twelfth birthday. But now that he's dead I won't go." Cecil watched in fascination as the child gutted the fowl and made short work of it. Once it was cleaned up, she rose to her feet and took it inside the house, returning after a while with a pitcher of water and a metal tumbler.

"Mama got these from Mr. Weatherly when he wanted to throw them away," she pointed at the utensils with her chin. Cecil recognized the utensils as having belonged to his grandmother. Mandy handed the tumbler to Cecil and poured out water with a trembling hand. "I would have given you some milk but we don't have any. Are you hungry? Ma left some bread for me to eat for lunch and the fowl will take a while to cook."

Cecil was starving but he wasn't about to deprive this little girl of her lunch. From what he could see, Mandy and her mother were really poor for he couldn't imagine anyone with means living in such a place or even working for Mr. Weatherly.

While his grandfather was alive this cottage had been well maintained as were all the other tenants' houses. No one had ever complained of a leaking roof, broken window or unhinged door. Grandpa Sinclair believed in taking care of his people, and he'd done well.

As soon as Cecil had arrived on the estate this morning and before he'd gone to the manor to confront Mr. Weatherly, he'd sneaked around the place just to see what state it was in. He'd nearly wept at the condition of the tenants' and workers' houses.

The fields which once used to droop with all manner of produce all year round except in the months when it snowed now lay bare and looked like a wilderness. Spring was midway but he could see that no planting had been done. In fact, the ground looked like it hadn't been tilled for years. He couldn't believe that his mother and Mr. Weatherly had left things to deteriorate and that was the question he'd wanted to ask them. But then his mother hadn't been at the manor and even now he didn't know if he would ever see her again.

"Drink your water," the little voice broke through his thoughts, "and after I've washed your wounds, I'll give you some bread to eat, then show you where you can lie down and rest. I'll cook the fowl, and when it's ready, I will wake you up to eat."

"I hope your Mama won't be too upset when she comes home and finds me in your house."

Mandy gave him a brief smile but lowered her eyes so he couldn't see the expression in them. She knew her mother would be very upset, but she didn't want the man to know. "Don't worry about my Mama, just drink your water," she said.

❄

Mandy was actually worried about what her mother would say when she came back home. Mr. Miller, as he'd told her his name after she served him a good portion of the cooked fowl and broth, was fast asleep in the corner of their living room. She'd taken one of the hay mattresses off their bed and laid it down for him, covering it with an old curtain. Then she'd covered him with one of the three quilts they had. She hoped he wouldn't get cold, and to prevent that she made sure the fire was burning hot and the room was warm. She had to use up a lot of firewood but she would get some more in the days to come.

Mandy walked softly to where Mr. Miller was asleep and looked down at him as he slept. She sighed, wondering where he'd come from and who had hurt him. He had the nicest green eyes, full of kindness like her Pa's had been. Who was he and why had he been so badly beaten up? Or maybe he'd tried to rob someone and got caught. Then she shook her head, Mr. Miller didn't look like a thief. He was badly hurt, and when he'd thought she wasn't looking at him, he'd winced from time to time, favouring his left side. His face was swollen and one eye nearly shut on account of the bruising from the blows he'd received, and his lip was split. Some blood was dried on it and Mandy felt sorry for him.

While it wasn't easy for her to trust a stranger, she felt that Mr. Miller was a kind man because of his eyes. Hadn't Pa once said that a person's eyes usually showed what was in their heart? Mr. Miller reminded her in some way of her father. He was tall and his green eyes showed kindness. His hair was thick and dark and really long, past his neck. It needed to be trimmed, and she wished she knew how to do it for then she would use her mother's little scissors and cut his hair for him because he couldn't do it alone. Mama had sometimes let her trim her father's hair, telling her she needed to learn in case she had to do it someday.

Mandy sighed again and walked away from the sleeping man. She didn't want him to suddenly wake up and find her standing over him, for he would think she meant him harm.

Where had this man come from and why had someone decided to beat him up so badly? If she hadn't found him, he might have died.

From the way he'd quickly devoured the bread and later the fowl and broth, it was clear that he'd been very hungry. Mandy hoped her mother would bring enough food for them. She'd left half of the fowl for their dinner. But even if Ma brought just a little food, they would make do with whatever they had. Hadn't Pa taught them to share whatever they had with those who needed it, no matter how little it was? Mr. Miller was too thin, the child thought. Someone ought to feed him well.

❄

It was getting dark, and Mandy was playing outside close to the door when she heard her mother's footsteps. The small lamp was lit and on the table. Mr. Miller was asleep and she didn't want to disturb him because he looked very tired. She stood up when her mother got closer and saw the anxious look on her face.

"Mandy are you all right? Why are you still playing outside and it's getting dark? Did you light the lamp?"

"Ma," Mandy hesitated, not knowing how to break the news that they had a visitor to her mother.

"What is it Mandy?" Mrs. Wood was carrying something in her hand. "Here," she handed the small package to Mandy. "For some reason I couldn't understand, Mr. Weatherly himself gave me some flour, sugar and oil. He also let me take all the pies that were left after his dinner."

Mandy took the package from her mother, then stood in the doorway as if to prevent her from entering the house. "Mandy, what's going on? Why don't you want me to enter the house? Did you burn or break something?" Then she laughed. "We don't have anything of value that would be missed." She placed her hands on Mandy's shoulders and gently but firmly moved her aside, opened the door and came to a complete stop.

"Who are you?" Cecil heard the fear in the woman's voice. He'd woken up just as Mandy's mother had arrived and listened as they spoke outside. The sleep had done him much good, even though his side was still very sore. From the look of things, he'd slept for more than six hours.

"Sir, I asked you who you are and what you're doing in my house," Mrs. Wood pulled Mandy close to her and stood close to the door as if ready to flee should Cecil make any sudden move.

"Ma, this is Mr. Cecil Miller, and he's my friend. I found him in the woods…"

"Mandy," her mother's voice was harsh. "I thought I told you not to go into the woods again, and you promised. But you went anyway and brought a stranger back with you. Do you even know who he is?"

Cecil cleared his throat, and two sets of eyes, one blue and one hazel turned to him. "Ma'am, I mean no harm and will leave right away because I don't want to distress you." Cecil struggled to get to his feet. His head felt light and he fought the darkness that threatened to overcome him again.

"No," Mandy pulled away from her mother and went to stand at the door. "Ma, tell Mr. Miller that he can't leave. Can't you see that he's badly injured and can't even stand up," for Cecil had fallen weakly back onto his temporary bed.

"Mandy," both her mother and Cecil called out together.

"No," she repeated, facing them. "Ma, tell him not to go. Stop him from leaving because he's still very weak."

"Mandy you shouldn't have brought this man to our house without asking me first."

"You weren't here and he looked like he was about to die. Also, remember what my Pa used to say," Mandy cast a glance toward Cecil and made an impatient sound, for he was once again trying to get on his feet. She hurried over to where he was, "Mr. Miller, sit down before you topple over." She pointed at one of the three chairs in the room, for Mr. Stiles had brought them two as he'd promised, and repaired the three-legged one so it was now complete. He'd also repaired their table and brought more hay in sacks. He had wanted to continue helping but her mother had firmly refused.

"Maybe Mr. Miller doesn't feel very comfortable here with us," her mother said.

Mandy shook her head, "Ma, Pa used to tell us to help everyone who needed our help. Are we not Christians? Do you remember the story that Jesus told his disciples about the man who was wounded on his way to Jericho? A priest and another man passed by and refused to help but the Good Samaritan stopped and helped him. Ma, we ought to be like the Good Samaritan and not the priest nor the Lev…" She grinned.

"Levite," Cecil offered, grinning back.

"But…" her mother started then stopped and sighed.

"Mandy," Cecil could see the fear on her mother's face and wished he had the strength to rise up and walk out of this house. He knew that if he tried hard enough he would succeed but he also acknowledged that he wouldn't get very far. And what if his pursuers were waiting for him to appear so they could cause him more harm?

Then an unpleasant thought came into his mind. What if they discovered that he was staying in this small cottage with this family? His presence might put Mandy and her mother in danger, and that wasn't something he wanted on his conscience. The last thing he wanted was to jeopardize the safety of these two innocent people. Were he stronger, then he could defend them should anyone attack, but in his current state, he would only create further trouble. He was still very weak, and his left side hurt terribly. At least the bruises on his face weren't so painful because Mandy had put salve on them, though it had stung at first.

Mandy knew that her mother didn't want Mr. Miller in their house. She heard her sigh, "Well all right then, Mr. Miller can stay, but only for a day or two. And I want him to stay out of sight so no one will see him. We don't want any trouble."

"Thank you, Ma'am, and I promise I won't be any trouble to you at all."

A smile broke out on Mandy's face. "Ma, Mr. Miller is really hungry. I brought back a fowl from the woods and cooked it. We shared the bread you left for me but I heard his stomach growling…"

"Mandy!" Mrs. Wood cast an apologetic look at Cecil. "I'm sorry but this one sometimes forgets herself and speaks without thinking."

"But she's a very kind girl and also mature beyond her years," Cecil said in a soft voice. "She knew what to do when she brought me here. You have a wonderful little girl and have brought her up well."

Cecil saw the slight puffing of the mother's chest and smiled inwardly. Every good mother likes hearing good things being said about their offspring. But whatever Cecil was saying was completely true. Very few eleven-year-old girls would have behaved in the way Mandy had. She was very responsible and he prayed that she would grow up into a good woman and not get ruined along the way.

"Thank you for saying that," Mrs. Wood was saying.

"It's only the truth that I speak."

"Ma," Mandy broke in, "thank you for letting Mr. Miller stay with us."

"But remember it's only for a day or two, and also don't let him go wandering about because we don't want any trouble."

"Yes, Ma."

※

The next three days were happy ones for Mandy because she wasn't lonely. Mr. Miller slept a lot during the day but during those times that he was awake, he told her stories about the army.

"If I was a boy I would join the army," she told him. "And then I would fight all the bad people in the world like the ones who hurt you."

"You're a good soul, dear Mandy, and may that never change about you."

"I don't like seeing you suffering," she bit her lower lip. "When my Pa was sick I used to hear him moaning in pain. He was coughing a lot of blood, and sometimes he couldn't even breathe. Ma said he was suffering so much, so she had allowed him to die. I was really angry with Ma for allowing Pa to die."

Cecil felt compassion well up within him. "My grandmother was also sick one day and she was also in a lot of pain. My grandpa also allowed her to die because she was really suffering, and he cried so much when she died. When a person is in a lot of pain we have to let them go."

"And what happened to your grandpa?"

"He died four years ago."

"Do you have a mother and a father?"

Cecil smiled at the child's curiosity and gave her the basic story. "My father died when I was a child, about three years old." He didn't know what to say about his mother because at this moment he had no idea if she was alive or dead.

"Do you miss him? I miss my Pa very much, and Mama is always crying when she thinks I'm sleeping. I wish he hadn't died and gone to heaven but Reverend Jones said he is happier up there than down here with us," she shook her head. "When I get children I will never leave them because I won't be happier up there and leave them here to be all sad."

"Mandy, life is so complicated."

"What does that mean?"

"It means that things are not always as easy as we think. Your father never wanted to leave you but the illness took him away. But you're a strong girl, and you need to take care of your mother always."

"Mr. Miller?"

"Yes?"

"Will you stay with us forever and never leave us again? You can take care of us the way my Pa used to."

"Mandy, you know that I can't stay here with you. But let's not talk about that," he touched the wound on his neck which had started bleeding again.

"Your neck is bleeding again," she said, rising to her feet and going into the inner room. She returned with a small white handkerchief which she held out to him. "Put this over the wound and press a little to make the bleeding stop."

"You're a little Florence Nightingale," Cecil said with a smile, receiving the piece of cloth. He noticed that it had some writing on it, and when he peered closely realised that it was Amanda's name. "Thank you for this handkerchief, it's very pretty."

"What is a Nightingale? Is it a bird?"

He threw back his head and laughed but was careful not to be loud. Someone might be passing outside the cottage and hear him and imagine all sorts of things. He didn't want to ruin Mrs. Wood's reputation. "Florence Nightingale is a great woman who helped a lot of injured soldiers during the Crimean War."

Mandy gave Cecil a blank look. "Was she a soldier like you?"

He shook his head, "No, she was a nurse, and because of her, many soldiers got better and didn't die. Maybe you can become a nurse when you grow up? Miss Nightingale started a nursing school and who knows, you might just become one of her students."

But Mandy shook her head, "I want to be a teacher so I can teach people how to read and write. Pa said if I study hard, then one day I might go and teach the queen's children."

"Teaching is also a very noble profession," Cecil agreed.

"Will you stay with us and teach me every day?"

"Mandy, you know that I can't stay. Let's not talk about that," Cecil said because he was feeling very raw inside. He'd never felt this comfortable since his grandfather died and he joined the army. "I have to leave as soon as I get stronger."

TROUBLE FOR SURE

❄

"Mandy," Cecil called softly to the child whose head was bowed over the table. "Please look at me."

"No," her voice was muffled.

"You know that I can't continue to stay here with you and your mother. As it is, I've been here long enough."

"But why?" Mandy's face was drenched with tears. She'd been crying silently ever since Cecil had pronounced himself well enough to leave that morning. She had spent the whole day looking very dull and Cecil felt terrible but he had other obligations.

"You know those men who hurt me," his voice was gentle and Mandy nodded. "They might find out that I'm staying here with you and then they'll come and harm you and your mother. Do you want that to happen?"

"But you could stay here and protect us," Mandy argued. She didn't understand why Mr. Miller had to leave so soon. Maybe her mother had said something unkind to make him want to go. "Ma, tell Mr. Miller that he should stay."

Cecil sighed; leaving was proving to be so much harder than he'd expected. The time to leave this small family had come, but he felt very reluctant to do so. Nevertheless, he knew that for their own safety and his, he had to leave. And also, he needed to return to his barracks, for he'd been away for more days than expected. But thankfully he still had a few furlough days left. The worst thing that could happen to a soldier was to be away from his barracks and be termed a deserter, whether by choice or not. He just wished that his heart wasn't so heavy.

"Mandy, I have another place where I should be," he looked to the child's mother for help but she merely shrugged. There was a curious look in her eyes and he decided to answer the unasked question. "I'm a soldier as I told you before and my furlough days are almost over. If I don't return, then I will be accused of deserting my post and could get into a lot of trouble."

"But will you ever come back to see us?" Mandy wiped her face and Cecil was glad he'd told her the truth. She was a very intelligent girl and it was clear that she understood that he had responsibilities and obligations to fulfil. But her question was a difficult one, and much as he didn't want to lie to her, he also didn't want to seem insensitive and hurt her. Cecil knew that he might never even return to this place.

Still, he had unfinished business with Mr. Weatherly up at the manor. The next time he came to this estate he'd be well prepared to deal with the man who had taken away his inheritance. He still didn't know where his mother was but that was something he would deal with when he returned to the barracks in Chelsea.

Cecil was sure that some of his colleagues knew of investigators who could help him find his mother's whereabouts. His mission was twofold; the first was to find his mother whether alive or dead. He wanted to know what Mr. Weatherly had done to her, and secondly he wanted to bring the man down and completely destroy him for what he'd done to them. And once the man had been dealt with he could then reclaim his inheritance.

"Mr. Miller?"

"Mandy, that's a very difficult question to ask Mr. Miller," her mother cut in. "As a soldier Mr. Miller might even be sent overseas and so might not be back in England for years."

"But he might die," Mandy rose to her feet and rushed to Cecil, throwing herself into his arms. He was seated on the strongest chair and held her on his lap as she wept on his shoulder. "I don't want you to die," she sobbed. "First Pa died and left me and now you're going away and I might never see you again."

"Mandy," Cecil felt a lump in his throat. "I'll make sure that I don't ever get killed and that's my promise to you."

"Please don't make such a promise to my daughter because no one knows the future," Mrs. Wood pleaded. "Mandy will be all right because she knows that life has to go on."

Cecil nodded, Mrs. Wood was right. He had no idea what the future held, and it wasn't right for him to make any promises to this child.

"Let me put it this way then," he said. "If for any reason I should ever get the chance of coming back here, I promise that I'll do so," he smiled at Mrs. Wood and was glad to note that Mandy was calming down. "I'll never forget your kindness to me and how you opened your home to me even when you didn't have to. You shared the little food and other resources you could barely spare, with me. I can't repay your kindness but God will reward you in His own way."

"Thank you," Mrs. Wood said.

"What will you give me so I know that you'll return one day? I gave you a handkerchief, and make sure you don't lose it. I embroidered my name on it even though it was so hard to do so." Mandy got off Cecil's lap and stood before him, hands clasped behind her back.

"Mandy!" Her mother's shocked tones made her take a step back.

"It's all right," Cecil laughed softly. "I don't have anything…"

"That ring," Mandy pointed at the ring on Cecil's small right finger "Leave me that ring and I promise to keep it safe for you until you return."

"Mandy, come here at once," her mother's voice brooked no nonsense. Mandy gave Cecil a sad smile and walked over to her mother. "Don't you know that it's bad manners to demand for gifts from people? Do you want Mr. Miller to think that you're a greedy little girl?" Mandy shook her head, her face turning red.

"It was my grandmother's ring which my Grandpa gave her on the day they got married," Cecil's voice was filled with much regret. On her death bed six years ago, his grandmother had made him promise that he would only give the ring to the woman who held his heart.

"I'm really sorry Mr. Miller, I don't know what's come over this one. She didn't mean to demand for a gift. Mandy, can you immediately apologize to Mr. Miller for behaving so badly?"

"I'm sorry, Sir," the girl said in a small voice.

"Think nothing of it."

Dinner that evening was a very quiet affair, and after brief prayers, Mandy and her mother retired to their bedroom, leaving Cecil still seated on the chair. His heart was really heavy and he knew that he would miss Mandy and her mother very much. This was the first time in four years that he had felt at home. It was like part of his heart was being ripped out of him and that surprised him.

Mandy tossed and turned for most of the night, glad that she had her own bed even if it was a tiny cot that Mr. Stiles had brought. She didn't have to disturb her mother with her restlessness. Her mother needed much rest because it was clear Mr. Weatherly was overworking her. If only they had somewhere else to go, the child thought.

Mr. Miller had been with them for four days and it was very clear that her mother hadn't been too pleased about the whole matter. Each day when she returned from the manor, Mrs. Wood would ask Mr. Miller if he was well enough to leave. It was as though she really wanted him gone.

Mandy was really surprised at the way her mother had been almost hostile to Mr. Miller. In the past, she'd always known her mother to be a very kind and welcoming person even when things were really hard for them. However, with Mr. Miller things were different, which troubled Mandy greatly. But because she was just a child and didn't understand what was happening with her mother, Mandy kept silent.

She eventually drifted off to sleep and it was still very dark when she suddenly woke up. It was pitch black in the small bedroom, a frightening darkness, and she could hear her mother's soft breathing indicating that she was fast asleep. Mandy was glad that she hadn't been disturbed because she really needed her rest. At least today she wasn't weeping into her pillow like she usually did. Exhaustion must have taken her over, and now she was dead to the world.

But something had woken her up, and Mandy felt as if there was someone standing at the foot of her bed. It wasn't an ominous presence, but it was still unnerving. She wanted to call out to her mother but was too scared to do so. So she pulled her quilt over her head, willing her heart to stop beating so hard, and she listened. But it was quiet and she once again drifted off to sleep.

When Mandy next woke up it was light outside and she felt as if her left hand had a weight on it. She could hear her mother in the next room, preparing their breakfast. She could smell the oatmeal porridge, which was usually all they had. Mandy sat up and looked at her left hand. The middle finger was weighed down by the ring that had been on Mr. Miller's hand, the one his grandfather had given his grandmother as he'd told her.

"Oh, Mr. Miller," Mandy felt tears of joy prickling her eyes. This was a sure sign that Mr. Miller would return one day. The ring was precious, and for him to have given it to her meant he would one day come back for it. She blinked rapidly, staunching her tears. She looked at the ring again and brought her hand to her lips, kissing it reverently. It was a small and nondescript gold band with a simple diamond to adorn it but it meant the world to the young girl that she had been charged with the care of such a treasure. Mr. Miller had entrusted this ring to her for safekeeping and she was going to make sure that she never lost it.

She had a feeling that when she finally went into the other room he wouldn't be there. But she had this feeling also deep down in her heart that one day in future she would see Mr. Miller again.

"Mandy are you awake?" Her mother called out.

"Yes, Ma," she scrambled out of bed and looked at the ring again. Though it had looked small on Mr. Miller's big hand, it was large for her finger, and she didn't want to lose it. Besides, she didn't want her mother to know that Mr. Miller had left her the ring, not after scolding her last night for asking for a keepsake from him. So she looked around for a safe place to hide the ring but found none. Then she pulled out a strand from the sack on her bed that covered the hay she slept on. She folded the long strand into three, slid the ring on it and then, after securing the ends with a tight knot just like her father had taught her, slipped it around her neck.

"Mandy!"

"Here I am, Ma," She quickly made her bed and then rushed into the other room, which she found that, apart from her mother, was empty.

"Mr. Miller left sometime in the night," her mother told her. "And he left us two gold sovereigns."

Mandy didn't know what gold sovereigns were and she didn't really care because Mr. Miller had left her a very precious gift that she would treasure with her whole heart until he returned to reclaim it. And that would be their secret, just the two of them. Mandy had a feeling that if she told her mother about the ring she would ask for it and say she was going to keep it for her. But she didn't want that because Mr. Miller had entrusted it to her care, and she felt very possessive over it.

"Did you hear what I said, Mandy? Mr. Miller is gone." Mrs. Wood was surprised at her daughter's indifference to Mr. Miller's absence this morning whereas she'd been so upset the previous day. She sometimes didn't understand her little girl.

"Did he wake you up to lock the door?"

Mrs. Wood shook her head. "No, when I woke up this morning I found that the key was on the floor close to the door. Mr. Miller must have locked the door from the outside and then slid the key under the threshold."

Mandy looked toward the spot where Mr. Miller had spent the last four nights. The quilt he'd been using was neatly folded and placed on top of the stuffed sack of hay. She sighed, feeling sad that her friend was gone. Now it was back to long, lonely days while her mother worked up at the manor.

"I'm sorry that he left without saying goodbye to you," Mrs. Wood saw the sad expression on her daughter's face.

But even though she was feeling sad inwardly Mandy had hope. Mr. Miller hadn't said goodbye to her. He'd only bid her farewell for now and she was sure the she would see him again. It was then that she realized he must have been the presence she'd felt standing at the foot of her bed in the deep of the night. He'd been there to bid her farewell in his own way and also to leave her his grandmother's ring. That thought comforted her.

"One day," she announced in a very confident voice, "I'll find Mr. Miller again and then I'll marry him. In that way he'll never leave me again," Mandy announced to her shocked mother, leaving her quite speechless.

❄

Mandy struggled against the heavy cloak of darkness. She felt very frightened because she knew that all this was her fault. If she hadn't pleaded with her mother to let Mr. Miller stay with them, then Mr. Weatherly wouldn't have found out about the stranger in their home.

Mandy wasn't sure how her mother's employer had discovered their little secret. In all the days that Mr. Miller had been with them, he'd never set foot outside the house unless it was dark, so he could use the outhouse. But just two days after his departure two burly men had suddenly appeared at their doorstep and hustled them out of the house.

"Why?" Her mother had cried out even as their few belongings were tossed onto the waiting cart. It was Mr. Stiles driving the cart just as he had six months before when he'd brought them to the cottage, but this time he wasn't friendly to them nor was he smiling. If anything he looked almost annoyed with them.

"Where are you taking us," her mother had asked fearfully as the men forced them to get onto the cart.

"To the place where worthless people like you belong," one of the men had said.

"I work for Mr. Weatherly and have done no wrong," her mother protested. "We can go by the manor and he'll vouch for me."

"Mrs. Wood, don't waste your time and ours. It was Mr. Weatherly himself who expressly instructed us to come and remove you from his property for he no longer has any need of your services."

"But we've done nothing wrong," Mrs. Wood held onto Mandy who was staring at the men with terror-filled eyes. "Mr. Burns, don't you have any compassion in your heart at all?"

"Anyone who associates with Mr. Weatherly's enemies also becomes his foes," Mr. Burns had said. "Jensen, make sure there's nothing left in there."

"Yes, Sir," Jensen said, throwing everything of theirs out of the cottage. He then locked the door and put the key in his pocket. "All done, and now we can get rid of these undesirables."

Together with Mr. Stiles who still hadn't spoken a word to them, the man called Jensen lifted their trunk onto the cart, uncaring that it was old and frail. Some things dropped out, and these he picked up and tossed onto the cart. Mandy had never felt so helpless as she watched her mother begging for clemency and being offered none.

Mandy knew that their secret was out, and her mother was being punished for offering Mr. Miller shelter. Mrs. Wood, on her part, wanted to shout and ask Mr. Burns why he would be loyal to a man who asked his wife to the manor in the absence of her husband. And there was nothing innocent in that visit as she knew. But that might make the man angry enough to hurt her and her daughter, so she kept silent.

Mr. Burns, Mr. Stiles and the third man drove them by cart nine miles away to the workhouse in Dudley. They were received by an unsmiling woman who asked for their names in a bored tone of voice after which she led them to an inner room. The only thing they were allowed to enter the room with was their small carpet bag which was searched by two young women who couldn't have been more than twenty years of age. Mandy saw them taking their nice things and slipping them under their aprons, and she knew she would never see them again. Her pretty hair brush that Pa had bought her for her tenth birthday and her mother's soft shawl that had been his last present to her just two months before his death were all gone.

But the worst was still to come. They were led to a courtyard where they found three other women and two children who were much younger than she was. All seven of them were told that before they could be admitted into the workhouse they had to be cleaned up and checked for lice. Mandy had never known such shame and humiliation as when they were stripped of their clothes and forced to wash from head to toe in the presence of two rough-looking women. The soap they were given to use was coarse and smelled awful.

Mandy saw her mother's downcast eyes as shame filled her and she felt terrible, keeping her gaze averted so she wouldn't look on her parent's nakedness. The water was ice cold, and the other two children screamed, but Mandy gritted her teeth and suffered in silence. No towels or cloths were offered for them to use for drying their wet and shivering bodies, and they had to stand still while their heads were examined for lice.

After all their properties were labelled and taken away, they were given coarse linen uniforms to wear, shoes and a shawl each, as well as bonnets. Then they were taken into a second waiting room where they were informed that after meeting with the administrators of the workhouse, they would be on probation for seven days, pending a doctor coming to ensure that they were in good health. He would examine them immediately and then again after the said seven days in probation.

After the doctor had poked and prodded them, another humiliating experience, he pronounced that she and her mother were in good health, and they were told to move to another room. Mandy saw the crestfallen faces of the other three women when the doctor announced that they were ill and had to be taken to the infirmary for further observation. That was the last she would ever see of the five.

Three people were in the next room waiting to receive them, two men and one woman. Mandy learned that these were the administrators of the workhouse. The Master of the workhouse was Mr. Spindle who introduced himself with an air of pompousness. He was middle aged and portly and his hair was thinning. It wouldn't be long before he was bald, Mandy had thought as she observed him. His eyes were grey and cold, making her shiver involuntarily. Something about the man made Mandy very uneasy and she had pressed close to her mother. The other man was the chaplain, Reverend Reid, who had kind brown eyes. He looked to be younger than Mr. Spindle and, though he wasn't very tall, he stooped slightly as if he was carrying a burden on his back. He had a soft voice and had introduced them to Mrs. Ridges, the women's matron. She was about the same age as Reverend Reid but her blue eyes were cold and she didn't look like she ever smiled.

"Clington Workhouse was set up by the Church of Saint Martha to help the poor so they can find purpose in their lives again," Reverend Reid, as he'd asked to be called, told them. "You'll be very happy here and after a season, when you've found your footing, you'll be able to return to the outside world and live your lives as normal. Please don't take this as a prison but as a transition house to a better life."

"We didn't ask to be brought here," Mrs. Wood had said tearfully. "We were taken out of our home by force and yet we're not criminals."

"Mrs. Wood, no one said you're criminals, and I sincerely apologize if you were made to feel as such. Your difficult circumstances of life caused a kind and concerned citizen to recommend that you be brought to us, but please don't worry, we'll take good care of both of you," the chaplain tried to reassure them. "It's better for you to be here where you get three meals a day, a bed to sleep in and a roof over your heads. Be thankful that someone cared enough to ensure that you and your daughter didn't end up on the streets." Reverend Reid smiled at Mandy. "And you child will be well educated so that when the time comes for you to leave this place, you'll have learned so much." Mandy didn't tell them that she knew how to read and write. "Mr. Weatherly is a godly man who cares about those in his community so you're very lucky."

Mandy knew that they had been brought here under false pretences and Mr. Weatherly wanted to look like a good person in the eyes of people when he was the one who was the cause of their troubles. She wondered why her mother wasn't speaking up and correcting the misconceptions of the administrators.

Mr. Spindle cleared his throat and she turned to look at him. He gave her a sharp and disapproving look, "And don't try to run away because that's the worst thing that anyone can do," Mr. Spindle said. "If the police catch you after you've run away, you'll be charged with theft."

"We're not thieves," Mandy burst out and the adults looked at her.

"If you leave the workhouse without permission, it means you're taking our uniforms and the other accessories with you, and those are on loan and not your property. Whatever you came in here with will be cleaned up and kept for you until the day you leave. So, if you walk out of here with our uniforms, that marks you out as a thief. And then the police will also charge you with vagrancy and throw you in prison. Believe me, you will pray and beg to be brought back here because this place is just like home, unlike the prisons."

They had lost their trunk because Mr. Stiles and the other two men had taken it away with them. After a week in the probationary dormitory, the doctor had examined them a second time. He pronounced them healthy and fit to work, and they were moved into the normal dormitory for women.

"How old is the girl," Mrs. Ridges had asked them on the seventh day when she was moving them to the regular dormitory. She was an unfriendly woman who looked cross, as if she were always being offended. In the seven days they'd been here, Mrs. Ridge would come to their dormitory three times a day to check on them. And Mandy had never seen her smile or speak a kind word to anyone.

"Ten years old," Mandy heard her mother saying and was quite surprised. She was about to correct her parent when she caught her eye.

Mrs. Ridges grunted. "Lucky girl for now; had she been above ten years old, then I would have taken her to the girls' dormitory to be with her age mates. But since she's ten, she gets to stay with you," the woman said. "At least she's small enough to share a bed with you so I don't have to look for an extra cot for her. As it is, all the dormitories are filled to capacity and you were lucky that a person just left and that's how you managed to get allocated a bed."

"Thank you, Ma'am," Mrs. Wood whispered as she drew Mandy close.

That was how they had ended up in this frightening place, and now Mandy was unable to sleep. The dorm was silent and she could hear their mates snoring, which made her wonder just how fast they fell asleep, as if they had no cares in the world. She was very scared and felt guilty for placing them in this situation. She missed that dilapidated cottage and even the nosy Mrs. Shaw. She wished they were back in their small and cosy house. Even if they hadn't had much in their cottage, it had still been home, a place where they were free and happy.

"Settle down and sleep," her mother whispered, drawing her close as they were facing the same side. She tugged at the frayed blankets and tucked the edges under the thin mattress to secure them. Mandy had noticed that some of the women had to share a bed and slept facing opposite sides of the bed. Only those with children didn't have to share beds with others. "Tomorrow will be yet another very busy and heavy day. We need all the rest we can get."

"Ma, are you angry with me?" Mandy just had to know. Even though the mattress on which they lay was thin, it was surprisingly comfortable and better than the hay they had used back on the estate. But she still missed the place she had come to think of as home.

"And why would you think that I'm angry with you?" The surprise in her mother's voice should have reassured her but it didn't.

"Ma, if I hadn't insisted on Mr. Miller staying with us, Mr. Weatherly wouldn't have found out about him and then sent us away. It's my fault that you're suffering like this and I'm so sorry, Ma."

"Oh, Mandy!" Her mother's arms tightened around her. "It's not your fault, and Jesus said that we're blessed if we suffer for doing the right thing. Your Pa would be so proud of you. We did the right thing when we helped that young man; otherwise, he might have died, so why should I be angry with you? Stop tormenting yourself with such thoughts and settle down. If your father were here, he would have told you that all things happen for a reason to those who believe in God."

"If Pa were still alive, then we wouldn't be here."

"That's very true, but at least we're together. I said you're ten years old so we wouldn't be put in separate dormitories. And if anyone asks you, tell them the same thing."

"Pa said we should never tell lies, Ma."

Mrs. Wood was silent for a moment. "So then go ahead and tell everyone your real age and watch as they drag you off to a separate dormitory and take you away from me. And who knows what kind of bad things might happen to you without me being there to protect you?"

"I'm sorry, Ma." Mandy knew that now she had angered her mother with her questions. She hated lying and determined that she would never open her mouth to answer any questions about her age. In that way she won't have to lie to anyone.

Mandy drifted off to sleep and it seemed like she'd only shut her eyes for a brief moment when a loud gong nearly made her jump out of her skin. While they were in the probation dorm she didn't ever remember hearing such a loud sound in the morning.

"What's that," she asked when she saw the others rising up from their beds. It was still dark in the dorm though a small lamp was burning at the far end of the room. Not every woman in this dormitory had a child or a baby. Those who did started cleaning their children and there was a lot of crying and fussing from the little ones who'd been woken up too early. Those without children were soon done making their beds and combing their hair and then walked toward the door to make a queue. The dorm monitor inspected them, and those who looked shabby were told to go back and neaten their appearance.

"This might be a workhouse, but you still have to look dignified," the young woman said. "For those of you who are new, my name is Miss Brenda and you'll address me as such at all times. I won't stand for slothfulness, untidiness or rudeness. Hurry up," she shouted and the women scurried around.

"That's the gong to wake us up so we can go for morning prayers before breakfast," their neighbour said when she spotted Mandy and her mother still lying in bed. "And Mrs. Ridges had better not find you still lying in bed when she comes in. Get up quickly before Miss Brenda comes around and catches you. She'll report you; then you'll be punished."

Mandy scrambled out of bed, and her mother followed more slowly. Once they had made their bed and straightened their uniforms, for they slept in them, all the thirty women in the dorm and their children formed a queue and were led out of the dorm in a single file. Mandy noticed that they went down two flights of stairs and entered into a large hall, which had long rectangular counter tops made of rough wood and the long benches were on only one side of each table.

"We all sit facing forward," the woman behind her mother whispered. "We're not allowed to engage in conversation while taking our meals, and so we all face in one direction."

Mandy followed her mother and they were shown their places, ten people to a table. She noticed that men and young boys came in through a separate entrance. This wasn't the same place they had taken their meals in while they'd been in the probationary dormitory, and she was surprised that there were so many people here. She wondered if all of them had been brought here by people like Mr. Weatherly or if they'd come here of their own free volition.

The one thing the child noticed on the faces of the adults, and especially the men, was the look of utter hopelessness. It was as though they had lost all will to live and merely existed, accepting their lot in life with resignation. It also seemed as if no one smiled and they all walked with their eyes downcast. Then something struck Mandy, it was not mere hopelessness, but shame that made the inmates bow their heads. Being in a workhouse meant that one had hit rock bottom, and she recalled something her father had told her just a few weeks before his death.

He'd started ailing, and getting out of bed and going to the coalmines to work was a great struggle for him. Yet every morning he would wake up, struggle to get his clothes on and leave for the coalmines, never missing a single day until the time he'd completely collapsed. That particular morning that came to the child's mind was one of the worst ones for Mr. Wood. He'd coughed for almost the whole night, and in the morning her mother had left very early to find some honey to soothe his chest. Mandy had come upon her father as he shuffled from the bedchamber to the living room. His pallor was sickly and he looked like he could barely walk. And she got very concerned when she noticed that he barely touched the oatmeal porridge that her mother had set out for their breakfast.

"Pa, if you're sick, why are you going to the mines? Can't you rest for a day?"

He'd given her a sad smile, "Mandy, one day you'll understand why I have to go to work even when I don't have the strength," and a bout of coughing assailed him, causing him to lean weakly against the wall. She rushed forward with a glass of water, which he drank, then handed back to her. "For a man to lose the ability and capability to take care of his family means that he's relegating them to great poverty. Every man must work hard, and for as long as I have strength in my arms and legs, I'll go to work so I can provide for you and your mother."

Sadly, just two days later he'd collapsed at the mines and been carried home. He was never able to return to work again till the day he died. She now understood what he'd meant, if a man couldn't take care of his family, then they would end up in terrible situations such as this one. She felt sad for everyone in this place because it was clear that they had nothing in life to call their own, save the clothes on their backs. And even these were on loan from the workhouse, so the tattered clothes they'd arrived in were all their worldly possessions.

Breakfast was a small hard bun, a slice of stale cheese and a bowl of tepid beef broth. Mandy was surprised that the inmates in this dining hall didn't queue to receive their food but found it already served and laid out on the table. No wonder the broth got cold so fast, because there had to be over fifty tables in the dining hall. Serving them from one end to the other obviously took time. Men sat on one side, and there was a wide aisle to separate them from women. Mandy and her mother were placed at separate tables, as Mandy had to sit with other children like herself.

They weren't allowed to touch the food until the morning prayers had been said, and by this time, the broth was cold and fat had congealed all around the bowl. The moment the prayers were over, everyone bowed their heads to start eating. Mandy scooped the first spoon of broth and was shocked to find a dead cockroach in it. She quickly dropped the spoon and grimaced with distaste.

"If you don't want that soup, may I have it?" the girl seated next to her whispered and she pushed the plate toward her. "Just know that lunch isn't any better, and if you choose what to eat, you'll soon starve." And saying thus, she quickly emptied Mandy's broth into her own bowl and then proceeded to ignore her for the rest of the meal. Mandy ate her bun and cheese, which were awful, but she was hungry.

Mandy had thought the workhouse wasn't so bad because in the probation dormitory the food had always been served hot, and it was plentiful. She looked around to see if she could spot her mother. Everyone was concentrating on their food, heads bowed and even the presence of large flies buzzing around the tables didn't deter them at all. Mandy couldn't imagine that this was how all mealtimes were going to be.

She was still looking around trying to find her mother when she sensed that someone was standing behind her. "You've already finished your breakfast," the person said and Mandy didn't know if it was a question or a statement. So she merely nodded when she realised that it was Mrs. Ridges.

"You can't leave the table unless everyone else is ready," she was told and once again she nodded.

Once everyone was through with their breakfast, they rose up to their feet. Mandy followed what the other girls were doing.

"Where are we going now?" She asked the girl in front of her when she noticed that they didn't return to the dorms.

"We have all been assigned places where we work," the girl said. "We're not supposed to be talking so just follow me."

Their long journey down two corridors ended up in a large sewing room. There were about ten long tables and five of them had sewing machines on them. Mandy forgot her discomfort for a while and stared in fascination at the contraptions.

"Have you never seen a sewing machine before?" someone scoffed. "Move before I knock you down."

Mandy hastily moved out of the way and stood on one side because she hadn't been allocated any duties yet. She wondered where her mother was working at this moment. Her Mama was a good seamstress and Mandy wondered why she hadn't been brought in here. Yet when they'd been registered she'd been asked if she possessed any skills and had said she was a seamstress.

"Don't just stand there," a loud voice roused Mandy out of her thoughts. "Do you know how to sew?"

"No, Ma'am."

"Then get over here at once and I'll show you what you can do," and Mandy joined her at the end of the sewing room. There were four large bins that were overflowing with clothes. "These are the charity bins and you have to sort the clothes out," the woman said, showing Mandy what to do.

PART II
INTO THE ABYSS

ENDLESS DESOLATION

❄

Mandy spent most mornings rummaging through the charity bins because that was the task assigned to her by the supervisor on the instructions of Mrs. Ridge. It was boring and sometimes downright disgusting because some of the clothes donated for charity were filthy, as if they hadn't ever been washed. But in the two years that she and her mother had been in Clington Workhouse, she had learnt not to complain about anything.

"Always remember that our lot is better than what so many others are going through," her mother would remind her whenever she murmured or complained. "Just think, some people have no roof over their heads and no food to eat. They sleep on the streets and are exposed to all manner of dangers. This place may not be pleasant, my child, but at least we have a dry roof over our heads, three meals a day and a bed to sleep in."

It was hard being happy all the time but she had promised her mother that she would try. Still, she never stopped thinking about her father and what their lives would be like had he lived.

Two Christmases had come and gone but Mandy hadn't allowed herself to feel anything for the holidays. Every Christmas Day would always be a reminder of what she'd lost. Reverend Reid had done his best both times to make some changes over the Christmas holidays, even bringing in musicians to entertain the inmates. But all that had passed over Mandy as she recalled all the other Christmases she had enjoyed with her father. And she'd wept through all the celebrations, just wishing they would be over and done with.

Her birthdays also came and went and her mother found her some small cupcakes to celebrate the milestones. She smiled just to please her mother but alone in the outhouse she had wept bitterly. Why had God allowed her to live this long if all she was going to see were days of despondency? Why hadn't God taken her life away at the same time that he'd taken her father's?

Each Sunday as she sat beside her mother in the dining hall for the week's church service, she closed her mind to everything that was being preached. Why believe in a God who had abandoned them to such a life? Sometimes it was Reverend Reid who gave the sermon and sometimes it was Mr. Spindle, the Governor as everyone referred to him. Once in a while even sour-faced Mrs. Ridges stood on the small platform and preached to them. Nothing seemed to penetrate the young girl's mind. It was as though a shroud was over her mind and she merely existed from day to day.

Mandy had learned how to keep a low profile and never draw any attention to herself in all the time they'd been here. Being noticed was the basis for trouble.

For some reason, Mrs. Ridges, the matron, hadn't sent Mandy to the dormitory for older girls even two years later, and she still slept on the same bed with her mother. Mandy had grown taller by two more inches and at fourteen was budding into a very beautiful girl, though she herself wasn't aware of the changes to her person. But her mother noticed her daughter's changing body, and Mrs. Wood lived in dread of her falling prey to the men who worked in the workhouse.

The male and female inmates weren't allowed to speak to each other, and in any case, they never had any chance to meet, so those didn't frighten Mrs. Wood. It was the staff, the cooks, bakers and even the medical officer, a young man with what Mrs. Wood thought was a roving eye who kept her on high alert. While males were forbidden from entering into the female quarters, Mrs. Wood had noticed that some of them found excuses to do so. They would claim to be coming to disinfect the dormitories or repair the beds and in the case of the medical officer, to examine sick inmates but their presence always made her very frightened. According to what she had heard, any male entering the female dormitory had to be in the presence of the matron or other female supervisor. Yet sometimes the men just entered the dorms without any female officers being present. Those were the ones who frightened her and she always tried to keep Mandy within her sight though it wasn't always possible to do so.

Mrs. Wood, like her daughter, kept her head bowed and rarely spoke. But she had a keen ear and knew everything that was happening around the workhouse. That was how she found out that Reverend Reid was taking leave of absence for an unspecified period and her heart knew fear like never before.

The chaplain was the one person who made life in this place bearable because he was a kind man who looked out for the interests of the inmates. He was also eager to see the inmates find meaningful employment outside the workhouse and so have their dignity restored. He also ensured that no inmates were abused by anyone and dealt with such complaints very harshly.

With him gone it meant that the inmates would be at the mercy of the master, Mr. Spindle, who Mrs. Wood knew to be a very cruel man. It seemed as if the man thrived on the pain and humiliation of those under his care. Mrs. Wood had heard it whispered that the man often whipped the male inmates just to show them that he was in control and then would threaten them with dire consequences if they reported the matter to Reverend Reid or any of the other guardians from the church who frequently visited the workhouse to ensure that the inmates were being treated well.

She had made only one good friend in the workhouse, whose name was Pauline Tucker, a woman who was in her forties. Mrs. Tucker had lost her husband to another woman. The two of them had then tried to have her murdered so they could wed in church, as bigamy was punishable by a prison sentence. Mrs. Tucker had managed to escape and travelled all the way from Southampton, over one hundred miles away. She'd tried to get gainful employment in Dudley but failed, and while loitering on the streets, she'd been arrested and brought to the workhouse.

"Where is Mandy," the said woman asked Mrs. Wood as they scrubbed the bathrooms together one morning. They were on their knees, though the floor was hard and very cold.

"Mrs. Ridges assigned her to the sewing room store to sort out the charity bins."

"Keep your eye on her at all times," Mrs. Tucker said in a low voice. "I don't like the way Mr. Spindle has started singling her out and separating her from the others."

Mrs. Wood raised a stricken face to her friend, "How do you mean?"

Mrs. Tucker cast a glance over her shoulder to see if anyone was listening to their conversation. The other women who had the same duties as them were busy on the other side of the large wash area. "A friend of mine who works in the sewing room told me that Mr. Spindle has taken to going there at least twice a day and calling Mandy out to the corridor. She told me that she tries to make sure the door is never shut so the man can't try any funny business on the young girls. This workhouse is large and old and there are many isolated rooms and corridors. Teach Mandy to only always use the well-trodden corridors. And no matter how tempted she may be, make sure she understands that taking shortcuts could prove very tragic for her."

Later that evening in the one hour after evening prayers and before bedtime, Mrs. Wood shared her fears with her daughter. "Are you ever alone in the sewing room," she asked. Mandy shook her head. "Who else comes to the sewing room with you?"

"Usually there are a number of women who make the uniforms we wear and some girls who work with me sorting out the charity bins."

"What about any males whether they be inmates like us or workers in this place?"

"I've never seen any males coming into the sewing room," Mandy wondered at her mother's questions. "Mama, why are you asking me all these questions?"

"Mandy," there was no easy way of telling her daughter. "You're growing up very fast and your body is also changing. In a few years you'll be a woman and I hope and pray that nothing will happen to harm you before then."

"Mama, I don't understand."

"You're growing up very fast and I'm really afraid for you."

"Why, Ma? Have I done something wrong?" She felt scared. Why was her mother speaking to her as if she'd done something that she wasn't supposed to do?

"That Mr. Spindle, whenever he calls you out where does he take you?"

Mandy frowned slightly, "We just stand outside the sewing room where the charity bins are."

"Does he make you walk alone on the corridors with him?" Mandy shook her head and her mother sighed in relief.

"Ma, that man frightens me so much," she shuddered. "I don't like it when he calls me out but Mrs. Ridges said that all of us should always obey whenever the governor calls. Mrs. Hannah keeps the door open and that makes me feel a little safer, but I don't like it when Mr. Spindle comes and calls me out. I haven't seen Reverend Reid around for the past few days, Ma. He makes me feel safe but Mr. Spindle frightens me." And her mother nodded, surprising her. "Ma, why are you nodding?"

"Because I'm happy that you're scared of Mr. Spindle; that will make you stay aware of whatever is happening around you. Be careful to never walk along strange corridors whether you're alone or with others you don't know. Only use the normal corridors, do you understand what I'm saying?"

"Yes, Ma."

"Even if a friend should tell you about or show you a shortcut, don't follow her, do you understand me?"

"Yes, Ma."

"Pauline, er, Mrs. Tucker told me that many girls have gotten into trouble when they walked down some of the old corridors. This is an old building and has many unused rooms and corridors which can be dangerous."

"I'll be very careful, Ma."

Two days later, Mandy was to remember her mother's warning. Two of the girls who worked with her sorting through the charity bins tried to convince her that they had found a shorter route to get to the dining hall from the sewing room.

"It passes by the mortuary," Claire Keen, a plain girl with buck teeth told her. "You just close your eyes as you slip by the morgue so you won't see the dead bodies in there," she urged.

"Claire is right," Ruth Foster joined in. "We always use that corridor even though it's dark and scary, but it's a shorter way to the dining hall. Come with us, Mandy, and we'll show it to you."

But heeding her mother's words, Mandy shook her head. "I don't mind going the long way with everyone else."

When she had first come to Clington Workhouse, Mandy had wandered around from time to time, like she used to in the woods back in Walsall and then Birmingham. She had discovered that this particular workhouse used to be an old monastery decades ago but it had been shut down after an outbreak of smallpox decimated a huge part of the population of monks who dwelt in it. And shortly after, a fire had broken out, burning down nearly all the buildings. When the church had acquired the property, they hadn't torn down the remaining buildings, instead building the current workhouse around them. That caused many corridors to exist and some were dead ends. It had seemed like a maze to Mandy and she'd been frightened one time when she was in a dark corridor and had heard strange sounds coming from one of the unused rooms. The guttural sounds had reminded her of when she'd once stumbled upon two wild hogs fighting in the woods. She'd fled before the animals spotted her but she'd never forgotten how frightening they had sounded.

From that day, she never again roamed around the workhouse. And she'd also never told her mother what she'd heard because she would have earned herself a scolding for wandering off. Now her two friends were trying to get her to walk down the corridor past the morgue. She knew the one they spoke of because it had been one of the places she'd roamed before, and according to her, it wasn't as close as they made it sound. She would stick to the known corridors, thank you very much!

"Mandy, are you coming with us?" Ruth called out as she walked toward the door.

"No, I'll use the same route that everyone else goes by."

"You're a fool," Claire hissed at her. "Who doesn't want to cut their work time in half and get across to the dining hall faster than everyone else?"

"Even if we're to finish our tasks early you know that we're not allowed to leave our work areas until the lunch and dinner gongs sound," Mandy pointed out. "And if we're found to have finished our tasks early we'll only be given more to do. I'd rather do whatever we're doing for as long as I can until the gong sounds."

And Mandy walked away when they continued to vex her to join them. She turned her back on the two girls and missed the cunning looks that were in their eyes.

Mandy was actually tired of working with the two girls because they rarely did much anyway. As soon as the supervisor's back was turned, they would resort to gossiping and badmouthing other people. Claire and Ruth never seemed to get any work done, and it fell to Mandy to ensure that all the bins were emptied in good time. The rule of work was that the team had to work together.

Even if one person finished the tasks assigned to them earlier, they weren't to leave the work area until the whole team was done. Their team was one of three and Mandy often admired the way the other teams worked. They always got their work done in good time and as soon as the gong sounded, they would file out together. No one slacked in their work and rarely were they ever reprimanded by Mrs. Ridges or Mrs. Hannah, their supervisor, unlike Mandy's team.

Mandy had tried to talk to the two girls about working harder and avoiding all the scolding, but they just wouldn't listen. It was as though they weren't even afraid of getting into trouble. Their bins were always the last to be emptied. So it was that the three girls spent far more time each day in the sewing room than was necessary.

One evening the gong sounded when Mandy was just finishing the last of the work that once again she'd had to do for the three of them. And as usual, theirs was the last team to leave the sewing room so they had to ensure that it was tidy and lock up. Mandy would then take the key to Mrs. Hannah who would in turn hand it over to Mrs. Ridges.

The sewing room emptied fast, and soon it was just the three of them left, along with two seamstresses who were also clearing their area up in readiness for the morrow.

"Let's use the shortcut," Ruth said, ignoring the fact that they had to clean up and lock the room together. She and

Claire were already at the door and ready to leave. Mandy was tempted to leave the sewing room just as it was and nearly gave in to the other girls' coaxing, but then her mother's words rang in her ears.

"No, I have to finish up here and then I'll catch up with you. Just go ahead and let me finish locking up." This she said because she knew that her teammates weren't going to help at all. If they left their area looking untidy there would be trouble in the morning. And the last thing Mandy wanted was to come to the attention of the matron and supervisor for the wrong reasons. The two seamstresses were also soon done and passed Mandy as she put away the final pile of clothes, giving her pitying looks she didn't understand.

"If you're late to dinner we won't cover for you and we won't protect your food from those who will grab at it," Claire warned.

"I'll hurry," Mandy put the empty bins away. They would be filled again in the morning. It was tedious and monotonous work, but like her mother said, their lot was better than many others in the world.

By the time she was done locking up, she was alone and had to run down the corridor so she wouldn't be late to enter the dining hall. She slipped in just before the dining hall door was shut. Any latecomers had to forfeit their ration for the day. Dining hall servers placed food on tables according to the numbers and it was usual for table mates to even steal someone's food. By the time Mandy got to the table she shared with Claire, Ruth and seven other girls, she found that her plate was empty and had been placed face down on the table. She saw the malicious glee on the two girls' faces and noticed that their plates seemed to have much more food than the others. Mandy couldn't report the two girls because she would get into trouble for coming late. And besides, who would believe her since she knew the other seven girls would never speak up, being too scared of Claire and Ruth.

It was clear that the two girls wanted to lead Mandy into a trap, and she didn't understand why they disliked her so much. No one gave her a single bite of food because they barely had enough for themselves. A small bun and half a bowl of broth was all they got for dinner. Mandy wanted to go to her mother who she could see seated several tables ahead of her. And she knew her mother would immediately hand over her own food to Mandy, but she needed it too.

That night the young girl couldn't sleep. "Are you ill?" Her mother asked when she kept tossing and turning.

"No, Ma, I'm very hungry."

"Didn't you take your dinner today?" And in hushed tones Mandy told her mother everything that had happened. "You should have come to find me," her mother told her. "And I would have shared my own food with you."

"Mama, you need to eat, too, and the food we're served is barely enough for one person," the girl sighed. "When Reverend Reid was here, we at least got food that kept the hunger pangs away. It's as if Mr. Spindle is deliberately starving all of us."

"Don't let anyone hear you saying that," her mother whispered. "You know that this place has a lot of people who want to get in that man's good graces. Keep your mouth shut and even if you hear anything, pretend as if you're deaf. I just wish you had let me know that your food was taken by those mean girls."

"Mama, I didn't want to get you or myself into any trouble. Remember we have to keep our heads down and not draw any unwanted attention towards ourselves. You know that the dining hall rules say that no one is allowed to stand up or move around until dinner time is over. And in any case, I was late."

"But that's because those girls didn't help you with the work," Mrs. Wood sounded cross. "What unpleasant girls."

"Ma please don't get angry. I'll be all right by morning."

"I'll see what to do for you in the morning. But stay away from those girls because they're nothing but trouble. Even if you miss dinner or lunch, come and find me for I'll always hide something for you."

"Ma, please don't starve yourself for my sake."

"I won't," her mother promised, "But I don't want you to go hungry either."

"How can you help me?"

Mandy heard her mother chuckle softly. "Have you forgotten how I used to hide food from Mr. Weatherly's house? Just make sure you never follow those girls anywhere. They're out to cause trouble for you. I'll ask Mrs. Tucker to show me their parents so I can speak to them and ask them to talk to their daughters."

"Ruth and Claire are orphans, Ma. That's why they're here. Their parents died months ago and the church decided to bring them here."

"Oh dear!" Her mother sighed. "That should make them more compassionate toward others and not so mean."

❄

Mandy soon learned to stay ahead of the two lazy girls. She would make sure that she finished her tasks, which involved sorting out the clothes which were brought in daily from the different churches around Dudley. The charity bins were never empty. Once Mandy was done separating the clean clothes from the filthy ones, she then had to separate male from female garments. And then further separate the two piles into the different sizes, for children, young boys and then adults, and did the same with the pile for the women.

Well, Claire and Ruth were actually supposed to separate the clothes into the different sizes but they spent their time chatting away. Mandy wished the supervisor assigned to their section of the sewing room would pay more attention to them but she was always away and the others didn't bother. It seemed as if no one wanted to do their work here and many times Mandy was also tempted to fold her hands and slacken in her duties. After all, if everyone didn't want to do their part, why should she?

But her father's words would always remind her never to be slothful. *"Remember my child,"* her father had told her once, *"The Book of Proverbs tells us that he who is slack in his work is brother to him who destroys. Slothfulness destroys, and you should never be a partaker of that vice, no matter how tempted you are."*

And thus Mandy was able to always finish all the tasks assigned to the three of them before the lunch and dinner gongs sounded and she was never late again.

❄

Mandy was so happy when, a few days later, Mrs. Tucker joined their dorm. And she arranged it such that she got the bed right next to theirs. Mandy had also found out why Mrs. Ridges hadn't sent her to the girls' dorm even after two years. Her mother, a very good seamstress was making clothes for the woman which she then sold to make money. It was their private arrangement and Mandy knew that her mother was being taken advantage of. None of the money made went into the workhouse coffers; instead, Mrs. Ridges pocketed it. And she never gave a single coin to Mrs. Wood, but she did let Mandy stay in the dorm with her. With Reverend Reid gone, Mrs. Ridges and Mr. Spindle ran the workhouse as if it was their personal home.

"I've been here for six years now," Mrs. Tucker told Mandy and her mother one Sunday after lunch. Sundays were the only days the inmates were allowed to go out into the courtyard and bask in the sun during the summer and spring. No work was done in the workhouse on Sundays. All they did was attend the morning service in the dining hall, then wait for lunch. After lunch, they were allowed to rest, and those who had obtained permission to leave the workhouse for whatever reason did so but had to be back before dinner time.

Mandy, her mother and Mrs. Tucker were seated on a bench and watched the other women milling about. Everyone looked hungry and thin, and the women with children suffered most, because these days they were only given food enough for one person yet they had children to feed. So many times the mothers went hungry as they gave up their food for the little ones. The women in the yard kept casting eyes towards the entrance as they were waiting for the lunch gong to summon them for their midday meal.

The sermon that morning, delivered by Mr. Spindle, had been long and boring, and Mandy felt ashamed that she'd dozed all through it. Her mother had had to keep pinching her so she wouldn't fall asleep.

"How is it that you've been in here for six years, Pauline," Mrs. Wood asked her friend. "Don't you ever want to leave? You're a good cook and I'm sure you can find meaningful employment, maybe in the home of a good family or even in a better institution. Or you could ask Mrs. Ridges to employ you as a cook in this place."

Mrs. Tucker gave her a tight smile, "Reverend Reid has tried on many occasions to find me meaningful employment," she hissed through clenched teeth. "When I first came to this place, I made the mistake of being very honest as to why I was destitute. My husband said I was barren after only six years of marriage and took another wife and then tried to get rid of me," Mandy had heard all that before. "Mr. Spindle tried to proposition me because according to him, I'm a desperate woman and would do anything to get ahead in life. I rejected him on more than once occasion, and he promised that he would get even with me. Hence my presence in this workhouse, and it seems like I'll never leave."

"But why do that?" Mandy asked dread filling her heart. Were she and her mother to be prisoners in this place for the rest of their lives? "Does this mean then you're a prisoner here?"

Mrs. Tucker laughed, "They try to make it seem as if we're free to come and go but that's not entirely true. Well, if a person gets employment on the outside, then they can leave. But the problem is, without employment it means ending up on the streets and the police are waiting to slap you with the offence of vagrancy. So unless you have somewhere to go, it's much safer to stay here in the workhouse with all its woes. But Mr. Spindle has often prevented us from leaving this place."

"How has he been allowed to get away with such wicked acts," Mandy asked. "Can't Reverend Reid and the other commissioners do anything to help those who want to leave?"

"Mr. Spindle has a roving eye despite the fact that he has a wife and children. When I rebuffed his advances he swore to get even with me. And I'm not the only one he's tormented like this. Every woman who rejects his advances is termed a loose and immoral woman. Even if we get the chance to go out and find work, we need a recommendation from Mrs. Ridges or Mr. Spindle. Usually Chaplain Reid leaves such matters to them because they are in charge of the day to day running of the workhouse. But Mr. Spindle has made it difficult for us to go anywhere because no one wants to employ one who has been termed a harlot. That's why six years after coming here, I'm still in this place and not likely to leave, unless a miracle occurs."

"But that's wrong," Mandy looked at her mother who hadn't spoken a word.

"Many decent folks out there are reluctant to take us in because Mr. Spindle has made us out to be harlots and immoral women. And as for the men, if they want to get out then there's one of two ways that Mr. Spindle will let them leave."

"What are they supposed to do?"

"Mandy, you're asking Mrs. Tucker too many questions," her mother rebuked softly.

"Let the child speak for she is growing up and has to know whatever is going on around her. You won't always be here to protect her, so the sooner she knows how to defend and look out for herself, the better."

Mandy didn't want to offend her mother, but Mrs. Tucker was right. If she had to survive in this place then she had to know what to do and what to avoid. "How do the men get the chance to leave?"

"Many of the men who end up here bring their families with them because they're too poor to support them. So if a man wants to be recommended for a posting outside the workhouse he has to submit to whatever Mr. Spindle tells him."

"And what's that?"

"First the man has to pay Mr. Spindle a certain sum of money and believe me, it isn't a small sum. Mr. Spindle sets the amount on the number of dependents that the man has. But as you know, everyone in here works for free and the men have nowhere to get the money from. The other way is that if the man has a wife and daughters then he's supposed to convince them to accept Mr. Spindle's amorous advances. Those men who love and respect their wives and daughters will never submit to such and prefer to continue staying here rather than dishonour their womenfolk. So Mr. Spindle then writes a report that they are nothing but thieves, looters and vagrants, unfit to rejoin society," Mrs. Tucker sighed. "Many of us no longer have any good reputations around here. But I would rather remain in here for the rest of my life than compromise my faith and virtue."

"But how is it that Reverend Reid doesn't know what that man is doing?" Mrs. Wood finally asked. "How have such evils been allowed to go on unnoticed and unpunished?"

"Chaplain Reid trusts Mr. Spindle very much and in his eyes the man can do no wrong. Haven't you heard the man preaching, looking very pious and holy," she spat to the side. "Do you know that Mr. Spindle is even a deacon in the church and everyone there trusts him? If you try to say anything bad about the man to Chaplain Reid chances are that you're the one who will get into trouble. So most people prefer to remain silent and suffer in silence."

Mandy thought about Mrs. Tucker's words as she lay in her bed that night. As was her usual practice, her hand reached for the hem of her uniform and she touched the ring that she'd sewn in it the very first day they had arrived at the workhouse. When they had been forced to strip for the disinfecting bath as one of the guardians had said, she had quickly removed the string on which it had been from around her neck and used it to hold her hair. But then she found out that she was to be shorn because she was still a child.

Since her mother had claimed that she was ten years old, Mandy had been ordered to the sewing room where a woman took a pair of scissors and cut her hair off, leaving her with short locks.

Mandy had stolen a needle and some thread and in the privacy of the outhouse, had untucked the hem of her dress, slipped the ring into it and, since it was small it fit nicely, and then sewed it up again. In that way she would never lose the ring. And she carried the needle and thread with her at all times, though she had to hide the items, for she wasn't allowed to take them out of the sewing room.

After their weekly bath they had to turn in their uniforms for dry cleaning and get freshly laundered ones. She would repeat that all over again. And she would never tire of doing it because she had promised Mr. Miller that she would keep the ring safe until he returned for it.

Mandy often wondered if Mr. Miller had made it safely away from Mr. Weatherly's estate after leaving the cottage. Or had the bad men caught up with him and harmed him?

If perchance he'd gotten clean away, was he even in England? And did he ever think about them? Would she ever see him again, now that they had left the estate and he had no idea where they were?

If Mr. Miller ever returned to Weatherly Estate and found them gone, would he give up on them and never search further? And would he even be brave enough to return after the beating he'd received at the hands of Mr. Weatherly's men?

The thought that she would never see Mr. Miller again filled her heart with so much despair that she found herself weeping silently.

Why had life changed so much for them after her father's death? If he were still alive, she was sure they would never have ended up in the workhouse. In spite of the low wages he'd received as a coal miner, he'd been able to give them a good life, albeit a simple one. But they had been very happy. With him gone, she and her mother were very vulnerable to people like Mrs. Ridges and Mr. Spindle and their wicked ploys.

With Mrs. Tucker's words ringing in her mind, she knew that they were probably safer in here than on the streets. Her mother was no longer the vibrant and happy woman she'd once been. And these days she no longer had much optimism.

With each passing day it seemed as if a little more of the light in her mother's eyes was dimmed. The grooves around her mouth deepened, and her forehead got more lined, as if she was always worrying about something. And with each passing day, Mandy's guilt grew deeper. Even though her mother had told her over and over again that she didn't blame her for their plight, Mandy couldn't forgive herself. It was because of her that they were here, and all because they had been kind to Mr. Miller. Had her father been wrong about always helping people even if it meant getting into trouble?

"Oh, Mr. Miller," she wept, "If only you were a good man and thought about us, you would come and find us and take us away from this place." She always daydreamed that Mr. Miller would travel to Birmingham and, finding them gone, would then comb every nook and cranny and find them here, then take them away to a wonderful life. But these were her own dreams and she knew that, if she ever shared them with her mother, she would be severely rebuked.

And before she slept that night, Mandy made a vow to herself that she would do all she could to get her mother out of this workhouse. And then she would go in search of Mr. Miller, give him back his ring and tell him how disappointed she was in him, that he wasn't a man of integrity.

❄

A few days later, word went around that the guardians and commissioners of the workhouse would be visiting and wanted to speak to the inmates about their experiences in the place. There was excitement in the air, and Mandy overheard some of the women in the sewing room discussing what they were going to report to the commissioners and guardians.

"The food is terrible," one woman was saying. She had to whisper but Mandy, who was pretending to rearrange the clothes bin was listening keenly. "When Reverend Reid was here, we would make our complaints and the very next day things would change."

"But the chaplain isn't here," a second woman said. "Those two wicked people won't let us talk to anyone about our woes."

"I'll still try," the first woman insisted.

Mandy paid attention and listened as they continued to bemoan Mrs. Ridges and Mr. Spindle's cruel treatment of the inmates.

It was Mrs. Tucker who confirmed that indeed the commissioners would be coming in a few days' time. The day before that great event was to take place, all the dorms were cleaned, and the inmates were forced to take their supervised baths and put on clean uniforms.

Early the next morning everyone waited with great expectations, and when the porter who manned the door told one person that the commissioners were here, everyone waited with bated breath. But the waiting was in vain as none of the inmates was called in to air out their grievances.

And dinner that evening was worse than before, and many of the inmates went to bed grumbling as usual. Mrs. Tucker, as usual, was the one who told Mandy and her mother what had happened.

"You should have seen them," she said, eyes filled with tears. She dashed them away angrily, uncaring that the dorm monitor could walk in at any time. Mandy wondered if the other women were already asleep or listening silently in their beds in the dark dorm. "A meal fit for a king was set out for them in the receiving area. Five men and three women showed up for the meeting. They ate like there was no tomorrow and when leaving I saw Mr. Spindle hand each of them an envelope. That's the reason no one bothered about us."

Mandy was a very troubled girl for many days after that. She knew that their lives were doomed. If those commissioners only came to eat and then be bribed to turn a blind eye to whatever was happening in the workhouse, there was no hope for them.

She tried to pray many times but found that she had nothing to say because she was very angry. Why would the loving God Mr. Spindle so piously preached about let His people suffer in this way?

Things were made worse in the workhouse when during the next week three children under five years old died. They all died in the night and in the morning their mothers woke up wailing loudly. That day everyone went around with bowed heads, grieved beyond words as they thought about those little ones and how their lives had been cut short.

"I will never have children," Mandy found herself telling her mother. "If bringing them into this world to suffer is what will happen, I'll find a monastery and join it and become a nun."

"Sh!" Mandy's mother twisted the girl's lips and she cried out. "Do you know that you're not supposed to speak things like that inside here?"

"Why stop me, Ma? This place is hopeless, this life is terrible and I wish I could just die."

Mrs. Wood started crying and Mandy felt deeply ashamed. "You want to die and leave me all alone like your father did," the woman wept.

"Ma, I'm really sorry, I didn't mean that," Mandy whispered. She hated hurting her mother but it seemed as if that was all she'd been doing since her father died. As she didn't want to continue causing her parent pain, she decided that she would run away from the workhouse.

But she had to make her plans very astutely. Just weeks ago two orphans had tried to run away. They'd been brought back and flogged in front of everyone and the inmates were warned that the next person who tried to escape would even be treated worse.

But she couldn't continue staying in here because she was sure that she would run mad. Even the education she'd been promised on the day she and her mother were brought in here was all a lie. For the first few months she and the other young children had been herded into what was supposedly the schoolroom, and for a few days a female teacher had come in to teach them.

Miss Lander was young and pretty, and Mandy had liked her. But just days after, she had left and no one had told them what had happened to the schoolteacher. Then Reverend Reid tried to take over the lessons but, with his other busy schedule, he was absent on more occasions than being in class. Soon the children were directed to go to work alongside their mothers, if girls, and fathers, if boys. They were promised that a teacher would be coming, but this was nearly three years down the line and nothing of the sort had happened. The schoolroom was now where men were trained to be cobblers.

This, the young girl thought as she forced herself to sleep, was the place where dreams came to die and lives were ruined forever. And she wasn't going to be a victim.

UNFIT FOR A LADY

Christmas that year came and went, and the inmates murmured under their breaths that nothing special had been prepared for them like in the days of Reverend Reid. But no one was brave enough to come right out and ask for any special privileges. And Mandy continued to make her plans to escape. She would do it during spring or early summer when it was warm and she could sleep under the bridges. The young girl told herself that, if she escaped during winter, chances of her freezing to death were high, especially if she didn't find a place to shelter from the harsh weather.

And the workhouse was filled to capacity and became overcrowded. Their rations also decreased further, but still no one complained loudly for fear of repercussions. Most felt that they were lucky to at least have something to eat no matter how insufficient. But many more children died, and Mandy wondered that no one cared about them. It was as if they had been forgotten by the world because no one ever came to find out what was going on. The burials for the dead children were done in the deep of the night, which caused Mandy to wonder even more. Sometimes the mothers returned from the cemetery, and Mandy saw broken women. Other times the mothers didn't come back at all, and Mandy wondered what had happened to them.

And the dorms became overcrowded too, with women having to sleep three or four on a bed and unlike when Reverend Reid was here; even those with children had to share. And somehow Mandy still escaped being sent to the girls' dorm, but she knew it was because of the agreement her mother had with Mrs. Ridges.

One evening, as Mandy was finishing up work in the sewing room, she suddenly felt a chilling presence. The women around her all fell silent and the supervisors pretended to be busy doing something in the farthest corner of the sewing room. It soon became clear what had happened when Mandy heard someone calling out to her.

"Miss Wood, a word with you please?" And Mandy stiffened when she heard that dreaded voice. When Mr. Spindle called a person it always meant trouble and she prayed that nothing had happened to her mother. These days they only met at bedtimes because Mrs. Ridges had become very strict.

"Miss Wood," the voice was firm. Mandy placed the last folded clothes in the right crate then turned and, with her head bowed, walked toward the door. Mr. Spindle held it open and urged her to step out into the corridor. He shut the door softly and dread filled Mandy's heart. The man could do anything to her out here and no one would know what was happening to her.

"How have you been, dear Miss Wood?" His voice was charming, but she was frightened. "Won't you at least look up at me and say hello?"

Mandy stared up at Mr. Spindle, her eyes burning with unshed tears and her lower lip trembling. He looked so powerful, so infallible and so merciless. She and the other inmates had found that he wasn't a man to be taken lightly. But what frightened her most was the ugly gleam in his eyes.

Her mother, being too shy to tell her much about what happened between men and women, had left it to Mrs. Tucker to educate her on the basics of life. And the woman had spared no words.

"Men will desire you."

"Desire to do what?"

"Desire to spoil you and ruin you. If a man comes close to you and touches you or looks at you in a certain way, his intentions aren't good. You're now a big girl and should know these things. A man will hurt you very badly and sometimes put you in the family way."

"I don't understand."

"Mandy, oh dear Mandy!" Mrs. Tucker had sighed. "Do you know how children come to be born into the world?"

"Mama said they were angels in heaven and when the time is right God sends them to come and live with people."

"I can't say that for sure but a man and a woman make a child together." And the woman had explained the intricacies of conception to a blushing Mandy. "So just know that if a man looks at you in a certain way, he wants to ruin you. Your body should only be for your husband and no other man. Be careful that no one entices you with words or gifts so that you give away the precious treasure that is your virtue. Flee from such temptations or dangers."

And now here was Mr. Spindle looking at her in the way that Mrs. Tucker had warned her about.

"You can be like your friends Clare and Ruth," Mr. Spindle was saying. "See, they no longer live here in the workhouse but are now rich young women. I made a good life for them out there and they will forever be grateful to me," he laughed.

Mandy realised that it had been a while since she had seen her nemeses. When they stopped coming to the sewing room again, she'd assumed that they had been assigned to work elsewhere in the workhouse. It surprised her to hear that they were no longer inmates but were instead wealthy women, and she wondered how that had come to be. Maybe Mrs. Tucker could shed some light on that and she purposed to ask her about what had happened to her so-called 'friends.'

"Do you know what I did?" Mandy shook her head. "I showed them that they can have a better life out of here," he laughed again, an ugly sound that made Mandy wince inwardly. "Aren't you the least bit curious how I did that?"

Mandy was, but she didn't want to continue speaking to this man who was frightening her. From the way he was rubbing his hands and licking his lips she had a rough idea. This man must have sought favours from Ruth and Clare and in return found them employment out of the workhouse. The thought made her grimace with distaste but she was careful not to let Mr. Spindle see the disgusted expression on her face.

"Miss Wood, I can make your life and your mother's very easy and you'll be very happy. One day, I'll have Ruth and Claire come in here to see you. Then you'll see how well they're doing. Their clothes, shoes, hats and purses are all very expensive and smart," he smiled. "And they have plenty of money too. Those two girls are living like queens while you wallow in this mire."

Still Mandy said nothing. She just wanted the man to finish speaking so she could return to the sewing room where she knew that tongues were no doubt wagging. It filled her with shame to think that the women in the sewing room were talking about her, probably speculating about her relationship with Mr. Spindle and despising her in their hearts.

"Pa, this was never what you wanted for me," the young girl thought as tears filled her eyes. *"You wanted me to have the best, but you didn't stay here to protect me and Mama."*

When Mr. Spindle noticed that the young girl wasn't paying much attention to him, he grabbed her chin, uncaring that he was inflicting pain on her and raised her face. He put his own close to hers and she nearly gagged at the foul stench he emitted from his mouth.

"Or I can do the opposite and make you think that you've visited the devil and his demons in the abyss." He dropped her chin when footsteps sounded as if they were coming their way. Mandy wished someone would come along so Mr. Spindle would be forced to let her go. But the footsteps stopped and then hurried away as if the person was retreating, and her heart sank. No help was forthcoming.

Mandy bowed her head, wishing she could be anywhere else but here. She longed to open the door and return to the sewing room, and she knew that speculation was rife as to what she and Mr. Spindle were discussing.

"Look at me," he ordered in a chilling voice and Mandy reluctantly raised her eyes again. "Think very carefully about the answer you'll give me."

Mandy made her eyes glaze over but still didn't say a word.

"You're a very beautiful woman," the man licked his thick lips and the look in his eyes made her skin crawl with loathing. "And if you make me happy then you'll have the world at your feet. I'm a very wealthy man and you'll want for nothing in your life ever again. You and your mother will live like queens out there in the world and you'll be the envy of your peers."

Mandy wasn't the least bit tempted by the man's offer. It shocked her that he didn't care that she was just a child. She was fourteen and would soon be fifteen in a few months' time, but everyone here thought she was two years younger. How could this grown-up man be lusting after her and she was just a child, barely a woman?

She wanted to scream and ask him if he had no shame at all, for she'd heard that he had daughters who were about her age. He was still speaking.

"Just think, if you let me come in to you say twice a week, I'll take you and your mother out of here, rent you a nice house and give you the life you deserve. No one will ever know."

"But God who sees all will know," Mandy said softly and saw the man's complexion change. He looked like one whose face had been covered in whitewash. "Can we really hide our deeds from the Most High God?"

"Don't make yourself out to be so pious," he sneered. "If you think that God cares then why are you here? Why hasn't that God helped you then? Or don't you know that the Bible says that God helps those who help themselves? Everyone has to find a way to help themselves in this life or end up living in a workhouse for the rest of their lives. Or is that what you want? To live in all this squalor when you could be enjoying your life like your friends out there?"

Mandy didn't know many Bible verses, and she wasn't sure if the verse Mr. Spindle quoted was even in it, but she knew the one Mrs. Tucker had taught her a few days ago. Even though she was still angry with God for their current circumstances, Mrs. Tucker had been sharing about the goodness of the Lord which doesn't change even if tribulations were rife. And she never stopped telling Mandy to be careful with her life and to guard her virtue with everything that was within her.

"Mandy, sin will separate a person from God, and then their life will be worse than we're even experiencing in here. The Bible says: Be not deceived; neither fornicators, nor idolaters, nor adulterers, nor effeminate, nor abusers of themselves with mankind, nor thieves, nor covetous, nor drunkards, nor revilers, nor extortioners shall inherit the kingdom of God."

And slowly and patiently the woman had explained what all those sins meant and how indulging in them would keep her away from heaven.

"Your Mama told me that you loved your father very much," Mrs. Tucker had said and Mandy nodded. "Your father is in heaven and the only way you'll get to see him again is if you go there. But if you let your life become full of sin then you'll never see him again. Remember that always whenever the temptation to sin comes your way. Nothing is worth losing eternal life over, Mandy."

She wanted to one day go to heaven and see her Pa again, but if she fell into sin then she would end up in hell instead. And she felt that Mr. Spindle was being dishonourable to her because she was still a child.

"Mr. Spindle, I'm still a child," she tried to appeal to any sense of morality in the man. After all, he was a deacon in church and preached to them every Sunday.

But he sneered at her, "You're a big girl who understands that life can change if she so wishes. I want to help you, but you're proving to be very stubborn."

Mandy shook her head, "That's not the kind of help my mother and I need, Mr. Spindle. I'm still a child and I don't think it's right for you to be talking to me like this."

"I can talk to you in any way I want, or do you think Reverend Reid is here to stop me?" He laughed cruelly, "The man is gone and it's doubtful that he'll ever return, so I now run this workhouse. My word is law around here and no one can stop me." An ugly look came over his face, and Mandy was really frightened. He looked like a demon and no longer a person. "Or do you think you're better than all the other women in this place? After all, if you were better than them then you wouldn't be here now, would you?"

Mandy bowed her head as the man spewed out more ugly words that made her feel very small indeed. When he'd run out of breath, he reached out a hand toward her, but she flinched and shrank back.

"I'm giving you two days to think about my offer, after which you'll see a side of me that you won't like. But knowing that you're a greedy little thing, I know that you'll soon succumb to me," he laughed again. "Now get out of my sight, you worthless woman."

Mandy opened the door and entered the sewing room, and once again everyone fell silent. She could see the curious looks in the women's eyes but ignored them and went to her work area.

"Oh Lord," she wept as she continued sorting out clothes from the bins. Who was going to help her and keep Mr. Spindle away from her? She didn't want to tell her mother because she didn't want to add to her sadness. The urge to run away became stronger but then she thought about something else. Maybe Mrs. Ridges could help, she thought.

Wasn't the woman always urging them to go to her if they had any problems with any of the staff and especially the men? Mandy just hoped that Mrs. Ridges was tough enough to stand up to Mr. Spindle the way she stood up to the other men in the workhouse, both inmates and workers. Everyone feared the woman as she intimidated them all.

Mandy decided to go and see Mrs. Ridges the next evening which was Sunday. She as well as everyone in the workhouse knew that Mr. Spindle usually went home to his family after Sunday lunch. That morning as he'd stood on the podium and preached about the Ten Commandments, Mandy bowed her head in shame. The man acted all pious, but he was actually a wolf in sheep's clothing. Something within her wanted to shout and tell him to stop being a hypocrite, another word Mrs. Tucker had taught her.

"Don't ever be a hypocrite, Mandy," the woman had warned. "They too have their place in hell because they pretend to be what they're not."

That evening after dinner, she was sure that he wasn't around, so she braced herself for what was to come and walked to the matron's office. Her mother and Mrs. Tucker were out in the yard for a short while before bed, and she excused herself saying she needed to find something. Mrs. Ridges was in her small office taking dinner when Mandy knocked at her door and was bid to enter.

"So Little Mandy, what ails you," The woman asked when Mandy entered the office. She had a few minutes before the lights would be put out in the dorms and she didn't want to get caught up in the darkness along the corridors.

"Mrs. Ridges what can I do about someone who has been bothering me?" Mandy asked, too nervous to even sit.

"Sit down child and tell me who this person is and I'll help you."

"I don't want to take up your time because you're having your dinner and also it's nearly time for the lights to be put out."

Mrs. Ridges laughed and the sound startled Mandy because she'd never heard it before. "Don't you worry a thing about that because I'll personally escort you to your dormitory," The woman reassured her and she felt relieved. "I'm here to help you and also watch out that no one harasses you at all. Now sit and tell me who this person is and I'll go and deal with them mercilessly," and she even plucked a drumstick off the chicken she was feasting on and handed it over to Mandy. Being hungry and having not seen such a luxurious meal for years Mandy briefly forgot why she was here and fell upon the drumstick tearing the flesh off and made short work of it. She even crushed the bone to suck the marrow inside and was soon left with pieces of the bare bone and licked her lips and fingers.

"Thank you." She longed for more but didn't want to look greedy. In any case, the woman had already cleared her own plate so there was nothing left on it.

"Now tell me."

And in halting tones the young girl told of her ordeal at the hands of Mr. Spindle and the threats he'd made to her. Then she suddenly fell silent when a chill seemed to permeate the room.

"You're nothing but a troublemaker and if I could, I would reach down your stupid throat and pull out the chicken you've just devoured, you ungrateful wretch," Mrs. Ridges' face turned really ugly. "Mr. Spindle is a respectable gentleman and for you to go around spewing such ugly falsehoods about a good man is wickedness."

"But I'm not lying…"

"Shut up, you worthless, insolent delinquent," the woman rose and towered over Mandy. "I have dealt with girls like you who think they are princesses and as such are entitled to special treatment," The woman moved from behind her desk and Mandy knew she was in deep trouble. "I've been very gentle with you and your mother, but it seems that all I've done is to breed an ingrate and a liar."

"I'm sorry," Mandy was so scared that she started crying, regretting why she'd even brought her complaint forward. She should have just kept her mouth shut and sought another solution, like running away. Yes, she should have just put her plans, feeble as they were, into action and escaped from this place, for now she was in deep trouble.

"Sorry? You'll soon know what it means to be sorry," Mrs. Ridges said. "Telling nasty lies about a God-fearing and respectable man is sin, and you'll burn in hell for that. And if I hear that you've told this nonsense to anyone in this place there will be big trouble. Do you understand?"

"Yes, Ma'am," Mandy said, trembling from head to foot.

"Now get out of my office, no," she grabbed Mandy's collar, almost choking her, "I have to deal with you myself." At her words Mandy knew fear like never before. She was frogmarched to the girls' dormitory where she was handed over to the monitor.

"And this is your place from today. Let me not catch you in the women's dormitory. I gave you an inch and you took a mile. That's why helping any of you delinquents is just a waste of time, you're always too greedy for more," and she shoved Mandy hard and she stumbled and nearly fell.

Mandy was sobbing loudly as the monitor showed her where she was to sleep. Being relegated to the girls' dormitory meant being separated from her mother. She knew that she wouldn't see her mother soon. And this place was terrible. Just before Clare and Ruth had left she'd overheard them talking about how crowded it was in here. It was even worse than her mother's dorm. Here four girls shared a narrow bed and even in the dimly lit room she could see the curious and pitying looks in their eyes. Ruth had claimed that the dorm was infested with mice and cockroaches which crawled all over a person's body as they slept, sometimes even biting them, and Mandy shuddered. A girl, Clare had added, had once even claimed to have seen a serpent slithering along the wall inside the dorm.

"Please," Mandy tried to make a last appeal to Mrs. Ridges. "I'm very sorry, let me go back to my mother."

"Up until now I've turned a blind eye even though I know your real age," she was told. "I've been patient with you because I thought you were a good girl. But now all that changes and this is where you'll stay for the rest of your life. And tomorrow you'll know just how wicked you've been to have made such terrible accusations."

Mandy heard murmuring, no doubt the other girls were wondering what she'd done.

Mrs. Ridges turned to the monitor. "If she gives you any trouble, use the whip and don't spare her. This wretched and worthless girl needs to learn her place in this world."

❋

Mandy wept the whole night, though she tried not to be overheard by the girl she shared a bed with. She was lucky to get a bed that had only one girl sleeping in it and soon understood why. The girl stank, and she gagged several times. It was clear no one else would share this bed with her.

"If you don't stop all that sniffling I'll toss you out of this bed," she was told and put a hand over her mouth to stifle her sobs. She didn't want to imagine what her mother must be thinking or feeling when she didn't see her coming to bed tonight. The guilt of adding to her mother's anguish after everything else was too much and she felt like her heart would burst with grief. But keeping in mind the threat from her stinking bed mate, she forced everything down. The moment she got a chance she would tell her mother and they would leave this place, never to return, and she would do everything humanly possible to make sure that such didn't happen to them again. And she slept with that thought in her head.

The next day, Mandy was to discover that being moved to the girls' dorm was just the beginning of her tribulations in the workhouse. Early that morning as usual, the gong sounded, and when she would have followed the other girls to the dining hall for prayers and breakfast, she found her path blocked by the monitor.

"You wait here," she was told in no uncertain terms and watched as everyone else filed out of the dorm. Once they were gone, the monitor turned to her. "The instructions I was given for you are that you're to report to the pit right away."

A few of the girls at the end of the queue heard what the monitor said and gasped, turning around to give Mandy pitying looks. But no one was there to help her and she wondered what kind of hell door she had opened by reporting Mr. Spindle to the matron.

"I don't know where the pit is," she said in a trembling voice.

The monitor, a woman in her early thirties laughed. "Oh have no fear, princess, I'll show you the place where you belong. And you will know what it is to cross Mrs. Ridges."

Mandy wasn't even allowed to go to the dining hall for breakfast but was led down a different corridor, the one that went past the morgue. This was the shortcut Ruth and Claire had urged her to use. The stench of decaying human flesh was in the air, and she averted her eyes as they went past the place where dead bodies were held until either a relative came to claim them, or if not, they were interred in the public cemetery.

There was a door at the end of that corridor and she guessed that all dead bodies were removed from the workhouse through it. The monitor pushed back three bolts and then opened it. It was raining outside and as soon as Mandy stepped out she cried out because her feet sunk into mire. The monitor laughed at her predicament and Mandy noticed that she had on thick galoshes. As Mandy trudged after her through the thick mire, tears fell fast and hard because she was being rained on and the woman didn't seem to care. The thin shawl around her shoulders was soon soaked.

The woman stopped outside a barn. Mandy had never been to this part of the compound of the workhouse, let alone knowing that it existed. The barn door opened, and the monitor pushed Mandy inside. The place stank and she felt her stomach heaving.

"You thought you were so good, that you were better than everyone else," the woman sneered. "This is where you'll be working for the rest of your life, princess. Let's see how beautiful you'll still be when you come out of here."

From all the squealing and grunting, Mandy guessed that she'd been brought to the pigsty. She couldn't believe that Mrs. Ridges had decided to punish her in such a manner. While the woman was cold and hardly smiled, Mandy hadn't thought that she was this cruel. And then to her further dismay, she saw Mr. Spindle standing at the far end of the barn talking to a rough-looking man. The pigs were still locked up in their stalls but they sounded angry and impatient, and from all the stampeding that was going on in the stalls, Mandy feared that they would bring the barn walls down.

The moment Mr. Spindle caught sight of Mandy his countenance changed and she knew that he was behind all her woes. She read the triumph in his eyes as he looked at her from head to toe, a slight sneer on his lips. Mrs.

Ridges must have told him about her complaint, and this was the result.

"How do you like this now?" he walked toward her, more of an exaggerated swagger that made him look ridiculous given his stature. If the situation hadn't been so dire, Mandy would have laughed out loud at the picture he made. She'd once seen a newspaper caricature of some self-important nobleman who'd been involved in a terrible scandal involving another man's wife. The funny pictures had showed him fleeing for his life through a first floor window of some building, his clothes clutched in his hands. For days the newspapers had been unkind to the man, and when she looked at Mr. Spindle he reminded her of those funny pictures.

"How do you like this now?" he asked smugly after he had dismissed the other man who was clearly the swineherd, for Mandy saw him open the stalls to let the pigs out. They rushed out, and Mr. Spindle hastily moved away as the animals rushed past him to go out of the barn and into the wet yard, uncaring that it was raining.

"There are fifty pigs in this barn and more are still being born. Your work henceforth will be to clean the stalls, feed the pigs with the leftovers from the kitchen, fill their troughs with water three times a day and take out the manure to the vegetable plot on the other side of the barn." And he laughed unkindly. "And just know this, pigs never make friends with humans, and given the chance the critters will even eat you up."

Mandy's shiver was involuntary even though she knew the man was trying to frighten her. She'd dealt with swine before and knew that they were very unpredictable creatures, but she'd never heard of them eating people. Maybe they did but she wasn't going to dwell on that or she would go out her mind.

"I gave you the better option, but how did you repay me?" he glared at her. "You tried to besmirch my good name and make me look bad. Do you know something," he snickered, "Mrs. Ridges is my wife's older sister, and she told me everything you said about me. Just know that you have brought this upon yourself with your foolishness." He walked around her and she wanted to cringe. "Now, do you have a better response for me?" He stood before her and licked his fat lips, looking like a toad she'd once seen basking on a rock at the pond.

Mandy spotted a shovel leaning against the wall and knew that it was what she would be using for mucking out the stalls. She ignored Mr. Spindle, walked to where the shovel was and picked it up. Seeing a pile of manure that the pigs had scattered in their haste to exit the barn, she walked toward it. It smelled foul but that was certainly better than standing to listen to what the unpleasant man was saying.

"You're still holding onto your stubborn stance, I see," and he drew closer. Mandy shovelled some of the manure and deliberately tossed it toward the man, who jumped aside, muttering angrily as a little of it got onto his shoes.

"You'll pay for your insolence," he hissed. "You'll soon know who I am and why it never pays to cross me." And saying thus, he turned on his heel and hurried out of the barn. Mandy waited for him to leave and was surprised to find that the monitor was still standing at the door watching her. She saw something in the woman's eyes like respect, but couldn't be sure. She had no idea what she was supposed to be really doing but getting rid of Mr. Spindle had been satisfying.

But then her shoulders fell because she had done something very foolish and knew that the man wouldn't let the slight go. She was now in a lot of trouble and would have to be extra careful. If only Reverend Reid would return!

The barn door opened and shut again and she knew the monitor had left. A few minutes later she heard voices and the barn door opened again. Mrs. Ridges came in and after her was Mandy's mother.

"Mama?"

"Mandy?" They shouted at the same time. Mandy dropped the shovel and raced to her mother and they embraced.

"Stop that at once," Mrs. Ridges shouted but they ignored her. "This is a place of work and not recreation." The two didn't hear her, being so happy to see each other again.

"I looked all over the place for you last night," her mother said. "Where were you and what are you doing here?"

"No more talking," Mrs. Ridges walked towards them. "I want this barn cleaned from top to bottom, the pigs fed and watered and all the manure removed to the vegetable farm before lunchtime or there won't be food for you. If you don't finish your chores by evening you won't get any dinner either."

It was backbreaking work, and Mandy wept silently when she saw her frail mother struggling to keep up. She was young and strong but her mother was really weak. For fear of punishment, Mrs. Wood worked as hard as she could. They didn't hear the lunch gong and nobody came to get them so they missed lunch. It was late afternoon before the monitor came and told them to stop working.

"Wash up before you return to the workhouse because the two of you smell worse than the pigs that live in here," she wrinkled her nose in disgust. "Whatever you did to annoy those two," the woman shook her head, "this is the worst form of punishment, and I've never known any woman to survive it. Men barely make it out of here alive and sane, so I really pity you."

Mandy and her mother put their shovels down and wiped their faces. It was true that they stank, but they had survived this first day. Though they had no idea what the future held they were determined not to give up.

Interestingly enough, no one had come to supervise their work, and the swineherd had made but few appearances throughout the day. So Mandy had been able to tell her mother the reason why they were in this place.

"Stand there," the monitor barked, pointing at one of the troughs and it was filled with murky water which the pigs had been splashing around in before they were herded back into their stalls by the swineherd. "Strip and wash yourselves so you can look like decent human beings."

Mandy felt humiliated because the woman apparently didn't care that anyone could just walk in and find them without their clothes on. But with nothing else to do, she obeyed the command, as did her mother. The water was very cold and the monitor took pleasure in pouring it on them using a small pail; never mind that it wasn't even clean.

"Scrub yourselves from head to toe," they were ordered and a piece of soap was tossed to them. It smelled terrible but at least it got them clean. "Now rinse those clothes you were wearing."

"What will we wear," Mandy asked.

"You'll put them back on, or do you want to give the residents of this workhouse a free show and parade yourselves around devoid of clothes?"

Uncaring that her charges were shivering violently from the cold water they had just washed in and their wet clothes, the woman led them to the backdoor through which they had come that morning and back into the workhouse. But instead of taking them to the dining hall as they had heard the gong sounding, she led them toward the kitchen's back door.

"You're not fit to sit with the others as the stench you're emitting will cause them to lose all the food they have eaten. You'll take your dinner in the yard behind the kitchen."

And the rations were so small that even a new-born baby wouldn't have had their fill. Having not had any breakfast or lunch, Mandy fell upon the bread and broth and even licked her bowl. Gone was the girl who had turned her nose up at the cockroaches in the broth when she'd first arrived. Hunger had taught her that rejecting food meant an empty stomach and sleepless nights. So these days she didn't care about the cockroaches or beetles, or even mice droppings in the food. If it looked edible then she would eat it.

"Here, you can have my share," her mother held her piece of bread out to Mandy. "No Mama," Mandy shook her head though she was still very hungry. "You need to eat so you can keep your strength up."

"I don't want to watch you starve to death," her mother was weeping softly as she looked at Mandy.

One of the cooks emerged from the kitchen and frowned when he found them sitting on the step.

"What are you doing here?" He asked in a rough voice. He was carrying something in a wooden pail.

"We were told to eat our food out here," Mandy said resignedly, waiting for more insults. But the man did a surprising thing. He approached them, looked around to see if anyone was watching and then he reached into the pail and scooped up some potatoes which he shoved into their bowls. "Eat as fast as you can because it isn't that hot. If you're found eating this food you'll get me into trouble," he said and disappeared from their sight.

The two needed no second bidding but ate as quickly as they could. For once in a long time they were replete. From the way it tasted so good, mother and daughter knew that this was the meal served to the administrators and other officers in the workhouse. Yet all the inmates ate food that was terrible and contaminated with all manner of dirt and insects. And they knew that such grace wouldn't happen again in a long time so they bowed their heads and made a prayer of gratitude for the man's kindness.

PERILOUS TIMES

❄

The next few months were torture for Mandy and her mother and seemed to pass very slowly. Her fifteenth birthday came and went, and she only remembered the day when Mrs. Tucker found her and brought her a small cake that evening just after dinner.

"I remembered your mother getting you a cake last year," the woman said. "Eat it quickly and then wipe your mouth," and she did so, but first broke off half of it and pressed it into her mother's trembling hand.

Mandy tried her best to make her mother's life as pleasant as she could, given their terrible circumstances. But she could see that her parent was just barely holding on and it pained her heart. The only good thing about working in the pigsty was that Mr. Spindle kept away from her and usually it was just the swineherd around, but he never paid much attention to them.

So Mandy and her mother got into the habit of kneeling down every morning as soon as they entered the barn and said a prayer for help and strength to work.

"Jesus suffered for us on the cross, and He set us free from all bondage," Mrs. Wood told her daughter a few days later. "We're suffering, but God sees our pain. In everything that happens to us, no matter how unpleasant we should give thanks."

Mandy nodded for she had resigned herself to their fate and stopped being angry with God. She just always prayed that they would be strong and safe and she had no idea how it happened but that evening when she returned to her dormitory the supervisor sent her to the older women's quarters.

"You're a big woman now, no longer a child, so I don't think you should be in here," she was told as she was escorted out.

Mandy found her mother and Mrs. Tucker whispering together and when they saw her, smiled broadly.

"What are you doing here?" Her mother asked.

"Ma, Miss Brenda sent me back here. I've been praying that this would happen," she said happily.

"But I already have three other bed mates," her mother said. Mandy could see the women huddled under the frayed blankets. It was still too early for them to be asleep but they lay still in the bed.

"One of those women can join us so Mandy can join you again, Mrs. Wood," Mrs. Tucker said. "There's only three of us so we can make room for a fourth person." And Mrs. Wood thanked the woman who slipped out of the bed to make room for Mandy. "We better get into bed quickly before Mrs. Ridges comes around to inspect the dorm."

And for a few days Mandy forgot about her tribulations because she was close to her mother once again.

However, her joy was short lived as work in the pigsty increased with the birth of nearly ten more piglets. If it weren't enough that they worked in the pigsty, Mrs. Ridge, clearly with instructions from Mr. Spindle, added to their daily tasks. They were made to clean all the chamber pots from the four women's dorms, nearly thirty of them. This had to be done very early in the morning before breakfast. And they had to scoop out the filth with their bare hands for they were denied the small trowels and brushes normally used for such work.

"He wants to break us," Mrs. Wood told her daughter one morning after they had received a thorough scolding for no reason at all from Mrs. Ridges. "But we're made of stronger stuff and will stand strong."

"Mama," Mandy looked at her mother and let the tears fall. "I'm so sorry that you're suffering all this because of me. I did this to you, and I'll never forgive myself."

Her mother looked gaunt and her skin was sallow. The coarse uniform hung on her thin frame like a sack. She was so emaciated that she could barely stand upright.

"Don't ever say that again, Mandy. This world is full of people who find pleasure in the sufferings of others. But one day all this will end. Now wipe away those tears. We don't want anyone to come by and see you crying and feel that they have succeeded in breaking our spirits. God will see us through all this and one day all will be well."

Mandy nodded and wiped her face, but inwardly she felt that death would be a relief for it would end their sufferings. But she was thankful that even in their punishment they were allowed to be together. In this way they were able to encourage each other with verses from the Bible and once in a while would even sing hymns. But of course they had to sing very softly because it seemed as if Mrs. Ridges hovered around just waiting for them to step out of line. Every time she found reason to scold them, meals were withheld from them.

As they scrubbed the chamber pots they heard the door to the backyard opening and quickly looked up. It was Mrs. Tucker and they smiled. Through all their sufferings the woman had remained steadfast in her friendship. And she had told them that she'd been put to work in the kitchen washing all the pots and pans. Whenever she got a moment she would sneak away from the kitchen and come to check on them. And she never came empty handed.

"How are you doing, my princess," she asked Mandy.

"I'm fine but Mama is only getting weaker. She won't go to the infirmary even though I know she should. See how ill she looks and please tell her to get medical attention."

"Today I bring you good news," Mrs. Tucker was beaming. "And don't mind, Mandy, your Mama will be alright."

"What is it?" They both looked at her expectantly.

"Reverend Reid is coming back soon," she said, clapping her hands happily.

That wasn't good news as far as Mandy was concerned. "Where has he been all these months," she cried out. "Doesn't he even care about all of us anymore? What happened to all his promises that this place would be a second home to all of us?"

"Child," Mrs. Tucker's voice was patient, "he lost his wife and daughter after nursing them for a very long time. She was his only child because they had tried for years without any success. Now he's all alone and you should understand that the man has been through some very trying times."

Mandy felt ashamed at her outburst.

"Anyway, Reverend Reid is soon coming back and it won't be long before he puts things right again. Mrs. Ridges and Mr. Spindle have been running this place to the ground, and I for one am glad that the chaplain is returning. Things are bound to change." She looked around and seeing no one pulled out a freshly baked loaf from under her skirts.

"Wash your hands quickly and eat this. I can't be away from the kitchen too long or someone will get suspicious."

The two women cleaned their hands as best as they could, using the same lye soap and water that they used to clean the chamber pots with. They shared the bread, said a short prayer and quickly devoured it. Mrs. Tucker bid them farewell and hurried back to her post before she was missed.

As always, whenever she had a moment, Mandy's hand went to the band of her drawers where Mr. Miller's ring now lay. It had found a permanent place now because the drawers were hers alone, unlike the uniforms which after being dry cleaned never returned to the previous owner. Touching the ring always gave her comfort even if these days she had to struggle to remember what the man looked like.

Would he remember her if he ever saw her again? Four years had gone by, and she knew she had changed from the small girl he'd known and was now on the threshold of womanhood. Her body, though thin, was filling out in places that made it obvious that she was grown up and no longer as small as she was when she came in here.

The one good thing that had come from their working in the filthy pigsty and also washing the chamber pots was that Mr. Spindle left her alone. He kept away from her but Mandy was still wary because such a man couldn't be trusted. She was sure that he was bidding his time for when he would find the chance to inflict pain worse than death on her. And she prayed daily that he would never get the chance. Mrs. Tucker's news suddenly took on new meaning. With the chaplain being around there would be no more harassment and if it happened she would do all she could to find a way to report it. She just hoped that the man wouldn't come back a changed person. Death had a way of robbing a man or woman of their joy and turning them into bitter and hard-hearted beings.

Then she smiled and her mother noticed, raising her eyebrows. "Reverend Reid is coming back," she said. Sooner or later she would find a way of getting to him and she knew that things would change. So she bent her head and scrubbed more chamber pots.

❄

Cecil patted the lining of his favourite coat and smiled. It was still there and safe too. It had survived the journey over land and the seas, four years of moving from place to place and now it was homebound and still safe.

His eyes skimmed over the waters of the Mediterranean Sea as they approached the Strait of Gibraltar to cross into the Atlantic Ocean and then toward England. Home at last, he thought, and to a new life.

And Cecil had reason to smile at last for various reasons. First, his efforts to bring Mr. Weatherly down had borne fruit. It had taken him nearly four years and most of his pay checks, but finally success was in his hands. It was both sad and happy news but he would deal with the former when the time came.

The detective that his colleague had put him in touch with had done a thorough job and obtained so much evidence against Mr. Weatherly. First, the detective had discovered that Grandpa Sinclair had been poisoned by Mr. Weatherly. What made Cecil a little afraid was wondering if his mother had been involved in his grandfather's death. He didn't want to imagine that it could be so. But she would soon be able to give him an answer because her whereabouts were now known.

This latter information caused his lips to tighten. For the past eight years his mother had been a patient in a mental institution. After fraudulently obtaining documents pertaining to Cecil's inheritance from her and possibly blackmailing her after the death of her father, Mr. Weatherly had then declared her to be mentally unstable. With the help of a doctor friend he'd then had her committed to the mental institution. If his mother was guilty of being an accomplice in the murder of Grandpa

Sinclair then she was paying for her sins. But if she was innocent then Mr. Weatherly would pay for his crimes and Cecil would get his inheritance back, all of it. It didn't matter that the estate had been plundered. He would rebuild even if it took him the rest of his life, and his grandfather would be proud of him.

Many people were going to pay for the crimes they had committed against him and his family and he couldn't wait to get home and see their faces as the truth confronted them.

Once again his hand went to his pocket and he pulled out the small white handkerchief from it. He'd held onto it for the past four years. The small pretty embroidery that was the border of the handkerchief and the name on it were still intact. He could count on one hand the number of times he'd washed the handkerchief. It was precious to him and he never let it out of his sight.

"Mandy," he whispered, wondering where she was. Probably still on the estate as her mother worked for Mr. Weatherly. Maybe the man had even offered her a position there. Or she was married to some local man by now, maybe one of the tenants or their sons. Many young girls in the countryside were usually married by the age of sixteen for that is what she would be right about now.

Four years had gone by and not once had he returned to Sinclair Estate. But in his defence he'd been overseas serving his country. As the treatment for malaria had been improved, the British troops had ventured further inland into Africa in search of gold, silver and other precious items. There had been much to be accomplished, but his tour of duty was now over and he was going home. He had already put in his application for retirement after serving in the army for eight years.

At twenty-six years of age, it was time for him to find himself a wife, settle down and have children. And he didn't think he could accomplish that while still serving overseas. Also, he needed to be there for his mother now that he'd found her and to restore his grandfather's estate, which was now his property.

He had no idea about his mother's state of mind, and she would definitely need a lot of care. That was the reason he needed a wife, so she could help him take care of his mother, the woman who had suffered at the hands of that treacherous Mr. Weatherly. He just prayed that she was innocent of murdering her father.

"Lieutenant Miller," Cecil turned around when he heard his name being called, to find his Commanding Officer, Captain William Dale coming towards him. He saluted the man and then stood at attention. "At ease, Lieutenant."

"Thank you, Sir," Cecil relaxed his stance. It was early afternoon and the weather was mild. The two men moved to the railing and leaned over as the ship continued on its voyage back to England. The sea was calm and seemed eager to see them on their way back home. In the distance he could see dolphins following their ship and smiled at their fun-loving nature. Mandy would love this, he thought, thinking of the little girl back in the cottage in the woods. Then he shook himself out of his thoughts and turned to his superior.

"It's good to see that you've recovered from the cold that assailed you," he said.

Captain Dale laughed, "I thought it would keep me bedridden and make me have to be carried home. My wife would have a fit and scold me for days on end."

Cecil liked Captain Dale because the man was not only a good commanding officer who treated the men under him with dignity and honour, but he was also a very strong Christian.

"I've received your request for discharge from the army once we get back home and that's why I've come to search for you, Lieutenant." His brow creased slightly, "Are you sure that's what you want to do?"

"Yes, Sir."

"You're a good soldier Lieutenant, and now that the Viscount Cardwell's reforms for the army have abolished the purchasing of promotions in the military don't you think you now stand the chance to get ahead in your career? You've served as a Lieutenant since you joined the army, and your rank has never changed. You deserve more, or is this the reason you're resigning from the army?"

Cecil shook his head, a half smile on his lips. "Captain Dale, if you recall, Sir, my own position was purchased for me when my grandfather paid for my commission into the army. So I'm not one to be hypocritical and speak against the practice that got me into service in the first place. The reason for my resignation is that my mother has been unwell and I'm all she has. Remember I once asked you to pray with me for her to be found," the captain nodded. "Her whereabouts are now known and I have to go and take care of her. I've been away from her since I was seventeen, nearly nine years ago, and she now needs me."

"I'm happy to hear that your mother has been found and also I'm sorry that she's been unwell. But believe me, with your flawless service record I could put in a word for you and you'll be able to serve at home permanently and not take on any more foreign postings. There are army barracks all over the country now and a single word from me and you can choose wherever you want to be posted."

"Much obliged, Sir," Cecil bowed slightly, "But my grandfather's estate, which is my inheritance, lies in shambles. I've been away for too long and need to return and put my own house in order."

The captain grunted while nodding slowly. "If that's the case, then I'll see to it that your discharge papers are expedited so you can make a smooth transition to civilian life."

"Thank you, Sir."

"I guess this means that you'll also be looking to settle down, get yourself a wife and some children," the man grinned, giving Cecil a knowing look.

"That's right, Sir."

The captain coughed, "You know that I have two daughters who are now of marriageable age. I know I haven't seen them in two years, since I last went home when my wife was ill." Cecil felt his face getting warm at the man's implication. "Catherine is twenty-two and her sister Harriet is nineteen. Having worked with you, I know that you're a good man who will make a fine husband for some lucky woman. Though I hate it that I'm losing you as a member of my team, it would be an honour to have you as my son-in-law."

Cecil cleared his throat. He'd met the Captain's daughters four years ago, before he shipped out, because they'd come to Liverpool to bid their father farewell. While they were pretty girls and very well behaved he didn't feel that either of them would suit him as a wife. And besides that, he'd been thinking a lot lately about the little girl who about five years ago had saved his life. She would be sixteen now and just the right age for a betrothal, he thought. But that would only be the case if she wasn't someone's wife yet.

"You seem like you want to say something."

Cecil pursed his lips, "There's a girl…"

"Say no more, Lieutenant," Captain Dale raised his hand. "You're an honourable and loyal man to have stayed true to that young woman you left back home in England. I pray that she, too, has stayed true to you."

"She has," Cecil croaked and the words nearly stuck in his throat because he really had no idea if little Mandy was still single. And did she ever think of him or consider him as someone who would be her spouse? At the time they had met, she'd been too young to even think of such things.

Even now he still had no idea why he'd left her his grandmother's ring. She'd been just a child then and he'd felt that she needed something to console her because she'd been so upset that he was leaving. But it didn't have to be his ring. He could as well have left her a handkerchief like the one she'd given him.

But over the years as he'd met a few young British and other European women overseas, he'd began to wonder. His grandmother had made him promise to only give the ring to the woman who captured his heart and no one else. It was a ring of love, she'd said, and deserved to be worn by the woman who loved him with her whole heart and he felt the same about her. She'd refused to give it to her own daughter.

Had he subconsciously left the ring with Mandy as a way of ensuring that he didn't give it to the wrong woman? Twice he'd come close to pushing things ahead with a British woman and then a young French woman, but something had held him back. And the young women had been expectant and then very disappointed when he'd made no move to take things any further than simple acquaintances. Out in the colonies where a number of European and British families had settled, it was difficult to find a suitable partner for their daughters. So the families came together often to throw balls and other functions where they invited all the military men serving in their areas. It had become obvious to Cecil that many families were on the hunt for suitors for their daughters. He grimaced slightly; it wasn't that the women weren't beautiful or well behaved. It was just that he hated to think that money or a prestigious position would be the reason why a woman fell in love with him. In his case he had no money, but his military position had still proved quite attractive to the two young women he'd nearly courted.

Well, as soon as he got home he would retrieve his grandmother's ring from Mandy and become serious about finding a wife for himself. Mandy surely wouldn't have waited for him because marriage and courtship had not once been on his mind.

While he was aware that many young men in Britain and Europe got betrothed to children while they were still in the cradle and then waited for them to grow up, that hadn't been the case between him and Mandy. She'd been there for him when he'd needed her, and that was all.

He prayed that, even if she was married, she had kept his ring safe. Perhaps she'd given it to her mother for safe keeping. He would soon know all that, for he would be back home in a few days' time.

"You seem to be in deep thought," Captain Dale's voice brought him back and he felt embarrassed that he'd quite forgotten the other man's presence. "She must be a special woman indeed."

Cecil shook his head, "I was actually thinking about my grandfather's estate and how badly it has been mismanaged while I've been away. The person Grandpa trusted to take care of things turned out to be a betrayer."

"I'm very sorry to hear that. I hope you find a way of putting things right again. Had it been during the early years of this century when the Regent ruled, all you would have needed to do was find yourself some wealthy suitor who comes with a title. That's what many impoverished young men did in those days to find wives to rebuild their estates that lay in ruins."

The thought filled Cecil with disgust even though he laughed with his captain who felt that he had made a good joke. He was glad that he didn't have to bow down to the pressures of such arrangements. Cecil believed in true love, where a man and woman had equal status in the relationship regardless of whatever financial backgrounds they both came from.

And then it suddenly occurred to him that this was the reason he'd shied off from getting serious with the two women he'd left in Cairo. Both of them had come from very wealthy families, and he'd met their parents, who were eager to have their daughters settle down. Being a British soldier, and an officer at that, had its attractions, and the two women, at different times of course, would have been happy to become Mrs. Miller.

The only trouble was that their parents' wealth would have put them above him and probably caused problems in the marriage. Being a soldier and having a grandfather like his had made Cecil the kind of man who respected and honoured people, yes, but never bowed down to another human being. Grandpa Sinclair had been a very honourable man but not a pushover. No one ever tried to make him feel like he was of no consequence, and he'd taught Cecil the value of being respected and esteemed.

"Don't ever use your wealth to oppress others, or become greedy in your quest for the things of this life," his grandpa had told him on many occasions. *"Wealth is a good servant but a terrible master and you must always know the difference."*

From his own observation, people with a lot of money and wealth often expected to be treated like little gods to be bowed down to and adored. Everything they said had to be law to those below them. Sadly, Cecil had watched as two of his officer brothers had succumbed to the lure of marrying into some of the distinguished families of Cairo and soon they began looking stressed.

They were now at the beck and call of their wives' families, and that had even affected their work, as they were expected to do whatever was required of them no matter how inconvenient it was. From time to time they had complained to Cecil though secretly, but with the deed already done, they had to grin and bear their lives after that. What made matters worse for one of the officers was when he'd been given an ultimatum, resign from the army and join the family business or end his marriage. Even at this moment Cecil knew that his friend was still struggling with the tough decision that he was required to make because he loved his wife and as well, he loved serving his country as a soldier. Whatever decision he made, he would lose out in the end.

According to Cecil, marriage wasn't to be tolerated as if it was a dose of malaria medicine to be taken. Marriage was forever, and one had to be with a partner who would keep them smiling all the days of their lives. Of course, all marriages had their own challenges for no one was perfect and that he knew very well. However, if two people genuinely loved each other then working the kinks and knots out of those challenges would be something done with much tolerance, perseverance and above all, love. Bowing down to a woman because of her family wasn't something he would ever do, even if he fell in love with such a one. It wasn't a situation of master and slave but equals all through.

His obeisance was to the Almighty God alone and none other. Cecil was a simple man with no title save the one given to him by the Royal Army. And he wanted a simple woman who would put up with him as he struggled to put his estate back in order. The woman didn't have to be rich, just hardworking and in love with him.

The Captain, seeing that Cecil was drifting off again in his thoughts, excused himself and left him to his own devices. Cecil knew that his friends and colleagues were puzzled at his need for isolation on this journey back home. But he felt distanced from the men he'd served with because right now their dreams and aspirations were headed in different directions. Many of them were excited about returning to the barracks and continuing with their careers as soldiers. Of course, when they got home, they would be furloughed for some time so they could visit their families, but they would return and continue to serve in the army. He knew that his time in the army was up, and he wasn't coming back again and had made his peace with that.

Cecil was just glad that, in his almost nine years of service, no major wars had broken out against Britain or her allies. They had lost a few men while overseas, but those had succumbed to malaria and other tropical diseases and not war. Though they had faced a lot of resistance in the interior where they had served, all these were minor rebellions that had quickly been quashed, and peace prevailed once again.

Cecil was also glad that his years in the army and serving in a foreign land had made him develop a hardness of spirit and self-reliance that had kept him going. While his friends used their pay checks to drink and have a good time in the foreign cities, he'd saved his money and lived frugally because he was determined to change things once he got back home. And his sacrifices had paid off. His pension and whatever he'd saved after paying the detective would push him forward and enable him to rebuild what had been destroyed on his estate.

"By the strength of the Lord Jesus Christ, you will rebuild the broken-down walls and be called the mender of the breaches," he recalled the Army Chaplain preaching to them one day not too long ago. Yes, he would rebuild the broken-down walls and mend the breaches on his estate. If the money he had wasn't enough, surely there was something he could sell and use to rebuild. The land had many large trees, and people needed timber for building and making furniture. He just hoped the forest hadn't been depleted in these years he'd been away. The last time he'd been on the estate he'd been running for his life and so hadn't had the time to walk around and see what damage Mr. Weatherly had done to the forest. Cecil knew that a man could fell trees at the centre of a forest while leaving the ones on the sides standing just to fool people.

Because of his lowly rank, his army pension wasn't much, but if he lived frugally then it would last until the estate became productive once more. His first endeavour after getting rid of the usurper would be to revive the sawmill and get it back on its feet. And he was praying that Mr. Weatherly hadn't sold off the machines his grandfather had purchased for the sawmill just months before his death.

The last time he'd been on the estate and nearly gotten himself killed he'd noticed that the sawmill had been shut down. It pained him to know that what Grandpa Sinclair had so painstakingly built had been reduced to shambles in no time at all. Was it malice that had driven Mr. Weatherly to plunder the estate or was it just gross mismanagement? He sighed as he shook his head, wondering if he would ever receive an answer to that question.

The thing that gave him much comfort was knowing that even if he wanted to, Mr. Weatherly couldn't sell a single inch of the land itself. While he might be able to dispose of everything else, the land was secured. According to his grandfather's will that the Scotland Yard detective had managed to find after a great search, the land couldn't be sold for ninety-nine years. Sixty were gone but thirty-nine were left, and the land would only be free once those ended. And Cecil was back to reclaim what was rightfully his, not to sell it.

"Thank you Lord for such a wise grandfather," he said as he retired to his cabin before the dinner gong sounded.

❋

They docked in Liverpool early on Sunday morning, and after bidding his colleagues farewell, he picked up his luggage and hailed a porter to help him find a taxi carriage to the train station. Cecil hated goodbyes because they made him feel weepy, so he'd made sure that everyone had left the ship before he disembarked. This was mostly because he knew that he might never see many of his colleagues again, as he was leaving for good. Captain Dale had promised him that in a few days' time his documentation would be ready and then he would be a civilian once again.

He was homeward bound, and not even the enticement of Liverpool and its bright lights caught his attention. Settling down in a first-class couch, Cecil found himself in the company of three other men. The compartment's luxurious seats were of deep blue velvet and he smiled and thought about the train ride Mandy had made to London with her father years ago. She'd mentioned travelling in a third-class coach and how crowded it had been. But the joy of seeing the Queen's city had overridden all the other discomforts they had experienced.

"I wonder what Mandy would think of this luxurious compartment," he thought as he settled down and made himself comfortable.

Since he'd arrived first in the compartment, he sat at the window and stared outside. Social norms dictated that he exchange polite greetings with his three travelling companions but as soon as those were dispensed with, it was back to staring outside at the passing scenery.

The last thing he wanted was to have anyone talking to him, so he leaned back, resting his head against the wall and closed his eyes. This was going to be a grand homecoming in very many ways.

NO WAY OUT

What started off as a small rash on the back of Mrs. Wood's right hand soon developed into a pus-filled sore that made her hand swell to the extent that she could no longer work as hard as she used to. And worse, it brought with it a feverish condition that the woman struggled with for days even as she tried to hide it from the supervisors. Mandy knew that her mother was ill but her parent charged her not to share the information with anyone, not even Mrs. Tucker. Each time the hand throbbed, her mother would beg her to drain it of the pus that had collected. And each time Mandy did this she wept over her mother's beautiful hands that were now gnarled.

Mandy and her mother both knew that if it was suspected that Mrs. Wood was seriously ill then she would be taken to the infirmary and admitted there. That would then leave Mandy vulnerable to assaults from Mr. Spindle or any of the other male workers who weren't respectful to the inmates.

Mrs. Tucker had told her about men sometimes attacking vulnerable girls and women, especially if they found them alone. That was the reason most of the young women and girls always walked in threes especially along the deserted corridors. It was even a regulation of the workhouse that no woman was supposed to be in any place alone.

"Ma, you look terrible," Mandy saw how pale her mother's face was one morning. They had hardly slept as her mother had tossed and turned the whole night because of the pain in her hand. "Is it your hand again?"

"Yes, and I barely slept last night," Mrs. Wood's face was contorted with pain, "but we can't stop working now or someone will notice, and then I'll be taken away."

They were shovelling pig manure and filling the buckets to take out to the vegetable garden. At least they didn't have to spread it out once they got it to the garden because that was the work of male inmates. It was raining heavily but no one would let them stop working. The barn was draughty, and the terrible weather was causing restlessness among the swine.

The swineherd didn't want to let the animals out because the last time it had happened they had run into the vegetable garden and trampled it down, uprooting the turnips and carrots since no one was there to stop them, as everyone had gone in to shelter themselves against the rain. He'd gotten into a lot of trouble and his wages were cut in half for nearly a whole month.

In the time they had been here, Mandy had quickly discovered that Hans, the swineherd was a lazy man. But he was good natured and once in a while in a rare show of kindness, he would help the women clean up the barn which was actually supposed to be part of his duties. But since Mr. Spindle was punishing Mandy and her mother and insisted on them doing it, the man felt like he'd been given time off.

Hans had surprised Mandy when he would give them food to eat. Whenever leftovers were brought for the pigs, he would sort through the large bins to find anything edible and share this with the two women.

"Hans, please let the pigs out," Mandy begged when a large sow bumped into her more than once. It was agitated, and she was afraid of what the animal might do. She was trying to keep the animals away from her mother because of the open sore on her hand. If the filthy animals smelled the pus and blood they might attack her mother and tear her arm off.

"It's raining, and last time the pigs destroyed the vegetable garden, and I got into trouble," Hans leaned against the barn door. "Pigs are very destructive."

Mandy felt sorry for the man but she was getting desperate. "Please open the door and lead them into the empty fields. I don't want them to attack my mother."

He scoffed at her, "These animals won't attack you or your mother. They're very tame."

"Please just keep them away from us so we can clean the barn. Lock them up in the other shed or something. We're getting far behind on our work and when Mrs. Ridges comes to check on us she'll be mighty cross and deny us dinner."

Hans gave her a cheeky look and then moved away from the wall, sauntering toward her. "What will you do for me in return," he winked at her, and Mandy was shocked. The man had never behaved in such a manner toward her before, so she'd always taken him to be a harmless fellow. But it was clear that he was just like the rest of the men she'd recently encountered, who made suggestive moves toward her.

"Mandy, come here," her mother called out in a weak voice. Mandy ignored Hans and his theatrics and rushed over to her mother.

"Ma, I'm here," Mandy was shocked to find her mother seated on the wet ground uncaring that the place was filthy. Tears were coursing down her hollowed cheeks.

"Mandy, I'm dying," Mrs. Wood said, her voice raspy. "My chest, my head and back hurt terribly."

"Ma, please don't say that," Mandy burst into tears. If her mother died, then her own life was as good as over. Even frail as she was, Mrs. Wood always did her best to protect her daughter from assault. People had come to know her as a very tough woman. "Ma, you can't leave me."

Mrs. Wood beckoned to her daughter to draw closer. "Promise me something," she whispered.

Mandy turned to find Hans observing them, a strange expression on his face that sent chills down her back. He wasn't to be trusted as Mandy had just discovered. It seemed that all his kindness had been pretence while he bid his time to begin making lewd suggestions to her. With her mother gone and she here in the barn alone with him, who knew what mischief he could get up to?

She knelt down beside her mother but made sure to keep him in the periphery of her vision so she could see if he tried to do anything. Vulnerable as they were, she was prepared to fight for their honour if the need arose.

A large sow rushed toward them and Mandy quickly pulled off her left shoe and threw it at the animal, which scampered away squealing loudly. Hans laughed and Mandy nearly took off her other shoe to hurl it at his face.

"You realize that these greedy animals will devour your shoe," he called out. "If you like I can retrieve it for you before they destroy it."

Mandy shrugged, ignoring the man's offer of help. She wanted no more favours from Hans or any other man because she was now aware that they came with unsavoury conditions attached to them.

She recalled her mother's words years ago when the cart driver, Mr. Stiles had offered to be stopping by their house to help them and even to bring them food.

"Mandy, no man ever does anything for a woman without expecting something in return," her mother had said. "While I agree that some men are gentlemen, as your father was, most aren't, and anything they do for you will have to be paid for."

"With money?" Mandy asked wide eyed. "But we don't have any money to pay Mr. Stiles and he knows it," She was so innocent and her mother gave her a sharp look.

"If only money was what they were after," Mrs. Wood had murmured. "Never get into the habit of accepting free gifts from people and especially men. Those gifts may seem innocent at first, but you may be led to compromise your integrity out of a sense of guilt. And if you owe people they always find a way of manipulating you into doing whatever they want, no matter how unpalatable it may be to you. The Bible even admonishes us to owe no man anything but charity. Unless it's the last straw, don't ever get into debt of any kind no matter how little or innocent it may seem."

And now her mother's words were being proved to be right.

When the swineherd realized that Mandy wasn't responding to his offer of help, he turned to walk away, out of the barn, He was whistling as he went. And then a shocking thing happened. As Hans opened the barn door, the largest hog knocked down the door to his stall and rushed out. Seeing that, the others also blew through their stalls and chased after him and it was a pandemonium.

Hans had his hand on the barn door when he looked back and saw the pigs bearing down on him. With a loud shout he tried to rush out and bang the door shut, but before he could do that, all the animals including the very little ones poured out of the barn, squealing and grunting as they fought to find their way out. Mandy's lips twitched maliciously. The man should have listened to her and released the pigs while they were still calm. For then he might have led them out to the empty fields on the other side of the compound. But with them running wild they were sure to end up in the vegetable garden again. She could hear his shouts and thought that it served him right.

"Mandy…"

"Yes Ma?"

"Promise me."

"What is it Ma?" Mandy forgot about the swineherd and the animals and turned to her mother. She put both arms around her mother who laid her head on her shoulder. It was clear that no work would be done today, but Mandy no longer cared about the punishment she would receive.

"Promise me that after I'm gone you won't spend a single day more in this place. That you'll find your way out and disappear."

"But where will I go, Ma?" The tears returned.

"You're a big girl now. Cut off your hair which has grown back, steal some men's clothing and disguise yourself. You worked in the sewing room sorting through all the clothes given to charity, I'm sure you can find a way of going there again and carrying out a set of them. But just promise me that you'll get out of this place before it sucks your soul out after I'm gone. Then find work somewhere else where you can fight back should anyone try to assault you."

"But, Ma…"

"Promise me," Mrs. Wood clutched her daughter's arm. Her thin fingers bit into Mandy's flesh. "Promise me."

"I promise, Ma," she tried to free herself but her mother held on fast, causing her to wince at the pain. "You're hurting me."

"That's because you think I'm joking and you're not taking me seriously. I have protected you but with me gone you'll be vulnerable to assault by anyone who cares to do it. Get out of here and don't die in here like me. There's something better for you out there, a good life. But you have to get out to find it."

"Ma, please don't say that you're dying. We came in here together and we'll leave the same way. Remember that you've always told me to be strong," Mandy was sobbing loudly. "Don't give up on us."

"Five years in this place," her mother said tiredly. "Twice I asked for permission to leave but my request was always denied, though I saw others being granted the chance to leave."

That was new information that Mandy was unaware of. "Who wouldn't let us out?" She couldn't believe that all these years there had been the chance for them to leave but they were still stuck in this place.

"Mrs. Ridges said that our case was special and if we tried to leave there would be trouble. I know that Mr. Weatherly paid them to keep us in here until we die."

"But why didn't you go to Reverend Reid?"

"Because each time I did he returned me to Mrs. Ridges because she dealt with the administrative side of things. Now I understand when Mrs. Tucker said she was also a prisoner because of Mr. Spindle's false accusations about her and others. Who knows what Mrs. Ridges told the chaplain about us such that he never once made a follow-up of the matter?"

"But why, Ma, what did we ever do to Mr. Weatherly that he locked us in here? If he didn't want you to continue working on the estate then he should have let us go but not imprison us in this place." Over the years Mandy had come to understand many things as she grew up and her hatred for the man increased.

"It was because of that young soldier that we helped," Mrs. Wood said. "I didn't want you to know anything at the time but I found out who he was."

"Are you talking about Mr. Miller?"

Mrs. Wood nodded. "Mrs. Shaw told me that Mr. Miller's grandfather had owned the estate before Mr. Weatherly."

Mandy wiped her eyes and looked at her mother, quite perplexed. "I don't understand." It didn't make sense to her. How was that even possible?

"Mr. Miller's father was killed when he was a small child about three years old, so his mother brought him back to the estate from Liverpool where they'd previously lived. Mr. Miller's father was a sailor who was lost at sea. When Mrs. Miller returned to the estate her father decided to bring up the boy as his heir," Mandy was listening keenly. "When Mr. Sinclair died, the estate was supposed to go to Mr. Miller but he was only seventeen and his grandfather wanted him to join the army so he could become a man, as the old man put it, according to Mrs. Shaw."

"So how then did Mr. Weatherly come to own the estate?"

"Mr. Weatherly was the estate steward or manager, and Old Mr. Sinclair trusted him, as did Mrs. Miller. They hoped he would continue to run the estate profitably and hold it for Mr. Miller until he returned from the army. Mr. Sinclair had purchased an army commission for Mr. Miller. The idea was for him to be in the army for about five years or so as a way of toughening him up so he could return and run the estate. But when Mr. Sinclair died suddenly, Mr. Weatherly convinced Mrs. Miller to become his wife. No one knows what happened but two weeks after the wedding Mr. Miller left for the army and didn't return until four years had gone by. That was the time he came to us."

"What happened to Mrs. Miller then," Mandy was sure that there hadn't been another woman at the manor. The information her mother was giving her was quite shocking.

Mrs. Wood sighed, "Mrs. Shaw told me that after about six months of being married to Mr. Weatherly the woman just suddenly disappeared. He told people that she had eloped with her lover."

"And was that true?" Mandy couldn't imagine Mr. Miller's mother being so flighty. But then people were strange and did stranger things.

Mrs. Wood shrugged, "No one knows anything but a few people who were loyal to Mr. Sinclair were concerned and questioned Mr. Weatherly extensively, even bringing in the police constable. In retaliation the man terminated their tenancies on the estate and chased them away. Many people left because they were afraid of him as he claimed to be related to Queen Victoria and was untouchable. The man began to make unwise investments and soon there was nothing of value in the manor. Mrs. Shaw suspects he was gambling the valuables away and then the sawmill shut down. It used to provide work for many people, and they moved to other estates or cities. No one wanted to work on the estate anymore because they weren't being paid. And Mr. Weatherly was very harsh with the tenants. If they didn't settle the rents he imposed, he kicked them off the estate. That's the reason nobody who knew him would respond to his advertisement for a cook and housekeeper. I was foolish to think we were going to live on a prosperous estate," she shook her head sadly. "Mandy, I failed you as a mother. Please forgive me."

"Ma, there's nothing to forgive because you did your best for us, but I messed everything up when I brought Mr. Miller to our house." They sat in silence for a little while. "Do you think Mr. Miller will ever return to take back the estate from Mr. Weatherly?" Her free hand went to the ring as it always did whenever she sought comfort. Would its owner ever return? Her mother shifted slightly and Mandy had to use both hands to hold her steady.

"It's highly doubtful. Before we were brought here I overheard Mr. Weatherly telling his two men, Burns and Jensen to do everything possible to find that young man and make sure he never spoke to anyone again. I fear that they may have harmed him because they were very vicious men. If he fell into their hands, that was the end of him."

Mandy's heart went to her throat. What if Mr. Weatherly had really succeeded in having Mr. Miller killed? Her hand again went to the band of her drawers. She touched the ring and deep sadness filled her heart. Would she ever see Mr. Miller again or had this ring been his parting gift to her forever? Had Mr. Miller known that his life was in danger and so had left her this ring?

"Mandy get out of here as soon as possible," Mrs. Wood said tiredly, then slumped.

※

Two days later Mrs. Wood collapsed on the way to the dining hall. She was immediately carried to the female sick ward. Mrs. Tucker found Mandy before she went out to the barn and informed her, and she was allowed to go and see her mother in the infirmary but had to return to her daily duties as soon as possible.

Even though Mrs. Tucker had told her that the chaplain was back she'd seen nothing of him for weeks. He was probably still mourning the deaths of his wife and daughter. The man had been away for close to two years and clearly he also had a lot to catch up on. But even with him being present now, nothing had changed. Everything was like before with Mr. Spindle and Mrs. Ridges running the workhouse, and the meals were small and as terrible as ever.

"Your mother has terrible infection in her blood caused by that ugly sore on her hand. We have tried to bleed her and also administered some drugs to her but if they don't work in three days to stop the sore from spreading then we'll have to refer her to Dudley General Hospital to have the arm amputated," the medical officer told Mandy.

"No," Mandy cried out in alarm. She couldn't imagine her mother losing her arm.

"That might be the only thing that will save her life. Infections like these only continue spreading and getting worse. If the arm isn't amputated, your mother could lose her life. Your mother is a very sick woman."

Mandy knew that her mother's illness stemmed from the filthy conditions they worked in. It was even a wonder that she herself hadn't fallen ill or gotten such an infection as her mother had. Seeing her mother lying in bed with her eyes closed and looking so pale put great fear in her heart. She looked half dead, and much as she didn't want to think about the chances of an amputation, maybe it would save her mother's life. She would see what happened in three days and then make a decision.

And the cause of all their tribulations was that wicked Mr. Spindle.

For the next few days Mandy continued working alone in the pigsty but her guard was up because she no longer trusted the crafty Hans.

"How is your mother doing," he came over to her late one afternoon just two days after her mother's admission to the infirmary and she stared warily at him. She was cleaning one of the stalls. "Don't look at me as if I'm going to harm you," he said. The tone of his voice told her that he was being honest and she could see something like regret in his eyes. He must have realised what he'd done a few days before and was probably trying to reassure her that he was harmless. But she would be very careful around him, and gone were the days of receiving anything from him.

"Mama is getting better and she'll soon come back to work again," Mandy told him with a false smile. She was really worried because her mother wasn't getting better and the sore was spreading. It had to be drained of pus and blood about five times a day and the hand was swollen to twice its normal size. Each time Mandy went to visit her mother in the ward she would find her groaning and writhing on the bed in a lot of pain.

"You look very worried," Hans told her. As soon as he'd heard about her mother, his manner toward Mandy had changed, and he did most of the work her mother had done before. Being a man, he was stronger and they got work done much faster, but she was still wary of him.

"Wouldn't you be worried if your own mother was ill?"

Hans shrugged, "I never knew my ma because I was left on a ship that came to Liverpool from Germany," he said. "Some sailor named me Hans, and I was brought up in a foundling home in Liverpool." He gave her a sad smile. "As a child I used to dream that one day my mother would come to the orphanage in a fancy carriage and take me away. When I turned fourteen one of the wardens told me my life story, and I knew that no mother would ever come for me. Imagine that in my foolishness I had held onto that hope for years. So I ran away and boarded the train without any money. The conductor finally caught up with me at Dudley but before he could raise the alarm I managed to jump off the train and ran away as fast as I could. Thank goodness it was slowing down to enter the railway station or I would have been badly maimed or even killed," he pointed at a long scar that ran from the back of his right leg down to his ankle. "I got this that day and will never forget the terrible pain I felt," he scrunched his face. "Reverend Reid found me lying in a ditch and very delirious. The wound was infected, and I was starving, and he brought me here. He put me to work in this barn, and ten years later, here I am. So I don't know what you want me to feel since I've never had a mother."

Mandy felt sorry for him. "Let's just finish the work," she said, not wanting to encourage him to continue talking to her.

It started raining a few minutes later and, because Mandy didn't want to get wet for the third time that week, she waited for it to ease. The dinner gong sounded, and she knew that if she didn't get there in time, she wouldn't get any food.

"Do you want me to walk you to the dining hall," he asked in a polite voice. The man was no doubt trying to make up for his past mistakes but Mandy didn't want to feel obligated to him in any way.

"No, I'll be all right. All I have to do is get in through that door and dash down the corridor."

"Make sure no corpses wake up and chase you," he said with a twinkle in his eyes and they both laughed at the joke.

After bidding Hans farewell, Mandy pulled her shawl over her head and dashed into the rain. Her feet squelched and splashed muddy water all over her dress and she prayed that no one would notice, for then she would be forced to go and change before dinner. And that would mean that she'd be late and find that her food had been shared by her tablemates. At least the cold and humiliating baths had stopped a while back. She ran to the door leading inside the workhouse, opened it quickly and then pushed back the bolts like Mrs. Ridges had told her to always do when she left the barn. She wasn't paying attention and so didn't notice the figure standing a few paces away in the semi lit corridor until it was too late.

"I've been waiting for you," the dreaded voice made her head snap upwards. "I told you that it was just a matter of time before you fell into my arms," Mr. Spindle laughed, an ugly sound that scared her. She knew that if she didn't get away then he would hurt her in the worst way possible. Her virtue was her treasure as her mother and Mrs. Tucker had kept emphasising to her and she knew that this man was out to rob her of it in whatever way he could.

The corridor was deserted as it usually was during mealtimes, and she knew that even if she screamed, no one would hear her. They were all probably in the dining hall taking their dinner. She should have taken Hans up on his offer to walk her to the dining hall. But would he have been her protector or would he have turned into an adversary?

"What did I ever do to you?" Mandy cried out, watching the man's every move. At least someone had placed lanterns along the corridor even though they weren't bright. So far the man hadn't taken a step in her direction but he was blocking her way so she couldn't go forward. She thought of retreating and running out back to the barn but she had shot the bolts back, securing the door. In the time it would take her to draw them Mr. Spindle would be upon her. The only way of escape was getting past him and running as fast as she could to the dining hall.

"You belong to me, and once I'm done with you no other man will ever want you," he said, and fear nearly paralyzed her. This man was evil, and she wondered why she'd had the misfortune of being in this workhouse.

THE ESCAPE ROUTE

❄

Mandy tried to think of some way to distract Mr. Spindle so she could get past him but failed. She had vowed that she would never let a man rob her of her virtue and if it meant dying in the process, then so be it. Her mother would mourn her but she would be all right, but that's only if the disease that was ravaging her body didn't kill her first. Hearing about Mandy's own demise might expedite her mother faster into the other world, but if that's how it was to be then she was prepared to die. Her virtue belonged to the man she would fall in love with and get married to, not some lecherous old man. But now it seemed as if she would never live to find a man, fall in love and get married, and the thought filled her with pain.

"When I asked you to become my mistress two years ago, you turned your nose up at me as if you were too good for me," he said scathingly. "Once I've had enough of you, I'll sell you to a brothel like I did your two friends and you won't choose whoever comes in to you. They tried to blackmail me but I proved to be cleverer than them." His words shocked Mandy to the core.

She'd always wondered where Claire and Ruth had gone after Mr. Spindle told her that he took them to find a better life outside the workhouse. So, the brothel was a better life, she thought, and pity filled her heart as she thought about what the two girls must be going through. Were they even still alive? Even though they'd been mean and at times downright cruel, she wouldn't wish their fate on her worst enemy. This man was evil through and through, and Mandy hoped that with her death, someone would repay him for his crimes. If she was to be the sacrifice so many young girls and women would be free, then so be it, but she was going to fight to the bitter end.

"You're mine," Mr. Spindle said and lurched forward intending to grab her. But she was alert and dodged him, managing to slip past him. He shot out a leg and tripped her, causing her to stumble. As she tried to regain her balance she felt him grab the back of her uniform. Because it was worn out and she'd been denied a new one as punishment, it came apart and she felt exposed as the wicked man laughed.

"No one will ever know what happened to you, because after I'm done, I'll lock you in the morgue and use you till I've had my fill of you. Then I will tell everyone that you died and after that I'll transport you to the brothel where I know I'll fetch a good sum because you're still young," and he raised his hand and backhanded her so she went flying and struck the wall with the back of her head and slid down to the cold, hard floor. He advanced, taking his belt off and then raised it intending to whip her.

Mandy screamed with all her might even though she knew it was hopeless. Maybe someone would hear her. She raised her hands to protect her face as she waited to feel the sting of the man's belt.

"Mr. Spindle," the harsh voice broke through and Mandy thought she was dreaming. God had answered her prayer and sent someone to save her. She watched in fascinated wonder as a man who she recognized as the Chaplain's assistant practically flew down the corridor and tackled Mr. Spindle whose hand remained raised even as his face conveyed his shock at being caught in such a situation.

The man grabbed Mr. Spindle's raised arm, snatched the belt out of it and twisted his arm behind his back, then pushed him away from Mandy.

"So all the stories that I've been hearing about you are true?" Reverend Reid was as white as a sheet, no doubt shocked at the sight he'd been about to witness. "While I was away you did terrible things, but I have been excusing you and saying that it's all lies." He turned to someone behind him. "Mrs. Tucker, thank you for making me aware of what this man has been doing. See to the young girl," he said.

Mandy was sobbing in relief, feeling weak when she imagined what might have happened to her had these people not come. Mrs. Tucker gave Mr. Spindle a look that said she wished him dead then rushed to Mandy and helped her get to her feet.

"He tore my dress," the terrified girl said, trying to hold the hanging pieces together, shame filling her heart at being exposed to the eyes of older men. Someone banged on the back door and Mrs. Tucker pulled back the bolts and opened it. It was Hans and he was armed with a shovel.

"I heard Miss Wood screaming," he said, taking in the scene before him. "I wanted to walk her to the dining hall now that her mother isn't here but she wouldn't let me." He gave Mr. Spindle an ugly look. "So you're back at it again."

Mandy didn't believe that the cheeky and normally mild Hans could look so fierce. Now she understood why he'd started hanging around her in the barn after her mother fell ill and was taken away. In his own way, the man had been protecting her and she cast him a grateful look.

"He threatened me," and Mandy told them about Mr. Spindle's harassment of her years ago and how he'd made her life so terrifying. She also told them about reporting to Mrs. Ridges and that's when their woes had begun.

"She's lying," Mr. Spindle screamed. "This woman is nothing but a harlot. She's been trying to seduce me but I rejected her and now she's out to cause trouble for me. She and that worthless oaf who is no doubt her lover have hatched this wicked plot to accuse me falsely."

"Silence!" The Chaplain commanded. "Don't let him get free," he told his assistant. Hans moved closer to where Mr. Spindle was being restrained, no doubt to prevent him from escaping. "This is an issue that can cause a lot of trouble for this workhouse," he turned to Mrs. Tucker. "Is the girl all right?"

"Did he touch you in any other way?" Mrs. Tucker asked Mandy, fear and anguish evident in her voice as she imagined the worst. "I promised your mother that I would look out for you, but I have failed. I've been watching out for you every day when you came out of the barn, but today there was much work to be done in the kitchen. When I didn't see Mr. Spindle in the dining hall I got worried and begged the Reverend to let me come and check on you." Once again, she cast an ugly glance at Mr. Spindle. "I'm so thankful we got here in good time. But I'm so sorry for not being there sooner for you, Mandy. What would I have told your mother had this wicked and evil man attacked you and succeeded?" she sniffed.

"Mrs. Tucker," Mandy didn't want the woman blaming herself. "He struck my face and tore my dress when I was trying to get away from him. He would have whipped me with his belt," and she repeated the threats he'd made about ruining her then selling her to a brothel like he'd done with Claire and Ruth.

"Is that what he told you?" The chaplain looked like he was about to cry when he heard about the other two girls. "That he sold Claire and Ruth to a brothel?"

Mandy nodded, feeling very tired. "Please may I go and see my mother?" She asked. She needed to see her mother and feel her comforting arms around her. It felt like she'd come through a long journey, and her soul was weary. But she also felt relief that the chaplain was here and knew without a doubt that Mr. Spindle would be dealt with very harshly.

"In a short while, my child," the chaplain spoke kindly to her. "I'm very sorry for the abuse you've suffered at the hands of this man. But rest assured that it will never happen again because Mr. Spindle is leaving this workhouse immediately. No such deviant of nature should be allowed to be around people, and especially vulnerable young girls like yourself," he glared at the man. "And be sure that his punishment will be befitting for his crime."

"I'm innocent and this girl is lying. I never did those things she's saying," Mr. Spindle cried out. "I've been a good governor and earned a lot of money for this place. How can you take the word of a harlot over mine? I'm a God-fearing man and a deacon in church. This woman seduced me, I tell you."

"Will you be silent," the chaplain roared. The noise attracted a few people who came to see what was going on. It was clear that dinner was over, and Mandy wasn't surprised because the rations were so small these days that it only took one gulp and everything was gone from the plate. "There have been many complaints about your terrible and wicked behaviour but I've always defended you. It has been your practice to coerce vulnerable women who depend on you to protect them. Some of them are very young and you've ruined their lives. Those who refused have either been forced or else you've tortured them in other ways like you did with this child. What kind of a man are you, Mr. Spindle, and yet as you say, you're a deacon in the church?"

"I didn't do anything," Mr. Spindle continued to protest his innocence.

"You'll leave the workhouse immediately and never return. Out of respect for your family I won't seek to prosecute you though you deserve it. But just know that the report I send to the church and the commissioners will state all your iniquities for I'm commencing an investigation into your gross misconduct especially in the months that I was away. I trusted you, Mr. Spindle, yet you've brought shame not only to yourself and your family but to this workhouse as well. Just be assured that you'll never again work in a workhouse, at least not in this county and the surrounding ones. Take him out," he instructed.

"You haven't seen the last of me," Mr. Spindle shouted as four men set upon him to help the assistant. They dragged him down the corridor and Hans followed, his shovel still in his hands. "You delinquent, this isn't the end of me and you. I'll find you and your mother and on that day you'll be very sorry."

"Ignore him child," the chaplain told the trembling Mandy as Mr. Spindle continued to curse and spew out ugly threats but soon his voice faded away. "He's not going to do anything to you because the law will protect you."

Mrs. Tucker took her apron off and wrapped it around Mandy from the back to cover her. Mandy's hand immediately went to the band of her drawers to make sure the ring was still there. It was and she felt comforted.

"You and your mother will never suffer in this workhouse again," Reverend Reid gave his promise. "I will make sure that you and all the other women are taken care of."

That day for the first time in five years, Mandy ate to her fill, and she was even allowed to stay in the ward with her mother for as long as she wanted to since the illness Mrs. Wood had wasn't infectious.

"Tomorrow you'll report to the kitchen where you'll be given light duties," the monitor told her that night when she went to bed. The woman looked ashamed at the way Mandy had been treated. Another surprise awaited her; she had a bed to herself as indeed was the case with the other women in their dormitory. Mrs. Tucker told her that even greater changes were coming. There was excitement in the air and it was palpable. Mandy wondered just how fast the chaplain had worked to change their living conditions. In a way she had been the sacrificial lamb that had brought down a wicked tyrant. As she heard the women chatting and laughing, a sense of relief engulfed her. She knew that Reverend Reid would do his best to protect all of them as he'd promised.

But even with the good things she was promised and the changes she saw including receiving a new set of uniform, shoes and a shawl, Mandy knew that she had to get out of this place and take her mother away. Even though Mr Spindle had gone, his cronies remained. Mrs. Ridges, for one, would most certainly seek ways to retaliate on behalf of her relative, and Mandy would never feel safe, not as long as the woman remained. And Mandy was also sure that there were others who wouldn't take too kindly to Mr. Spindle's dismissal. There were those who had profited and benefited greatly from his crooked ways. With their source of plunder now dried up, who knew how angry they would be?

Early the next morning after breakfast and before she reported to her new work station, Mandy went to see her mother.

"Mandy," her mother whispered.

"I'm here, Ma," she smiled. "How are you feeling today?"

"Much better, though I still feel weak. You still look worried, even though that man is gone from our lives for good." She raised her hand "And my hand is healing nicely, too, so please stop looking so anxious. There will be no need for an amputation as the doctor had feared. God has spared my life and limbs."

And in a low voice Mandy told her mother everything about the previous evening, leaving nothing out. Last night she'd been too tired, and her mother had looked drowsy, so though she'd sat with her for a long while she, hadn't told her anything apart from the fact that Mr. Spindle had left. Now she gave her the full details.

Mandy also mentioned the threats Mr. Spindle had made against them as he was being thrown out of the workhouse and she shared her concerns about those who had been on his side, especially Mrs. Ridges.

"So Ma, you need to get better quickly so we can get out of here."

Mrs. Wood gave her a sad smile, "Why don't you find a way to go and leave me here? I'm still very weak and will only slow you down and get you into trouble."

"Ma, I told you that I would never leave you behind. Even if I have to carry you out of here that's what I'll do. We came in the two of us and we'll leave the two of us. Papa would never forgive me if I left you in here."

But it would take another four weeks before Mrs. Wood was strong enough to rise up from her bed. In that time she received special care and Mandy was glad to see her mother getting better. She told her about the plans she'd made for them to leave.

"Do you think we'll be allowed to get out," Mrs. Wood asked.

Mandy smiled and her mother's heart skipped a beat. Mandy had become very beautiful even if she wasn't aware of it, and innocence shone from her eyes. Her mother feared that the outside world would be worse than it was in here.

After Mr. Spindle's departure, many reforms had been implemented and in the short span of four weeks a lot had changed and things were so much better now, including the food both in quality and quantity. The dormitories had been decongested, as many families that had otherwise been held in the workhouse because of Mr. Spindle's maliciousness were released. The chaplain took over all the administrative duties that Mr. Spindle had been doing and strictly supervised Mrs. Ridge and the other officers. In those four weeks many women and men got good recommendations and were soon being offered meaningful employment by those who had once rejected them. Yes, those reforms had done much good for the inmates. But Mandy still wanted to leave.

"Mrs. Tucker told me that all I need to do is to request for leave to visit a sick relative and we'll be granted permission to go."

"But we don't have any sick relatives and I don't like you lying to get your own way, Mandy. Remember who you are and what you stand for."

Mandy wanted to remind her mother about the lie she'd told five years ago regarding her age. But this wasn't the time and besides, it had worked out for their good, at least for a while. Her mother had probably felt that she was doing the right thing at that time.

"Ma, I need to get you out of here by any means possible. We've been here for too long and I'm not spending my next birthday in this place."

"But things are changing now," Mrs. Wood argued. "And didn't you say that the chaplain promised to find you a good position outside the workhouse?"

"That's right, but there are still people in this place who are sympathetic to Mr. Spindle and feel that he was treated unfairly. Mrs. Ridges is just biding her time and then she will come after me again. Remember what happened when Reverend Reid was away for months. Nobody knows what will happen in future, and if Mrs. Ridges gets the chance to retaliate against me, don't you think she'll do her worst? It was because her brother-in-law was shamed, as she sees it, and that has definitely affected her sister's marriage in a bad way. Reverend Reid didn't want the matter broadcast outside the walls of the workhouse, but you know how it is with gossip and large populations. And the newspapers are full of mockery for Mr. Spindle and you can imagine what his family must be going through. No, Ma, this place is no longer safe for us because I will always be blamed for what is happening to Mr. Spindle."

"No, my child, you weren't responsible for that man's tribulations. His sins found him out and he brought all that trouble upon his own head."

"Ma, you sound as if you don't want to leave this place again."

"Truthfully, I don't."

"But why? A few weeks ago you were begging me to leave. What has changed now?"

"A few weeks ago I wanted you to leave because Mr. Spindle was becoming too wicked and cruel and I was terrified that he would hurt you. And he would have but for the grace and mercy of the Lord. But now that Reverend Reid is back and knows everything, don't you think he's being very careful about how this workhouse is being run? Even those accomplices of Mr. Spindle's, including Mrs. Ridges, are most probably being investigated and their time will come. She will soon get what she deserves, so now they are treading carefully and can't hurt you. We don't have to leave."

"Mama, Reverend Reid is only one man and there are about five hundred of us, not counting the workers. Do you think one man is able to pay attention to all of us and protect us?"

❋

Cecil nearly wept when he saw his mother for the first time since he'd left home nine years before. She was so thin, to the point of gauntness, and it seemed as if all life had been sapped out of her. Her eyes were dull and soulless.

When he'd arrived and asked for Mrs. Miller, he was informed that there was no patient present who went by that name. But when he asked for Mrs. Weatherly, he was shown to the common area where visitors were received. He found her seated alone on a bench outside on the veranda, and she was staring at the road, a blank look on her face.

The hospital was old and the buildings were in terrible condition, but at least it was clean.

"How long has my mother been like this," he asked the nurse who was standing by his side. "Can she really hear me or is her mind gone forever?" He'd been informed that his mother was completely out of it, a total lunatic.

"Mrs. Weatherly…"

"Her name is Mrs. Miller. Rachel Miller," Cecil's tone was firm.

"Oh!" the nurse looked flustered. "The person who brought her here told us that he was her husband and gave his name as Mr. Paul Weatherly."

"He lied," Cecil said and felt his stomach churning with rage. He wanted to rush to Sinclair Estate and rip Mr. Weatherly's throat for having nearly destroyed his mother. The man had lied when he'd seduced her, and the marriage certificate they had signed was fake, among other things. "My mother's name is Mrs. Miller and the man who brought her here did so under false pretences," he approached his mother. "The doctor who signed the forms that committed her to this institution has been arrested and confessed that he was bribed to do so." And the man had also confessed to aiding Mr. Weatherly to poison Grandpa Sinclair for he'd been the old man's personal doctor. Truly a person's worst enemies were those of his own household!

"Careful, Sir, Mrs. We… er Miller is very violent and in the past has hurt two orderlies. No one approaches her, and when left alone to her devices she's harmless. She also hasn't spoken a word in nine years. Mr. Weatherly said that she tried to murder him while he slept, and fearing for his life, he had to call the doctor in and that's why your mother was brought here. She is violent, Sir." The nurse sounded like she was panicking.

Cecil smiled sadly as he drew even closer to his mother. "She can never hurt me because she's my mother," and to prove his point to the nurse he sat on the same bench as his mother and took one of her lands that lay lifeless on her lap. "Ma, it's me, Cecil. Do you remember me?"

At first it seemed as if she was hard of hearing but then she turned her head and looked into her son's eyes. "Three thousand, four hundred and sixty-eight," she said at last.

"Ma?" Cecil looked at his mother in confusion.

"Those are the number of days that you've been gone from me," she said, sounding completely lucid.

Cecil was stunned and then began to laugh. "Oh, Ma!" He hugged her, feeling how thin her body was. She was just skin and bones, and he wanted to weep. He pulled back and drew the shawl closer around her. He was still laughing as he remembered that his mother had always been very good with numbers. His grandfather used to say that had she been born a boy she would have been a fine Eton scholar.

"Well, I never," the shocked nurse put a hand to her heart. "Mrs. Miller hasn't spoken a word, at least not in my hearing, for the past nine years."

"Mama," Cecil held her by the shoulders and looked into her eyes. "I'm here now and everything will be all right. I'm sorry for leaving you at the mercy of that wicked man. Please forgive me."

Rachel Miller raised up a trembling hand and touched her son's cheek. "You tried to warn me, but I thought you were just being childishly jealous."

Cecil kissed the palm of her hand, feeling strong emotions welling up within him. "I should never have left you to deal with that scoundrel all by yourself."

"If you had stayed, he would have murdered you like he did my father," tears welled up in her eyes and then fell. "I found out that he was responsible for Papa's sudden death, and when I confronted him, he said no one would ever believe me. He said he would tell people that I had tried to murder him and was the one who had made all the plans to get rid of my father so we could take away his wealth," she pulled away and covered her face with her palms. "It was better that you were gone and out of reach where he couldn't hurt you. I always knew that one day you would find me."

Cecil turned his head and realised that the nurse was still there, and she seemed very interested in their conversation. So he stared pointedly at her, his expression conveying to her that she was no longer needed. With a slight nod and a red face, she left them alone.

"Five years ago I returned to the estate," Cecil told his mother, startling her.

"What?"

"I thought I would find you there but you had disappeared. Mr. Weatherly went about telling people that you had eloped with your lover."

"That man was always very cunning but my father seemed to trust him, so I did, too, only for him to turn around and betray us all. After the wedding he told me that if I didn't let you go to the army then he would finish you like he'd done my father. It wasn't long before he decided to get rid of me too. A second death in a matter of months would have raised suspicions so the best thing was to bring me to this place. And Dr. Cartwright helped him, too, and was one of our witnesses on the day we supposedly got married. Mrs. Burns was the other witness."

"Mr. Weatherly was never legally your husband, Ma, and the certificate of marriage that you have is fake. Dr. Cartwright is trying to protect his own reputation and so has confessed everything to the police. But the man's days as a medic are finished, and even if he's not put in prison, the shame and scandal will drive him out of town. And I for one won't miss him," Cecil said unkindly.

"I heard you telling the nurse all that," Mrs. Miller shook her head. "How could I have been such a fool?"

"Why then did you just sit in this place and let everyone think that you were a lunatic?"

Mrs. Miller's sigh was full of regret. "I guess I felt that I deserved all that I was getting. This was my penance for having been a very foolish woman. But after I lost your father I never looked at another man. You and Papa were all I had, and when I thought of you leaving me after Pa died, I felt lost. I was always that woman who thought she needed a man to protect her."

"Oh, Ma!"

"Did you see that man when you returned to the estate five years ago?"

Cecil nodded. "And not only did I see him but he set his men on me and they would have killed me but by the grace of God, I managed to escape out of their clutches. They chased me through the woods but I was too fast for them even though I was badly injured." He was silent for a moment. "I thought that was the end of me, for sure. But after I collapsed, a little girl and her mother helped me. The child found me and took me home, which happened to be Old Mrs. Elizabeth's cottage. They nursed me back to health, and when I was better I left. Right now, I'm on my way to the estate to reclaim it and also find out if Little Mandy and her mother are all right. I've been praying that Mr. Weatherly didn't discover that they had helped me because he would most definitely harm them. That's just the kind of person he is, wicked and vindictive."

"Oh Cecil, please go and make sure that they are all right. And I'm ready to testify against that man for what he did even if I get into trouble myself."

"But not before I get you out of here and to a safe place. If that man has an inkling that I'm back and have been here, he might try to harm you either himself or through those that he bribed to keep you here. Somehow I don't trust that all the workers in this place are good people. For you to have been kept here all these years means that Mr. Weatherly has been keeping his eye on you. I pray that Dr. Cartwright will be found guilty and then sentenced to spending many years in prison. I'm sure you're not the only patient he had committed through falsifying medical records. Someone in this place has also certainly been reporting about you to Mr. Weatherly so I'm not letting you stay a single moment more in this place."

❄

Knowing that Mrs. Ridges would never give her and her mother permission to leave the workhouse even for a few hours, Mandy knew she had to think of a way of coming up with a good reason for that to happen.

Then an idea came to her when she noticed that Chaplain Reid and Mrs. Ridges took lunch together every day in the private parlour where visitors to the workhouse were often received.

So she bid her time and one afternoon when they were in the middle of taking their meal, she carried their dessert in. She'd begged Mrs. Tucker to let her do it even though her own duties in the kitchen were to wash dishes and clean the counters. That was as much as she was given to do. To Mandy it was like a dream. After all the rigorous and strenuous work that she and her mother had been forced into, this was like being on holiday. .

"Oh, Miss Wood, Amanda Wood it is, right?" She nodded. The chaplain smiled kindly at her. "I hope you've recovered from your terrible ordeal at the hands of Mr. Spindle."

Mandy was watching Mrs. Ridges and noticed her lips tightening, but then the woman sensed her gaze and gave her a false smile. This made Mandy distrust her even more. Just like Mr. Spindle had done before, it was clear that Mrs. Ridges was a pretender. She could be one thing in the presence of the chaplain so as to look good before him but Mandy saw through her guise.

Five years of ill treatment taught a person a thing or two. And besides that, she'd learned how to stay out of the woman's way, especially since the chaplain's return, because she didn't want any more trouble.

"Miss Wood, how is your mother doing," Mrs. Ridge jumped into the conversation, obviously pretending to be concerned.

"She yearns for the sunshine," Mandy got her opening. "Now that it's summer I wish I could take her to the park to see the ducks and just see life outside this place. We haven't set foot outside this place in the five years we've been here," Mandy made her tone mild so she wouldn't seem as if she was accusing anyone of having kept them locked up for all that time.

"My dear, why don't you do just that," the chaplain agreed. "You can get a day pass for tomorrow and return in the evening because there will always be a place for you here. And here," he reached into his pocket and pulled out two silver coins. "Take these two shillings and buy something nice for your mother."

"Thank you so much, Sir." Mandy hadn't seen money in such a long time that she'd almost forgotten what it looked like. So she found herself staring at the coins in her hand and wondering what she could get with them.

"Go on, come and see me tomorrow with your mother and I'll sign you both out. But make sure you don't stay out too long because your mother may not be too strong."

"Yes, Sir."

"And soon I'll find a good place for you and your mother to go and work so that you can become independent again. Just make sure that when you go out there, you don't get into trouble."

"Yes, Sir, and thank you very much."

PART III
COMING HOME FOR CHRISTMAS

JUST REWARD

❄

His mother was safe, as he'd taken her to the home of a friend of his grandfather's. Colonel Watson had served with his grandfather in the Royal British Navy and fought in the First Opium War against China. Grandpa Sinclair had saved Colonel Watson's life and the man had never forgotten the favour. It was his mother who told him about the elderly retired soldier.

"I'm angry at you and your mother," the elderly colonel told Cecil and his mother when they arrived at his home in Cheltenham. "Why didn't you come to me as soon as my good friend was murdered? I would have dealt with that imbecile and none of this trouble would have happened." He fixed his eyes on Mrs. Miller. "To think that you languished in a mental institution for nine years as if you were a deranged person," he shook his head. "Your grandfather would never forgive me if I didn't take vengeance on the persons who put you there. I can't believe that Cartwright turned into a rogue and murdered his own friend and had you committed."

Cecil had no response and his mother also kept silent. But the colonel was glad to keep Mrs. Miller with him for a few days. Due to gout he'd lost his right leg and now had a wooden one. However, he was still a spry man and wanted to accompany Cecil to Birmingham for the facedown that was coming. But Cecil managed to deter him, much to his wife's relief.

"If you run into any trouble just send me a telegram and I'll be there faster than you can imagine and we'll take that man down together. I wish you Godspeed."

"Much obliged, Colonel."

With the reassurance that his mother was safe with friends Cecil travelled to Birmingham. The colonel had insisted that he should find a certain judge who was an old friend of Grandpa Sinclair's and let him know everything. So it was that when Cecil arrived at the estate he was accompanied by the judge, two police constables and his grandfather's lawyer's grandson.

Mr. Colts was also a lawyer after his grandfather and when Cecil had arrived at his home the man had expressed joy that he was still alive. "My grandfather served yours for years and they both died in the same year," he told Cecil. "I was away at Cambridge and only returned four years ago to find that everything was in shambles. I tried to reach out to Mr. Weatherly to find out whatever was going on because my grandfather had left me instructions to take over all his clients," he shook his head regretfully. "Unfortunately one of the clerks working for my grandfather at the time was bribed by Mr. Weatherly. I trusted that man but in my absence he and his crony caused a lot of damage. It has taken me these four years to straighten out all those messes. The clerk is serving a long sentence for fraud and mismanagement of many other clients' inheritances and trusts."

"Why wasn't Mr. Weatherly prosecuted alongside his accomplice?"

"Because I had no evidence that you or your mother were even still alive," he said. "When the detective from the Scotland Yard reached out to me a few months ago it was a great relief to hear that you were both alive. I knew then that all the wrongs that had been done would be righted, Mr. Miller…"

"It's actually Lieutenant Miller," one of the police constables corrected Mr. Colt. "I mean no disrespect, Sir," The man's face turned red. "Lieutenant Miller, whatever you need, you can count on me to provide it so you can take your inheritance back."

"Thank you very much, Mr. Colt."

When they arrived at the estate, it was a Saturday. It was midmorning, and the female servant who opened the door didn't ask them any questions when they asked for her employer. She immediately led them to the living room where they found Mr. Weatherly with a woman. The two looked shaken when they saw the group of people walking in very unceremoniously.

"I remember you," Cecil told the woman. "You're Mrs. Burns and your husband is one of the men who beat me up five years ago."

The woman looked like she was about to swoon but they all ignored her, concentrating on Mr. Weatherly whose face was as white as a sheet, and he seemed to have been struck dumb. He made no protestations at all the charges read to him by one of the constables.

"You'll remain in custody until the hearing of your cases in two weeks' time. Just know that all your accomplices are facing long sentences and have confessed all that they did because you bribed them," the judge put in. "During that period we'll search for more witness who will testify against you. One thing I can tell you without a single doubt in my mind, Mr. Weatherly, is that you're facing a long sentence."

And just like that, it was over for the man who had murdered Grandpa Sinclair, committed his mother to a mental institution and defrauded Cecil of his inheritance. It was a bittersweet victory, because even if Mr. Weatherly would be in prison for a long while and get his just due, Grandpa Sinclair was gone forever.

When Mrs. Burns realised that things were going badly for her lover, she slipped out of the manor unnoticed.

As the man was being led out of the manor by the constables, with Mr. Colt and the judge following to make sure he was taken to the right place for him, Cecil called out to the servant who'd opened the door for them.

"Yes, Sir," the middle-aged woman responded, entering the living room while wiping her plump hands on her apron. "You called for me."

"How long have you worked for Mr. Weatherly?"

"Just one week, Sir. And I was just telling myself that I want no trouble with someone who does strange things and also has the police coming into his house. I determined that as soon as he paid me my wages I was going to resign," she twisted her lips. "Well now who will be paying me my wages for the days I've worked?"

"Why were you determined to resign from this position?"

"When I came to take this position people warned me that Mr. Weatherly was not normal. And I found that to be true. The man wasn't sleeping, and the first night I was here he gave me a mighty fright."

Cecil frowned, "What did he do?"

"I found him standing on the balcony with a rope in his hands and thought he wanted to end his life," then she chuckled, "Turns out he was letting the woman down through the balcony because her husband was sleeping in the living room." She shook her head. "Such strange goings on in this house! But it was either working here or ending up in the workhouse," the woman shuddered visibly. "I thought things would be better for me here, but it turns out that I was wrong."

"Do you know if Mrs. Wood and her daughter still live in the cottage at the edge of the woods?"

The servant shook her head, "I don't know much about this estate but one thing is for sure. That cottage had been empty for years, according to the tenant I spoke to. Mr. Weatherly had sent me to collect rents from the tenants and I met her."

"Would the person or any other of the tenants have any idea of the whereabouts of Mrs. Wood, the woman who lived in that cottage about five years ago?"

The woman shrugged, "You would have to ask her. Mrs. Shaw is the last person remaining on this estate and she stays because, like me, the only other option for her is the workhouse. Everyone else left before I got here, so when I went around collecting rents there was none to get. Not that the man believed me," she scoffed. "He accused me of colluding with the tenants to rob him of his dues. I told him to go out and see for himself, but he never sets foot outside this house. But the woman and her husband come and go as they please."

Cecil remembered Mrs. Shaw because he used to play with her children. "Has Mrs. Shaw no family left? I thought she had four sons who are about my age."

"Mr. Shaw died two years ago, a broken man because of the way Mr. Weatherly mistreated him. After the sawmill was shut down, he and many others lost their jobs, and life became very difficult. And the four sons of whom you speak all moved away years ago. She has no idea of where they could be. Mr. Weatherly threatened them when they came to the manor to ask about the whereabouts of Mrs. Miller and her son. So they fled like many others but the parents stayed. Now the poor woman has no one and it's just by the grace of God that she's been surviving."

"Don't you worry, Mrs…?"

"The name is Emelda Pitch, Sir."

"Well Mrs. Pitch, I am Cecil Miller, the rightful owner of this estate. I'm back now and things will get better. You don't have to worry about who will pay your wages anymore."

A huge smile broke out on the woman's face. "Now I see the resemblance to the old man from the portrait paintings Mr. Weatherly asked me to burn up. He was searching in the attic and found them, quite a number and gave them to me to get rid of."

"And did you destroy them?" Cecil felt his anger rising. Mr. Weatherly had wanted to erase all traces of his grandfather, no doubt because of his guilt after murdering him.

"No Sir, I took them to Mrs. Shaw when the man was sleeping. I reckoned that one day the rightful owners of this manor would return and require them back."

"You did well, Mrs. Pitch; would you consider staying on and working for me? I may not be able to offer you much in the way of wages at the beginning because you can see the state of the estate."

"For a gentleman such as yourself and because I respected your grandfather very much, I would work for no wages. Even though I never personally met Mr. Sinclair, his fame went far and wide and we all mourned his death." She paused for a moment. "All I need is that you put some food on the table for me, a roof over my head and a bed in a warm room that has no draught."

Cecil smiled kindly at the woman. "Rest assured Mrs. Pitch that you'll get your full wages at the end of the week once I know what they are. I'll see to the repairs as soon as possible so you can have a comfortable room and have no fear, there will always be food on the table for us. What was Mr. Weatherly paying you?"

"One shilling per week," she said.

Cecil was shocked because that was gross underpayment and he wondered what the man had paid Mrs. Wood when she was here five years ago.

"Well, I will make that five shillings a week, which means one pound a month. My army pension may be small, but I can afford to feed us and pay you five shillings a week until such a time as the estate becomes prosperous again then that amount will increase."

Mrs. Pitch stared at Cecil as if he'd just offered her the moon on a platter. He felt guilty that he wasn't able to pay her better, yet here she was looking at him like he had offered her the wages that royal servants earned.

"Thank you, Sir," she managed to get out after a few minutes of staring at him wide mouthed. "Never in my life have I ever earned such wages. Would you like me to prepare anything for you? Mr. Weatherly used to lock up all the food in his bedchamber but with him gone it's all there for us now," she tightened her lips. "The man was such a miser."

Cecil shook his head, "Not right now, Mrs. Pitch. I would like to go and see Mrs. Shaw and make sure that she's all right. Would you know who served in this house before you?"

Mrs. Pitch shook her head, "As far as I know there hadn't been a servant here for some months until I came. I understand Mrs. Burns was hclping out but," she chuckled, "well, Mrs. Shaw would know. She's a well of information that one."

❄

And Cecil found out that Mrs. Pitch was right. Mrs. Shaw was quite a well of information, and in under one hour he had a grasp of everything that had been happening on the estate for the past nine years.

"Mrs. Wood was a gentle woman," Mrs. Shaw said when Cecil's questions kept returning to the widow and her daughter. "It's a pity what was done to her five years ago." She fell silent, a sad look on her face. "The story was that she saved a young man from death and Mr. Weatherly had her committed to a workhouse, together with sweet little Mandy. Can you imagine the gall of the man? Having a genteel woman and her child committed to that terrible place just because they were kind to another human being?" Her tone was indignant.

The information shocked Cecil. He knew that Mr. Weatherly was a terrible man and the most he would have expected was that he would have sent Mrs. Wood away. But to have her committed to a workhouse and with her child was even worse than sending them away penniless.

"Would you have any idea of which workhouse he sent them to?"

Mrs. Shaw shook her head. "I would tell you to find that Burns fellow and ask him because until just a few days ago he worked for Mr. Weatherly, doing all his dirty work."

"I saw Mrs. Burns at the house," he offered.

Mrs. Shaw made a sound of disgust. "That one, flighty as a bird with its feathers on fire! She was the reason Mr. Weatherly and her husband had a terrible falling out a few days ago. Then two days ago, his body was found in a ditch, poor fellow. Serving that man and doing his wicked deeds for years, only to end up dead in a ditch."

"What happened to him? Could he have stumbled while drunk and got himself killed?"

"That's what the constable thought at first until the coroner saw those marks around the poor fellow's neck. He was strangled for sure and then dumped in the ditch. I think the body was too heavy to be disposed of so someone just tossed him there. And I'm very sure that it was all on account of that woman."

"That's terrible but it doesn't tell me where I can find Mrs. Wood."

"There was another fellow who worked with Burns," she scrunched her face. "Yes, folks around here called him Jensen. He disappeared a year ago and rumour was that he stole some money from Mr. Weatherly. But with that man who knows, maybe he finished him off the same way he did with Burns. And if that was the case then I'm most certain that Burns was involved in his death. Those two were the ones who carried Mrs. Wood and Little Mandy out of here and took them away. And in the end they both got what they deserved; just punishment for wicked men."

"I just wish I knew where I could find that Jensen fellow so he can tell me where he took them."

"You could ask Mr. Weatherly himself."

"I would rather search the whole world and turn every stone over rather than talk to that traitor. If I see that man again I may not be responsible for my actions," Cecil said fiercely.

"Between Birmingham and London and Manchester are tens of workhouses. If you're to search through all of them it would take you months to find Mrs. Wood and Mandy."

Cecil felt defeated. He was sure that his detective friend could help in his search for Little Mandy and her mother but that would eat into his scarce resources. He needed all the money he had to begin putting the estate to rights. Reviving the sawmill was first priority then also make a few urgent repairs to the manor and pay Mrs. Pitch. There would hardly be anything left over after all his expenses.

Mrs. Shaw saw the pain and anguish on his face. "Or you could do what I've been doing lately," the middle aged woman said.

He turned agony-filled eyes to her. Somehow he felt that he had failed Mandy and her mother but he didn't know what to do or where to start searching for them. "How do you mean?"

"Do you believe in God, Lieutenant Miller?"

He nodded, "Yes, Ma'am."

"And do you believe that God answers the prayers of those who believe in Him?"

"Yes," which was quite true. He'd prayed to find his mother alive and that had been answered. He'd also prayed to find a way of having his inheritance restored without any more bloodshed and that too had happened. So he nodded harder, "Yes, Mrs. Shaw, I believe that God answers prayers."

"Good," she smiled. "Then you can pray, like me, that your loved ones will return home to you."

"I never said anything about them being my loved ones, I was only expressing concern for their wellbeing," Cecil felt uncomfortable at the woman's intense stare. Her watery silver eyes were fixed on his face as if she were trying to see through to his soul. Then she apparently saw something in his eyes that satisfied her for she nodded, chuckling softly.

"You've been playing with that small kerchief ever since you got here," and Cecil's face turned red when he looked down at his hands. He hadn't even been aware that he'd pulled the small handkerchief out of his pocket. "I remember Little Mandy used to sit with me and make a fuss about learning how to embroider flowers on handkerchiefs. Her mother said it kept her out of trouble.

One day we made a few of those and she said she would keep them to give to her friends," Mrs. Shaw looked at him. "You must be her friend, but how did you get that handkerchief?"

Cecil told her that he was the man Mandy and her mother had rescued five years ago.

"That makes sense now. Mandy would be about sixteen now, a fine young girl indeed and ripe for marriage. And as for you asking about that child and her mother, it means that you care. There used to be many tenants on this estate and you played with their children, my sons included. But apart from general question that you've asked, I haven't heard you inquiring about any of them or their whereabouts like you've done with that little girl and her mother. But by now five years later, Mandy is no longer a child."

Cecil didn't have a rejoinder to the woman's observation.

"Pray that if it's His will, the Lord will lead them back to you," she tilted her head to one side. "Though I'm a bit puzzled."

"What about?"

"Is it the child you yearn to see or the mother?"

❄

Cecil didn't have to answer Mrs. Shaw's question because it was obvious to him. He'd barely thought about Mrs. Wood except in a general way. It was Little Mandy who had taken up most of his thoughts for the past five years. Each time he'd touched the handkerchief, which was many times a day, he would wonder what she was doing. Had she become an obsession and was he becoming one of those men who ran after little girls?

He grimaced with distaste. No, his relationship with Mandy had been that of a good friend and over the years he'd been concerned about their wellbeing. And when he was leaving he'd left two gold sovereigns for them just to tide them over.

All through he'd only thought about Mandy as a little eleven-year-old girl. But now he had to start seeing her as a young woman of sixteen years. And like Mrs. Shaw said, ripe for marriage.

Cecil had plenty of time in the coming days to think about Mrs. Shaw's words. And whenever he had a moment he found himself going to the cottage which had been his place of refuge after he'd fled from Mr. Weatherly's men. And now those men hadn't ended up well.

The elements hadn't been kind to the little cottage and it looked worse than it had five years ago. But like a sturdy oak that weathered all seasons, the little cottage stood there defying nature itself.

In order to get around the estate and check on what needed to be done, Cecil had purchased an old mule because his grandfather's prize horses were long gone from the stables. On his rounds on the estate he'd seen many of the buildings that had once graced the landscape and they were now nothing more than ruins and inhabitable only by foxes and other creatures of the wild.

But Mandy's cottage, as he'd come to think of it, surprisingly still had both windows and the door standing. It was as though the little house had waited for the return of those who had once lived in it.

Then Cecil laughed. Mrs. Shaw had gotten into his head. But as always, his hand went into his pocket. The small white handkerchief was in its rightful place in the left pocket of his shirt and close to his heart.

He got down from the mule and tethered it, leaving it enough slack so it could graze peacefully. Then he spotted a stick, which he picked up. He remembered the one Mandy had handed him five years ago so he could use is as a support as he leaned on her. He was about to toss it aside, then decided to hold onto it.

And he was going to have to stop thinking of Amanda as Little Mandy. Five years later and she was now a woman as Mrs. Shaw had pointed out. He prayed that life had been kind to her and her mother. Life in a workhouse wasn't as glamorous as those who ran such places wanted the world to think. He'd recently read in the newspapers about the shocking evils that went on in some of those institutions. So daily he prayed that Mandy and her mother had escaped the terrible misdeeds of such wicked people. But he was worried because, knowing Mr. Weatherly, he'd probably found the worst workhouse and had them committed there, just like he'd found the worst mental hospital and had his mother locked up in there.

"Father," he found himself praying as he used the stick in his hand to beat down the small shrubs around the cottage. "Please bring my loved ones home, if it be Your will to do so."

He would return with a shovel and hoe and make the place habitable because he had faith that his prayer would be answered.

IS THIS HOME?

❆

Mandy worried her lower lip while she stood at the small grate stirring the pot of stew that was over the fire she had lit a little while ago.

After all they had been through in the past five years, once again they had ended up in their little cottage on Mr. Weatherly's estate. No, the estate rightfully belonged to Mr. Miller as her mother had told her.

A smile curved her lips as she thought about their arrival just that morning. It had been nothing like the first time they'd come here. This time there had been no Mr. Stiles to bring them here on his cart. They had sneaked onto the estate, quite dismayed to find that the path they had once used was now overgrown with shrubs.

"It looks like no one has used this path in years," her mother said. "We might have been the last people to use it."

"But don't you think that's a good sign then, Ma? It means that Mr. Weatherly or his people never venture out this way, so they won't have any way of knowing that we've returned, at least not for a few days."

"I fear that the smoke may alert someone as to our presence and then we'll get into trouble. But we have to find a way of preparing our meals."

"Then we'll light the fire for cooking at night only. No one will be able to detect the smoke then. In any case, once we find our friends they will help us."

Mrs. Wood sighed. "Mandy, you saw the state of the manor even as we were sneaking into this place. It's even worse than before, so you can imagine what the tenants' houses must look like now. Five years ago they were in a state of disrepair, and Mr. Weatherly never cared. What do you think has happened since then?"

They had expected the cottage to no longer exist but when they had come to the small clearing, they'd been surprised. While it was still dilapidated, in fact looking worse than they had last seen it, the wonder was that their little cottage was still standing. And it seemed as if someone had cleared the area around the cottage and the small outhouse which now had only one side of the wall still standing. Afraid that someone might be living in the cottage, possibly a tramp or an outlaw or fugitive, they had prepared themselves for flight.

But upon opening the door and entering the cottage they had found it swept clean but empty. There were no signs that anyone had lived in it for years, yet the windows and door still stood. The two women looked at each other with questions in their eyes that they could find no answers to. Of course, all the furniture and utensils they had left behind five years ago when they were hustled out of the house were gone now. Nevertheless they had the few utensils they'd been using for the past few weeks after escaping from the workhouse. Life had to start somewhere.

"Mandy," her mother came to stand next to her.

"Yes, Ma?"

"You've been stirring the beans in that pot for a while now, lost in thought and your hand playing with the string around your neck. What are you thinking about?"

Mandy took the ladle out of the pot and then turned to smile at her mother. "Ma, do you ever wonder where he is or if he's even still alive?"

Her mother nodded, knowing of whom Mandy spoke. "I always pray that Mr. Weatherly never caught up with him. That young man deserved a better life than what he got."

"I wonder if he would even remember us, or would he pass by us if we met him now?"

Mrs. Wood smiled, "Don't think about the impossible, Child. There are other matters to ponder, like where we'll go from here."

"I think of nothing else," Mandy said softly. "I'm just glad that you didn't die in that workhouse at Dudley, Ma." And she put her arms around her mother. "God spared both of us from terrible things, and here we are. I think He will continue to guide us until one day we find a place to settle, a place we'll call home forever."

"And He spared us too in Manchester," Mrs. Wood said.

Mandy nodded as her thoughts took her back in time to four weeks before.

❄

Like he'd promised, Chaplain Reid gave Mandy and her mother permission to leave the workhouse on a Saturday morning.

"Make sure you return while it's yet light. I don't want the two of you wandering around in the dark because these are dangerous times," he'd cautioned.

"We'll hurry back," Mandy said.

"Your mother has been ill and, even though it's summer, the evenings can get very cold," Reverend Reid reiterated. "Get back here in good time because you know how cumbersome all the paperwork for re-entry can be. And being a Saturday there are

many who seek shelter even if for a night only. I don't want you to miss your beds."

"Yes, Sir," Mandy said, head bowed. She didn't want to look directly at the Chaplain, lest he see that she wasn't telling him the truth. She had no intention of ever returning to this place.

The previous evening she'd showed her mother the two silver coins that Mr. Reid had given her. "What's the value of these two coins, Ma?"

"That's two shillings," her mother told her, "Which is also twenty-four pence and quite a bit of money to be found in here. Why did Mr. Reid give the money to you?"

"He said that I should buy you something nice but I think we can put it to better use," Mandy's fingers folded over the coins. "Ma, do you think this money can get us to a place like Manchester?"

Her mother shook her head. "We need ten shillings each to board the train to Manchester from here."

Mandy's face fell. She had only two shillings with her. Where were they going to get eighteen more? She couldn't run the risk of them remaining in Dudley even if they left the workhouse. They might be arrested as vagrants and also Mr. Spindle might still be waiting to take his revenge on them.

And also, chances of Mr. Weatherly finding them were great. They'd already lost five years of their lives and who knew what more suffering he would impose on them if he were to find them outside of the workhouse? She wanted her mother to be safe and

Manchester was the best option. Dudley, nice as it seemed, was a place of a lot of adversity and getting away was the only way they would be safe.

So Mandy decided on Manchester City. It was a large city and with the many factories that were to be found there, there were bound to be positions open for them in one of the factories. She would search for something easy for her mother to do like work in a knitting factory. Mandy would never let her mother do any more strenuous work. She'd nearly lost her and now she was very protective. When it came to herself, she would even carry stones if need be to provide a living for them. She didn't mind doing all the hard work because she was strong and now it was her turn to take care of her still fragile mother.

Ever since Chaplain Reid had returned, things had gotten so much better for her and her mother. And Mrs. Tucker who now worked in the kitchen made sure that they always had sufficient food to eat.

Mandy purposed in her heart that never again would they see the inside of a workhouse, not as inmates at least.

"Don't look so downcast my dear child, two shillings is still a good sum and it's better than nothing," her mother fumbled under her own garments and brought out two gold sovereigns. "Remember the money that Mr. Miller left for us when he left? This is it. I've been holding on to these for a rainy day."

Mandy stared at her mother in stunned surprise. "You've had this money all this while?"

"Five years," her mother said triumphantly. "And no one ever found it on my person," she giggled and Mandy was glad to see a glow in her eyes. Life was returning to her mother and that was why she needed to get her out of here before something else happened to completely extinguish it.

"Ma, how did you achieve that?"

Mrs. Wood laughed, "Remember I worked for the stingy Mr. Weatherly and would hide food from his house. Two small coins were nothing in comparison with the packets of food that I had to sneak out of the manor so we wouldn't starve. I thought of giving the money to you when I fell ill but since I still hadn't taught you the value of money I decided to save them for a rainy day such as this."

And with the money they purchased two tickets and travelled to Manchester. When they got to the big city it seemed as if the heavens above their heads were open to pour down blessings on them after all their sufferings. Before they'd even left the station Mandy decided to check on the notice board. It was full of advertisements of all kinds and some even made her laugh. Men were searching for wives, and she rolled her eyes. Just as she was about to give up and leave she saw something that caught her attention. It was an advertisement for the position of a scullery maid at one of the large estates which was about a mile out of the city.

She felt that it would be better to live on an estate even though the wages offered were paltry. They would be safe on an estate because of the security that its owners provided rather than renting a small room in one of the slums where their adversaries could easily find and harm them. At least on an estate they wouldn't be exposed too much. And she would make sure that they never went into town until many months or even years had passed and people had forgotten about them.

And as soon as Mrs. James, mistress of the estate, interviewed Mandy, she offered her the position on the spot. So she became one of the four scullery maids on that large estate. A small cottage was also offered and her employer didn't mind that she lived with her mother. Not knowing the full value of money, Mandy thought the ten shillings wages per week was a lot of money and her mother smiled indulgently.

Mandy would happily have worked on the James Estate for years because her employer was kind and there was always plenty to eat and even take home to her mother. But the banes of her life were her employer's two sons.

Tobias and Charles James were the apples of their mother's eyes and could do no wrong, according to Adelaide one of the other scullery maids.

"They tease and bully us," Adelaide said. "But Mrs. James turns a blind eye to all they do. The boys are eighteen and seventeen but she says they are still children and don't mean any harm. But I'm afraid one of these days they may go far and then we'll have trouble for sure," Adelaide had said.

Mandy worked hard because she wanted her mother to have the best. And she did her best to steer clear of the two young men who liked coming to the kitchen to bully the staff. They made *disparaging remarks about the female staff and just to prove that they were untouchable they would find small reasons to slap and manhandle the male staff.*

Mandy despised anyone who used their strength to bully others, but she would simply purse her lips and carry on with her work. She was here to make money and not get into fights or quarrels with her employer's children.

And then trouble came calling. Mandy had been working on the estate for a month when the boys decided that it was time to teach her a lesson because she'd rebuffed their advances many times.

She was leaving the manor after work and on her way home when the two young men suddenly appeared out of nowhere. Seeing the ugly gleam in their eyes reminded her of when Mr. Spindle had looked at her in that evil way back at the workhouse. Mandy knew that they were out to make mischief and evil was intended for her person.

She had in her hands a small pail containing the food that the cook had packed for her and an old umbrella. Mrs. James had given the old umbrella to her because the woman no longer had any use for it. She was a generous woman, letting her servants have whatever wasn't used in the manor.

That was how Mandy had furnished their small house and they had many pots and pans, two beds, three old but comfortable seats and a nice round table. Their new home was heavenly, according to Mrs. Wood.

When the young men came upon her and stopped her, she begged them to let her go.

"I don't want any trouble from you," she told them. "I work at your house and your mother trusts me to be prudent at all times."

Tobias the older man laughed, "Look at this peasant acquiring airs all of a sudden. We're the law around here and if you want to keep your lowly position, then you'll do as we say."

"My brother is right; if you refuse to give in to us, then tomorrow you'll be tossed out on your ear. A woman such as yourself will soon find your way to a brothel in desperation unless you give in to us."

Mandy sighed sadly, wondering why people had to be so cruel. They were doing almost exactly what Mr. Spindle had done, threatening her, and she'd had it.

When Tobias made the first move towards her, she hurled the pail of still hot food at him and it splattered all over his face, momentarily blinding him. He screamed and fell to the ground, hands over his face. When his brother saw this he lunged at her but she was prepared. Mandy swung the umbrella as hard as she could and struck him. All rage rose up within her and even when the young men were down on the ground and begging for mercy she didn't hear them. All she could see was Mr. Spindle's face and the suffering he'd subjected them to for close to five years and she had nearly lost her mother then. She didn't even realise that she was also screaming just as loudly as the two young men.

A male worker passing by heard the racket and ran to investigate. He was shocked to find Mandy standing over the bleeding young men, still swinging her umbrella. It took him a few minutes to calm her down. He then helped the boys to their feet and supporting them, took them back home.

That's when Mandy snapped back to reality and looked down at the bloody umbrella. What had she done? She would be arrested and charged as a criminal and yet she'd only been defending herself. But in the world of the wealthy, a nonentity like her didn't have any rights and they would accuse her of trying to murder her employer's sons. Dropping the umbrella as if it was a hot rock, she ran home.

"Mama, there's trouble on the mountain," *she was gasping while grabbing whatever she could and stuffing it into an old carpetbag, another gift from Mrs. James.* "We have to get out of here."

"Mandy, what has happened," *her mother was shocked at her appearance.* "Slow down and tell me."

"Ma, we have to get out of here before those men decide to come and exact their revenge on us," *and she told her mother everything that had happened, right from the bullying when she'd first set foot in the manor.* "And their parents, especially Mrs. James, will come and put me in jail. Ma, hurry please."

As they collected their few belongings there was a knock at the door and terror filled their eyes and hearts.

"Miss Mandy, it's only I," the servant who had stopped her from badly injuring the two young men called out. Mandy quickly opened the door for him. "Good thing you're leaving," he said when he saw their luggage.

"Where are the boys?" Mandy asked fearfully. "Are they dead?"

The man chuckled. "Nothing of the sort, and they'll soon recover from this ordeal. Only the shame of being beaten up by a woman who is smaller than them will live with them forever," he howled with laughter. "You gave them the beating that all of us have been wanting to do for a long time. I'm buying you time so you can get away and not be arrested."

"Did you take them home?"

"No. I took them to my cottage because my mother is a medicine woman and told them that she would treat them. Bless my Gypsy mother's shrewdness," he wiggled his eyebrows and Mandy giggled. "Mama gave them some concoction that has them sleeping for now. By the time they wake up and return to the manor, you should be as far away as possible from this place."

Mandy hugged the man and then quickly stepped back. "I don't have anything to pay you with but I will be praying for you. Thank you for helping us."

"We won't speak of the matter in public but to all of us here at the manor, Miss Mandy Wood, you'll always be a heroine. Those boys got what they deserved, and none of us will be sad on that account."

And collecting their few belongings, the young man showed them a secret path out of the estate, one that poachers used, and took them to the train station. Mandy gave him five shillings from her three weeks' wages. It was a pity that she would have received her wages the next day.

While they were at the station it was Mrs. Wood who had suggested that they return to Birmingham. "Our friends on Mr. Weatherly's estate will help us until we decide where we'll go. They will hide us for a few days until we can make a decision. At this point, I'm even ready to board a ship and travel to America."

"Mandy, the food is burning," her mother's words brought her back to the present and she quickly took the pot off from the fire.

She looked at their few utensils, what they had been able to carry from Mrs. James' estate and sighed. What if the young men never recovered from the beating or got badly maimed, would she be a fugitive for the rest of her life?

❄

Cecil was feeling restless and couldn't quite settle down even after bringing his mother home. Colonel Watson had insisted on coming with them and, when he saw the state of the manor and indeed the whole estate, he'd been really angry.

"You should have let me come with you when you came to find that scoundrel. I would have had his head on a platter by now," the man said fiercely.

Mrs. Miller had spent the past three days moving from room to room. Sensing that she needed to be alone, Cecil left her to her own devices.

From time to time he heard a loud sniffle and once a wail and he knew that she had found something else that had reminded her of her parents and especially her father. Mrs. Pitch also stayed out of her way.

Colonel Watson hadn't been satisfied with the information that Mr. Weatherly had been charged with his friend's murder, committing an innocent woman to a mental institution, forging a marriage certificate and other documents so he could grab the estate. The colonel had pulled all the strings he could and all the valuables that Mr. Weatherly had stolen from the house were found. He hadn't sold them as people thought, but had stashed them away. It was clear that Mr. Weatherly had known that he wouldn't get away with his crimes forever. So he'd built a nest egg for himself over the years.

Of course, he'd pawned off a few of the valuables, but these were traced and recovered, to the dismay of those who had them in their possession. And what's more, much of Mrs. Miller's mother's jewellery was found in the possession of Mrs. Burns, who Mr. Weatherly had set up in a small cottage. Along with that had been found a trunk full of money, coins of all denominations and even a few notes. Once the money was counted out in the presence of Colonel Watson and Mr. Colts, Cecil's lawyer, it was found to be quite a substantial amount.

Cecil had gone over the estate's books from the time Mr. Weatherly had come to work for his grandfather and found that the man had been a crook right from the start.

When Mrs. Burns was threatened as an accomplice, she confessed that her husband had murdered Jensen and then in turn had been murdered by Mr. Weatherly. She was able to give directions as to where Jensen's body was buried right on the estate. When the police constables went to the named location they found the skeletal bones of the man. Because he'd been buried in a cave near the river, the body was well preserved and his clothes identified his person.

Mrs. Burns told the magistrate and constables that Mr. Weatherly had promised her that once he'd disposed of her husband, they would sell all they had looted from the estate and move to Paris to begin a new life.

"You're a very foolish young woman," the magistrate had told the weeping woman. "And you're lucky we found you when we did. Mr. Weatherly would have disposed of you in the same manner he did with your husband and anyone else who stood in his way. You knew of his crimes and yet you kept silent, making you his willing accomplice."

"But he threatened me," she cried.

"If you say so, but I see a woman who was nothing but an opportunist. You'll serve a shorter sentence than his, but you will spend some years in a prison cell and think about your life then."

Colonel Watson insisted that all the money found in Mr. Weatherly's possession be returned to Cecil so he could rebuild the estate, and he'd nearly wept with joy. Now he could restore the estate to what it had been before and even make it better.

All these thoughts were going through Cecil's mind as he sat in the parlour. Colonel Watson had returned home with promises of visiting again. His mother was somewhere around the house and he could hear Mrs. Pitch singing loudly and tunelessly in the kitchen. Now that they could afford good food, the woman was in her element. He appreciated her because she was a hard worker and determined to please, reminding him of Mrs. Wood.

Yet there remained the question of Mandy and her mother. With his coffers full, Cecil was ready to spend whatever he could to find them.

He heard footsteps and then his mother entered the parlour. She looked so much better now, and it was clear that Colonel Watson and his wife had taken really good care of her. Mrs. Pitch was also determined to fatten her mistress, as she said with a twinkle in her eyes and enticed her with delicious meals. It had angered Cecil to find that

Mr. Weatherly had given all his mother's lovely clothes to his mistress. Mrs. Burns, in a show of remorse had offered to return them but Cecil rejected them. His mother didn't deserve to be treated the way the man had, and he didn't want her to use the clothes that his mistress had worn for the past nine years. She deserved a new wardrobe, and he'd gotten her one.

"Have you heard any news about the women you seek?" Mrs. Miller asked her son as she sat down and poured herself a cup of tea from the pot that Mrs. Pitch had brought in a while ago. It was still hot.

He shook his head, "They seem to have fallen off the face of the earth. When Colonel Watson asked Mr. Weatherly about them he gave the name of the workhouse in Dudley. Two police constables were sent there but found that Mandy and her mother weren't there."

"So the man lied," Mrs. Miller twisted her lips. "You shouldn't have trusted that man to tell you the truth."

"On this occasion he spoke the truth, Mama. But from what the constables found out, Mandy and her mother escaped from the workhouse slightly over a month ago. They aren't anywhere in Dudley, or someone would have seen them, so they must have decided to move to another city, possibly London. Mandy spoke of her father promising to take her there."

"Will you continue searching for them?" His mother asked and he nodded. "I'm glad you were able to recover much of what that wicked man stole," Mrs. Miller looked shamefaced. "I failed you as a mother, Cecil."

"Ma, not that again," he said. "Please forgive yourself as I've forgiven you. And I know God has also forgiven you, so you need to let it go. It's time for us to rebuild our lives again."

"I pray that my parents will forgive me," she sniffed.

"Knowing Grandpa and Grandma, they forgave you a long time ago."

"At least there's money for you to use to search for Mrs. Wood and her daughter."

"Well, the same detective who found you is working on that, but I'm also taking Mrs. Shaw's advice."

"What advice is that?"

"Mrs. Shaw is an amazing woman. When I first returned and she told me about Little Mandy and her mother, she advised me to pray for their return. Her own four sons left home not long after I joined the army because Mr. Weatherly threatened them when they asked about us. She hadn't seen or heard from them for years. On that day that I went to see her, she told me that she was praying for the Lord to lead them back home." Cecil smiled, looking very boyish and excited, which touched his mother's heart. "Ma, all Mrs. Shaw's sons have returned home and even sent me applications to become our tenants."

"That is wonderful news," Mrs. Miller wiped her face. "If I hadn't trust that man, our tenants would never have left, and this estate would be very prosperous."

"Ma, in everything let us give thanks. We lost Grandpa yes, but the Lord preserved us, and we'll rebuild and rise again. I think there's a lesson in there for all of us and all who will hear of it." He took a deep breath. "Worldly possessions bring no lasting happiness and can grow legs and walk away from a person. But what's in here," he touched his heart, "That's what is important."

"You've become a very wise man, my son."

"I thank God that we're getting things back together again."

"And have you been praying as Mrs. Shaw advised?"

"Yes Ma, and if it be the Lord's will, then Mandy and her mother will return some day." He got a faraway look in his eyes. "When I last saw her, Mandy was just eleven years old and barely reached to my waist. I wonder if she's grown any taller."

"Five years is a long time and a girl of sixteen is no more a child but a budding young woman, ripe and ready for marriage."

Cecil sighed, "I pray that wherever they are, those two are all right." He rose to his feet.

"Where are you going?"

"I want to ride around just to make sure that Mrs. Shaw's boys are taking care of the fence like I asked them to. Even though they're our tenants, I've given them some tasks like making sure the estate boundaries are secure. With the money I'll pay them they will be able to rebuild their own lives."

"Where have they been all these years?"

Cecil sighed, "They ended up in Manchester working at a steel mill. It was really hard and gruelling work but with very little pay. Many times they wanted to return home to their mother but feared the repercussions. Then a few weeks ago they saw the newspapers with news about Mr. Weatherly's downfall. They didn't hesitate any longer."

"Don't ride too far, it's getting late and I don't want you out in the dark."

Cecil grinned but decided that he would humour his mother. She had no idea of the kind of danger he'd been in while serving in Egypt. He was a grown man who could take care of himself but he didn't say any of that.

"I want to ride by the sawmill. An engineer recommended by Colonel Watson is checking the machines over to see whatever needs repairing and what needs to be replaced."

"You've done well, my son. Your grandfather knew what he was doing when he named you his heir. Thank you for forgiving me and bringing me back home."

"Ma, this will always be your home, and I'm just glad that I found you."

❄

When Cecil left his mother, he wanted to ride out and check on Mrs. Shaw's sons before going to the sawmill. But as he headed in that direction he decided to go and take a look at the cottage as he always did.

"Mandy, come back home," he murmured as he rode his new horse. Having money had its perks for he'd replaced the old mule with a younger stallion. And with time he would once again restore his grandfather's stable and fill it with thoroughbreds.

He thought he smelled something burning like beans but dismissed it as being his own imagination. When he got closer to the cottage, however, he saw a wisp of smoke rising from the chimney he'd cleaned a few days ago.

"That's strange," he thought, because the cottage was supposed to be empty. Then his lips tightened, perhaps it was some vagabonds who were up to no good, or even poachers. Glad that he'd brought one of his revolvers with him, he prepared himself to deal with any unpleasant characters.

He patted his coat where the gun was and sighed. Mr. Weatherly had taken his rifle and revolvers that he'd left at home when he'd joined the army, but they had all been recovered.

With the estate being very large, he knew poachers and vagrants had had a field day, but no more. He wouldn't be surprised to find a tramp or fugitive living in the cottage, which was empty.

And that was one reason he'd decided to take on many more tenants so they could keep the estate safe. Things would be different and the whole estate would be occupied with his people.

He didn't want to startle the person into running away because he wanted to teach the intruder a lesson. He just hoped the person hadn't lit a fire and left it unattended. Bush fires in summer had been known to cause a lot of destruction to property When growing up, his grandfather had always emphasized on the need to look out for any unattended wild fires.

As Cecil came closer to the cottage he heard voices, female voices and his heart began to beat rapidly. Dare he hope?

TASTE OF VICTORY

❄

The knock at the door jarred both women and they looked at each other, terror in their eyes. Had Mr. Weatherly already discovered their presence on his land and sent his goons once again to harass them? They hadn't been here even six hours and already trouble was standing at their doorstep.

"Ma," Mandy whispered as they huddled close together in the front room. At least they'd had the good mind to shut the door and lock it. "What do we do now?" She shouldn't have lit the fire to prepare their dinner and then left it burning as they prepared for bed. It was still light outside but they were exhausted from their flight from Manchester and wanted to rest. Someone must have seen the smoke and come to check on what was going on.

"Let's be very quiet and perhaps the person will go away and then we can escape."

Then a thought struck Mandy, "Ma, if it's Mr. Weatherly's men, won't they just break the door down and force their way inside?" And the thought of that terrified Mandy because she knew men like that wouldn't hesitate to hurt her and her mother very badly. They felt very defenceless and vulnerable. Mandy felt so helpless and angry at the same time because as a woman she was at the mercy of men's whims.

The knock sounded again and this time it was loud and impatient. Mandy looked toward the grate and spotted a thick piece of firewood. She would go down fighting for their virtues and lives if need be. She refused to be a victim all the time. This time she was going to fight. "Open the door," she told her mother in a firm voice.

"You want me to open the door?" Mrs. Wood looked at her daughter in surprise.

"Ma, we've got to stop being afraid all the time. I'm tired of always being a victim. If I have to fight for our lives then so be it."

"Let me open the door then," her mother said. Her intention was to delay whoever it was at the door so as to give Mandy time to escape through the window in the other room. "Mandy, I'll hold them here. Go to the other room and be ready to escape. Get out of the window and run as fast and as far away as you can. Don't on any account stop for any reason until you're safe."

"Yes, Ma."

Mrs. Wood took a deep breath then called out. "Who is it?"

"Mrs. Wood, please open the door," the women were shocked because it was a strange deep voice, not sounding at all like Mr. Weatherly's men. And the person was even being polite. "I mean you no harm."

Mandy held the thick stick in both hands, ready to swing as hard as she could to defend them. "Ma, open the door. We can't live in fear forever."

"Very well," and Mrs. Wood pushed back the two rusty bolts and turned the key. It wasn't as if they could even stop a determined person from entering the house because the door wasn't that strong. Mandy was glad that it was still light outside.

Mrs. Wood opened the door and then gasped.

"Ma?" Mandy raised the stick in readiness but then started lowering it again. Her mother's stance wasn't one of fear, more of surprise. "Who is it?"

"You won't believe me even if I tell you," Mrs. Wood said and stepped aside to let the person in. "Please come in, Sir."

Mandy's brow creased as the tall man came into view, and then she got rooted to the spot. The tall, well-built man who entered their small house took her breath away, and her eyes widened. She couldn't understand why her heart was racing as if it wanted to beat right out of her chest.

Never had the presence of a man made her feel the flurry of butterflies in the pit of her stomach and her knees suddenly became weak. She wished there was a chair in the cottage, for she would sink into it and not rise up again until the stranger was gone. What was happening to her?

Mandy was so lost in trying to understand what was going on that she didn't immediately notice that the man had been struck as speechless as she was.

Cecil blinked rapidly to make sure he was seeing right. The last time he'd been in this cottage Mandy had been a little girl. But the beautiful woman who stood before him took his breath away. And for Cecil, that was the moment he really fell in love for the first time and also the last for his heart told him that he had found his mate.

"Mandy," his voice came out in a whisper.

"You know my name?" Mandy looked at her mother who had a strange smile on her face. "Ma, you know him?"

Mrs. Wood laughed, a happy sound that warmed Mandy's heart. The last time she'd heard her mother laugh in such a manner was years ago when her father was still alive.

"Mandy, don't you recognize your friend, Mr. Miller?"

"What?" Mandy thought she would swoon. This handsome and very strong looking man standing before her was her Mr. Miller. No, she shook her head, he wasn't hers. The man she'd thought about every day for the past five years had looked lanky and weak. The last time she'd seen Mr. Miller he hadn't been this tall. This man was strong and of robust health and his skin was flawless. No bruises marred his visage like before.

"Are you about to swoon," there was laughter in Cecil's voice as he reached out his arms and grabbed the woman who looked like she might fall at his feet. "Surely, my face isn't as frightening as it was last time when you rescued me and saw all the bruises, blood and gashes."

"Mr. Miller," Mandy felt as if she was in a dream. "Dear Lord, if this is a dream, let me never wake up," she murmured and he laughed, a rich sound that made her heart beat even faster. "Is it really you?" She had to touch him to make sure and her hand went to his face.

"As I live and breathe, it's me, my Little Mandy," Cecil murmured, feeling like he wanted to weep for joy.

"Not little anymore," Mrs. Wood said, moving away from the door. "I'm sorry we have no chairs so we can't even offer you a place to sit. We just got in today and haven't even settled down." Her eyes moved around the room. "As you can see, this place was stripped bare when we left five years ago. I doubt that anyone has lived here since."

"I thought some vagabonds had made this their dwelling and were out to cause trouble," Cecil said.

"I still can't believe that it's you," Mandy realised how inappropriate it was for her to still be in the arms of a man who wasn't her husband. He could be engaged or even married by now because five years was a long time. And the thought filled her with pain and brought her dreaming to a stop. She moved out of his arms.

Cecil noticed when Mandy's countenance changed. "Aren't you happy to see me?"

Mandy's response was to reach under the collar of her dress and bring out the string. She pulled it over her head. "I kept the ring safe," she said, holding it out to him. He would need it for the woman in his life, she thought.

"You kept it all these years?" It was her mother who spoke, sounding surprised. "I never knew that you had the ring that you had asked for, nor did I ever see you wearing that string around your neck when we were in the workhouse."

Mandy smiled, still holding the ring out to Cecil. "When we first got to the workhouse I sewed it into the hem of my uniform because I was afraid that someone would take it away if they saw it. You remember how those bad girls stole your shawl and my hairbrush," she twisted her lips. "Those were the last things Papa gave us before he died and we never got them back. Had someone seen this ring they would most certainly have taken it away from me. I felt that it wasn't safe around my neck, however because we had to change out of our uniforms every week on laundry day. And since we never got back the same dresses I sewed it into my undergarments," and she blushed as she thought about it.

Cecil stared at the ring in Mandy's hand. He too couldn't believe that she had kept it safe all this while. As a child she could have so easily lost it but yet here it was, and with the woman he'd fallen in love with. Grandma was right, this ring belonged to the person who held his heart. But since he didn't know much of what had happened to her he chose to be cautious and keep his feelings to himself, at least for now.

"And I too have something you gave me," he reached into his top left pocket for the small handkerchief, but it wasn't there. "I must have left it at the manor in my other coat," he said.

"The manor!" Mandy gasped. "What are you doing there and are you all right?" She feared for him. What if Mr. Weatherly hurt him again?

"It's a long story which can only be told when we're sitting down over a cup of tea and delicious scones made by Mrs. Pitch." He looked around the empty room; then his eyes went to the small pot and few utensils close to the grate. "I thought I smelled beans burning," he said and Mandy blushed. "That smell and the wisp of smoke was what brought me quickly to check on the cottage."

"I burnt our dinner," she said.

He laughed, then shook his head, "You can't ever live here. I've been searching for you, and Mrs. Shaw told me to pray for you to return."

"We were afraid that Mr. Weatherly would send his hoodlums to assault us, so we didn't intend to stay for long. Tomorrow we were going to look for our friends and I'm glad Mrs. Shaw is still here. We were going to ask them to hide us for a few days until we'd decided on where to go next."

Cecil laughed, "You never have to fear again. Mr. Weatherly will spend the rest of his life in prison. He narrowly escaped the hangman's noose and that was because Colonel Watson said it would be too easy for him. A man like that needs to feel pain for a long time," Cecil waved his hand, "Pardon me for rattling on."

"Colonel Watson?" Mandy asked.

"Like I said, it's a long story which needs to be told in the comfort of a good home. Gather up all your belongings for you're coming to live in the manor with me."

Mother and daughter exchanged happy looks.

"I also found my mother and brought her back home with me," Cecil said as he walked toward the door.

"Where was she?" Mandy felt happiness flooding her heart. Mr. Miller looked so happy and at peace and it warmed her heart.

"As I said, it's a long story and I need to go back to the manor and make ready for you. I need to get the servants to prepare rooms for you, so pack whatever you have and await my return."

"Your ring," Mandy called out just as Cecil was about to step out of the cottage.

"Hold it for me and I'll be back for it and you." And he closed the door behind him. They listened as his footsteps faded away, then rushed into each other's arms.

"Oh Ma, did you see him?"

Mrs. Wood chuckled, "I was here the whole time, my dear child."

"Mr. Miller is still alive and he now lives at the manor," Mandy's eyes glowed. "And he wants us to go and live with him."

"Yes, but remember that our place in life is different from his, Mandy. Mr. Miller is probably only doing this out of the kindness of his heart. Maybe he's offering us positions in his house as servants now that he's the master of the estate."

Mandy knew that what her mother said made a lot of sense but she couldn't help feeling excited. She slipped the string back around her neck, feeling comforted that Mr. Miller hadn't taken it from her. Even if he had someone else in his life she would ask him to let her keep the ring that had comforted her through all those hard days in the past.

"Let's pack whatever we have…" Whatever else Mrs. Wood was about to say was cut off when there was a soft knock at the door.

Mandy grinned as she rushed to open the door, very sure that Mr. Miller was back to bring them to the manor. "Mr. Miller, back so soon?" She flung open the door with a broad smile, expecting Mr. Miller.

"You thought you could hide from me forever."

With her reaction slowed by the shock of seeing who was on the threshold, Mandy didn't think of shutting the door fast enough and Mr. Spindle wedged himself in the doorway.

"Go away," she whispered as he shoved her aside and entered the room. He smelled of the sweat of many days and stale alcohol and his clothes were tattered. His hair was unkempt and he'd grown a beard that was shaggy and made him look like a lunatic. There was a wild look in his eyes that terrified Mandy and she knew that trouble had come to them for sure.

"Is that any way to treat the man who only ever wanted the best for you?"

Mandy stepped back and thought of rushing toward the door but Mr. Spindle noticed the glance and moved backward, laughing unkindly.

"Don't even think about it because I've got you now."

"How did you find us," Mandy was still in shock and asked in a whisper. She wanted to go over to where her mother also seemed rooted to the floor but was afraid that, if she moved, Mr. Spindle would lunge at her.

And Mr. Miller had gone back to the manor, so he couldn't help them. By the time he returned, Mr. Spindle would have done much harm to them. Why, oh why hadn't he stayed to wait for them?

"You destroyed my life, and my reputation was shattered forever," Mr. Spindle said. "The newspapers made fun of me and called me all sorts of names, and everyone treated me like a pervert. These few months have been hell for me because my wife and her family tossed me out of my own home. I knew that you would eventually leave the workhouse and return to this place because rats like you usually return to their former breeding ground. When I found out that you had left the workhouse I came here expecting to find you. For the past one month I've been roaming around hoping that you would show up and you did. Today when I saw you at the train station I followed you. This is my time to exact my revenge on you and you'll be sorry for what you did to me."

His eyes were red and Mandy knew that she was in the presence of a man possessed by a very foul spirit. He didn't seem human at all. She wanted to scream but her throat felt closed up.

Mr. Spindle lunged at Mandy and with a sharp cry, Mrs. Wood leapt forward to defend her daughter.

"Not again," she screamed.

But having been ill for a long time and still weak, the woman was no match for the demented tramp. He struck her hard, throwing her backward and she reeled back, struck the back of her head on the wall, then slithered down to the floor where she lay stunned.

"Don't hurt my mother," Mandy didn't think twice but charged at her assailant like a mad woman.

"You think you can fight with me," Mr. Spindle jeered and backhanded her hard. She fell across the room. He spotted the thick piece of firewood and picked it up.

"I'll kill you both," his voice was sinister, "But before that, I'll have my way with you and take by force the virtue that you denied me all this while. I'll break your legs so you won't be able to move as I do whatever I want to do with you, and when I'm done, no one will ever look at you because you'll be dead," he laughed and raised the stick.

Mandy curled her legs as she heard her mother moaning and pleading for mercy but Mr. Spindle was like one possessed of the devil. She raised her hands, praying that the blow he struck would be fatal and she would die immediately. She wept as the thought about the happiness that had been in her grasp, only to be snatched away from her again. Was she born cursed?

"Lord please help us," she sobbed as she closed her eyes and waited for the first blow to fall.

※

Cecil hadn't gone far when he reached into his trouser pocked and found the white handkerchief Mandy had given him five years ago.

"Well, what do you know," he laughed. His feet faltered and he thought to himself, 'Why am I leaving Mandy and her mother behind and yet they don't have much to pack? The servants can easily prepare the rooms while we're taking our tea.'

"Oh how foolish I am," he slapped his forehead, turning to retrace his steps toward the cottage. As he drew closer he heard someone cry out in pain and his heart nearly stopped.

Without a thought as to his personal safety he pulled his revolver out and got ready to use it, sensing that Mandy was in danger. He quickly opened the door which mercifully wasn't locked and the sight that met his eyes was one he would never forget.

Both women lay on the floor in different parts of the room, and a tramp stood over Mandy, a thick stick raised in readiness to strike her. Cecil knew that if that blow landed it would break her bones. And the dirty looking scoundrel was uttering obscenities and curses.

Cecil quickly put his revolver back in his holster and then slowly moved forward. As the evil hand started to descend, Cecil was immediately at the tramp's side and grabbed it.

Mr. Spindle had been so caught up in the haze of revenge and hatred that he didn't hear the door opening until it was too late.

"What…" caught by surprise Mr. Spindle lashed out, and the stick struck Cecil's shoulder and he winced at the pain. But that was the only blow the younger man allowed to land on his body. With a roar of rage he charged and soon the cottage was filled with guttural sounds like two wild animals fighting. At first Mandy thought Mr. Spindle would overcome Cecil and she grabbed the stick which had nearly been used on her.

But then she saw that Cecil was winning the fight as the two men wrestled and her heart cheered him on. She dropped the stick and then crawled to where her mother still lay stunned.

"Ma," she wept because her mother looked like she was slipping into unconsciousness. After being ill, now she was badly hurt. Would her mother survive this latest attack by the mad man who was obsessed with her? She heard heavy breathing as the two men continued with their scuffle but Cecil proved stronger. He was younger, healthier, faster on his feet and also sober, things that Mr. Spindle wasn't.

Cecil grabbed Mr. Spindle's right arm and twisted it behind his back reminding Mandy of what had happened back at the workhouse many months ago. Rage filled her heart as she thought about what this man had wanted to do to them. Would they never be free of this man's obsessive cruelty? What had she ever done to him for him to have pursued her relentlessly in the past and even now? Would she never be free of his bullying and wickedness?

"Let me be," Mr. Spindle turned his head just as Cecil slammed him into the wall until the cottage shook and bits of sod fell from the walls.

"You'll be sorry you ever set your hands on a woman, and not just any woman, my woman," Cecil growled fiercely, turning the man to face him. He held the front of Mr. Spindle's shirt and slammed his fist hard into his face. "You deserve to die for what you wanted to do to my woman," and Mr. Spindle slid to the floor. He grunted once then slumped into unconsciousness.

Cecil was taking no chances, so he rolled the unconscious man onto his stomach and pressed his knee into his back.

"Mandy, get me something to bind this worthless scoundrel with."

Mandy scrambled to her feet and ran to where their scanty belongings were and pulled out a thin sheet. She ripped it into strands which she handed over to Cecil. Cecil made short work of binding Mr. Spindle's hands behind his back and then his ankles too. Once he was sure that the man was secured for now, he rose to his feet.

"Are you all right? Is your mother alright?"

But Mandy didn't seem to hear him. Her eyes went to the thick stick which Mr. Spindle had dropped when Cecil had charged at him. She walked over to it, bent down and retrieved it, flexing her fingers around it. She had a glazed look in her eyes as she tightened both palms around it. Rage once again welled up within her and she ignored her mother's soft cry, not recognizing that she'd regained consciousness. She approached the man on the ground.

This man had tormented her for five years and when happiness was within her grasp, he'd returned to snatch it away again. One blow to his head would end his miserable life and he would never hurt anyone else again.

"Mandy," the strong voice penetrated through her rage and she stopped next to the bound man who was just stirring. As if he sensed danger, he opened his eyes and a resigned look entered them. It was as if he looked into Mandy's eyes and saw that his end had come.

"Mandy!" Cecil's voice was sharper and Mandy blinked. Tears stung her eyes then she raised them to Cecil's. The expression in his eyes said he understood her pain and rage but his gaze also urged her not to strike the man.

"Striking a man to defend yourself when he has attacked is understandable," Cecil said softly, holding Mandy's gaze and willing her not to look at the man who lay on the ground. "But this fellow isn't worth it and he's bound like a trussed up chicken. If you strike and kill him while he lies helpless at your feet, you'll never live with yourself and the guilt that will follow."

And as he said this, Cecil reached tentatively for the thick stick still clutched in Mandy's trembling hands. She let go and soon found herself enclosed in the protective circle of Cecil's warm embrace.

"There now," Cecil held the young woman and stroked the back of her head as she sobbed. But his eyes were also on the prisoner just in case the man broke free. The strands from the sheet weren't a very good restraint and a strong man could easily snap them and get free.

Footsteps sounded outside and someone knocked on the door. Cecil didn't recall shutting it when he'd rushed in to save his woman and he braced himself for more trouble. His stance relaxed when he heard the voice of Andrew Shaw.

"Andrew, get in here at once," he called out. The door was pushed open and a man with a bushy beard entered.

"Lieutenant, my lad found your horse wandering around and got worried," the man said, taking in the scene before him. "What happened here?" his eyes widened when they settled on the trussed up man.

"This tramp came into this cottage and attacked Mrs. Wood and her daughter, Where is your lad now?"

"I told him to wait outside when I heard voices in here because I wasn't sure what was going on."

"Good. Send him to bring the police constables, and I'll tell you everything once this scoundrel has been arrested. He's a trespasser and assailant and I want him dealt with severely."

"Yes, Lieutenant," he rushed out to do as bid. Mandy heard him urging his lad to hurry, and then he was back in an instant.

"I don't trust this fellow," Andrew Shaw said and stepped closer to where Mr. Spindle was lying, standing guard over him. The prisoner tried to wriggle and when it seemed like he might break free Andrew knelt on him, pressing him back to the floor. He groaned.

They had to wait for nearly twenty minutes before Andrew's son returned with two constables. They had handcuffs and quickly secured the prisoner as Mr. Miller explained what had happened. Mandy was still staring at the whole scene in shock, not believing that once again God had saved her from the demented man. Mr. Spindle cast an ugly look at Mandy and opened his mouth.

"Say one word," one of the burly constables said. "I dare you to open your foul mouth and say one word and see what happens to those teeth you have remaining in there."

And Mr. Spindle wisely kept his mouth shut, no doubt fearing for his teeth. The two constables with Andrew and his lad behind them followed.

"Lieutenant, I'll make sure this man gets what he deserves," the police constable said.

"Thank you."

Cecil turned to Mandy's mother who was struggling to get to her feet. He went over and helped her up and them with his arms around both women he led them out of the cottage.

"Come let me take you to the manor where it's safe," he said. "Leave everything as it is, and someone will come and collect these things and bring them to you."

REST FOR THE WEARY

Four Months Later

F"I haven't celebrated Christmas for almost six years now," Mandy told Cecil months later as they stood in the parlour watching as two servants brought in a large fir tree. The men placed it in one corner of the newly tiled room.

Ever since Queen Victoria's husband had introduced Christmas trees at Windsor Castle nearly two decades ago, every household in England followed the tradition. A box of coloured cloth sat in one corner of the room and Mrs. Pitch was baking cookies and gingerbread men to hang on the tree. The smell of Christmas was in the air, and Mandy wanted to weep for joy. But this was also a sad time for her because she was reminded of how it used to be when her father was still alive.

"We celebrated Christmas in the army, but there wasn't much pomp. Still, we used to get invited to the homes of many of the families who had chosen to settle down in Cairo. But I also remember how jolly Christmas used to be when my grandmother was still alive," Cecil said, then turned when Mandy sighed. "What happened to stop Christmas for you?"

"My Pa died on Christmas Day six years ago, and life was never the same for Ma and me again." She closed her eyes, seeing the day as it had been. "There was a storm that day and lightning struck a tree in our yard. Pa loved that tree, and whenever the weather was good we would sit out there and drink lemonade and cookies while greeting everyone who passed by. I thought that losing the tree would be the worst thing that happened that day, but then I realised that we had no food in the house, nothing to eat. Mrs. Fount, our neighbour was hosting Christmas that year but there was no money to buy flour to bake cookies for us to take over to her house. All the money had gone to buy Pa's medicines and pay all our debts because Pa had stopped working nearly two months before. And the next five Christmas Days were spent in the workhouse. The first two years weren't so bad because Reverend Reid always made sure we got a treat during meal times. There were some celebrations and Reverend Reid even brought in some musicians to entertain us." She fell silent.

Cecil could hear the pain in her voice and wanted her to stop but he knew that she had to let out all her feelings in order for true healing to begin.

"When Reverend Reid's wife and daughter fell ill he had to leave to take care of them. He stayed away for nearly two years but they still died. In that time things were terrible and Christmas was no longer the same again. Rations decreased and there were no musicians. It was as if Christmas had gotten lost and I never thought I would celebrate it again."

"Mandy, I'm so sorry that you missed out on so much."

"But we're free now and here I am, looking forward to this Christmas Day," she smiled. "And Mr. Spindle will know what it is like to be on the other side of the workhouse as an inmate and not a governor."

When Cecil had found out who Mr. Spindle was and how much he'd made Mandy and her mother suffer in the workhouse, he'd called upon Colonel Watson for his help. And together they had brought pressure to bear on the commissioners of the workhouse and a thorough investigation was conducted. The man's atrocities, including how he often sold young women to brothel owners, came out. The newspapers had a field day!

And the sentence for his crimes was for him to become an inmate in the workhouse, the same one he'd ruled over like a king. And the conditions placed on his residence there were worse than those in a prison for he was to be isolated from others and watched over like the criminal that he was.

"No please," Mr. Spindle had screamed in the courthouse as his sentence was passed down to him. "Take me to prison, I won't survive in the workhouse. Mercy please."

But the judge's ruling had been final and he was to spend an unspecified period of time in the workhouse.

"So that you can become human, and compassion can return to that depraved heart of yours," the judge had said. "I want you to taste of the pain and punishments you inflicted on those you were supposed to protect and tell me how it feels."

Mandy and her mother had more cause to smile because Mrs. Ridges had also been investigated and narrowly escaped joining her brother-in-law in the workhouse. Instead she was given the choice of imprisonment for her own crimes or transportation and she'd chosen the latter, too ashamed to face her family again. In as far as Mandy knew, Mrs. Ridges was now a resident of Australia and with no hopes of ever returning.

Mrs. Pauline Tucker was promoted, much to the joy of the residents of the workhouse because she was a kind woman who had tried to look out for them. She was now the matron and life at the workhouse was so much better than it had ever been. Anyone else who had ever been associated with Mr. Spindle or Mrs. Ridges also found themselves in trouble as they were relieved of their duties and sent away. The worst offenders found themselves facing prison time.

When things had settled down at the workhouse, Mrs. Tucker and Reverend Reid had visited Mandy and her mother at their invitation. They had shared their ideas and the reforms that were taking place at Dudley Workhouse to make it a better place for its inmates.

Cecil realized that Mandy was lost in her own world so he gently nudged her with his elbow and she turned to him. "You know that I like to see you smiling," he said, raising her chin and looking into her eyes. "So this year I want to give you the best Christmas Day you've ever had. We'll have a large celebration, and for you Christmas will come alive again."

❄

Cecil didn't spare any expense for Christmas because firstly he had the money that had been his grandfather's, and now his own coffers were filled. Also, the sawmill was up and running, and in just a few months it was already beginning to show a profit. It wasn't much but he had hope that things would get better.

Colonel Watson had recommended to him a good manager and the man was honest and very hardworking.

Mrs. Wood and Mrs. Miller had become fast friends and worked together with the servants to make Christmas

Day a very grand affair. With nearly fifty new tenants on the estate Cecil was confident that they would all prosper.

And as it had been during his grandparents' time, every tenant received a gift of foodstuff, enough to make their lives comfortable for a few weeks as they settled down properly. And there was much candy for the little ones because Mrs. Pitch and Mandy decided that they too deserved to celebrate.

Everyone ate and drank to their fill and even had something to carry back home. Reverend Reid was there to bless the first Christmas at the manor in nearly ten years and there was much joy and celebration.

Once the guests were gone and it was just Cecil and Mandy and their mothers left in the parlour, he held out his hand to her. "Where is my ring?" He asked her. In the months since he'd saved their lives he hadn't spoken about the ring and Mandy had wondered whether he remembered it.

But she had seen something unravelling before her eyes. Expecting Mr. Miller to tell her that he had someone in his life, nothing of the sort had happened. Instead he'd paid so much attention to her, always seeking her out. Of course, he would always make sure that one of their mothers was around, for propriety's sake.

"Mandy, my ring?"

She reached for the string around her neck and pulled it over her head. She untied the knot and slipped the ring to her palm, held it for a few seconds then passed it to Cecil.

Cecil took the ring and held it in his hand. "My grandmother told me to give this ring to the woman who holds my heart," he said. "Five years ago, even without knowing what I was doing, I left the ring with Mandy when I was returning to my duty station. At the time all I wanted was to comfort the little girl who had saved my life. She was really upset that I was leaving. She'd given me a handkerchief to cover the bruise on my neck and I left her my ring." He reached into his pocket and pulled out the white handkerchief. "I kept this little piece of cloth with me, close to my heart and didn't understand what I was doing." He smiled tenderly at Mandy and she felt shy. "Her name is embroidered on it and every time I looked at it, I thought of the little girl who had such a big loving heart. I had no idea that heaven was working to bring the two of us together in a totally different way."

"Mr. Miller…"

"Over the years I felt like Mandy was close to me whenever I held this tiny cloth in my hand. But in my mind, she was still the small eleven-year-old girl. And then this past summer I returned home and she came back and I saw her again," he took a deep breath. "When I saw her I fell in love with her on the spot. She had grown into a very beautiful young woman. She had also proved to be a good custodian of grandma's ring. My grandfather gave this ring to my grandmother and she called it a ring of love. They were together for more than thirty years, and when she died, my grandpa's life was never the same again. And because Mandy has been such a good custodian of this love ring, what better way to reward her than to make sure that it stays permanently on her finger?"

The two mothers clapped happily.

"Say yes, Mandy," her mother urged her.

Mandy gave her mother a quick glance. "Ma, how can I say yes to a question that hasn't been asked yet?"

"Oh," Cecil grinned broadly. "Amanda Jane Wood—you remember I know all your names—will you be my beloved wife, to have and hold for the rest of our lives?"

Mandy looked to her mother for direction and the woman nodded happily. But she was afraid and it showed on her face. She was only sixteen and Mr. Miller was a worldly man who could have any beautiful woman that he wanted. Was she really the right mate for him and would their marriage be happy? What did she know about being a wife to such a man as him?

"I know that I'm ten years older than you Amanda, but I'm in love with you. It may have started off as friendship, but the Lord knew that we were meant for each other. I want to marry you and have a family with you."

"Right now?"

Cecil shook his head, "I love you so much and don't want to imagine spending another day without you. But you're still very young and need to find your feet first. So we'll remain in courtship for two years until you turn eighteen. You're still too young for me to just impose wifehood and then motherhood on you."

"You're prepared to wait for me for two years?" Mandy was surprised by Cecil's words. "What will we be doing in that time?"

"I'll be building our estate while you'll serve as an apprenticed pupil teacher because you once told me that you wanted to be an educator and enlighten the minds of little ones. At the end of your apprenticeship you'll take the Queen's scholarship exam and if you pass you'll go on to training college."

Mandy felt like her heart was about to burst. Her father's dream for her was coming true through this man that she loved with her whole heart.

"But will I be allowed to work as a teacher when we get married?"

"Why not? Our estate is growing and we have many young families coming up. One of my dreams is to have a school right here on the estate, and we will need good teachers. So, if you work hard enough, you'll be the first headmistress of Sinclair School For Enlightened Boys and Girls."

"Really?" Her eyes glowed and she didn't realise how beautiful she looked. Cecil felt a pang of regret that he couldn't immediately make this beautiful woman his wife. But it was all for her good and his, and their generations to come. England and the world were changing and the turn of the century would soon be here, and he wanted a wife he could be proud of.

"You've made me so happy though I'm worried that two years might be too long for you to wait."

Cecil picked her hands up and kissed them, then placed her right one over his heart. "They will be as nothing because of the love that I have for you," he said. "And am I not in a better position than Jacob who had to wait seven years for the woman he loved, though at first he was given the wrong one? I have only two years which will pass quickly."

"Oh Mr. Miller!"

"The question first is Do you love me, Mandy? I might be making assumptions here and yet you're not in love with me."

Mandy stared at the man she loved with her whole heart, noting the tension around his lips. He'd stopped smiling and his body was stiff, almost as if he was preparing himself for rejection.

"Oh, Mr. Miller," she said, and forgetting all propriety she threw herself against him in delight. "I love you, you silly man, I love you so much and my heart belongs to you. This feels like a dream to me because I never thought it would come true."

"My dearest girl," Cecil could now breathe again. "The question has been asked," he gently pushed her away, mindful that their mothers were watching them. "I await your answer."

"It's yes," Mandy laughed happily. "My answer will always be yes, I'll be your wife."

"You've made me a very happy man indeed. I love you so much Mandy, my little Mandy."

"And I love you, Mr. Miller."

"Cecil, my darling. Call me Cecil from now going forward."

EPILOGUE

Two Years Later

Mandy opened her eyes to the sound of chirping birds. Today was her wedding day, and even nature seemed to celebrate this with her. She knew that it would be a very special day for it was in the third week of spring.

She slipped out of bed, wrapped a robe around her and sat in a chair by the window. She could hear sounds of laughter and rose to open the balcony doors. She leaned over the railing and a smile broke on her face.

Her mother, Mrs. Miller, Mrs. Pitch and Mrs. Shaw were out on the front lawn making sure that the servants were doing the right thing. Some were arranging the flowers while others took care of the chairs on which the invited guests would sit.

Being spring, Mandy had begged Mr. Miller to let them have the celebrations on the front lawn, the reception that is. It was wide enough to fit almost one hundred people, which was roughly the number of guests they were expecting. Though they had tried to make it a small affair, the tenants and their mothers had conspired together and now it had turned into this lavish affair.

When Colonel Watson had heard about the wedding, he and his wife had packed up their bags and moved to the manor. Mandy laughed when she thought about the vivacious old man who made life jolly around the manor. No one could believe that he'd lost a leg because he was all over the place, taking on the role of Cecil's grandfather.

As Mandy watched, Mrs. Watson joined the other women, and they all looked up and waved at her. She waved back, then went in and took her seat once again, thinking about her life for the past two years.

Just as Mr. Miller had promised, he'd found her a teacher apprenticeship at the local school. And he made sure there was someone to drop her there and bring her back home whenever he himself couldn't do it.

Because Mandy was a determined young woman and because she wanted to make her Ma and Pa, and most of all Mr. Miller, proud, she'd worked really hard. Just six months into her apprenticeship, the master of the school had recommended that she take the Queen's Scholarship Exam, which she passed with flying colours.

When she was admitted at Cheltenham Ladies College for further training, no one was happier than Mr. Miller himself. Even though the school provided quarters for the women, her family wouldn't hear of it, least of all Colonel Watson.

"You will live with us until such a time as you graduate," had been his words and that was final. And Mandy had found a new father in the man. To honour him, she'd asked him to give her away today, and he had shed one or two tears seeing as he had no daughters of his own, only six sons.

Her bedroom door opened, and Mrs. Tucker walked in. "There you are," the woman had a tray in her hands which she placed on the small table in the bedroom. "Your groom says you should take this cup of tea and dainty cakes, then get ready for him. He asked me to come and make sure that you have everything you need."

Mandy smiled at the woman who had been like a second mother to her all these years. Whenever she had days off from her duties at the workhouse, Mrs. Tucker visited them, and the Sinclair Estate had become her second home.

Just last year she had received news that her husband, the man who had abandoned her, had given up his wayward life, returned to the church and put away his mistress. He returned to Mrs. Tucker and, after months of patiently wooing her, she had accepted him back. And she looked so much happier as they now both worked at the workhouse, he the governor and she the matron.

"I have more than I need," she said. "Mr. Miller has been more than generous to me."

Mrs. Tucker chuckled, "Don't you think it's time you changed the way you address your soon-to-be husband?"

Mandy grinned. It was true that she had never been able to bring herself to call the man she loved by his first name, no matter how much he begged her to. She didn't think it was appropriate and especially since they weren't married yet.

"I like to tease him and make him feel old."

"Well, as long as you're both as happy as Mr. Tucker and I are then so be it." The woman quickly stripped the bed. "After today this will no longer be your bedroom."

Mandy felt a flutter in her stomach. In the past two years Mr. Miller had showed her what true love was when he supported her career, and on the day that she had graduated from college, he'd been the proudest man on earth.

"This one is for you, Pa," Mandy had held up her diploma and wept tears of joy in her mother's arms.

And Mandy had been glad that they had waited for two years to get married. Apart from her achieving what her father had always dreamed for her, she had also been working on her own heart. It had been very hard to forgive all those who had wronged her and that had stood between her having a satisfactory Christian life. It had been hard to humble herself, but in the past two years all that had changed.

The day she had finally opened up her heart and decided to forgive everyone was the day she'd felt as if she was reborn. All pain, bitterness and anger had drained out of her heart to be replaced by compassion and deep love for people.

In an act of contrition and after confessing to the colonel, he and his wife had accompanied her to Manchester to visit the James Estate. She had repented and asked the two young men for their forgiveness.

She'd been surprised when Toby and Charles too had begged for her forgiveness, telling her that her actions toward them had changed their lives. They had taken a good look at themselves and hated the men they had become. Mandy had returned a very happy soul indeed.

In that same frame of mind, she'd prepared herself to travel to Dudley to face Mr. Spindle and tell him that she had forgiven him. Unfortunately just a day before she was to go there, the man was found dead and lying face down in the pigsty where he'd tortured her and her mother.

According to Mrs. Tucker, Hans had come in that morning and found the pigs congregated in one corner of the barn. Wondering what was happening he'd tried to draw closer but the animals were so hostile that he'd had to get help. A few men from the workhouse came to help him and that's when they had found Mr. Spindle's mangled body. If Hans hadn't come in when he did the pigs would have made short work of his flesh.

Investigations were still going on and it was suspected that some of the inmates whose lives he'd made a living hell had turned on him. But they were all being mum and Mrs. Tucker told Mandy that the investigators were just about giving up because they were being taken round in circles.

"But at least you had the idea of going to forgive him and did it in your heart and made peace with God," Mr. Miller had comforted her when she expressed her regrets at not being able to look her nemesis in the eye and tell him that she'd forgiven him and even ask for his mercy.

Mr. Miller and his mother had also forgiven Mr. Weatherly who was just a broken man spending the rest of his life in prison.

Footsteps came up the stairs and the door opened. Her mother walked into the room. "Your groom is ready and pacing nervously at the bottom of the stairs."

Mandy was also glad that their wedding had been delayed because it had given Mr. Miller enough time to finish renovations on Sinclair Estate and also repair the tenants' houses as well as build new ones. Much had been accomplished in the past two years with Mr. Miller also opening a bakery and grocery store to be run by both mothers who were in their element. And the small cottage where it had all begun was also renovated, and that was to be their private love nest starting from today.

"I want us to have a place which is just for the two of us," Mr. Miller had told her just yesterday. "In years to come when our children and grandchildren ask us how we met, we'll have the little cottage to show them where this journey all started."

Nearly half an hour later Mandy was ready. "Mama, I'm ready," she said as she donned her veil, a gift from Mrs. Shaw. It was made from intricate lace and Mandy had wept when the woman had brought it to the manor.

Tears came to her mother's eyes as she fluffed the veil. "Your Papa would be so proud of the woman you've become, Mandy. You've been through so much since his death but that didn't take away your sweet nature. And more than that, you've fulfilled his dream for you."

"Mama, that's because you've always been there to guide me," she hugged her. "Now shall we go down so I can get married?"

Reverend Reid was officiating the wedding and when Mandy and Mr. Miller had bestowed the honour upon him, he'd actually wept with joy.

The exchanging of vows would be done in the parlour downstairs in the presence of family and very few other witnesses, after which they would all move out to the front lawn for the reception, a lavish affair indeed.

Cecil was pacing the downstairs lobby when he looked up and saw his bride standing at the top of the stairs. Because of his leg, Colonel Watson was waiting at the bottom of the steps for Mandy.

"Pull yourself together Lieutenant," the man chuckled. "And remember to breathe."

"She just takes my breath away," Cecil of said of the beautiful woman who was gliding down the stairs. She looked so radiant. He was so happy and couldn't stop smiling. The colonel sent him to the parlour to wait amidst a lot of protesting but laughing while he did so.

And it was a moving ceremony where bride and groom were lost in a world of their own. After exchanging rings and their very first kiss, they moved out to the lawn where they were received with loud cheers.

Their tenants and neighbours as well as invited guests were all present for the reception, bestowing gifts of all kinds on the newlyweds.

Someone had brought a fiddle along and another produced a flute. Mandy laughed and clapped when she saw Chaplain Reid twirling her mother around on the lawn. And Mr. Albert, the sawmill manager, a middle-aged widower reached for Mrs. Miller who blushed delightfully.

"Are you happy, my darling," Cecil whispered to his new bride as they sat at their place of honour on the podium that had been erected for them. He delighted in the joy he saw on her face. He knew that if it were ever required of him, he would walk on hot coals for this woman because he loved her more than he loved his own life.

"I'm thinking that in the next few months we may have two more weddings," Mandy said, pointing at their mothers and their partners.

"Would you mind?"

Mandy shook her head as she turned to look into her husband's intense eyes. How had she been so blessed? Now she understood what the Bible meant where it said that in all things men ought to rejoice, and all things work together for good for those who love the Lord. She'd lost her Pa and life had been so hard, but it had all been pointing to this day.

"My mother seems happy and Reverend Reid seems to have recovered from the loss of his wife. They're both still strong and he has a very kind heart, so Mama will be happy with him." She touched his cheek. "And do you mind about Mama Miller and Mr. Albert?"

"Not at all, for he's a good man, unlike that cunning Mr. Weatherly. I see how happy Mama is and besides, any person recommended by the Colonel is a man of integrity." He took her hands and kissed her palms. "Our mothers have suffered enough and they, too, deserve all the happiness they can get."

"You, too, deserve all the good things in life for all the happiness you've brought into my life, Cecil," and she earned herself a resounding kiss. "What was that for," she asked breathlessly when he let her go. She noticed that people were giving them knowing looks, and she blushed.

"That's the first time in the seven years I've known you that you've called me by my first name, and that earns you a kiss."

Mandy smiled in deep satisfaction. She sent up a prayer of gratitude and thanksgiving for all the blessings she had received. Who would have thought that her father's death would lead to the long and hard journey that she had travelled and had now ended in bringing her so much love and happiness?

She snuggled close to her husband as they watched all the merrymaking that was taking place on this very special day. It was a very glorious day indeed because she was this soldier's beloved forever.

❄

THANK YOU FOR CHOOSING A PUREREAD BOOK!

We hope you enjoyed the story, and as a way to thank you for choosing PureRead we'd like to send you this free book, and other fun reader rewards...

Click here for your free copy of Whitechapel Waif
PureRead.com/victorian

Thanks again for reading.
See you soon!

LOVE VICTORIAN ROMANCE?

If you enjoyed this story why not continue straight away with other books in our PureRead Victorian Romance library?

Read them all...

Victorian Slum Girl's Dream

Poor Girl's Hope

The Lost Orphan of Cheapside

Born a Workhouse Baby

The Lowly Maid's Triumph

Poor Girl's Hope

The Victorian Millhouse Sisters

Dora's Workhouse Child

Saltwick River Orphan

Workhouse Girl and The Veiled Lady

OUR GIFT TO YOU

AS A WAY TO SAY THANK YOU WE WOULD LOVE TO SEND YOU THIS BEAUTIFUL STORY FREE OF CHARGE.

Our Reader List is 100% FREE

Click here for your free copy of Whitechapel Waif

PureRead.com/victorian

At PureRead we publish books you can trust. Great tales without smut or swearing, but with all of the mystery and romance you expect from a great story.

Be the first to know when we release new books, take part in our fun competitions, and get surprise free books in your inbox by signing up to our Reader list.

As a thank you you'll receive an exclusive copy of Whitechapel Waif - a beautiful book available only to our subscribers...

Click here for your free copy of Whitechapel Waif

PureRead.com/victorian

Printed in Great Britain
by Amazon

少年探偵　　　　　10
鉄塔王国の恐怖
江戸川乱歩

もくじ

- のぞきカラクリ ……… 6
- 深夜の妖虫 ……… 13
- 鉄塔王国 ……… 20
- しのびよる怪物 ……… 28
- 奇怪な消失 ……… 35
- 落とし穴 ……… 43
- 探偵七つ道具 ……… 50
- 運転台の怪物 ……… 57
- 魔法のつえ ……… 64
- 黒いこびと ……… 68
- 丸ビルの妖虫 ……… 76
- 小林少年の危難 ……… 79
- のぞきじいさん ……… 83
- あやしいぬけがら ……… 88
- 四人の警官 ……… 94
- 明智探偵の登場 ……… 100

- おばけ屋敷 107
- あやしい女こじき 113
- 地下室の妖虫 117
- 見知らぬ少年 122
- 怪自動車 127
- 名探偵の知恵 132
- ふしぎな尾行 136
- そびえる鉄塔 139
- 山小屋の主 146
- ハトと縄ばしご 150
- カブトムシ大王 154
- むちのひびき 161
- 老魔術師の正体 164
- ワシのえじき 169
- 妖虫の最期 176
- 解説　戸川安宣 181

装丁・藤田新策

さし絵・佐竹美保

少年探偵

鉄塔王国の恐怖

江戸川乱歩

のぞきカラクリ

明智探偵の少年助手、小林芳雄君は、ある夕方、先生のおつかいに出た帰り道、麴町の探偵事務所の近くの、さびしい町を歩いていました。

麴町には、いまでも焼けあとの、ひろい原っぱがのこっています。かたがわは、草のはえしげった原っぱ、かたがわは、百メートルもつづく長いコンクリートべい。もう、うすぐらくなったその町には、まったく人どおりがありません。気味がわるいほど、しずまりかえっています。

ヒョイと、コンクリートべいのかどをまがると、そこに、みょうなものがありました。車の上に、四角い、大きな箱のようなものがのせてあって、その箱のまえがわに、三センチほどの、小さな丸い穴がよこに五つならんでいるのです。そして、その車のそばに、ひとりの白ひげのじいさんが立っていました。

頭も白く、口ひげも白く、そのうえ、長いあごひげが胸までたれ、しわくちゃの顔に、昔はやった、小さな玉のめがねをかけ、そのおくに、ゾウのようなほそい目がひかっています。着ているのは、三十年もまえにつくったような、古いかたの、はでな格子じまの洋

* 東京都千代田区の町名。このころは屋敷町だった

服で、それに、でっかいドタ靴をはいて、腰のうしろで両手をくみ、ニヤニヤ笑いながら立っているのです。

人どおりもない、こんなさびしい町かどで、なにをしているのだろうと、小林君は、おもわず立ちどまって、そのみょうなじいさんの顔をながめました。

「ハハハ……、おいでなすったね。わしは、さっきから、きみのくるのを待っていたんだよ。」

じいさんは、歯のぬけた口を大きくひらいて、顔じゅうを、しわだらけにして笑いました。

「ぼくを、待ってたって？　人ちがいじゃありませんか。」

小林君が、びっくりしていいますと、じいさんは、まじめな顔になって、

「いや、人ちがいじゃない。きみに見せたいものがあるんだ。この箱は、なんだか知っているかね……。知るまい。いまから三十年も四十年もまえの子どもたちが、よろこんで見たものだ。のぞきカラクリといってね。まあ、いまの紙しばいみたいなものだが、ほら、そこに、丸い穴があいているだろう。その穴からのぞくのだ。そうすると、おもしろいけしきが見える。穴にはレンズがはめてあるから、中のけしきが、まるでほんとうのけしき

7

小林君は、昔のぞきカラクリというものがあったことを、聞いていました。これが、それなのかとおもうと、ちょっと、のぞいてみたいような気もするのです。そこで、おもいきって、五つならんでいる丸い穴のひとつに、目をあててのぞいてみました。

小林君は、あっとおどろきました。じいさんがいったとおり、レンズのはたらきで、箱の中には、まるでほんとうのけしきのようにひろびろとした山や森がひろがっていたからです。

飛行機にのって、大きな山を上のほうからながめているようなけしきでした。たぶん、オモチャの木なのでしょう。それが何百本も森のようにかたまっていて、ほんとうの深山を見ているようです。

そのふかい森の中に、黒い建物が立っています。西洋のお城のような、まるい塔のある建物です。それが、ぜんぶ鉄でできているようにまっ黒なのです。そのお城も、紙かすい鉄板でつくったオモチャなのでしょうが、レンズのかげんで、まるでほんとうのお城のように見えるのです。

「よく見なさい。きみはいま、日本のどこかにある山の中を、のぞいているんだよ。鉄のお城が見えるだろう。これも、ほんとうにその山の中にあるのだ。ほーら、どうだね。ふし

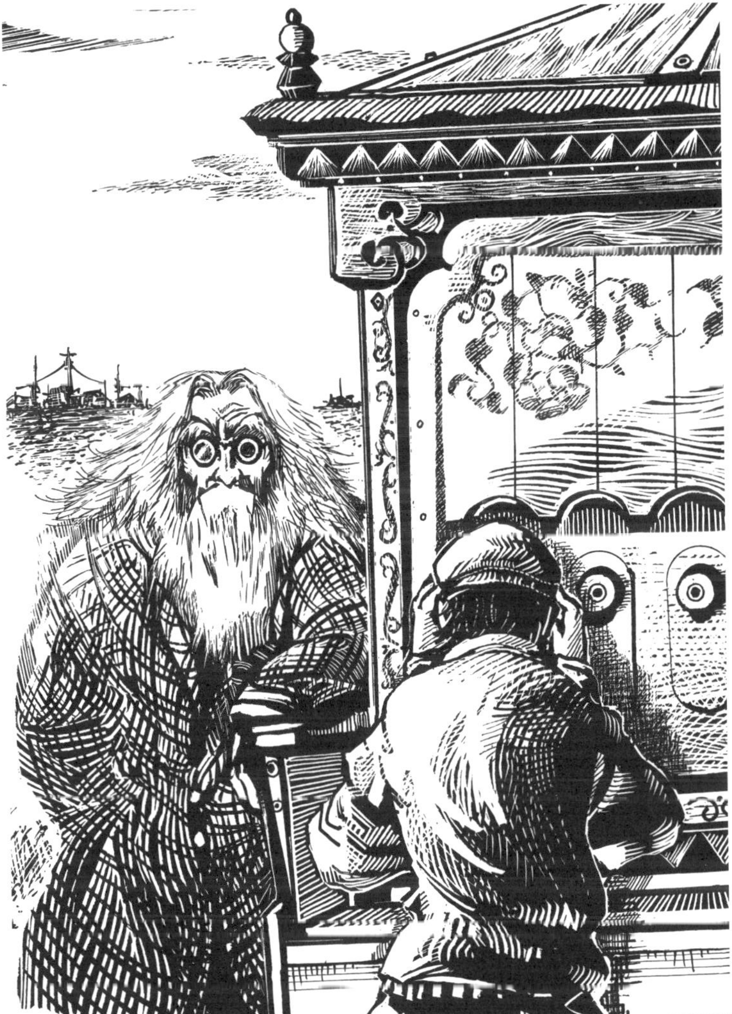

「ぎなことが、おこってきただろう。」

じいさんが、しわがれ声で、そんなことをつぶやきました。すると、のぞきカラクリのお城に、ギョッとするような異変がおこったのです。

お城のまるい塔の上に、なにかがモゾモゾ動いているのが見えました。それが、塔のふちをのりこえて、塔の壁をジリジリとはいおりてくるのです。

それは、おそろしくでっかい、一ぴきの黒いカブトムシでした。塔の窓の大きさにくらべると、そのカブトムシは人間ほどもあります。

人間ぐらいの大きさのカブトムシが、塔をはいおりてくるのです。頭のてっぺんから、一本の黒い大きなツノが、ニューッとつきだしています。小林君は、それを見て、西洋の怪談にでてくる、一角獣という怪物をおもいだしました。大きさといい、形のおそろしさといい、カブトムシというよりも、一角獣の怪物といったほうがふさわしいのです。

この巨大なおばけカブトムシは、やがて塔をはいおりると、森の中を、だんだんこちらへ近づいてきました。すると、森のしげみの中から、ヒョイととびだしたものがあります。一ぴきのシカです。怪談を見て、逃げだしたのです。そのシカが、カブトムシより小さく見えたのですから、怪物の大きさがわかるでしょう。

カブトムシは、シカの姿を見ると、いきなり、おそろしいかっこうでとびかかりました。

まるで大グモが、巣にひっかかったハエにとびかかるような、ものすごいいきおいでした。シカは、カブトムシのがんじょうな前あしにおさえつけられて、そこへ、よこだおしになってしまいました。おそろしさに、身うごきもできないで、死んだようになっています。シカが動かなくなったのを見ると、怪物カブトムシは、ひとあしあとにさがって、あの大きなツノをグッと下にむけて、シカのよこばらめがけて、パッとつきかかっていくのでした。

小林君は、のぞき穴から目をはなしました。おそろしくて、見ていられなかったのです。目をはなしてあたりを見ると、そこはもとの夕ぐれの町でした。原っぱがあり、コンクリートべいがあり、のぞきカラクリの箱をのせた車、白ひげのじいさん。ああ、よかった。いまのは、ほんとうのけしきではなかったのだと、胸をなでおろしました。まるで、こわい夢を見たあとのような気持ちです。

まさか、この箱の中に、あんな山や森があるはずはありません。みんなオモチャのつくりものです。カブトムシもシカもオモチャで、かんたんな機械じかけで、動いていたのでしょう。それが、レンズのかげんで、いかにも、ほんとうのように見えたのです。

「ハハハ……、どうだね。おもしろかったかね。」

白ひげのじいさんは、小林君の顔を見つめて笑いました。そして、ふしぎなことをいう

のでした。
「いまのけしきを、よくおぼえておくんだよ。これはのぞきカラクリだが、ほんとうに、こういう山や森があるんだ。黒いお城も、あのでっかいカブトムシもね。……きみは、いまにきっと、おもいあたるときがある。やがてこの世に、おそろしいことがおこるのだ。ウフフフ……、それじゃ、小林君アバヨ。」
 じいさんは、そういいすてて、車のハンドルをにぎると、そのままむこうへ遠ざかっていき、やがて町かどをまがって見えなくなってしまいました。ふしぎなことに、のぞきカラクリをのせた車は、すこしも音をたてませんでした。そして、じいさんと車とは、まるで夕もやの中へ、とけこんでいくように感じられたのです。
 小林少年はぼうぜんとして、もとの場所につっ立っていました。なにかキツネにばかされたような気持ちです。いまのは、ほんとうのできごとだったのでしょうか。それとも、まぼろしでも見たのでしょうか。
 小林君は、なんだか背中のへんが寒くなって、ブルッと身ぶるいしました。夕闇はいよいよ深くなって、まわりからヒシヒシと、夜がせまってくるのが感じられるのでした。

深夜の妖虫

そんなことがあって数日ののち、真夜中の銀座通りに、じつに前代未聞の、おそろしい事件がおこりました。

中学二年の山村志郎少年は、銀座うらの小さなお菓子屋さんの二階に部屋をかりて、おかあさんとふたりきりで住んでいました。おかあさんは裁縫がじょうずなので、あるデパートの仕立部につとめているのです。

ある晩のこと、真夜中に、山村君のおかあさんが、きゅうにおなかがいたくなり、ひどく苦しむので、少年はお医者さまへ電話をかけるために、近くの公衆電話へかけつけました。

さいわい、お医者さまは、すぐ来てくださるというので、ひと安心して公衆電話を出ようとすると、ガラス戸の外に、なにか黒い木の枝のようなものが、動いているのに気づきました。

へんだなと思って、ドアをひらくのをためらっていると、木の枝のようなものが、ガラスとすれすれのところに、近づいてきました。よく見ると、それは、ピカピカと黒びかり

13

にひかっている棒のようなもので、その棒のさきがほそくなって、そのさきに、ネズミのしっぽぐらいの太さの、小枝のようなものが何本も、てんでに、クシャクシャとはえているのです。そして、そのネズミのしっぽみたいなものが、まるでムカデのあしのように動いているのです。

山村君は、それを見ると、ゾーッとこわくなって、立ちすくんでしまいました。すると、黒い棒のようなものが、だんだんのびてきて、それがかぎのようにまがっていることがわかりました。棒は根もとのほうほど太くなっているのですが、それが、すっかりあらわれると、なにかまっ黒な、びっくりするほど大きなものが、ガラスのむこうに姿をあらわし、つぎには、二つのギョロギョロした目で、山村君をにらみつけました。

いや、そればかりではありません。その黒い大きなやつは、おそろしい、まっ黒なヤリのようなツノを持っているのです。太さは、根もとのほうで、さしわたし五センチもあるかとおもわれ、長さは五十センチもありそうです。その黒びかりのした、とんがったツノで、いまにも公衆電話のガラスをつきやぶろうとしているのです。

「ワワワワ……」

山村少年は、なんともいえぬさけび声をたてました。そして、そのまま気をうしなって、公衆電話のコンクリートの床に、クナクナとくずおれてしまいました。

14

しばらくして気がつくと、もうガラスの外には、なにもいません。それじゃ、今のは夢だったのかしらと、おそるおそるガラス戸をひらいて、外をのぞいてみました。なにもいません。

そっと、外へ出てみました。そこにあるのは、シーンとねしずまった町ばかりです。山村君は、うちのほうへかけだしました。そして、まがりかどまで来て、ヒョイと銀座のおもて通りのほうを見ると、ずっとむこうのかどに、へんてこなものがうごめいているではありませんか。

山村君は、ギョッと立ちすくんだまま、もう身動きもできなくなりました。

やっぱり怪物がいたのです。真夜中で、ネオンは消えているけれども、街灯があります。その光にてらされて、巨大な怪物の背中が、まるでウルシのように黒びかりにひかっているのです。

それは、カブトムシを万倍も大きくしたような、見るもおそろしいばけものでした。カブトムシのキングコングです。頭のさきから、ニューッと太いツノのはえた、一角獣のような怪物です。

そのとき、山村少年のうしろから、コツコツと靴の音がしました。またしても、ギョッとしてふりむきますと、それは、ばけものではなくて、パトロールのおまわりさんでした。

15

おまわりさんは、まだ怪物に気づいていないのです。

山村君は、それを見ると、ほっと安心して、いきなり「ワーッ」と、泣き声をたてながら、おまわりさんの腰にすがりついていきました。ふいをうたれて、おまわりさんもびっくりしましたが、山村君が、しっかりすがりつきながら、かた手で指さすほうを見ると、こんどは、おまわりさんが石のように立ちすくんでしまいました。

しかし、このおまわりさんは、勇気のある人でしたから、逃げだすようなことは、しませんでした。山村君に、おうちに帰るようにささやいておいて、自分はひとりで怪物のほうへ、用心しながらジリジリと近づいていきました。

山村少年は、そんなさいにも、おかあさんの病気のことはわすれなかったので、そのまままろめきながらおうちへ帰りましたが、下のお菓子屋さんの人に、怪物のことを話したので、たちまちさわぎが大きくなりました。深夜の銀座に、カブトムシの怪物があらわれたことが、となりからとなりへとつたわり、屈強な男の人たちが、手に手にこん棒などを持って、家の外へとびだしてきたのです。

その人たちが、山村少年におしえられた場所へかけつけたとき、夜のしずけさをやぶって、パーンと、ピストルの音がひびきわたりました。おまわりさんが、怪物めがけて発砲したのです。

そのとき、怪物はもう銀座の大通りへ、はいだしていました。それをおっかけるおまわりさん。さわぎを聞きつけて、近くの交番からとびだしてきたおまわりさんがふたり、そのあとからずっとおくれて、こん棒などを持った町の男の人たちが、こわごわつづいているのです。それからずっとおくれて、こん棒などを持った町の男の人たちが、こわごわつづいているのです。その人数もいまでは、十五、六人にふえていました。

真夜中の二時ごろですから、銀座にはまったく人通りがありません。電車の通らないレールばかりが銀色にひかって、どこまでもつづいています。あの人通りのおおい銀座が、夜中にはこんなにもさびしくなるのかと、おどろくほどです。昼間、にぎやかなだけに、夜のさびしさはこわいようでした。

そのひとけのない大通りの、銀色の電車のレールの上を、クマのように大きなカブトムシのばけものが、たくさんのあしをいそがしく動かして、おそろしい速さで走っているのです。

二度、三度、ピストルがなりわたりました。しかし、怪物は鉄でできているのでしょうか、たまがあたっても、カーンとはねかえるばかりです。

そのとき、深夜の客をのせた一台の自動車が、むこうから走ってきました。

その自動車の運転手は、人通りのない町を、気をゆるして運転していたのですが、ふと

＊都電（路面電車）のこと。現在、荒川線だけが走っている

気がつくとヘッドライトの光の中に、おそろしい怪物の姿を見て、びっくりぎょうてんしてしまいました。

とっさには、何ものとも見わけられませんが、ともかく、まっ黒にひかった大グマほどもある、長いあしの何本もはえた怪物です。二つの大きな目が、ヘッドライトをうけて、ギョロギョロとひかっています。そのうえ、頭のてっぺんに、おそろしいツノがとびだしているのです。その怪物が、グッと頭をさげて、するどいツノで、自動車にむかって、いどみかかってくるように見えたのです。

うしろの座席にいた客の紳士も、怪物に気づきました。そして、あっとさけんだまま、クッションの上にうつぶせになってしまいました。

こちらから見ている人たちは、自動車がカブトムシにぶつかってくれれば、いくら怪物でも、きっときずつくだろうと、手に汗をにぎっていたのですが、自動車は、怪物の前五メートルほどにせまったとき、キーッという音がして、急停車しました。運転手がブレーキをふんだのです。

すると、つぎの瞬間、じつに奇怪なことがおこりました。

巨大なカブトムシは、前から、つきすすんでくる自動車をものともせず、そのまま走りつづけていましたが、それが急停車しても、すこしも速度をかえず、グングン前にすすん

18

で、いきなり自動車の前部にはいあがったのです。

運転手は、すぐ目の前にせまってくる一角獣のツノを見ました。そして気が遠くなってしまったのです。

こちらから見ていると、怪物は、自動車のまっ正面から、車体の上にはいあがり、その屋根をのりこえて、自動車の後部へおり、そのまま、また電車道を走っていくのです。長いあしを、めまぐるしく動かしながら、大きなすうたいを、はこんでいくのです。

怪物と、おまわりさんや町の人たちとのへだたりが、だんだん遠くなっていきました。人間の二本の足では、とても怪物におっつけないばかりか、怪物はすこしもつかれるようすが見えないのです。

怪物は銀座四丁目の四つかどを、数寄屋橋のほうへまがりました。しばらく走りつづけるうちに、数寄屋橋の交番から、ふたりのおまわりさんが、とびだしてきました。そして、ピストルをさしむけながら、怪物のゆくてに立ちふさがったのですが、カブトムシはへいきで、まるで機械のように、そのおまわりさんたちをめがけて、つきすすんでいきます。パーン、パーンと二発の銃声がひびきました。しかし怪物は、すこしもひるみません。そのまま走りつづけて、おまわりさんたちを、左右にはねとばしてしまいました。

ふたりのおまわりさんは、おそろしいきおいで地面にたたきつけられ、きゅうに起お

＊ 銀座と有楽町の境にかかっていた橋。一九五八（昭和三十三）年になくなった

あがることもできません。あのするどいツノでつきさされなかったのが、まだしも、しあわせというものでした。

怪物は、あれよあれよというまに、数寄屋橋をわたり、きゅうに右にまがったかとおもうと、どこかへ見えなくなってしまいました。おまわりさんや、町の人たちが、橋をわたって、そのへんを、くまなくさがしまわったのですが、あの怪物のいやらしい姿は、もう、どこにも、見あたりませんでした。まるで消えうせたように、いなくなってしまったのです。

鉄塔王国

そのおばけカブトムシの、つやつやしたまっ黒な背中には、骸骨の顔のような、白いものがついていました。『黄金虫』という小説の金色のカブトムシや、死頭蛾という大きなガの背中にも、骸骨の顔がうきだしていますが、あれらと同じようなおそろしいもようが、この巨大なカブトムシの背中にもついていたのです。小林少年があとになって、そのことを新聞記者に話したものですから、翌日の新聞には、その絵が大きくのせられました。地獄からはいだしてきた、おそろしい妖虫の姿でした。

＊アメリカの作家エドガー・アラン・ポーが書いたミステリー

しかし、銀座の夜のできごとがあってから二週間ほどは、なにごともなくすぎさりました。妖虫はあの晩数寄屋橋のところで、かきけすように見えなくなったまま、一度も姿をあらわさないのです。

ところが、二週間ほどたったある夜のこと、荻窪の高橋太一郎さんのおうちに、おそろしいことがおこったのです。

高橋さんは、昭和鉄工会社の社長さんで、荻窪のおよそ三千平方メートルも庭のある、広い屋敷に住んでいました。家族は、主人の太一郎さん夫婦と、ふたりの男の子だけで、数人のお手つだいさんや書生をおいているのです。ふたりの男の子の兄のほうは、壮一君といって中学二年生、弟のほうは、賢二君といって小学校四年生でした。

その晩七時ごろ、高橋さんのところへ、木村というお友だちから、電話がかかってきました。主人の太一郎さんは、ちょうどおうちにいましたので、電話に出ますと、
「いま、村瀬というわたしの会社のものがおじゃまするから、会ってください。くわしいことは村瀬から聞いてくださるように。」
ということでした。

まもなく、その村瀬という男がやってきました。村瀬は三十歳ぐらいの、やせた人相のよくない男でしたが、懇意な木村さんのおつかいだというので、応接間にとおしてていね

＊ 他人の家にせわになって、家事を手つだい勉強する人

21

いにもてなしました。
　主人の太一郎さんとあいさつをすませて、むかいあって、安楽イスにこしかけましたが、村瀬という男は、だまって主人の顔を、ジロジロ見ているばかりで、なかなか用件をきりだしません。
　木村君からは、まだ何もきいていないのですが、どんなお話ですか。」
　太一郎さんが、さいそくしますと、村瀬はニヤリと笑って、みょうなことをいいました。
「ぼくは、じつは木村さんのつかいではありませんよ。」
「え、それじゃ、さっきの電話は？」
「あれは、ちょっと木村さんの名をかりてぼくがかけたのです。ぼくは、*声色がうまいでしょう。」
　村瀬は、タバコの煙をフーッと吹きだして、そううそぶいています。
「なんだって？　それじゃ、きみは、木村君の名をかたったんだな。」
　太一郎さんは、おもわず身がまえをして、テーブルの上のベルのボタンに手をのばしました。書生をよぶためです。
「おっと、ベルをおしちゃいけない。あんたとふたりきりで話したいんだ。ベルをおせば、

＊人の話し方や声をまねること

「これが火をはくぜ。」

村瀬は、すばやくポケットからピストルを出して、太一郎さんに、ねらいをさだめました。

村瀬は、とび道具を持ちだされては、どうすることもできません。太一郎さんは、そのままあいてをにらみつけて、じっとしているほかはありませんでした。

「では、用件を話そう。」

村瀬は、とくいらしく、ペラペラとしゃべりはじめました。

「鉄塔王国……といっても、あんたにはわかるまいが、そういう名前の小さい王国が、日本のある山の中にできているんだ。世界でだれも知らない小さな王国だ。深い深い山の中に、まっ黒な鉄の塔がそびえている。そこに一つの別世界ができている。おれは、その鉄塔王国の首領、いや、王さまの命令で、あんたのところへやってきたんだ。

王さまから、お金持ちのあんたにたいして、一千万円を寄付してもらいたい。いくら別世界の王国でもかでもない。鉄塔王国にたいして、一千万円を寄付してもらいたい。いくら別世界の王国でも、金がなくてはやっていけないからね。それで、時間と場所をきめておいて、現金で一千万円、おれに手わたしてもらいたい。これが、今晩の用件だよ。どうだね。返事を聞きたいね。」

* 現在の約二億円

村瀬という男はそういって、ピストルの筒口をあげたりさげたりしながら、主人の顔を見つめるのでした。

太一郎さんは、あんまりとほうもない話に、あっけにとられてしまいました。そして、こいつは気でもちがっているのではないかと考えました。

「さあ、返事はどうだね。」

「ハハハ……、そんな金は出せないよ。この日本の中に、べつの王国ができたなんて、だれが信じるものか。それに、一千万円という大金は、わしには、きゅうにどうすることもできないよ。」

太一郎さんは、まともに答えるのもバカバカしいような気がしました。

「ふーん。あんたは、おれのいうことを、でたらめだと思っているんだな。それじゃ、もっとよくわかるようにいってやろう。鉄塔王国では、小さい子どもが入り用なんだ。たちのよい子どもを集めて、みっちりしこんで、りっぱな兵隊にするんだ。鉄塔王国の近衛兵にしあげるんだ。だから、一千万円がいやなら、あんたの次男の賢二君を、山の中の王国へつれていくが、それでもいいかね。

どうして、つれていくというのかね。それには、すばらしい武器があるんだ。あんたは、今から二週間ほどまえ銀座にあらわれた、でっかいカブトムシのことを、知ってるだろう。

＊ 君主の近くにつかえ、その警護にあたる兵

あれが、鉄塔王国のまもり神だ。あれはカブトムシの戦車だよ。ピストルのたまだってはじきかえす鋼鉄の戦車だ。そればかりじゃない。あれは魔法つかいだ。幽霊カブトムシだ。みんなの見ているまえで、スーッと煙のように消えてしまうんだ。それがしょうこに、いつかの晩のカブトムシは、数寄屋橋で消えたまま、どうしても見つからなかったじゃないか。

鉄塔王国には、こんなおそろしい武器があるんだよ。その武器でもって、子どもたちをさらっていくんだ。頭のいい、かわいらしい、じょうぶな子どもばかりをさらっていくんだ。警察の力でも、ふせぐことはできない。あいては魔法つかいなんだからね。さあ、子どもがかわいければ、一千万円だ。どちらとも、あんたの心まかせにするがいい。」

聞けば聞くほど、でたらめのようで、太一郎さんはどうしても、この男のことばを、信じる気になれません。おばけカブトムシの事件で、世間がさわいでいるのをさいわいに、こんなつくり話をでっちあげたとしか、おもえないのです。

「まよっているね。むりはない。それじゃ一日だけ待つことにしよう。あすの夕方、おれの方から電話をかける。五時から六時までのあいだ、かならずうちにきめてくれ。もし、そのとき、あんたがうちにいなければ、賢二ぼうやをちょうだいする。これははっきりことわっておくよ。」

村瀬と名のる男は、それだけいうと、イスから立ちあがって、庭にむかった大きな窓の方へ、あとじさりに歩いていきました。

「まだ、ベルをおしちゃいけない。おれの姿が見えなくなるまで、じっとこしかけているんだ。でないと、このピストルが火をはくんだぜ。」

そこの窓には、あついビロードのカーテンが、床までたれていました。村瀬は、そのカーテンのあわせめをまくって、むこうがわに姿をかくしました。しかし、そのまま、窓から出ていこうともせず、カーテンのあわせめから、ピストルのさきを出して、じっとこちらをねらっています。カーテンの下からは、彼の靴が見えています。そうして立ったまま、しんぼうづよく、身うごきもしないで、こちらのようすをうかがっているのです。

そのふしぎなにらみあいが、じつに長いあいだつづきました。太一郎さんは、安楽イスにかけたまま、カーテンのかげに身をかくしたまま、ふたりともまるで人形のように動かないで、五分間もじっとしていたのです。

しかし、太一郎さんは、もうがまんができなくなりました。そっと手をのばして、テーブルの上のベルを、つよくおしておいて、いきなりドアの方へかけだしました。いまにも、カーテンのピストルが、火をはくのではないかとビクビクしましたが、そんなようすも見えません。

ドアをひらくと、むこうからかけてくる書生に、出会いました。
「あいつは、ピストルを持って、カーテンのかげにかくれている。フランス窓のカーテンだ。だれか庭へまわれ。そして、はさみうちにするんだ。」
　書生に命じておいて、太一郎さんはそっとドアの前にもどり、そのすきまから、カーテンの方を見ました。あいてはやっぱり、もとのままの姿でした。カーテンのすきまからはピストルが、カーテンの下からは二つの靴が見えています。さっきから、すこしも動かないのです。
　なんだかへんです。しかし太一郎さんは、まだ部屋の中へとびこんでいく決心がつきません。そこに立ちすくんでいるばかりです。
　しばらくして、カーテンのあたりに、ガチャンという音がしました。ギョッとして見つめていると、いきなりカーテンがさっと左右にひらかれ、そこから、書生の姿があらわれました。村瀬ではなくて、書生です。そして、村瀬はどこへ行ったのか、かげもかたちもないのでした。
　あっけにとられていると、書生がニコニコして、カーテンのはしを持ちあげてみせました。するとそのカーテンのはしに細い糸で、さっきのピストルがぶらさがっているではありませんか。それから床に目をやると、そこには二つの靴がぬぎすててありました。カー

テンがしまっているあいだは、いかにもそこに人が立っているように見えたのです。村瀬というみょうな男は、靴をぬぎすて、ピストルをカーテンにぶらさげておいて、とっくに窓から逃げさっていたのです。

ただ、逃げだしたのでは、書生たちがおっかけてくるでしょうし、警察に電話をかけられ、*非常線をはられる心配もあります。それをふせぐために、うまい手品をつかったのです。

しのびよる怪物

高橋太一郎さんは、その晩のうちに、事のしだいを警察にとどけましたが、あまりにとっぴな事件なので、警察でも、気がおかしくなった者のしわざと考えたらしく、いちおう高橋さんの屋敷のまわりを、警戒することにはしましたが、事件を深くしらべようともしないのでした。

高橋さんも、鉄塔王国などというバカバカしい話は、信用できませんので、翌日村瀬から電話がかかってきても、とりあわないことにきめました。やくそくどおり村瀬からは、二度も三度も電話がありましたが、そのたびに書生が出て主人は外出し

＊ 火事や犯罪事件が起こったとき、一定の区域に一般の人の立ち入りを禁止し、警官を守りにつかせること

ていて、ゆくさきがわからないとことわったのです。

ところが、事件があってから三日目の夜になると、つぎつぎと、村瀬という男のいったことが、けっしてでたらめでなかったことがわかってきました。つぎつぎと、おそろしいことがおこったのです。

高橋さんの次男の、小学校四年生の賢二少年は、その晩、じぶんの勉強部屋で、机にむかって本を読んでいました。まだ七時ごろですが、さびしい屋敷町ですから、あたりはシーンとしずまりかえっています。おうちが広いので、ほかの人たちの声も聞こえません。

この勉強部屋は、壮一にいさんとふたりでつかっているのですけれど、そのにいさんもどこかへ行っていて、賢二君はひとりぽっちなのです。

いっしょに本を読んでいますと、机の上のどこかで、カリカリと物をひっかくような、かすかな音がしました。へんだなとおもって、そのへんを見まわしましたが、べつに変わったこともありません。しばらくすると、またカリカリと、こんどはごく近くから聞こえてきました。賢二君は、なんだか気味がわるくなって、じっと机の上を見ていますと、電気スタンドの台のむこうから、黒い小さなものが、はいだしてきました。カブトムシです。

よく見ると、そのカブトムシには、頭のてっぺんから、ニューッと一本のツノがはえて

いました。そして、背中にみょうな白いもようがあります。
賢二君(けんじくん)は、そのもようを見て、おもわずゾーッとしました。それは、骸骨(がいこつ)の顔(かお)にそっくりだったからです。

賢二君はこわくなって、イスから立ちあがりました。そして、遠くから机(つくえ)の上を見ていますと、はいだしてきたカブトムシは、一ぴきだけでないことがわかりました。二ひき、三びき、四ひき、五ひき、あとから、あとからとはいだして、今まで賢二君の読んでいた本の上を、ゾロゾロと歩いているのです。しかも、そのたくさんのカブトムシの背中には、みんな、骸骨の顔のようなもようがあるのです。

賢二君は、もうたまらなくなって、勉強部屋(べんきょうべや)から逃(に)げだしました。そして、茶の間の方へ走っていきますと、むこうから壮一(そういち)にいさんがやってきました。

「なんだい、まっさおな顔をして。どうかしたのかい。」

「カブトムシ、骸骨のもようのあるカブトムシが、ぼくの机の上に……」

賢二君は、にいさんにすがりつくようにして、べそをかきながらいうのでした。

「ふーん、骸骨のもようだって？ よし、にいさんが見てやる。いっしょにおいで。」

中学二年の壮一(そういち)君は、さすがにいさんらしく、しっかりしていました。

ところが、ふたりが勉強部屋にひきかえして、賢二君の机の上を見ますと、ふしぎなこ

とに、さっきまであんなにゾロゾロはっていた、たくさんのカブトムシが、どこにも見えないのです。机の下や、ひきだしの中まで、しらべてみましたが、一ぴきも見つかりません。ゆうれいのように、消えうせてしまったのです。

あとで、そのことを、ふたりがおとうさんにお話ししますと、おとうさんの太一郎さんは、へんな顔をして考えこんでおられました。いよいよ、あの村瀬という男が、いやがらせをはじめたのかと、なんだか心配になってきたからです。

やはり、そのおなじ晩の十時ごろのことです。こんどは書生の広田が、おそろしいものを見たのです。

広田青年は高橋さんに見こまれて、大学へかよわせてもらい、学校から帰ると書生としていろいろな用事をしているのです。その広田が、いつものように門のしまりをして、うちの中にはいろうとすると、庭のほうに、なにかゴソゴソ動いているものがありました。

その晩は月が出ていたので、庭の木や草は、霜がおりたように、白く見えていました。その庭の中を、なにか大きな黒いものが、ゴソゴソと裏手のほうへはいっていくのです。イヌやネコではありません。もっとへんてこなものです。

広田は足音をしのばせて、そのあやしいもののあとをおいました。なんだか、おそろし

い夢にうなされているような気持ちでした。

月の光は、庭いっぱいにふりそそぎ、コンクリートの西洋館の裏側を、白々とてらしていました。その中を、黒い巨大な怪物が、ゴソゴソとはっていくのです。まっ黒な背中、そこに白くうきだしている奇怪なもよう、まがった長いあし、グーッと上をむいた黒い一本のツノ、ギラギラひかる二つのまるい目。広田は、そのものの正体を見きわめると、ギョッとして、おもわずその場に立ちすくんでしまいました。

そのとき、怪物のほうでも、はうのをやめて、じっと動かなくなりました。そして頭をグーッとまげて、二つのひかる目をこちらにむけたのです。

広田ははっとして、建物のかげに、すばやく身をかくしました。

「見つかったかもしれない。怪物は、あのおそろしいツノをふりたてて、こちらへむかってくるのではないだろうか。」

とおもうと、胸がドキドキしてきました。

怪物は、しばらくのあいだ、頭をこちらにねじむけて、じっとしていましたが、広田に気づいたわけでもないらしく、そのまま、またむこうむきになって、長いあしでゴソゴソとはっていきます。広田は建物のかげのまま、しんぼうづよく、それを見まもっていました。

怪物は、月光の中をはいつづけて建物に近づき、一つの窓の下にとまりました。それは

32

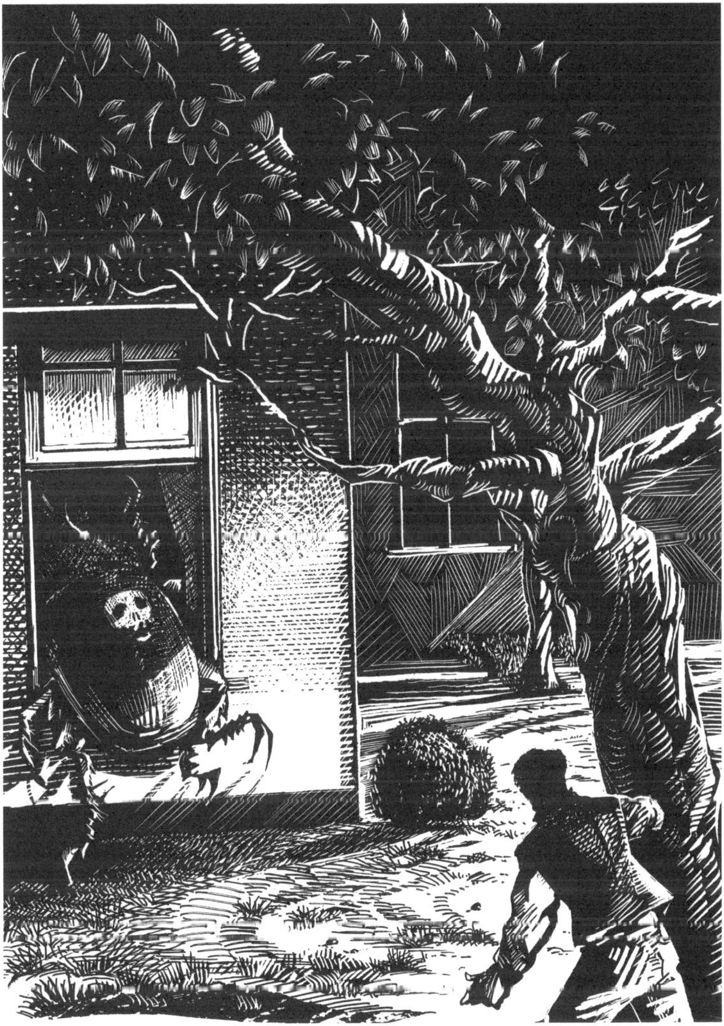

壮一、賢二兄弟の勉強部屋の窓です。広田は、それを見て、さてこそと、おもわず両手をにぎりしめるのでした。

怪物の前あしが、壁にかかりました。そして、ゴソゴソやっているうちに、やつは後あしで、すっくと立ちあがったのです。前あしは、窓のしきいにとどき、二つの目が窓の中をのぞいています。

怪物が立ったので、背中がまともに見えるようになりました。その大きな、つやつやひかる背中が、月光にてらされてぶきみにかがやいています。

そして、そこに、あの骸骨の顔が、まるでリンのように青白くひかっているのです。

広田は、夢を見るここちでした。この世に、こんなおそろしいけしきが、またとあるでしょうか。

彼は、月光にてらされたこの巨大な妖虫の姿を、一生わすれることができないでしょう。

勉強部屋の窓のガラス戸は、半分ほど上のほうにおしあげられ、ポッカリと黒い四角な穴になっていました。部屋の中の電灯は消えていて、だれもいないらしいのです。

怪物は、左右に首をふって、ギロギロひかる目で、部屋の中のようすをうかがっていましたが、やがて、そのツノのはえた首を、グッと窓の中へさしいれるようにしました。そ

れといっしょに、長いあしを、いそがしく動かしたかとおもうと、いつのまにか、怪物のからだは、地面をはなれて壁をよじのぼり、グイグイと窓の中へはいっていくのです。

やがて、おしりだけが、窓の外へはみだしていましたが、それも、窓の中へかくれてしまいました。ぶきみな長いあしを、モガモガやっていましたが、それも、窓の中へかくれてしまいました。怪物は、ついに兄弟の勉強部屋へ、侵入してしまったのです。

村瀬という男は、うそをいいませんでした。賢二少年は、今にも、かどわかされようとしているのです。しかも、あの見るもおそろしい妖虫の長いあしにだかれて、どこかへ、つれさられようとしているのです。

奇怪な消失

ぶきみな妖虫の姿が、賢二少年たちの部屋の中に消えてしまうと、広田は、にわかにあわてだしました。もう夜の十時なので、勉強部屋にはだれもいません。にいさんの壮一君も弟の賢二君も、べつの部屋で寝ていたからです。しかし、カブトムシは、その寝室までも、ゴソゴソとはっていくかもしれません。そして、賢二君を、あの長いあしでつかんで、どこかへつれさるかもしれないのです。

広田はそれをおもうと、もうじっとしていられません。いきなり、勉強部屋の外にかけよって、今しがたカブトムシのはいっていった窓によじのぼり、まっ暗な部屋の中へ、はいっていきました。

部屋のすみに身をかがめて、じっと耳をすましても、なんの音も聞こえません。あれだけの大きな虫が、もし部屋の中にいるとすれば、なにか音がするはずです。それが、シーンとしずまりかえっているのをみると、怪物はもう、部屋から廊下のほうへ、出ていったのかもしれません。

広田は、おずおずとスイッチのところへ近よって、パッと電灯をつけました。やっぱり、部屋の中にはなにもいません。怪物は、廊下へ出てしまったのです。

「たいへんです。だれか来てください。カブトムシが、カブトムシが……」

広田は、おもいきりどなっておいて、死にものぐるいの勇気をだして、廊下へとびだしていきました。

廊下には電灯がついているので、一目でわかります。左は行きどまりですから、右のほうを見ればよいのですが、長い廊下には、なにもいません。廊下のむこうには、居間や茶の間や寝室があるのですが、広田のどなり声に、そのほうから、主人の高橋さんが、びっくりして廊下へかけだしてきました。そのうしろに、おくさんやお手つだいさんの姿も見

えました。寝ていた壮一・賢二兄弟もねまきのまま、外へとびだしてきました。
「広田、どうしたんだ。なにごとだ。」
高橋さんが、大声でたずねました。
「カブトムシです。おばけカブトムシが、この廊下へはいこんだのです。」
広田は、息をきらしています。
「どこに？ 廊下にけ、なにもいないじゃないか。」
「ほかへ行くひまはありません。ぼくはすぐあとから、おっかけたのですから。そちらの茶の間のほうへは行かなかったでしょうね。」
「くるはずがないよ。わたしたちがいたんだからね。」
「すると、どこにも、逃げ道はないはずですね。ふしぎだなあ。」
「おまえ、夢でも見たんじゃないのか。」
「いいえ、けっして夢なんかじゃありません。」
広田はそこで、庭で見たことを、てみじかに話しました。
「広田さん、おとうさんの書斎のドアが、すこしあいてるよ。あの中、見たの？」
壮一少年が、目ばやくそれに気づいて、遠くから声をかけました。

みんなの目がそのドアを見ました。たしかに、四センチか五センチはひらいているのです。この廊下の、勉強部屋から茶の間までのあいだには、右側に主人の高橋さんの大きな書斎が一つあるきりで、左側はずっと壁になっているのです。もし、怪物が逃げこんだとすれば、この書斎のドアのほかにはないわけです。

「書斎の窓には、格子がはまっている。もし、ここへはいったとすれば、袋のネズミだ。」

高橋さんはそういって、広田に目くばせをしました。ドアをあけてみよという意味です。

広田は、ドアのそばに近よりました。しかし、それをひらくのには、よほどの勇気がいります。彼は、そこに立ちすくんだまま、しばらくためらっていました。

するとそのとき、そのドアが、ひとりでに、すこしずつひらきはじめたではありませんか。中からひらいているのです。

それを見ると、人々は、ギョッとして、あとじさりをしました。あのおそろしい妖虫が、まがったあしでドアをひらいて、みんなの前に、とびだしてくるのだと、おもったからです。

ドアは、みるみる大きくひらいていきました。中はまっ暗です。その闇の中からヌーッと出てきたのは、おばけカブトムシではなくて、意外にも、もうひとりの書生の青木青年

でした。
「アッ、青木君か。カブトムシを見なかったか。」
高橋さんが、しかりつけるようにいいました。
「いいえ、この部屋になにもいません。」
「きみは、まっ暗な書斎で、なにをしていたんだ。」
「本だなの本をおかりしにはいったのです。いつでも、かってに読んでいいとおっしゃったものですから。本をさがして、電灯を消して出ようとすると、廊下がさわがしくなったので、ちょっと出そびれていたのです。」

青木はそういって、手に持っていた一さつの本を見せました。法律の本でした。
「そうか。それならいいが、しかし、おかしいな。広田は、人間ほどの大きさのカブトムシが、この廊下へはいこんだというのだ。そして、わたしたちと広田とで、はさみうちにしたわけだから、逃げ道はこの書斎のほかにはない。ところが、きみはなにも見なかったという。どうもふしぎだ。ねんのために、書斎の中をしらべてみよう。」

高橋さんが、さきに立って書斎にはいり、スイッチをおして電灯をつけました。広田と壮一君とがそのあとにつづき、青木は本を持って、どこかへ立ちさりました。

書斎の中には、なにもいませんでした。机の下や本箱のうしろなども、じゅうぶんさが

しましたが、なにもいないのです。窓をひらいて、格子をしらべてみましたが、どこもこわれてはいません。

「おい、広田君。きみはやっぱりまぼろしでも見たんだろう。もし、カブトムシが家の中にはいったのなら、これほどさがして、見つからないはずがないじゃないか。きみは、今夜はどうかしているよ。」

高橋さんが、にが笑いをしていいました。しかし、広田は、あの怪物がまぼろしだったとは、どうしても考えられません。たしかに妖虫がはいこんできたのです。しかも、それがあっというまに、煙のように消えうせてしまったのです。

広田は、なお、あきらめきれないように、書斎の中をグルグル歩きまわっていましたが、ふと、大机の前に立ちどまると、その上にひろげてある手紙の用紙のたばを、じっと見つめました。

「あっ、これ、先生がお書きになったのですか。」

とんきょうな声に、高橋さんもそこへ近よって、用紙を見ました。

「わたしじゃない。そこには白い用紙がおいてあったばかりだ。」

「それじゃ、やっぱりそうです。あいつが、書きのこしていったのです。」

その用紙には、らんぼうな大きな字で、つぎのように書きなぐってありました。

> 今夜は、気づかれたので、このまま帰る。だが、賢二君はかならずさらってみせるから、そのつもりでいろ。

そして、その文句の下に、子どものいたずらのようなへたな絵で、一ぴきの黒いカブトムシが書いてありました。
「壮一、これは、おまえのいたずらじゃないだろうな。」
高橋さんが、壮一少年をよんで、その用紙を読ませました。
「ちがいます。ぼくでも賢ちゃんでも、そんなもの書きません。」
「青木はどうした。まさか青木が書いたのでもあるまいが……」
高橋さんは、そういってあたりを見まわしましたが、書生の青木の姿が見えません。
「青木君、青木君。」
高橋さんの声におうじて、壮一、賢二の二少年も、かんだかい声でさけびました。
「青木さーん……」
すると、どこか遠くで、「ハーイ」という声がして、バタバタと階段をおりる音がして、

41

やがて、青木が両手で目をこすりながら、そこへやってきました。
そして、ときならぬ夜ふけに、みんなが書斎に集まっているのを、がてんがいかぬという顔つきで、キョロキョロしています。
「青木君、どこへ行ってたんだ。」
「はい、ぼく、自分の部屋で、寝ていました。」
「なに、寝ていたって？　バカをいいなさい。いましがた、この書棚から本をさがして、出ていったばかりじゃないか。」
「いいえ、ぼくは書斎へはいったおぼえはありません。たしかに、自分の部屋で寝ていたのです。」
「まさか、きみは、一度もねむったまま歩きまわる夢遊病者じゃあるまいな。」
「そんなことは、一度もありません。」
さあ、わからなくなってきました。青木がほんとうに寝ていたとすると、さっき書斎から出ていったのは、何者だったのでしょう。あれは青木とそっくりでした。あんなによくにた別人があるのでしょうか。
読者諸君も考えてみてください。頭のいい読者には、この謎が、もうとけたかもしれませんね。

これはでたらめではありません。ちゃんととける謎なのです。しかし、それをとくのは、もうすこしあとにしましょう。

落とし穴

高橋さんは、すぐに、このふしぎなできごとを、電話で警視庁の捜査課にしらせました。
捜査第一課の中村警部とは、心やすいあいだがらだったからです。
その晩のうちに、中村警部が数名の刑事をつれてしらべに来てくれましたが、けっきょくなんの手がかりも発見されず、むなしく引きあげるほかはありませんでした。書生の青木は、きびしくしらべられましたが、自分の部屋で寝ていたのは、うそでないことがわかりました。
すると、もうひとりの青木は、いったい何者だったのでしょう。さすがの中村警部にも、それは想像がつかないのでした。
中村警部のはからいで、その夜から数名の刑事が、高橋さんの家のまわりを、たえず見はってくれることになり、賢二少年はしばらく学校をやすんで、うちにとじこもっていることにしましたが、なにしろ、あいてはおばけみたいなやつですから、ゆだんはなりませ

ん。

事件のあったあくる日の午後、壮一少年は、学校から帰ると、おとうさんの部屋へ行って、相談をもちかけました。

「おとうさん、ぼく考えてみたんだけど、こういう事件は、やっぱり明智小五郎探偵にたのんだほうがいいんじゃないでしょうか。中村警部もえらいけど、明智探偵はもっとえらいんでしょう。」

おとうさんは、しばらく考えたあとで、

「うん、それもいいだろう。それじゃ、わたしが明智事務所へ電話をかけて、つごうを聞いたうえで、広田をつかいにやることにしよう。広田なら、わたしたちよりも、よく事情を知っているんだからね。」

といって、さっそく電話をかけましたが、明智探偵は、ちょうど事務所にいて、午後四時ごろに来てくれという返事でした。

時間を見はからって、広田は自動車にのって千代田区の明智事務所をたずねました。玄関のベルをおすと、ひとりの青年が、中からドアをひらきました。広田が名前をいいますと、青年は、

「わかってます。お待ちしていました。どうかこちらへ。」

44

といって、さきに立ちながら、
「広田さん、きょうは用心しないといけませんぜ。うちの先生は、ひどくふきげんです。さいぜんから書斎にとじこもったきり、お茶を持っていっても、ぼくを入れてくれないほどですからね。」
と、注意してくれます。
「小林という有名な少年助手のかたがいましたね。あなたは小林君ではないのでしょう。」
と、たずねると、
「ああ、小林ですか。きょうは、遠くへつかいに行って、るすです。先生のおくさんもお手つだいさんもつれておでかけで、うちには先生とぼくとふたりきりですよ。ぼくは、ちかごろ先生の助手になった近田というもんです。これでも名探偵のたまごですよ。」
と、この青年、なかなかおしゃべりです。
やがて書斎の前に来ると、助手はかるくドアをノックして、「高橋さんのおつかいの人です」と、大きな声でいいました。
すると、中からドアがほそめにひらいて、明智探偵のモジャモジャ頭の顔がチラッとのぞき、
「つかいの人だけ、おはいりなさい。近田、きみはベルをならすまで用事はない。あっち

「へ行っていなさい。」
と、なるほど、ふきげんらしい声です。
中にはいってみますと、写真でおなじみの明智探偵が、きょうも黒い背広を着て立っていました。明智は、広田が部屋にはいるのを待って、ドアにピチンとかぎをかけました。
そして、正面の大デスクのむこうがわにまわると、そこのイスに、どっかりこしかけて、客には、「おかけなさい」ともいわず、だまってこちらをにらみつけています。
広田はていねいにおじぎをしてから、デスクの前のイスに、おずおず腰をおろしました。
「どんな用件だね。」
いつもニコニコしている明智とはちがって、まるで、にがむしをかみつぶしたような顔です。
「電話では、くわしいことを、お話ししなかったと思いますが、じつは、このごろ新聞でさわいでいる妖虫事件です。」
妖虫事件といえば、名探偵は、きっとひざをのりだしてくると思ったのに、いっこう、そんなようすも見えません。
「うん、それで。」
と、さきをうながすばかりです。

そこで広田は、ゆうべのできごとを、くわしく話しましたが、明智は、なにを聞いても、すこしもおどろかないのです。無表情な顔で、うん、うんと聞いているばかりです。

「賢二ぼっちゃんを、まもることが第一ですが、そのうえ犯人がつかまれば、こんなありがたいことはありません。どうでしょう、ひとつ、この事件をおひきうけくださいませんでしょうか。」

広田はそこでことばをきって、じっと返事を待っていましたが、明智はやっぱり、こちらをジロジロ見ているばかりで、なにもいいません。なんだか、うすきみがわるくなってきました。

「どうでしょうか。先生、ぜひごしょうちねがいたいのですが……」

「きみはぼくに、それをたのみたいというのかね。」

明智の目つきが、きゅうに変わったように見えました。声もちがってきたようです。広田はなぜかドキッとしてあいての顔を見つめていますと、明智はますますへんなことをいいだしました。

「きみに聞くがね。きみはいったい、だれと話をしていると思っているんだね。」

「むろん、先生とです。先生に、事件のご依頼に来たのです。」

「先生って、だれだね。」

「明智小五郎先生です。」

広田は、あまりバカバカしい問答に、おもわず声が高くなりました。

「ホホウ、明智小五郎。ぼくが、その明智小五郎だとでもいうのかね。」

広田は、びっくりして、イスから腰をあげました。

「あなたは、明智先生じゃないのですか。」

「わしが明智先生に見えるかね。」

「え、なんですって。」

「おれが明智に見えるかと、聞いたのさ。ハハハハ……、おれも変装がうまくなったものだなあ。アハハハ……」

その笑い声をきくと、広田は、はっとあることに気づきました。

「さては、きみは、おばけカブトムシの同類だなっ。」

「ハハハ……、そのとおり。きみは、なかなか頭がいいよ。」

「で、ぼくをどうしようというのだ。」

「ちょっと、とりこにしておくのさ。おっと、逃げようったって、逃げられやしないよ。そうそう、そこに立っていなさい。いま、明智探偵の発明したカラクリじかけをお目にかけるからね。名探偵さん、いいものを発明しておいてくれたよ……」

48

そのことばもおわらぬうちに、おそろしいことがおこりました。広田青年の足の下の床板が、スーッと消えてしまったのです。あっというまに、広田のからだは、下へ下へと、おそろしいいきおいで落ちていきました。めまいがして、なにがなんだか、わからなくなったかと思うと、ガクンと、背骨がおれるようないたみを感じて、そのまま気が遠くなってしまいました。

「ハハハ。どうだね、穴ぐらのいごこちは？　きみはゆうべ、カブトムシを見つけて、さわぎたてた張本人だ。きみさえいなければ、うまくいったのだ。そのばつだよ。まあ、そこでゆっくり寝ていたまえ……」

そして、バタンという音がしたかと思うと、あとは墓穴のような、暗闇にとじこめられてしまいました。それは、ほんとうの明智探偵が悪人をとらえるためにつくっておいた、落とし穴だったのです。

さて、にせの明智探偵は、広田をとじこめておいて、これから、なにをしようというのでしょうか。

探偵七つ道具

広田青年は、あっというまに、穴のそこに落ちこんで、なにかにひどく腰をぶっつけたかと思うと、そのまま気をうしなってしまいました。それから、どれほど時間がたったかわかりませんが、ふと気がつくと、あたりは真の闇で、たおれたからだの下は、かたいコンクリートの床でした。

腰のいたさをこらえて、すこし起きなおり、手であたりをさぐってみましたが、なんの手ごたえもありません。あんがい広い地下室です。

広田は、このまま暗闇の中で、うえ死にしてしまうのかとおもうと、ガタガタからだがふるえるほど、こわくなりました。まるで、あつい黒ビロードのきれで、目かくしでもされたような暗さです。

そのときです。広田は、うえ死によりももっとおそろしいことに、気がつきました。地下室には、なにかがいるのです。かすかに、なにものかの動いている音が聞こえます。そいつが、ジリジリとこちらへ近よってくるらしいのです。

広田はゾーッとしました。骸骨もようのある大カブトムシをおもいだしたからです。あ

のおそろしいカブトムシが、このまっ暗な地下室に待ちかまえていて、広田に危害をくわえようとしているのではないでしょうか。

ガサガサと、はっきり聞こえます。こちらへはいよってくるのです。その音が、だんだん大きくなってきました。もう一メートルほどのところへ、近づいているのです。

「だれだ！ そこにいるのは、だれだ！」

広田は、おもわず大声をたてて、身がまえをしました。

すると、ふしぎなことに、怪物が人間のことばで答えました。

「高橋さんのうちの広田さんでしょう。ぼくですよ、ぼくですよ。」

「ぼくって、だれだ。」

こちらは、まだゆだんしません。とびかかってきたら、とっくみあいをするつもりで、身がまえしています。

「ウフフフ、あやしいもんじゃありませんよ。小林ですよ。明智探偵の少年助手の小林ですよ。ほら、さわってごらんなさい。」

広田は手をのばして、さわってみました。毛織りの学生服の手ざわりです。金ボタンもついています。だんだん上のほうへ手をやると、少年らしい、やわらかいほおがありました。

「ああ、それじゃきみは小林君か。ほんとうに、小林君だろうね。にせものじゃないだろうね。」

「にせものじゃありませんよ。にせものにこりているので、ねんをおしました。にせものじゃなかったら、こんな地下室にとじこめられているはずが、ないじゃありませんか。」

広田は、明智探偵のにせものにこりているのにりかを、おしました。

「ふーん、すると、きみも、悪人のために、ここへ落とされたのか。」

「そうですよ。あいつ、なんて変装がうまいんだろう。ぼくも、ほんとうの明智先生だとおもって、ゆだんしたのです。そして、落とし穴へ、落とされてしまったのです。」

「明智探偵事務所には、もとからこんな落とし穴があったの？」

「ええ、あったのです。先生は、悪人をとらえるために、この落とし穴をつくっておかれたのです。それを、あべこべに、敵に利用されたのですよ。」

「それじゃ、ほんとうの明智さんはどこにおられるのだろう。まさか、明智探偵まで、敵のとりこになったのじゃあるまいね。」

「二、三日、旅行中なのです。べつの事件で、大阪のほうへいかれたのです。きょうかあす、お帰りになるはずだったので、ぼくは、にせものにだまされたのですよ。あいつが、先生とそっくりの顔と、そっくりの服で、いま帰ったよって、はいってきたものですか

「ふーん、きみまでだますとは、よくよく変装のうまいやつだね。だが、この落とし穴は、ぬけ道でもないのかね。なんとかして、ここを出るくふうはないのかね。」

「ぬけ道なんてありませんよ。ここへ落ちたら、もうおしまいですね。天井まで四メートルもありますよ。はしらもなんにもないから、のぼりつくこともできません。」

そのとき、ガタンという音がしたかとおもうと、天井からパッと光がさしこんできました。おどろいて見あげますと、落とし穴の四角な板がすこしひらいて、そこから人の顔がのぞいていました。

のぞいているのは、さっきのにせ明智でした。

「いいこころもちだよ。ヒヤヒヤとすずしくってね。それに、広田さんという話しあいてをおくってくれたので、とうぶんたいくつしないよ。」

「ハハハ……、ご両人、なかよく話しているね。どうだね、落とし穴のいごこちは？」

「ハハハ……、まけおしみをいってるな。だが、安心したまえ。きみたちを殺しやしない。こっちの仕事のすむまで、二、三日のしんぼうだよ。二、三日で、うえ死にするわけもないからね。」

「ぼくたちは、だいじょうぶだよ。それより、きみこそ、用心するがいい。いまに明智先生が帰ってくるからね。そうすれば、きみはすぐつかまってしまうんだからね。小林少年も、なかなかまけていません。

「ウフフフ、まあ、熱をあげているがいいさ。……まあ、おれのほうの仕事は、これからすぐはじめるんだからね。明智先生、まにあえばいいがね。……まあ、その暗闇の中で、ふたりでなかよく話でもしていたまえ。それじゃ、あばよ。」

そして、パタンとふたをしめ、止め金をかけてしまいました。地下室の中は、また、もとのまっ暗闇です。

「ねえ、小林君。あいつは、これからすぐ高橋家へいって、賢二ぼっちゃんを、どうかするにちがいない。明智さんはとてもまにあわないだろう。それをおもうと、ぼくはじっとしていられないよ。ねえきみ、どうかして、ここをぬけだすくふうはないだろうか。」

広田は、賢二少年の身のうえが、心配でしかたがないのです。

「ぬけ道なんかないけれども、ここを出るくふうはあるんですよ。」

小林少年は、ニコニコ笑っているような口ぶりです。

「えッ、それはほんとうかい。どうして？　どうしてぬけだすの？」

するとそのとき、小林君のからだから、パッと強い光がかがやきました。懐中電灯で

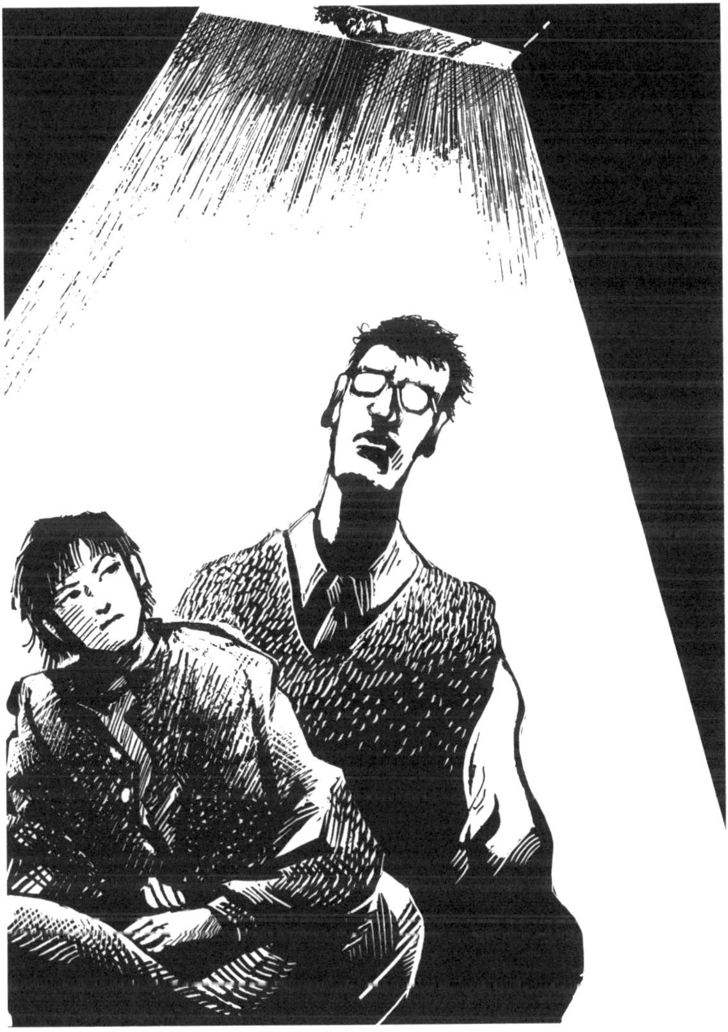

「アッ、きみ、懐中電灯もってたの？」

「探偵七つ道具のうちには、むろん、懐中電灯がはいっています。ごらんなさい。これがぼくの七つ道具です。ほらね、ぼくはどんなときでも、胴巻きのように、この袋を腹にまいているのですよ。」

小林君はビロードの大きな袋から、いろいろな品ものをとりだして、コンクリートの床にならべ、それを懐中電灯でてらしてみせるのでした。

そこには、七つどころか、十いくつの、ひどく小さな、こびと島の道具とでもいうようなものが、ズラリとならんでいました。

てのひらにはいるような小型写真機、指紋をしらべる道具、黒い絹糸をよりあわせて作った、まるめればひとにぎりになる縄ばしご、ノコギリやヤスリなどのついた万能ナイフ、虫めがね、錠まえやぶりの名人が持っているような万能かぎたば、それから、なんだかわからない銀色の三十センチほどの長さの太い筒など。

小林少年は、その銀色の筒を手にとって、みょうなことをいいだしました。

「これ、なんだかわかりますか。手品の種ですよ。ぼくの魔法のつえですよ。これと、この絹糸の縄ばしごさえあれば、こんな穴ぐらなんか、ぬけだすのは、ぞうさもありません

よ。」

広田青年は、小林君の手から懐中電灯をとって、天井をてらしてみました。高さは、四メートルはあります。落とし穴の板は、ぴったりしまって、鉄のカンヌキで落ちないようになっています。四方の壁からは、ずっとへだたっていますし、手がかりになるようなものは、なにもありません。たとえ、縄ばしごをなげてみたところで、どこにも、ひっかかるものがないのです。

小林君の手品とは、いったい、どんなことでしょう。わずか三十センチの銀色の筒が、なんの役にたつのでしょう。

運転台の怪物

小林君と広田青年が、地下室でこんな話をしていたころ、一方、高橋さんのおうちの玄関に、ひとりの紳士がおとずれていました。もうひとりの書生の青木が、とりつぎに出ますと、

「ぼくは明智小五郎です。おつかいがあったので、おじゃましました。」

というのでした。

青木が奥へそれをつたえますと、主人の高橋さんは大よろこびで、明智と名のる紳士を応接室にとおしました。

「やあ、よくおいでくださいました。新聞などの写真で、お顔はよく知っています。つかいのものからお聞きくださったでしょうが、わたしの次男の小学校四年生の子どもが、カブトムシにねらわれているのです。先生のお知恵で、なんとか、子どもをたすけていただきたいとおもいまして。」

「それはうかがいました。ぼくのところへつかいにみえた書生さんは、もう帰っているのでしょうね。ちょっと、ここへよんでくれませんか。」

明智探偵は、ソファにゆったりともたれて、タバコに火をつけながらいうのでした。

「いいえ、書生の広田は、まだ帰りません。先生といっしょじゃなかったのですか。」

「いや、書生さんは、ぼくがじきにおうかがいするというとよろこんで、いそいで帰ったのです。自動車で帰るといっていましたから、まだつかぬというのは、へんですね」

高橋さんは、書生の青木をよんで広田をさがさせましたが、どこにもいないことがわかりました。

「へんだなあ。まさか、こんなさいに、より道なんかしているはずはないが、先生よりもよほど前に、おたくを出たのですか。」

「そうですね。ぼくよりも三十分ほど前にです。電車にのったとしても、とっくについているはずです。これは、ひょっとしたら……」
「え、なんとおっしゃるのです?」
「カブトムシの怪物団のために、さらわれたのかもしれませんよ。大カブトムシが、賢二君の部屋へしのびこむのを、さいしょに発見して、さわぎたてたのは広田君でしたね。そのふくしゅうかもしれませんよ。」
「あのがんじょうな広田が、苦もなくさらわれるか知れたものではありません。高橋さんは、かよわい賢二少年など、いつさらわれるか知れたものではありません。」
した。
「先生、広田がさらわれたとすると、いよいよ、すててはおけません。賢二をたすけてください。なんとか、うまい方法はないでしょうか。」
「そうですね。ともかく、賢二君をここへよんでみてくれませんか。」
「高橋さんは、また書生の青木をよんで、賢二君を応接室へつれてこさせました。
「やあ、きみが賢二君ですか。おじさんが来たから、もうだいじょうぶですよ。さあ、もうとこちらへいらっしゃい。」
明智はニコニコしながら、賢二少年をまねいて、その肩へ手をかけました。しかし、手

をかけたかとおもうと、探偵は、はっとしたようにきびしい顔になりました。
「賢二君、ちょっと、そちらをむいてごらんなさい。きみの背中に、なんだかはっている。」
賢二少年が、きみわるそうにしてうしろをむくと、その学生服の背中に、黒い大きな虫が、モゾモゾとうごめいていました。
「あっ、ドクロのもようだ。」
書生の青木が、とんきょうな声をたてました。それはドクロもようの、一ぴきのカブトムシだったのです。
明智がサッと手ではらうと、カタンという音をたてて、妖虫は床に落ち、あおむけになって、ぶきみなあしをモガモガやっていましたが、そのうちに、クルッとひっくりかえって、そのまま、部屋のすみのほうへ、かけだしていくのでした。
賢二少年はもちろん、おとうさんの高橋さんも、顔色をかえていました。
「まえぶれだ。あいつが、やってくるというまえぶれだ。明智さん、もうぐずぐずしてはいられません。はやく、なんとかしなければ……」
高橋さんは、今にもあのおそろしい大カブトムシが、窓からしのびこんでくるのではないかと、うしろを見ながら、おびえたようにいうのでした。

「広田君が、帰ってこないこととといい、今のカブトムシといい、どうもこのまますててはおけませんね。」

明智はそういって、しばらく考えていましたが、

「高橋さん、東京都内に、ごしんせきがあるでしょう。いちじ、賢二君をしんせきにでも、おあずけになってはどうでしょうか。さいわい、ぼくの自動車がおもてに待たせてありますから、あなたと賢二君とが、人目につかぬように、いそいでそれにのりこむのです。ぼくも、いっしょにのります。そして、あなたのさしずなさるところへ、車を走らせるのです。」

高橋さんは、賢二君をここのうちにおくのも心配だし、といって、外へつれだすのも、なんとなく気味がわるいとおもいましたが、こういうことには、なれている名探偵が、くりかえしすすめるので、ついその気になりました。そこで、高橋さんは、奥さんとも相談したうえ、賢二君を、下谷のしんせきにあずける決心をしたのです。

書生の青木に見はらせておいて、高橋さんと賢二君と明智探偵は、すばやくおもての自動車にのりこみました。高橋さんが小声で、行くさきをいいますと、自動車はすぐに走りだしました。

高橋さんは、自動車のうしろの窓から、しばらく町をながめていましたが、だれも、あ

「高橋さん、タバコならここにあります。さあ、ごえんりょなく。」

それは西洋の葉巻きタバコでした。

高橋さんはタバコずきで、ことに葉巻きは大好物でしたから、それをうけとって火をつけると、スパスパとやりはじめました。

「いかがですか、その味は？　ぼくはタバコだけは、ぜいたくをしているのですよ。」

「いや、けっこうです。ひさしぶりに、うまいタバコを吸いました。ありがとう。」

走る自動車の中には、むらさきの煙が、もやのようにただよい、葉巻きのさきが、だんだん白い灰になっていきました。

それから五分ほど自動車が走ったころ、高橋さんの口から、半分ほどになった葉巻きが、ポロッと座席の床に落ちました。となりの賢二君がびっくりして、おとうさんの顔を見ま

とをつけてくるようすはありません。あとから、走ってくる自動車もありません。このぶんなら、まず安心だと、そっと胸をなでおろすのでした。

しばらくすると、たしかに入れておいたはずのピースの箱がありません。和服の両方のたもとをさがしましたが、むこうのはしにこしかけていた明智探偵が、そのようすに気づいて声をかけました。

すと、おとうさんは、うしろのクッションに頭をグッタリとよせかけて、かすかにいびきをたてて、眠っているのでした。
「おとうさん、おとうさん。」
賢二君がいくらゆり起こしても、目をさますようすがありません。なんだかへんです。こんな場合に眠ってしまうなんて、日ごろのおとうさんらしくもありません。
「賢二君、いくらよんだって、おとうさんは起きやしないよ。」
明智探偵が、今までとはちがった、らんぼうなことばでいいました。
「なぜです。なぜ起きないのです。」
賢二君は、なんだかギョッとして、聞きかえしました。
「葉巻きをのんだからさ。あの葉巻きにはね、麻酔薬がしこんであったのだよ。ハハハハ。」
賢二君は、むちゅうになってさけびました。
「だれです？　おじさんは、だれです？」
「わからんかね。賢二君、ほら、ちょっと前を見てごらん。」
ぶきみな声に、おもわず、前の運転席を見ました。
「あっ……」

63

賢二君は、おそろしいさけび声をたてたかとおもうと、いきなり眠っているおとうさんにしがみついて、そのひざに顔をかくしてしまいました。

運転席には、なにがいたのでしょう。いままで人間だとばかりおもっていた運転手が、いつのまにかおそろしい姿に、かわっていたのです。

そいつには、おそろしい長いツノがありました。まっ黒な背中には、大きな骸骨の顔が、こちらをにらみつけていました。ああ、この自動車は、あのおそろしい妖虫が運転していたのです。

そいつが、長いツノをふりたてて、グッとこちらへふりむきました。おさらほどもある、大きな二つの目が、怪光をはなって、賢二君をじっと見つめました。

魔法のつえ

お話は、すこしあとにもどりまして、時間でいえば、にせ明智探偵が高橋さんのおうちへたずねて来るよりもまえのことです。

そのころ、明智探偵事務所の地下室では、にせ探偵のために、にせ明智探偵が高橋さんの書生の広田とが、地下室をぬけだす相談をしていました。

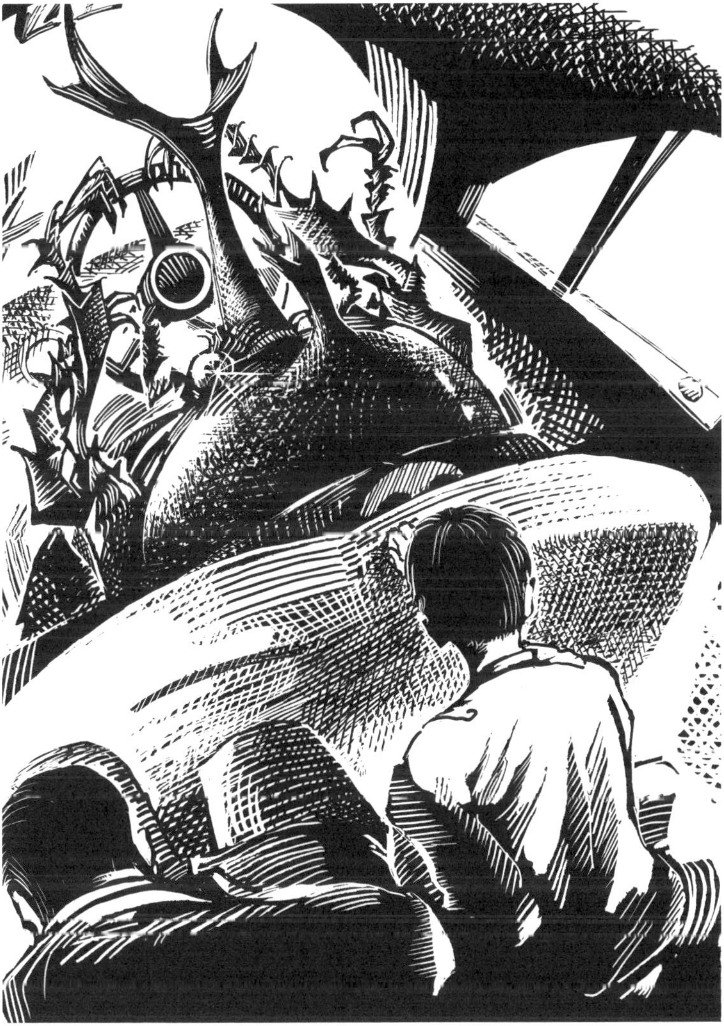

まっ暗な地下室の床が、まるくポッとひかっています。小林少年の懐中電灯を広田が手に持って、床にならんでいる探偵七つ道具を、てらしているのです。

小林少年は、その七つ道具の中から、銀色にひかった三十センチほどの長さの筒をとりあげて、説明するのでした。

「これは魔法のつえですよ。たった三十センチの筒が、たちまち、三メートルにのびるのですよ。」

「へー、ほんとうかい？」

広田はびっくりしています。

「ほら、ごらんなさい。のびるでしょう。手品師の持っているつえと同じしかけです。」

銀の筒をサッとふると、倍の長さになり、もう一度ふると、三倍の長さになり、四倍、五倍、六倍と、いくらでものびていくのです。それは写真機をのせる三脚と同じしかけで、銀色の筒の中に、すこしほそい第二の筒があり、その中にまた、もっとほそい第三の筒があるというように、十本の筒がかさなりあっていて、それを、つぎつぎとひっぱりだせば、おしまいには、十倍の長さにのびるしかけなのです。

「ね、わかったでしょう。この長い棒があれば、地下室をぬけだすことなんか、わけもありませんよ。」

小林少年は立ちあがって、その銀色の長い棒を、天井の落とし穴のふたのほうへのばしました。

「懐中電灯で、天井をてらしてください。」

広田が、いわれたとおり天井をてらします。そのまるい光の中に、落とし穴のふたをとめている金具が見えます。

小林君はせのびをして、長い棒のさきで、その金具を、よこからたたくようにして、とうとう、はずしてしまいました。すると、バタンと音がして、落とし穴のふたが下にさがり、そこに四角な口がひらきました。

小林君は、七つ道具の中の、絹糸の縄ばしごを、てばやくほぐして、かぎになった金具のついている一方のはしを、天井の四角な穴になげ上げ、うまくそこへ、ひっかけました。金具は、なにかにひっかかったら、けっしてはずれないように、できているのです。じょうぶな黒い絹糸を、何十本もないあわせて、四十センチぐらいのかんかくで、大きなむすび玉が、いくつもついているわけなのです。

「ぼくらを、ここに落とした悪者は、もうでかけたにきまっています。上には、だれもいません。ぼくが、さきにのぼりますから、広田さんも、すぐあとからきてください。」

小林君は、なれたもので、まるでサルのように、ほそい縄ばしごを、スルスルとのぼっていきました。広田は、小林君のように、うまくはのぼれませんが、それでもやっと上の部屋にたどりつきました。

「あいつは、どこへでかけたんだろう？」
「きまってますよ。明智先生になりすまして、高橋さんのうちへのりこんだのです。そして、なんとかうまくごまかして、賢二君をつれだすつもりです。さあ、いきましょう。グズグズしていると、賢二君がどんなめにあうかもしれませんよ」

小林君はそういいながら、もう、おもてのほうへかけだしていました。

黒いこびと

それから、小林少年が、賢二君を助けるためにどんな計画をしたか、それは、しばらくおあずけにしておいて、お話をもとにもどし、賢二君がにせ明智のためにさらわれた、自動車の中のできごとになります。

運転台に、人間と同じぐらいの、巨大なカブトムシがすわっているのを見て、賢二君は、麻酔薬で眠っているおとうさんのひざへ、顔をかくしてしまいました。すると、となりに

こしかけていたにせ明智が、賢二君の肩をトントンとたたいて、
「なにをこわがっているんだ。よく見てごらん。ほら、ね、なんにもいやしないじゃないか。」
と、笑いながらいうのでした。賢二君は、その声に、おもわず顔をあげて、こわごわ運転台のほうを見ましたが、これはどうしたことでしょう。そこには、もとの運転手が、ちゃんとすわっているではありませんか。おそろしいカブトムシは、かき消すように、見えなくなってしまったのです。

では、賢二君はさっき、まぼろしを見たのでしょうか。いや、まぼろしではありません。たしかにカブトムシでした。背中に骸骨もようのある、おそろしいカブトムシでした。

カブトムシは、またしても魔法をつかったのです。あいつら、虫の国のふしぎな魔法の力で、思うままに姿をあらわしたり、消したりすることができるのかもしれません。

そのあいだにも、自動車はずっと走りつづけていたのですが、そのとき、西側が森のようになった、ひどくさびしい道にさしかかりました。

「よし、ここで、とめて……」

にせ明智が、運転手に命令しました。自動車はブレーキの音をたてて、きゅうにとまり

「手をかしてくれ。このおやじさんを、ちょっと、このおやしろの中へ、寝かせておくんだ。朝になれば、しぜんに目をさますだろうからね。」

怪人物は、そんなことをいいながら、眠っている賢二君のおとうさんを車の外に出して、ふたりがかりで、エッチラオッチラ、暗い森の中へはこんできました。

そのあいだに賢二君が逃げだす心配はありません。運転台には、まだひとりの助手がのこっていたからです。そいつが、こわい顔で賢二君をにらみつけています。とても、逃げられるものではありません。

それにしても、ここはいったいどこでしょう。まだ東京を出はなれたとはおもわれません。さっき、にせ明智が「おやしろ」といったのをみると、この森は、なにかの神社をとりかこんだ森なのでしょう。東京の町の中にも、こういう神社の森は、いくらもあるからです。

賢二君のおとうさんは、その社殿の縁側にでも、おきざりにされるのでしょう。そんなに寒い気候ではありませんから、かぜをひくようなこともないでしょうが、賢二君は心配でたまりません。

そのときです。自動車のうしろのほうで、なんだか、みょうなことが起こりました。まっ暗なので、はっきりはわかりませんが、自動車のうしろの荷物を入れる場所の鉄板のふたが、そうっとひらいたようです。そして、その中から、小さな黒い人の姿があらわれました。

黒いこびとです。そのこびとが、まず、自動車のうしろのタイヤのところにうずくまって、しばらくなにかやっていたかとおもうと、スーッと空気のもれる音がして、タイヤがペチャンコになってしまいました。

こびとは、つぎにはもう一つのうしろのタイヤ、それから前の両方のタイヤと、リスのようにチョコチョコと走りまわって、たちまち、車の四つのタイヤを、みんなペチャンコにしてしまいました。

あとでわかったのですが、このこびとは、よくきれる大きなナイフをタイヤのうすいところへつきさして、空気をぬいてしまったのです。空気がぬけるたびに、自動車がグンとしずむような感じになるものですから、運転台にいた助手の男は、「おやっ、へんだぞ」といいながら、ドアをあけて、車をしらべるためにおりてきました。助手が右側へまわったすきに、こびとは左側の後部の窓に近づいて、そのガラスを、コツコツとたたきました。

中にいた賢二少年がびっくりして、ガラスの外を見ますと、そこに、ひとりの少年の顔が笑っていました。そして「だいじょうぶだよ。安心したまえ」というように、コックリとうなずいてみせるのでした。

この少年こそ小林君でした。彼は、明智探偵事務所をとびだすと、高橋さんの家にかけつけて、そのおもてに待っていた、悪人の自動車の、うしろの荷物入れにしのびこんでいたのです。そして悪人どもが賢二君のおとうさんを、神社の森へはこんでいるすきに、タイヤをきずつけて、自動車を動けなくしてしまったのです。さすがに、少年名探偵の小林君でした。

小林少年は、窓の外から賢二君に、安心するようにあいずをしておいて、そのままいちもくさんに、どこかへかけだしていきました。どこへ行ったのでしょうか。

そこへ、森の中から、にせ明智と運転手とが帰ってきました。

「おい、なにをウロウロしているんだ。どうかしたのか」

助手の男が、自動車のまわりを、なにかブツブツいいながら歩きまわっているのを見て、にせ明智が声をかけました。

「どうも、わからないのですよ」

「なんだって、四つともパンクした？ タイヤが四つとも、パンクしちゃったんです。」
そんなバカなことがあるもんか。よくしらべてみ

ろ。夢でも見たんじゃないか。」
　どなりつけながら、にせ明智は懐中電灯を出して、タイヤをしらべていましたが、いきなり、びっくりしたようにさけびました。
「タイヤにナイフをつきさしたんだ。おい、きみ、そのへんに、だれかかくれているんじゃないか。タイヤをだめにして、自動車を動かないようにしたやつがいるんだ。きみはそれを知らないでいたのか。」
　しかられて、助手は首をかしげながら、のろまな声で答えました。
「そういえば、なんだかこびとみたいなやつが、あっちへ走っていきました。暗くてよくわからなかったけれど……」
「なにっ、こびとだって？　それじゃ、もしかすると……」
　にせ明智は、悪人だけに、頭もよくはたらくのです。彼は、地下室にとじこめておいた小林少年のことを、ハッとおもいだしていました。
「しかたがない。このまま、運転するんだ。なあに、車がこわれたって、かまいやしない。グズグズしていると、たいへんなことになる。」
　にせ明智は、いそいで後部にのりこみ、運転手に、スタートするように命じました。
「だが、すぐつぶれらまいますぜ。とても遠くまではいけませんよ。」

「かまわん。ともかく、出発するんだっ。」

自動車は、ガタンガタンと、へんな音をたてながら動きだしました。しかし、百メートルも進むか進まないうちに、にせ探偵が、またしてもおそろしい声でどなるのでした。

「とめろ。車をとめるんだっ。見ろ、むこうのやつらが、へんなやつがいる。あれをなんだとおもう。」

ずっとむこうの町かどのぼんやりした街灯の下に、いく人かの人かげが見えます。さきに立っているのは、小さな子どもでした。そのあとに、制服の警官が、ひとり、ふたり、三人、まだまだ、おおぜいあとにつづいているように見えます。遠くてよくはわかりませんが、さきに立っているのは、どうも、小林少年らしいのです。

「いけないっ。子どもは、ほうっておいて逃げるんだ。あとにひきかえして、森の中へ、そこから別の町へ、通りぬけるんだ。いいか。むこうのやつらに、気づかれないようにしろっ。」

にせ明智が、自動車をとびだすあとから、運転手と助手もつづいて、三人は風のように、もときた道を走るのでした。

しばらくすると、数人の警官隊が小林少年をさきに立てて、自動車のところへかけつけました。

74

「賢二君、だいじょうぶか。」

小林少年が、窓の中をのぞきながらさけびました。賢二少年は、小林君を見たことがありませんけれど、味方にちがいないとおもったので、自動車の外にとびだして、うしろを指さしながら、

「逃げたよ。三人とも、あの森の中へ逃げたよ。」

と、おしえました。

それから、ふたりの少年は、警官たちといっしょに、神社の森にたどりつきましたが、いくらさがしても、悪人たちの姿は、もうそのへんには見あたりませんでした。しかし、賢二君のおとうさんはすぐ発見され、ぶじにたすけることができました。

こうして小林少年の知恵によって、賢二君はすくわれたのです。おとうさんもぶじでした。

悪人たちはとりにがしても、まず、成功といわなければなりません。

やがて、麻酔薬の眠りからさめたおとうさんは、ことのしだいを聞いて、小林少年のてがらをほめたたえ、くりかえしくりかえし、お礼をいうのでした。

丸ビルの妖虫

しかし、鉄塔王国の怪人は、一度失敗したぐらいで、あきらめてしまうようなやつではありません。失敗すればするほど、しゅうねんぶかく、くいさがってくる、おそろしい悪人です。

それから一週間ほどたった、ある朝のことです。東京駅のまえの丸ビルの中に、ギョッとするような事件がおこりました。

朝の六時をすこしすぎたころでした。まだ会社員は、ひとりも姿を見せません。大きなビルディングの中は、まるで死んだ町のように、がらんとして、しずまりかえっていました。

その、ひとけのない、一階のひろい通路を、ひとりの用務員さんらしい老人が、ほうきとバケツを持って、二階への階段の下まで歩いてきました。そして、ふと階段を見あげたかとおもうと、電気にでもかかったように、ピッタリ立ちどまったまま、身うごきもできなくなってしまいました。目はとびだすほど大きくなり、口はポカンとひらいて、まるで、あおざめたろう人形のような顔になってしまったのです。

通路の両側の商店も、一けんも店をひらいていません。

それもむりはありません。その階段の上には、世にもおそろしいばけものが、うごめいていたからです。

それは、人間ほどの大きさの、一ぴきのまっ黒なカブトムシでした。そいつが、自動車のヘッドライトほどもある二つの目を、ランランとひからせ、するどい長いツノをふりたてて、ゴソゴソと、階段をはいおりてくるではありませんか。

この妖虫は、いかめしいずうたいのわりには、おそろしくぶきようなやつです。エッチラオッチラ、まるで、よっぱらいのようなかっこうで、さも、なんぎらしく、階段をおりてくるのです。

そうして、二、三段、はいおりたかとおもうと、ズルッと足をすべらせました。ぶきような大カブトムシは、そこでふみとどまる力もなく、そのまま、おそろしいいきおいで、階段をすべり落ちたのです。立ちすくんでいる用務員さんの目の前へ、サーッと落ちてきたのです。

「ヒャーッ……」

用務員さんは、なんともいえない、きみょうなさけび声をたてて、その場にしりもちをついてしまいました。

大きなビルには、いないように見えても、どこかに人がいるものです。このさけび声を

聞いて、そうじ婦さんだとか、とまりこみの会社員などが、ふたり、三人、五人と、どこからかかけつけてきました。

それらの人々も、通路にもがいている異様な怪物を一目見ると、やっぱりまっさおになって、そこに立ちすくんでしまいました。

巨大なカブトムシは、階段から落ちたひょうしに、背中を下にして、あおむきにひっくりかえると、なかなか起きなおれないものです。小さなカブトムシでも、一度あおむきにひっくりかえると、なかなか起きなおれないものです。

まして、こんな大きなずうたいのやつですから、きゅうには、起きあがれないとみえて、みにくい腹をまる出しにして、長いあしをモガモガやりながら、ひどく苦しがっているのです。

しかし、その苦しがるようすが、じつにおそろしいのでした。なめらかな背中とはちがって、グジャグジャした腹のほうは、なんともいえない、いやらしい形です。それを見ていると、ゾーッとして、はぎしりがしたくなるほどです。

ところがそのとき、またしても、じつにふしぎなことがおこったのです。妖虫の腹が、スーッとたてにわれてきたのです。そして、そのわれめが、だんだんひろくなって、その中から、なにかべつのいきものが、はいだしてきたではありませんか。

78

それは、リンゴのようにつやつやしたほおの、ひとりの少年でした。大カブトムシの腹の中に、人間の子どもがはいっていたのです。それが腹をやぶって、びっくりしている人びとの前に、姿をあらわしたのです。

小林少年の危難

「なあんだ、子どもがはいっていたのか。」

ほんとうの怪物だとばかりおもっていた人々は、少年の姿を見て、すこし安心しました。

少年は、カブトムシの腹から外に出ると、グッタリとその場にたおれてしまったので、人々はかけよってたすけおこし、今まで少年がはいっていた、巨大なカブトムシのからだをしらべました。

それは、ほんとうの虫ではなくて、うすい金属を革でつなぎあわせてつくったもので、中はからっぽで、そこへ少年がはいって動いていたのです。

「なあんだ、びっくりさせるじゃないか。きみはどうして、こんないたずらをしたんだ。このおばけカブトムシの衣装を、いったい、どこから手にいれたんだ。」

ひとりの会社員が、少年をだきおこしながら、しかるようにいうのでした。

少年は、さっき階段を落ちたとき、どこかをうったらしく、いたそうに顔をしかめながら答えました。
「いたずらじゃありませんよ。ぼくは、悪者のためにカブトムシの中へとじこめられたのです。」
「悪者だって？」
「ええ、鉄塔王国の怪人です。」
　それを聞くと、人々はおもわず顔を見あわせました。鉄塔王国というふしぎな怪物団のことは、新聞に書きたてられていたので、だれでも知っていたからです。
「それじゃ、夜中に銀座通りを歩いていた大カブトムシは、こんなこしらえものだったのか。中に人間がはいって、動いていたのか。」
「そうかもしれません。そうでないかもしれません。あいつらは魔法つかいですから、なにをやるかわかりません。ぼくを、こんなものにいれて、ビルの中へころがしておいたのも、なにかわけがあるのです。カブトムシなんて、こしらえものだとおもわせて、ゆだんさせるためかもしれません。」
「それにしても、きみはどうして、こんなめにあったんだ？」
「しかえしですよ。新聞に出ていたでしょう。カブトムシの怪物団は、高橋賢二という少

年を、どこかの山の中の鉄塔の国へ、さらっていこうとしたのです。それを、ぼくがじゃまをして、とりもどしたものですから、ぼくにしかえししたんです。ゆうべ、町を歩いていると、だれかがうしろからくみついてきて、ぼくの口と鼻に、麻酔薬をおしつけたのです。そして、ぼくが気をうしなっているあいだに、このカブトムシの衣装を着せて、丸ビルへかつぎこんでおいたのです。

　けさ、気がついてみると、ぼくは、カブトムシのよろいの中にとじこめられて、二階の廊下にころがっていました。カブトムシの目のところに、ガラスがはめてあるので、外は見えました。ビルの中だということも、すぐわかりました。ぼくは、さけび声をたてましたが、だれもきいてくれません。階段をおりたら、人がいるかもしれないとおもったので、はいおりようとしたのです。でも、こんなよろいみたいなものをつけているので、うまくおりられません。足がすべって、ころがり落ちてしまったのです。」

「ふーん、それじゃ、たいしてしかえしにもならないね。きみが階段をおりないで、じっとしていたら、そのうちに二階の会社の人たちが出勤してきて、きみをたすけるにきまっている。そうすれば、きみはひと晩、カブトムシのよろいを着せられたというだけじゃないか。」

　いちばん年とった会社員が、ふしんらしくいうのでした。

すると少年は、さもくやしそうな顔をして、
「ところが、ぼくには、大きなしかえしになるのですよ。ぼくの名誉がメチャメチャになってしまうのですよ。」
「きみの名誉だって？ そんなにきみは、名誉の高い子どもなのかい？」
「そうです。ぼくは少年名探偵として、悪者どもにおそれられているんです。それが、こんなはずかしいめにあっちゃ、ぼくは先生にだって、あわせる顔がありません。」
少年はなみだぐんで、くやしがっています。
「先生だって？ きみの先生というのは、もしや……」
「そうですよ。明智小五郎先生です。ちょうど先生は旅行中なのです。そのるすのまに、こんなはずかしめをうけたのです。」
「するときみは、あの名高い少年助手の……」
「小林です。……みなさん、ぼくはきっと、あいつらをつかまえてみせます。明智先生といっしょに、この怪物団をほろぼします。見ててください。きっとです。ぼくをこんなめにあわせたやつを、やっつけないでおくものですか。」
小林少年ときくと、人々はびっくりしたように、このかわいらしい子どもの顔をながめました。ああ、これが、明智探偵の片腕といわれる少年名探偵だったのかと、にわかに

人々のあつかいがちがってきました。

「そうか。きみがあの有名な小林君だったのか。まあ、部屋にはいってやすみなさい。そして、電話で警察にれんらくするがいい。」

年とった会社員は、そういって、小林君の手をとると、自分の会社の応接室へあんないするのでした。

のぞきじいさん

怪物団の、ぶきみないたずらは、これだけではすみませんでした。その同じ日の夕方、高橋賢二少年のおうちには、もっとおそろしいことがおこるのです。一週間まえ、小林少年にたすけられた賢一少年のうえに、またしても、あやしい魔の手がおそいかかってくるのです。

その日のおひるすぎ、賢二君が、にいさんの壮一君にまもられて、ちょっとおうちの外へ出ますと、その町かどに、異様な箱車を引いた白ひげのじいさんが、待ちかまえていました。

それは、このお話のさいしょに出た、あのきみょうな白ひげのじいさんで、引いていた

のはあのときののぞきカラクリの車でした。これが、その日のおそろしいできごとのまえぶれだったのです。

白ひげをはやし、はでなしまの洋服をきたじいさんは、ふたりの少年が出てきたのを見ると、ニコニコしながら手まねきしました。

「さあ、きみたち、ここへおいで。そしてこののぞき穴から、中をのぞいてごらん。ふしぎなものが見えるから。」

ふたりの少年は、このじいさんを見るのははじめてですから、べつにうたがいもせず、箱車のよこについている、ふたつののぞき穴に、それぞれ目をあててのぞいてみました。

すると、箱の中には、石をつみかさねた、いんきな、広い部屋がありました。西洋のむかしの、古いお城の中とでもいうような感じです。それが、ひろびろとして、まるでほんとうの部屋のように見えます。

のぞき穴にはレンズがはめてあるので、小さな模型が、何百倍にも大きく見えるわけです。

「きみたち、これをどこだとおもうね。日本のどこかの山おくにある鉄塔王国のお城の中だよ。見てごらん。今におもしろいことがはじまるから。」

じいさんが、やさしい声でいいました。

すると、石の部屋の一方の入り口から、なにかしら黒い虫のようなものがはいだしてき

84

ました。それが一ぴきだけではありません。つきからつぎと、十何びきも、ゾロゾロはいだしてきたのです。それはカブトムシでした。みんな、背中に白いもようがあります。よく見ると、あの気味のわるい骸骨の顔ではありませんか。壮一君も、賢二君もびっくりして、のぞき穴から、目をはなそうとしました。ところが、どうしたことか、首が動かないのです。目をはなすことができないのです。

それは、ふたりの頭を、じいさんの大きな両手が、グッとおさえつけていたからです。

「もうすこし、がまんして見なさい。なにもこわいことはない。カブトムシは、箱の中から出られやしない。今に、おもしろいことがおこるから、よく見ているんだよ。」

じいさんは、ふたりの少年の頭を、おそろしい力でおさえつけたまま、声だけはひどくやさしいのです。

レンズのはたらきで、一ぴきのカブトムシが、人間ほどの大きさに見えます。それが十何びきもはいだしてきたのですから、じつにものすごいありさまです。

少年たちは、こわいけれども、見たい気持ちもするので、おさえつけられたまま、目もつぶらないでいました。

するとやがて、たくさんのカブトムシの中の一ぴきが、コロンとひっくりかえって、腹を上にして、もがきはじめました。賢二君たちは知りませんが、それは、同じ日の朝、丸

ビルの中で、小林君のはいっている大カブトムシがひっくりかえったのと、そっくりのかたちでした。

やがて、レンズのむこうのカブトムシも、腹が二つにさけたのです。そして、その中から、ひとりの少年があらわれたのです。おやっとおもって、見つめていますと、十何びきのカブトムシが、つぎつぎとひっくりかえり、つぎつぎとおなかがさけて、中からひとりずつ、かわいらしい少年があらわれてきました。そして、その少年たちは、列をつくって、石の部屋の中をグルグルまわりはじめたのです。

「どうだね。おもしろいだろう。これは鉄塔王国のカブトムシ少年隊だ。賢二君、きみもいまに、この少年隊にはいるのだよ。そして、カブトムシのよろいを着せられて、訓練をうけるのだ。アハハハ……」

じいさんは、長い白ひげをピクピクふるわせながら、大きな口で笑いました。そして、賢二君たちの頭をおさえていた手をはなしました。

自由になったので、おもわずじいさんの顔を見あげますと、しわくちゃのじいさんは、大きな口をひらいて、赤い舌をヘラヘラさせて、いつまでも笑いつづけています。その顔が、童話に出てくる魔法つかいとそっくりに見えました。

ふたりの少年は、まるで背中に氷でもおしつけられたようにゾーッとして、いきなりお

86

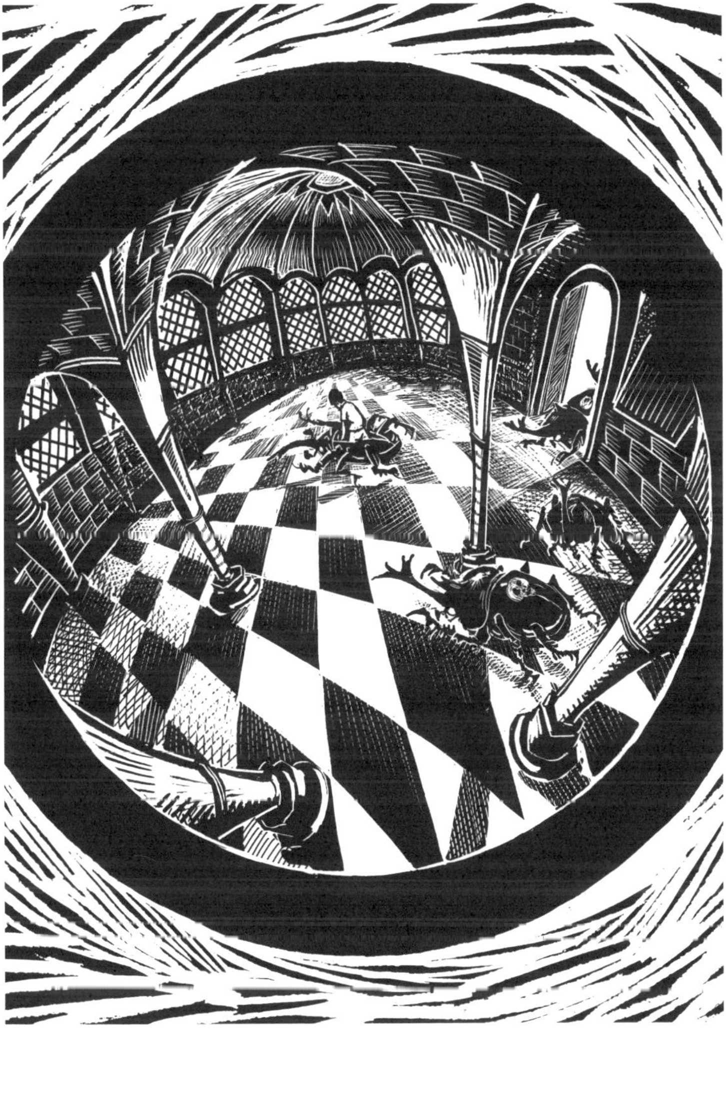

うちのほうへかけだしました。うしろからじいさんの笑い声がおっかけてくるようで、気が遠くなりそうでしたが、やっとのことで、おうちの中へとびこむことができました。
いきせききってかけつけてさがしこんできた、ふたりの少年の話を聞くと、おとうさんや書生などが、その町かどへかけつけてさがしましたが、あのあやしいじいさんも、箱車も、どこへいったのか、かげも形も見えませんでした。賢二君たちは、まぼろしを見たのでしょうか。それとも、あのじいさんは、ほんとうの魔法つかいだったのでしょうか。

あやしいぬけがら

その日の夕方、賢二少年は、おうちの二階のおしいれの中にある、昆虫標本の箱をとりにあがって、二階の広間の外を通りかかり、ガラスのはまった障子から、ふと中をのぞくと、みょうなものが目にはいりました。
それは十五畳の日本座敷で、いつもつかわない部屋ですから、広間の中はうす暗く、ものの形もままになっているうえ、もう日がくれるじぶんなので、はっきり見わけられないくらいですが、その床の間の上に、大きな黒いものが、寝そべっているように見えたのです。

「書生」の青木はかわりものですから、ときどきへんなことをします。だれもいない二階の広間にかくれて、ひるねをしていることもめずらしくないのです。賢二君は、ひょっとしたら、青木が床の間に寝そべっているのではないかと思いました。それで、そっとはいっていって、「ワッ」といって、おどかしてやろうと考えたのです。

賢二君は音のしないように、障子をあけて、足おとをしのばせながら、そのうす暗い床の間へ近づいていきました。

ぼんやりしていた、黒い大きなものが近づくにつれて、だんだんはっきり見えてきました。ああ、それはなんだったのでしょう。賢二君は、ギョッと立ちどまったまま、身うごきができなくなってしまいました。心臓がパッタリとまってしまったようで、からだじゅうからつめたい汗がながれました。

そこには、あのおそろしい巨大な妖虫が、うずくまっていたのです。自動車のヘッドライトのような目を、ギョロリとさせて、今にもこちらへとびかかってくるようなしせいで、うずくまっていたのです。

賢二君はじっと立ったまま、怪物とにらみあっていました。逃げようとして身うごきしたら、とびかかってきそうで、逃げることがおそろしいのです。ながいにらみあいでした。しかし、妖虫はすこしも動きません。賢二君がうしろをむい

89

て逃げだすのを、じっと待っているかのようです。

それには、ひじょうな勇気がいりました。しかし、賢二君は、やっとその勇気をふるいおこして、あとも見ずに部屋をかけだすと、ころがるように階段をおりました。そして、ワッと泣きだしたのです。「どうした、どうした」と、みんなが集まってきましたが、まだしてもカブトムシがあらわれたと聞き、その場所があまりへんなので、おとうさんも、きゅうには信用しません。賢二君は、こわいこわいとおもっていつづけて、頭がどうかしたのではないかと、心配になってきたのです。しかし、ともかく、ねんのための書生をつれて、二階の広間をしらべてみることにしました。

三人でその部屋にはいっていきますと、なるほど、床の間にへんなものがいます。

「おい、電灯をつけなさい。」

書生のひとりがスイッチをおしますと、パッと部屋が明るくなりました。それと同時に、三人はおもわず「あっ」と声をたてて、廊下へとびだしてしまいました。たしかに巨大なカブトムシが、そこにうずくまっていたからです。

障子のこちらから、そっとのぞいていますと、怪物は、まるで床の間のおきもののように、すこしも動きません。いくら待っていても、こちらへはいだしてこないのです。

「へんですね。あいつ、死んがいじゃないのでしょうか。」

書生の広田が、廊下の戸袋のところにあった長い棒を両手にかまえて、勇敢にも部屋の中へはいっていきました。妖虫と一騎うちをやるつもりなのです。

用心しながら、ジリジリと怪物に近づいて、いきなり棒をふりかぶると、やっとばかりにうちおろしました。

すると、怪物はブルンと身ぶるいしたように見えましたが、べつに動きだすようすもありません。それに、なんだかみょうな手ごたえでした。まるで、ひらいたこうもりがさをたたいたような感じがしたのです。

広田は、勇気をふるいおこして、棒を片手ににぎったまま床の間にあがって、怪物の背中に手をかけました。そして、ゆり動かすようにしたかとおもうと、いきなり、とんきょうな声をたてました。

「なあんだ。ぬけがらか。先生、こいつ、中はからっぽですよ。」

それを聞くと、高橋さんと書生の青木も、部屋にはいってきました。

「からっぽだって？」

「ええ、セミのぬけがらみたいなもんです。しかも、これは、ほんとうのカブトムシでなくて、ビニールをはったこしらえものですよ。」

それから、三人でよくしらべてみますと、太い針金を、かごのように組みあわせて、そ

91

れに黒くひかったビニールをはりつめた、つくりものであることがわかりました。頭としりを持って、グッとおさえつけると、小さくおりたたむこともできるのです。

その朝、小林少年がとじこめられたカブトムシの衣装とは、つくりかたがちがっていました。怪物団はこういうものを、いくつも持っているのにちがいありません。

「しかし、なぜ、こんなものが、床の間においてあるのでしょうか。ただ、おどかしのためでしょうかね。」

書生の青木が、ふしぎそうにいいました。高橋さんはしばらく考えていましたが、やがて、ひどく心配そうな顔になって、

「いや、ただのおどかしじゃない。怪物団のやつが、その中にはいって、やって来たのだ。そして、ここで皮をぬいで、うちの中のどこかへ、姿をかくしているのだ。むろん、賢二をかどわかすためだ。おい、すぐ警視庁へ電話をかけてくれ。中村警部をよびだすんだ。」

そのとき広田がまた、とんきょうな声をたてました。

「あっ、こんな紙きれがありました。カブトムシの腹の下に、おいてあったんです。」

ひろいあげて、よく見ますと、その紙きれには、鉛筆でつぎのような、おそろしい文句が書きつけてありました。

今夜じゅうに賢二君を、つれていく。こんどこそ、まちがいない。おれたちは、かならず知らせるがいい。だが、なんの役にもたたないだろう。早く警察にやってみせる。

そして、文章のおわりに、黒いカブトムシの絵がかいてあるのです。

三人は、いそいで、階下におりました。広田は賢二君をまもる役目をひきうけ、青木は電話室にとびこむと、捜査課の中村警部をよびだしました。

中村警部が電話口に出たので、高橋さんは受話器をとって、カブトムシのぬけがらのことと、怪物団の予告文のことをつげて、すぐきてくれるようにたのみました。

高橋さんは、カブトムシの怪人が、うちの中にかくれているといいましたが、はたして、そうだったでしょうか。怪人の予告文には「警察をよべ」と書いてありました。もしうちの中にかくれていたら、警察に来られては、つかまってしまうではありませんか。

では、怪人はどんな計略を、考えだしたのでしょう。床の間のぬけがらは、いったい、どういう役目をはたすのでしょう。やがて、中村警部のひきいる、警官の一隊がやってきます。そして、おそろしい知恵くらべがはじまるのです。やがて、怪物団の思いもよらぬ

魔術が、人々をあっといわせるときがくるのです。

四人の警官

中村警部は、高橋さんの話を聞くと、ひじょうにおどろいて、すぐ、部下の警官と刑事を四人ほどさしむける。わたしも、あとからいくつもりだという返事でした。

まもなく日がくれて、外がまっ暗になったじぶん、おもてに自動車のとまる音がして、ふたりの制服警官とふたりの私服警官がはいってきました。

私服警官のひとりが出した名刺には、警部補正木信三と印刷してありました。

四人は高橋さんから、いっさいのようすを聞きとると、まず二階の広間からはじめて、うちの中はもちろん、庭のすみずみまで、くまなくしらべまわりました。しかし、どこにもあやしい人間は発見されませんでした。

「裏庭に、みょうな足あとがあります。人間の足あとではありません。大きなカブトムシでも歩いたような、気味のわるい足あとです。それから、二階の屋根へ、はしごをかけたあとがあります。庭の土にふたつ、深いくぼみができているのです。あいつは、そこからに階へのぼったのでしょう。はしごはだれかが、もとの場所へもどしたようです。すると、

あいぼうがいたのですね。そいつの足あとらしいものも、のこっています。しかしあやしいやつは、どこにもいません。われわれが来ることを知って、逃げてしまったのでしょう。」

正木警部補は、三人の部下といっしょに応接間にもどってきて、主人の高橋さんに報告しました。

「ところで、おたくの人たちを、全部ここへ集めていただきたいのですが。ねんのために、ひとりひとり、たずねてみたいとおもうのです。」

そこで、うちじゅうの人が応接間に集められました。主人の高橋さんのほかに、賢二君のにいさんの中学生の壮一君、書生の広田と青木、お手つだいさんなどでした。

「これでおたくのかたは全部ですか。」

正木警部補が一同を見まわしてたずねました。

「いや、このほかに、もう三人います。賢二がカブトムシを見て、熱を出してしまったものですから、部屋に寝させて、わたしの家内と、もうひとりのお手つだいさんがつきそっているのです。」

「ああ、そうですか。よろしい。賢二君には、こちらから出むいて、話をきくことにしましょう。」

警部補は、そういって、そばにいた部下に目くばせしますと、私服と制服の警官のふた

95

り、いそいで、賢二君の部屋のほうへ立ちさりました。
　それを見おくって、正木警部補は、ポケットから手帳をとり出すと、いろいろとたずねましたが、今までわかっていることのほかに、新しいことは何も聞きませんでした。
　そこへ、さきほどの制服と私服の警官が、大きなカブトムシのぬけがらを、ふたりでかかえて帰ってきました。
「これは証拠物件として、警視庁へ持って帰るほうがいいと思いますが……」
「うん、そうしよう。自動車の中へ入れておいてくれたまえ。で、賢二君はどうだった。」
「これということもありません。ただ二階へあがったとき、なんの気なしに広間をのぞくと、あいつがいたので、びっくりして、下へかけおりたというだけです。そのまえには、べつに、あやしいものも見なかったようです。」
　それをきくと、正木警部補は主人の高橋さんにむかって、
「おたくのしらべは、これで、いちおうすみました。邸内には何者もかくれておりませんから、今のところ、心配はありませんが、なにしろ魔法つかいといわれるやつのことですから、よほど用心しないといけません。われわれは、これから、おたくのへいの外や、となり近所を、しらべてみることにします。そして、見はりのものは、表門と裏門とに、の

こしておくつもりですが、賢二君には、いつもだれか、ついていてください。けっしてひとりぼっちにしてはいけません。では、ちょっと、しつれいします。」

警部補は、部下をひきつれて応接間を出ました。高橋さんは、玄関まで見おくりました。

大カブトムシのぬけがらをおりたたみもしないで、ふたりがかりでかかえた警官が、それを自動車に入れているのが見えました。そして、なにか運転手にさしずをしているようです。

高橋さんは、玄関からひきかえすと、熱を出して寝ている賢二君のことが心配ですから、ふすまをひらいたのですが、ひらいたかとおもうと、高橋さんは、「あっ」といったまま、そこに立ちすくんでしまいました。

お手つだいさんが気をうしなって、ころがっています。そのひたいから血が流れているのです。高橋さんのおくさんは、手足をしばられ、さるぐつわをはめられて、たおれています。賢二君のふとんの中は、からっぽです。どこかへ、いなくなってしまったのです。

「おーい、だれかきてくれ。早く、だれか……」

高橋さんは、廊下に出て、大声でどなりました。すると、バタバタと足音がしてふたりの書生がかけつけてきました。

97

「いまの警官たちが、近所にいるはずだ。早くよびもどしてくれ。賢二がさらわれましたといって。」

書生たちがかけだすあとについて、高橋さんは電話室にとびこむと、警視庁をよびだそうとしましたが、いくらダイヤルをまわしても、手ごたえがありません。耳にあてた受話器からは、なんの音も聞こえません。おりもおり、電話がこしょうをおこしたらしいのです。電話をあきらめて、玄関へとびだしていきますと、外から帰ってきた書生たちにであいました。

「どうだ、警官は見つかったか。」

「うちのへいの外を、ぐるっとまわってみましたが、どこにもいません。近所のうちをたずねても、だれも知らないというのです。警官たちは、警視庁へ帰ってしまったのじゃないでしょうか。」

「そうか、しかたがない。きみ、うちの電話はこしょうだから、おとなりの電話をかりてね、警視庁の中村警部をよびだしてくれたまえ。早くするんだ。」

書生の広田が、おとなりの門の中へとびこんでいきました。高橋さんは、それを待つのももどかしく、「いや、わしがかけよう」といいながら、広田のあとをおってかけだしていきました。おとなりの電話は、すぐに、警視庁に通じました。高橋さんは、電話口にし

がみついて、
「捜査課ですか。中村警部はおられませんか。わたしは高橋太一郎というもんです。……ああ、中村君ですか。中村警部はおらんのですか。たいへんなことがおこったんだ。きみがよこしてくれた警官たちが、帰ったあとで、賢二が見えなくなったんだ。あのさわぎで熱を出したものだから、寝かせてあったのだが、そのふとんがからっぽなんだ。」

すると、中村警部の声が、みょうなことをいいました。
「モシモシ、あなた高橋太一郎さんですね。なんだかお話がよくわかりませんが、わたしからだといって、だれかが、そちらへ行ったのですか。」
「なにをいってるんだ。今から一時間ほどまえに、きみに電話でたのんだじゃないか。それで、きみが四人の警官をよこしてくれたんじゃないか。」
「待ってください。ちょっと待ってください。たずねてみますから。……あ、モシモシ、いまたずねてみましたが、捜査課からは、だれもあなたのおたくへ行ったものはありませんよ。たしかに警視庁のものだったのですか。」
「そうですよ。制服がふたりに、私服がふたりだった。その中に警部補がいてね、正木信三ぞうという名刺をくれましたよ。」

「え、マサキ シンゾウですって、正木信三ですね。高橋さん、こりゃこまったことになりましたね。ぼくのほうには正木信三なんて警部補は、ひとりもいないんですよ。その四人の警官は、賊の変装だったかもしれません。ともかく、おたくへまいります。くわしいことは、そちらでうかがいましょう。」

「それじゃ、待っています。大いそぎできてください。」

そこで電話がきれました。いったい、これはどうしたわけなのでしょうか。

明智探偵の登場

高橋さんは、そのまま家へ帰りましたが、なにがなんだかさっぱりわけがわかりません。一時間ほどまえに、たしかに警視庁へ電話をかけたのです。ダイヤルをまわすと、交換手の女の声で、「こちらは警視庁です」と、はっきりいいました。いくら魔法つかいの犯人でも、ダイヤルで自動的につながる電話を外からどうすることができましょう。まったく不可能なことです。これが第一のふしぎ。

第二のふしぎは、いつのまに、どうして、賢二君をさらっていったか、ということです。あれがにせ警官にしても、四人のものは、高橋さんの見ているまえを、どうどうと出ていっ

たではありませんか。賢二君をつれさることなど、できるわけがありません。

では、四人のほかに、べつのやつが裏庭からでもしのびこんでいったのでしょうか。それも、考えられないことです。さっきの警官が賢二君の部屋へ行ってから、高橋さんが同じ部屋へ行くまでに、十分ぐらいしかたっていません。裏庭からしのびこんで、お手つだいさんをなぐりたおし、おかあさんをしばってさるぐつわをはめ、それから賢二君にもさるぐつわをはめて、窓からかつぎだし、裏のへいをのりこえて逃げるというようなことが、たった十分でできるでしょうか。それに、へいの外は道路ですから、夜でも人通りがあります。人の通るすきを見て、へいをのりこえなければなりませんから、それにも時間がかかるはずです。とても、ふつうの人間にできることではありません。

いくら考えてもわかりません。やっぱりカブトムシの怪人は魔術師です。魔術でなくては、こんな、はやわざができるわけがないのです。

高橋さんは、書生に医者をよばせて、気をうしなっていたお手つだいさんの手あてをしてもらい、賢二君のおかあさんも、さるぐつわや縄をとって、ひと間にやすませました。そして、賢二君のようすをたずねてみましたが、いきなり、うしろから目かくしをされてしばられたから、なにもわからなかったという答えでした。お手つだいさんも話ができ

101

るようになったので聞いてみますと、これも、あっというまになぐられたので、あいての服装などは、まるでおぼえていないというのです。

そんなことをしているうちに時間がたち、やがて玄関にベルの音がして、中村警部の声が聞こえました。書生に応接間へ通すようにいいつけておいて、高橋さんがはいってきますと、応接間には中村警部のほかに、ふたりの背広の男がいました。そのひとりのほうが、なんだか見たような顔なのです。高橋さんはおもいだそうとしましたが、どうもおもいだせません。それを見てとって、中村警部が紹介しました。

「ごぞんじないでしょうが、こちらは、私立探偵の明智小五郎さんです。明智さんはやっぱりわれわれにも関係のある事件で、大阪のほうへ旅行しておられたのですが、それがうまくかたづいたので、きょう東京に帰られて、警視庁へおよりになったのです。さっきの電話の話をしますと、ひじょうにおもしろい事件だから、自分も、いっしょに行ってみたいといわれるので、おつれしたわけです。こちらは、わたしの部下の刑事です。」

「ああ、あなたが明智先生でしたか。なんだか見たようなお顔だとおもいました。新聞の写真でお目にかかっていたのですね。カブトムシの怪人のことは、ごぞんじでしょう。あなたのおるすちゅうに、あいつは、あなたにばけて、ここへやってきたのです。そして、わたしと賢二を自動車にのせてつれだしたのですが、あなたの少年助手の小林君のはたら

102

きで、ぶじにすみました。わたしは、あなたのお帰りをどんなに待っていたかしれませんよ。」

高橋さんが、うれしそうにいいますと、明智もニコニコして答えました。

「そのことは、小林が大阪へ電話をかけてくれましたので、くわしく知っています。とんだやつに見こまれて、あなたもご心配でしょう。じつはもっと早く帰るつもりだったのですが、あちらの仕事がてまどって、一週間ものびてしまいました。しかし、もうだいじょうぶです。わたしは、とうぶん、このカブトムシ事件に全力をつくすつもりです。賢二君は、きっととりかえしておめにかけます。」

「ありがとう。それで、わたしも、どんなに心づよいかわかりません。」

高橋さんは、名探偵の自信にみちたことばに、すっかりうれしくなって、たのもしげに、その顔を見あげるのでした。

「それに、けさ、小林が丸ビルで、ひどいめにあっています。小林ははずかしくて、わたしにあわせる顔がないといって、しおれています。そのかたきうちもしなければなりません。」

こい眉、するどい目、高い鼻、にこやかな、しかし、ひきしまった口、有名なモジャモジャのかみの毛、名探偵は、そのモジャモジャ頭を指でかきまわしながら、はげしい口調

でいうのでした。

高橋さんは、明智探偵と中村警部に、今夜のできごとを、くわしく話しました。

「それにしても、警視庁の電話番号のダイヤルをまわして、ちゃんと捜査課が出たのに、中村君がにせものだったというのは、じつにふしぎです。またあいつらは、賢二をいったいどうしてつれだしたか、それについて、あなたがたのお考えが聞きたいのです。」

と、ふたりの顔を見くらべました。すると中村警部が、首をかしげながらいうのです。

「わたしも、電話のことは、ふしぎでしかたがありません。もしや、捜査課に犯人のなかまがまぎれこんでいて、わたしの声をまねたのではないかと、よくしらべてみましたが、交換手は、だれも、高橋さんからわたしへの電話をとりついだおぼえがないというのです。つまり、あなたは警視庁のダイヤルをまわされたが、出たあいては、警視庁ではなかったわけですね。」

「しかし、もし、電話線が、まちがったところへつながったのなら、警視庁ですと答えるはずがないじゃありませんか。中村君の口まねをしたやつは、悪人にきまっているが、わたしのまわしたダイヤルで、悪人の電話にうまくつながるなんて、そんなことはできないことですよ。」

「それは、そうですね。じつにふしぎだ。」
　警部も腕をくんで、考えこんでしまいました。
　ふたりの話をだまって聞いていた明智探偵は、そのとき、「ちょっと、しつれい」といって、どこかへ出ていきましたが、しばらくすると、ニコニコしながら帰ってきました。
「わかりました。電話の秘密がわかりましたよ。ちょっと庭へおりてごらんなさい。」
　明智はそういって、さきに立って廊下へ出ると、庭のほうへおりていきます。高橋さんと、中村警部と、その部下の刑事も、わけはわからぬけれど、ともかく明智のあとにしたがいました。
「高橋さん、あの庭のすみに、小さな小屋がありますね。物置きですか。」
「そうです。がらくたが、ほうりこんであるのですよ。」
「あの中に、私設電話局ができていたのです。」
　明智が、みょうなことをいいました。
「え、私設電話局ですって？」
「ここに懐中電灯があります。これで物置きの中を見てごらんなさい。」
　高橋さんは、いわれるままに懐中電灯をうけとると、物置き小屋の戸をひらいて、中をのぞきこみました。

「ほら、天井から二本の電線が、たれさがっているでしょう。あのさきに、電話機がとりつけてあったのです。それから外へ出て屋根をごらんなさい。むこうのおもやの屋根から、この小屋の屋根へ、やっぱり二本の電線が引っぱってある。わかりましたか。この二本の電線は、ほんとうは、あすこに立っている電柱につながっていたのです。それを切りはなして、この小屋へ引っぱり、電話機をすえつけて、私設電話局をつくったのです。あとになって秘密がばれても、犯人はすこしもこまらないのですからね。

犯人は電話機を持って逃げたが、電線はそのままにしておいたのです。

つまり、犯人のひとりが、この小屋にかくれて、あなたが警視庁へ電話をかけるのを待ちかまえていたのです。ダイヤルはどこをまわしても、みんなここへつながるわけですからね。そして、ひとりで警視庁の交換手の女の声色をつかったり、中村君の声色をつかったりしたのです。

目的をはたすと、電話機をとりはずして、それをかついでスタコラ逃げだしたというわけです。敵ながらあっぱれですね。じつにかんたんな、うまいやり方を考えたものじゃありませんか。」

「ふーん。」

高橋さんは、おもわず、うめき声を出しました。

「そいつのあいずで、あの四人のやつが、やってきたんだな。しかし、明智さん、まだ一つ、かんじんなことが、わたしには、どうしてもわかりませんが……」
「賢二君を、どんなふうにして、つれだしたかということでしょう。」
「そうです。」
「それなら、わけのないことですよ。わたしは、あなたのお話を聞いたときに、その秘密がわかりました。賢二君がつれだされるのを、高橋さん、あなたはその目でごらんになっていたのですよ。」
「高橋さんと中村警部は、この名探偵のことばにびっくりして、顔を見あわせました。そういわれても、まだわからなかったからです。

おばけ屋敷

　高橋さんは、ふしぎでたまらぬという顔つきです。明智はニコニコしながら、
「これも、あいつらの手品ですよ。賢二君は、あなたの目のまえで、つれだされたのです。それが、あなたには見えなかったのです。」
「え、わたしの目のまえを？　それはいったい、どういう意味です。」

「手品ですよ。じつにうまいことを考えたものだ。にせ警官がカブトムシのぬけがらを、ふたりでかかえて出たといいますね。さっきのお話では、ビニールでできた、そのカブトムシのからだは、こうもりがさのように、小さくおりたためたというじゃありませんか。そうすれば、なにもふたりでかかえなくても、ひとりで持てるはずです。それをおりたたみもしないで、もとのかたちのままで、ふたりでかかえていったというのは、へんではありませんか。」

高橋さんは、それを聞くと、みょうな顔をして、しばらく目をパチパチやっていましたが、はっと気がついて、顔色をかえました。

「あっ、それじゃ、あの中へ賢二を……」

「そうです。そのほかに考えようがないのです。賢二君をしばって、さるぐつわをして、カブトムシのぬけがらの中にとじこめたのです。だから、おりたたむことができなかったのです。ふたりがかりでなくては、はこべなかったのです。」

「ああ、そうだったのか、そこへ気がつかないとは、わたしはなんというバカだったのでしょう。カブトムシが小さくおりたたためることは、書生に聞いて知っていました。しかし、あいてを警官だと信じていたので、そこまでうたがわなかったのです。まんまと手品にひっかかりました。じつに、とりかえしのつかない失敗でした。」

高橋さんはそういって、さもくやしそうにうつむくのでした。　中村警部は、気のどくそうな顔で、
「高橋さん、そんなにがっかりなさることはありません。われわれは、賢二君をとりもどすために全力をつくします。明智さんも、きっと、ほねをおってくださるでしょう。」
と、なぐさめ、それから三十分ほど、賢二少年のゆくえをさがしだすてだてについて、いろいろ話しあっていましたが、そのとき、書生の広田が、顔色をかえてとびこんできました。……こちらへ、つなぎましょうか。」
「たいへんです。電話が、カブトムシから電話がかかってきました。
　高橋さんは、それをきくと、おもわず立ちあがりましたが、また、こしかけて、
「うん、こちらへ、つないでくれ。」
と、卓上電話の受話器をとりあげました。
「もしもし、きみはだれだね。……うん、わしは賢二の父の高橋太一郎だ。」
「おれはカブトムシだよ。わかるかね。ウフフフフ……。おい、高橋さん、さっそくだが、とりひきの相談だ。賢二君と、このまま一生わかれてしまうか、一千万円か、どちらかだ。きみの身分で、一千万円はたいした金額じゃない。かわいい賢二君を買いもどしたらどうだね。」

「わしは、いま手もとに、そんな大金はない。」

「あした一日でできるだろう。きみが銀行にどれほど預金があるか、株券をどれほど持っているか、おれはちゃんとしらべているのだ。あすの夕方までに一千万円をつくるのはわけはない。」

「賢二は今、どこにいるのだ。」

「東京にいる。おれは手あらいことはしないから、心配しないでもよろしい。しかし、身のしろ金を持ってこなければ、きみはかわいい賢二君と、一生あうことができなくなるのだ。」

「身のしろ金を、どこへ持っていけばいいのだ。」

「今、くわしく教える。紙とえんぴつを用意したまえ。……いいかね、あすの晩、九時だ。ちょっきり九時にくるのだ。場所は、新宿駅から八王子街道を、西へ一キロ半ほど行くと、右に常楽寺という大きな寺がある。その寺のうしろの墓地のうらに、*戦災でやられたままになっている大きな屋敷のあとがある。コンクリートのへいがこわれて、中は草ぼうぼうのばけもの屋敷だ。建物は焼けてしまったが、洋館のレンガの壁だけが、少しのこっている。その壁の中へはいってよくさがすと、地下室への階段が見つかる。それをおりて、地下室へはいるのだ。おれはそこで待っている。」

＊ 空襲など戦争による災害

「賢二を、そこでひきわたすのか。」

「そうだ。一千万円の札たばとひきかえだ。現金でなくちゃいけない。ちょっとかさばるし、重いけれども、ふろしきづつみを二つにして、両手でさげれば持てないことはない。きみひとりになるのだ。そして、ふろしきづつみをさげて、墓場の裏手までくればいい。おれはまちがいなく地下室で待っている。暗いから懐中電灯を持ってきたほうがよろしい。おれ……常楽寺の前まで自動車できてもかまわない。だが、そこでおりて自動車を帰し、きみ高橋さんはそこまで聞くと、ちょっと電話の送話口をおさえて、明智と中村警部に相談しました。

「ともかく、しょうちしたと答えておいてください。」

中村警部が、ささやき声でさしずしました。

「よろしい。あすの晩九時までに、一千万円の現金を持って、その地下室へ行くことにする。きみのほうも、賢二をかならずつれてくるのだぞ。」

「だいじょうぶだ。いまきみは、だれかと相談したね。……警察は、われわれの出あいの場所を知ったわけだね。だから、よろしくいってくれたまえ。中村警部がそこにいるんじゃないかね。よろしくいってくれたまえ。……警察は、おおぜいで、おれを待ちぶせして、つかまえようとするだろうね。しかし、それはよすようにいってくれたまえ。おれのほうには、あらゆる準備ができているのだ。

111

つかまるようなへまはけっしてしない。それよりも、そんなことをすれば、きみは永久に賢二君にあえなくなる。中村君にも、よくいっておくんだ。じゃあ、まちがいなく、九時だよ。」

そこで、ガチャンと電話がきれました。

「しかたがありません。わたしのまけです。身のしろ金を用意して、賢二とひきかえることにしましょう。」

高橋さんが残念そうにいいました。

「警察としては、身のしろ金などおだしになることをおすすめはできません。しかしこのチャンスをはずすと、賢二君をとりもどすことがむずかしくなります。こちらはこのチャンスを、うまく利用するのです。わたしの部下の、うできぎの刑事を十人ばかり、そのばけもの屋敷の地下室のまわりにはりこませます。

むろん、みんな変装をして、あいてにさとられぬようにします。そして、あなたが賢二君をとりもどすのを、たしかめたうえ、怪人団をまわりからかこんで、ひっとらえてしまいます。お金もとりかえします。しかし、お金はにせものではいけません。あいても、じゅうぶん用心しているでしょうから、にせものと気づかれたらおしまいです。やはり、ほんとうの札たばを用意してくださらなくてはいけません。ねえ、明智さ

ん、このほかにてだてはないとおもいますが……」

中村警部が相談するようにいいますと、明智はあまり乗り気でもないようすで、

「警察としては、そうするよりしかたがないでしょうね。しかし、あいてを逃がさないようにしてください。賢二君をとりもどすまでは、けっしてあいてに気づかれてはいけません。刑事諸君に、そのことはよく注意しておいてください。」

明智は、それをなんどもくりかえして、ねんをおすのでした。

あやしい女こじき

そのあくる日の夕方のことです。常楽寺のうらの、草ぼうぼうのおばけ屋敷の、こわれたコンクリートべいのそばを、酒屋のご用聞きといったかっこうの、三十ぐらいの男が、あたりをキョロキョロ見まわしながら歩いていました。それは中村警部の部下の刑事の変装姿でした。

空はいちめんの雲にとざされ、風ひとつないどんよりとした日でした。歯がかけたように、こわれているコンクリートべい。その中の、ひざまでかくれるような草むら。うしろのほうには、常楽寺の墓場が、うす暗い木立ちの中に、チラチラと見えています。あたり

は、シーンとしずまりかえって、人っ子ひとり通りません。
「なるほど、こいつはおばけ屋敷だ。なんて気味のわるいところだろう。」
ご用聞きにばけた刑事は、そんなことをつぶやきながら、そっと中へはいっていきました。ところが、一歩足を入れたかとおもうと、彼ははっとしたように、やにわに、草むらの中へ身をかがめたのです。なにを見たのでしょう。
やはり塀ぎわの、ずっとむこうの草むらの中に、なんだか黒いものが、うごめいていました。草のあいだから、首だけ出してじっとそのほうを見ていますと、やがて、それはふたりの人間であることがわかりました。じつにきたならしい姿をした人間です。ああ、わかりました。こじきです。こじきがこんなところに、やすんでいたのです。ひとりは女こじき、ひとりはその子どもでしょう。十四、五歳のきたない少年です。そしてよく見ると、女こじきはかた手で腹をおさえて、からだを二つにおるようにしてうずくまっているのです。赤ちゃけたかみの毛は、スズメの巣のようにモジャモジャしていて、顔はあかでよごれてまっ黒です。着物とも言えないようなボロぎれをからだにまとい、縄でおびをしています。
子どもこじきは心配らしく、女こじきの背中をさすって、なにかいっているのですが、

114

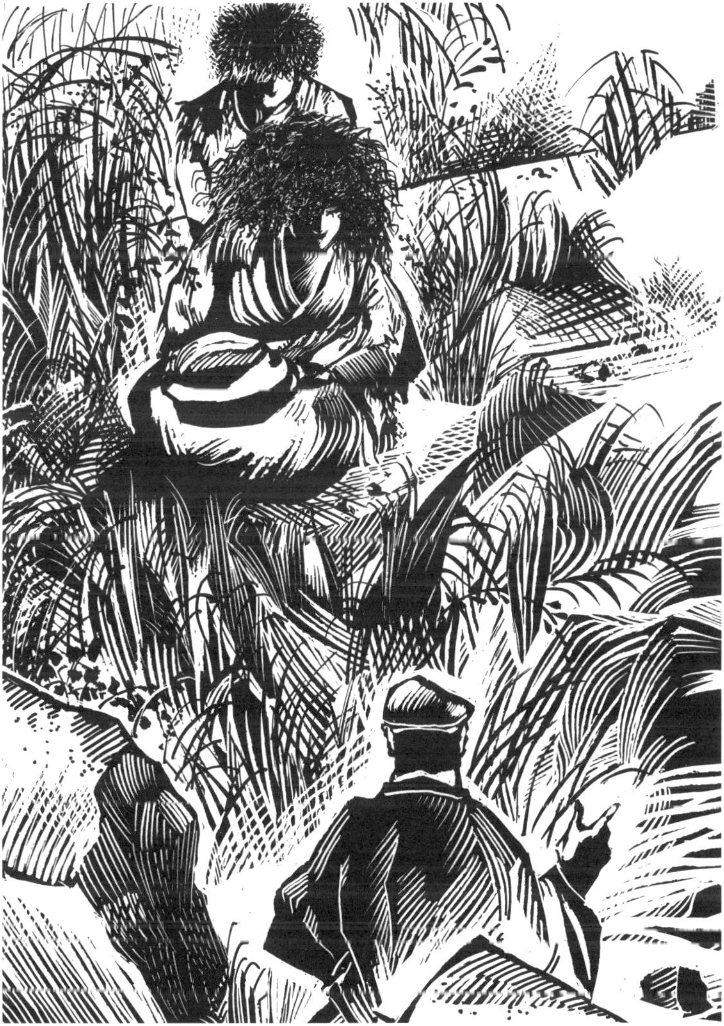

これも、黒くよごれたボロボロのシャツとズボンで、顔はまっ黒です。
「どうしたんだね。腹でもいたいのかね。」
ご用聞きにばけた刑事が、女こじきの顔をのぞきこみながらたずねました。
「うん、おっかあのしゃくがおこったんだ。おめえジンタン持ってねえか。あれのむと、なおるんだがな。」
少年こじきが、ジロジロと刑事の顔をながめながら、ぶえんりょにいうのです。
「ジンタンなんて持ってないね。そんなにいたいのかい。」
「なあに、たいしたことねえんです。じきによくなります。」
女こじきが、うつむいたままかすれた声で答えました。
「そうか、病気ならしかたがないが、日がくれないうちに、ほかへ行ったほうがいいよ。今夜は、このばけもの屋敷に、おそろしいことがおこるんだ。おまえたちが、ここにいると、ひどいめにあうかもしれないよ。」
刑事はそういって、あたりを見まわしながら、へいの外へ出ていきました。ふたりのこじきも、それから二十分ほどすると、どこかへ姿を消してしまいましたが、あとになって、このこじきは、にせものだったことがわかるのです。何ものかが、女こじきと少年こじきにばけていたのです。ふたりは、いったい、だれとだれだったのでしょうか。また、なん

のために、このばけもの屋敷へ来ていたのでしょうか。

地下室の妖虫

　さて、その夜の九時かっきりに、高橋さんは、おばけ屋敷の地下室の階段をおりていました。札たばのはいったふろしきづつみの一つをこわきにかかえ、一つを左手にさげ、右手には懐中電灯を持って、足もとをてらしながら、一段一段、おずおずと階段をおりていきます。

　まだ雨はふっていませんが、いつふりだすかわからないような、まっ暗な夜です。道もない草むらをかきわけて、ここまで来るのもやっとでした。高橋さんは、りっぱな実業家ですから、おばけをこわがるような人ではありませんが、それでも、なんとなく気味がわるいのです。それに、地下室に待ちかまえているあいてが、例のおそろしいカブトムシだとおもうと、なんだかゾーッとしてくるのでした。でも、かわいい賢二君をとりもどすためですから、どんなことでも、がまんするつもりです。

　コンクリートの階段はひびわれて、そのあいだから草がはえているので、うっかりすると、足がすべりそうになります。高橋さんは、用心しながら、だんだん深くおりていきま

した。
「懐中電灯をけすんだっ。」
足の下の穴の中から、気味のわるい声がひびいてきました。高橋さんはビクッとして、立ちどまりましたが、それは地下室に待っている怪人の声とわかったので、懐中電灯をけしてポケットに入れ、
「わしは高橋だ。賢二はそこにいるのだろうな。」
とたずねました。見ると、地下室の中からボーッとあかりがさしています。電灯ではありません。ろうそくの火のようです。
「賢二君はここにいる。きみはひとりだろうね。」
「ひとりだ。やくそくにはそむかないよ。」
「よし、おりてきたまえ。」
高橋さんは階段をおりきって、地下室へはいりました。やっぱりろうそくでした。部屋の中ほどに古い木箱がおいてあって、その上に一本のろうそくが立っているのです。
そのろうそくのむこうがわに、なんだか黒い大きなものが、モゾモゾとうごめいています。高橋さんはギョッとして、逃げだしそうになりました。
そこには、おばけがいたのです。まっ黒なやつが、大きなまんまるな目で、じっとこち

らをにらんでいたのです。それは、あの人間よりも大きなカブトムシでした。

それはビニールのこしらえものなので、中には人間がはいっているのですが、そうと知っていても、こんなさびしい穴ぐらの中で、この巨大な妖虫とさしむかいになるのは、気持ちのよいものではありません。

「ウフフ……、おれの姿が、おそろしいんだな。なあに、きみをとってくうわけじゃない。安心したまえ。おれは顔を見られたくないんだ。だから、こんな姿でやって来たんだ。きみをおどかすつもりじゃないよ。」

カブトムシの、大きなツノの下のみにくい口の中から、その声がきこえてくるのです。中に人間がはいっていることは、いうまでもありません。

高橋さんも、それを聞くと、おちつきをとりもどしました。

「賢二は？　賢二はどこにいるんだ。」

「よく見たまえ、おれのうしろの部屋のすみっこにいる。泣き声をたてられるとうるさいから、さるぐつわがはめてある。きみにひきわたすまでは、このままにしておくよ。」

ろうそくの光があわいので、今まで気づかなかったのですが、いわれてみると、部屋のすみに、小さい姿がうずくまっていました。賢二君はかわいそうに、うしろ手にしばられて、てぬぐいで、しっかり口のへんをしばられています。さっきから、おとうさんの姿を

見ていたのでしょうが、立ちあがることも、声を出すこともできないのです。たった一日のあいだに、なんだかひどくやせたように見えます。
「さあ、ここに、やくそくの一千万円を持ってきた。これをやるから、はやく賢二の縄をといてくれ。」
「よし、金はたしかにうけとった。まさかにせ札ではなかろう。きみは、そんなこざいくをする人とはおもわない。しかしもしにせ札だったら、おれのほうには、ちゃんと、しかえしのてだてがあるんだだから。……それじゃ、賢二君はかえしてやる。おれは、こんな不自由なからだだから、きみがここへ来て、縄をといて、かってにつれていくがいい。」
 いかにも、カブトムシの足では、縄をとくこともできないわけです。そこで、高橋さんは、気味のわるいカブトムシのそばをよけるようにして、部屋のすみに近づき、賢二君の縄をとき、手をとって、立ちあがらせました。そして、さるぐつわのてぬぐいをほどくと、そのまま、賢二君をひったてるようにして、階段をかけのぼり外に出ると、いきなり、ポケットの懐中電灯をとりだしてスイッチをおし、原っぱのほうにむかって、ふりてらしました。
 それがあいずでした。闇の中から、草むらをはうようにして、黒いかげが、あちらから

もこちらからも、地下室の入り口にむかって、かけよって来ました。いうまでもなく、中村警部の部下の刑事たちです。

すこしも音をたてないで、黒い人の姿が、ひとり、ふたり、三人、五人、十人、たちまち地下室の入り口に集まりました。暗くてよくわかりませんが、夕方のご用聞きにばけた刑事も、その中にいるのでしょう。十人が十人、てんでに、いろいろなものにばけています。刑事や警官らしい姿の人は、ひとりもおりません。

地下室は一方口です。この階段のほかに出口はありません。もう怪人は、袋のネズミです。こちらは十人、あいてはひとり、いかなる魔法つかいの怪人でも、とてもかなうものではありません。

声もたてず、刑事たちは、つぎつぎと階段をおりていきました。ろうそくはもとのままに、にぶい光をはなっていました。巨大な妖虫も、もとの場所にうずくまっていました。

刑事たちがはいっていっても、あいてはすこしも動きません。シーンとしずまりかえっています。あまりしずかにしているので、なんとなく気味がわるくなってきました。

「ぼくたちは警察のものだ。さすがの怪物も、まんまとわなにはまったな。」

ひとりの刑事が、人声でどなりつけました。すると、ああ、これはどうしたことでしょう。カブトムシが大きなツノをふりたてて、いきなり、

「ワハハハ……」

と笑いだしたのです。おかしくてたまらないように、いつまでも笑っているのです。

刑事(けいじ)たちは、あっけにとられましたが、もうグズグズしている場合(ばあい)ではありません。さきに立っていた三人の刑事が、ひとかたまりになって、いきなりカブトムシのからだにとびかかっていきました。

すると、そのとき、じつにきみょうなことがおこったのです。カブトムシのからだが、三人の刑事の手の下で、グニャグニャとへこんでいったのです。

刑事たちは、たおれそうになるのをやっとふみこたえて、おもわず「あっ」と、おどろきのさけび声をたてました。

カブトムシのからだは、からっぽだったのです。中の人間は、いつのまにか消(き)えうせていたのです。では、いま、あんな大きな声で笑ったやつは、いったいどこへいったのでしょう。カブトムシのぬけがらが、笑うはずがないではありませんか。

見知らぬ少年

地下室には一つしか入り口がありません。その入り口の前には、たえず人がいました。

そこからは、ぜったいに逃げられないのです。では、ほかに秘密の出入り口でもあるのかと、刑事たちは地下室のすみずみまでしらべましたが、ネズミの出入りする穴さえありません。怪人は煙のように消えうせてしまったのでしょうか。

「おやっ、これはなんだろう。」

それを聞くと、うしろのほうにいた高橋さんが、賢二君の手をひいて、そこへ出てきました。

ひとりの刑事が、地下室の床においてある、一つのふろしきづつみを指さしました。

「あっ、これは賢二とひきかえに、あいつにやった一千万円の札たばです。」

と、ふろしきの中をしらべてみましたが、

「たしかに、わたしの持ってきたまま、そっくりのこっています。あいつは、かんじんのお金をわすれて、逃げだしたのでしょうか。これはいったい、どうしたわけでしょう。」

高橋さんは気味わるそうに、あたりを見まわすのでした。刑事たちも、いよいよわけがわからなくなって、だまって立ちすくんでいました。

そのときです。とつぜん、どこからかへんな笑い声がひびいてきました。

「アハハハ……。高橋さん、きみがわるいのだよ。やくそくにそむいて、刑事なんかつれ

123

てくるからさ。おれのほうでは、こんなこともあろうかと、ちゃんと用意をしていたんだ。もう金はほしくない。そのかわり、賢二君を遠くへつれていくのだ。山の中の鉄塔王国へつれていくのだ。……それじゃあ、あばよ。」
 そして、ふしぎな声は、パッタリととだえてしまいました。
 だれもいないのに、声だけが聞こえてきたのです。高橋さんも刑事たちも、おばけの声でも聞いたように、ゾーッとして、たがいの顔を見あわせるばかりでした。
 それにしても、今の声はわけのわからないことをいいました。お金はほしくないから、賢二をつれていくというのですが、お金もここにあるし、賢二君も、ちゃんとここにいるではありませんか。あれはいったい、どういう意味なのでしょう。
 高橋さんはそのとき、ギョッとして、手をひいている賢二君の顔を見つめました。
「ちょっと、その懐中電灯の光を……」
と、そばの刑事にたのんで、その光を賢二君の顔にあててもらいました。少年はキョトンとして、こちらを見あげています。パッと明るくてらしだされた顔。
 その顔は賢二君にそっくりでした。しかし、どこかしらちがっているのです。じっと見ていると、だんだん、そのちがいがひどくなってくるのです。

「おい、おまえ、賢二じゃないのか。いったいきみは、どこの子だ？」
　高橋さんが、はげしい声で、しかりつけるようにたずねました。
「ぼく、木村正一だよ。賢二じゃないよ。」
　少年は、やっぱり、キョトンとしています。
「どうして、賢二の替え玉になったんだ。わたしは、きみを賢二だとおもいこんでいたんだよ。」
「ぼく、学校の帰りに、へんなやつにつかまって、ここへ、つれてこられたのです。そして、口と手をしばられたんです。でも、がまんしていれば、いまに高橋さんという人が来て、その人につれられていけば、おうちへ帰れるし、それから、エンジンで動く大きな船のオモチャを、くれるっていうやくそくだったんです。おじさんは高橋さんだから、ぼくに船をくれるんでしょう。」
　木村というこの少年は、あまりりこうでないようです。怪人にうまくごまかされて、それを信じているらしいのです。
「そうだったか。それにしても、きみはあのカブトムシのおばけが、こわくなかったのかね。」
「こわかったよ。でも、しばられてるので、逃げだせなかった。それに、ぼくをここへ、つ

れてきたへんなやつが、逃げると殺してしまうといったんです。」

少年のいうことは、うそではないようでした。それならこの少年は、悪人のために、替え玉につかわれただけで、べつに罪はありません。

「よし、それじゃあ、きみはうちへつれていってあげよう。しかし、船のオモチャはだめだよ。おじさんは、ひどいめにあったのだ。それどころではないのだ。賢二という、きみとよくにた子どもを、さらわれてしまったのだからね。」

高橋さんは、くやしそうにいいました。こんなよくにた替え玉さえいなければ、だまされはしなかったのにと、この少年が、にくらしくなってくるのでした。

ああ、賢二少年は、やっぱり、鉄塔王国とやらへつれさられてしまったのです。お金さえやれば、ほんとうの賢二君を、かえしてくれたのかもしれないのに、刑事たちをつれてきたばかりに、怪人にうらをかかれて、とりかえしのつかぬことになってしまいました。

高橋さんは、中村警部をうらめしく思いました。警部さえ、刑事をはりこませるようなことをしなければ、こんなことにはならなかったのです。

それにしても、名探偵明智小五郎は、いったいなにをしているのでしょう。小林少年は、どこにいるのでしょう。

さすがの名探偵も、今夜のことは、見通しがつかなかったのでしょうか。

怪自動車

みんなが、うまい考えもうかばないで、地下室に立ちならんだまま、ぽんやりしていたとき、うしろの階段から、なにか黒い影のようなものが、地下室へおりてきました。
「だれだっ、そこへきたのは、だれだっ。」
ひとりの刑事が、それに気づいて、いきなり懐中電灯をさしつけながらどなりました。
その電灯の光の中にうきだしたのは、きたない女こじきでした。夕方、ご用聞きに変装した刑事が、原っぱで出あったあの女こじきでした。
「なあんだ、こじきか。いまごろ、どうしてこんなところへ、やってきたんだ。この地下室で寝るつもりなんだろう。いけない。いけない。外へ出ろ。さあ出るんだ。」
べつの刑事が、女こじきを、らんぼうにつきとばそうとしました。
ところが、こじきはつきとばされるどころか、刑事の手をはねかえして、グングン前にすすんできます。みかけによらず力のつよいやつです。そして、高橋さんの前まで来て、みんなのほうにむきなおり、ニコニコ笑いだしたではありませんか。

127

「こいつ、頭がおかしいな。こらっ、ここはおまえなんかの来る場所じゃない。出ていけ。出ないと、ひどいめにあうぞ。」

刑事にどなりつけられても、女こじきはへいきです。そして、へんなことをいいだしました。

「ここは、ぼくの来る場所だよ。ぼくが来なければ、きみたちでは、どうにもできないじゃないか。」

それは、はぎれのよい男の声でした。またしても、わけのわからないことがおこりました。

女こじきが、男の声でしゃべっているのです。

「ハハハ……、わからないかね。ほら、これを見たまえ。」

女こじきはそういいながら、手をあげて頭の毛をつかみ、グッと上に持ちあげました。すると、きたないかみの毛がスポッとぬけて、その下から男の頭があらわれたではありませんか。女のかみの毛は、カツラだったのです。

下からあらわれたのは、モジャモジャの男の頭でした。顔はススでもぬったようにまっ黒でしたが、よく見ると、どこか見おぼえのある顔でした。

「あっ、それじゃ、あなたは……」

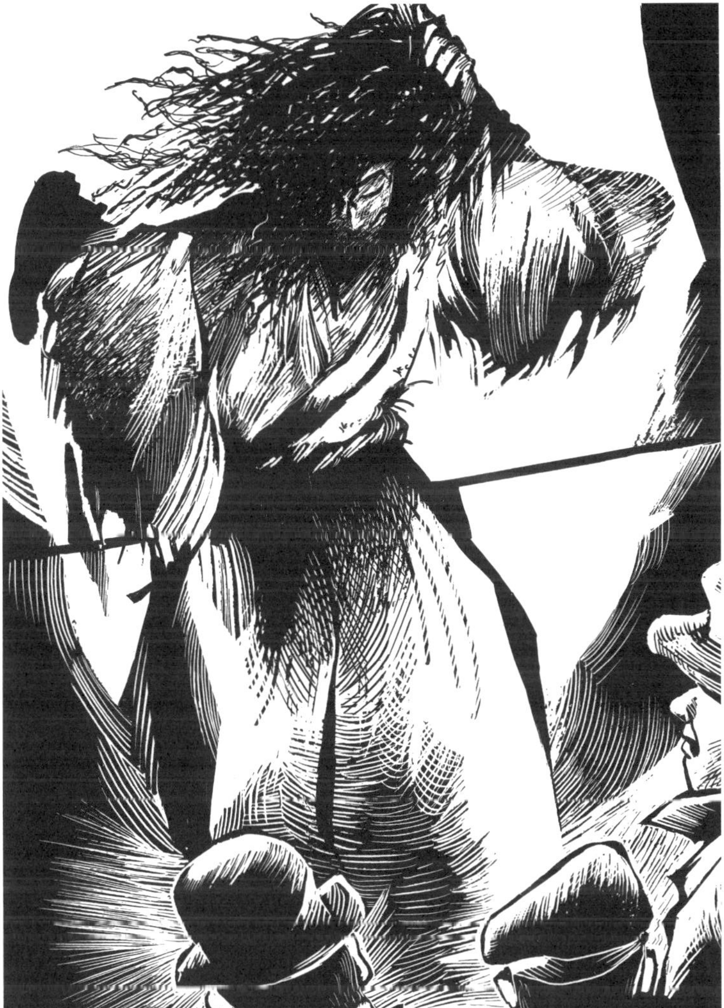

「明智小五郎です。おわかりになりましたか。」

ああ、そのきたない女こじきは、名探偵明智の変装姿だったのです。高橋さんも刑事たちも、あっけにとられて、しばらくは口をきくこともできませんでした。

「ぼくは、ここへ刑事諸君をはりこませたら、かえってあぶないとおもったのです。怪人団は、もう一つ、おくの手を考えるかもしれないとおもったのです。それで、だれにも知らさず女こじきにばけて、夕方からこの原っぱを見はっていました。そして、まんいちの場合には、とびだしてくるつもりだったのです。」

明智は、まるで演説でもするように話しはじめました。

「高橋さんが、札たばのふろしきづつみをさげて、地下室へはいっていかれるのも見ていました。それからしばらくして、高橋さんが、ひとりの少年をつれて出てこられたのも、刑事諸君がそこへかけつけて、地下室へおりていくのも見ていました。そして、そっと入り口の階段に近づき、中のようすを聞きますと、少年が賢二君の替え玉だったことや、怪人が消えうせたことがわかりました。

ところが、ぼくは一度も目をはなさないで、この地下室を見はっていたのに、だれも、ここから出ていったものはなかったのです。この地下室には、階段のほかに出入り口のないことはたしかです。

暗くなってから、原っぱのむこうに、一台の自動車がヘッドライトを消してとまっていました。ぼくは、ふと思いあたることがあったので、その自動車に注意していたのについ今しがた、それが、どこかへ走りさったのです。さっき、この地下室で、だれもいないのに怪人の声が聞こえましたね。あの声のすぐあとで、その自動車は出発したのですよ。この意味がわかりますか。」
「では、その自動車に怪人団のやつらが、のっていたとおっしゃるのですか。」
　高橋さんが、おもわず聞きかえしました。
「そうです。怪人団の首領が、のっていたのだろうとおもいます。」
「それを、あなたは、逃がしてしまったのですか。自動車に気づいていながら、なにもしなかったのですか。」
「いや、なにもしなかったのではありません。そこにいるご用聞きにばけた刑事さんは、女こじきが、ひとりの子どもこじきをつれていたことを、知っているでしょう。あの子どもこじきは、どこへいったとおもいます。怪人の自動車のどこかにかくれて、尾行しているのです。ひじょうな冒険です。しかし、あの少年ならだいじょうぶですよ」
「あっ、それじゃあ、あの子どもこじきは、先生の助手の小林君だったのですよ。」
　ご用聞きに変装した刑事が、とんきょうな声をたてました。

「そうです。小林はリスのようにすばしこくって、よく頭のはたらく少年です。こういう尾行は、おとなにはできません。からだの小さい少年でなくては、うまくいかないのです。小林はヒルのように、くっついたらはなれませんよ。そして、怪人団の本拠まで、ついていくでしょう。鉄塔王国がどこにあるかをたしかめるまでは、はなれないでしょう。こじきにばけた小林は、大きなきれの袋をさげていました。その中には、いろいろなものがはいっているのです。それをつかって、小林は、きっと目的をはたすでしょう。ぼくは、あの少年の力を信じているのです。」

それを聞いて、みんなはやっと安心しました。あの名助手の小林少年が尾行したのなら、けっして怪人を逃がすことはないだろうとおもったからです。

名探偵の知恵

「それにしても怪人は、どうして、この地下室から逃げだせたのでしょう。それから、だれもいないのに声が聞こえたのは？……わたしには、なにがなんだか、さっぱりわかりませんが、明智さん、あなたはそのわけがおわかりですか」

高橋さんが、みんなの聞きたいとおもっていたことをたずねました。

「ぼくはそのわけを、自動車が走りさったときに、とっさに気づいたのです。すこしおそすぎたかもしれません。しかし、怪人団の本拠をつきとめるためには、おそいほうがよかったともいえるのです。ちょっと待ってください。ぼくの考えがあたっているかどうか、いま、たしかめてみますから。」

明智はそういって、足もとにつぶされたようによこたわっていた、大カブトムシの上にしゃがみました。そして、そのぶきみな口に手をかけてグッとひらき、口の中へかた手を入れて、しばらくなにかやっていたかと思うと、やがてそこから、小さな器械のようなものを取りだしました。その器械には長いひもがついていて、口の中からズルズルとひきだされてくるのです。

「これです。これは小型のラウドスピーカーですよ。怪人が、自動車の中にあるマイクロフォンにむかって口をきくと、その声が、このラウドスピーカーから出るというしかけです。それで、カブトムシの中に人間がいて、ものをいっているように感じられたのです。

むろん、自動車とこの地下室のあいだには、長い電線がひいてあったのです。草にかくしておけば、電線など、だれも気がつきませんからね。

それで、むこうの声が、聞こえたわけがわかりました。しかし、こちらの声が、自動車の中までつたわらなければ、問答ができません。それには、この地下室のどこかに、マイ

133

「クロフォンがしかけてあるはずです。」

明智はそういって、刑事の懐中電灯をかりて、地下室の中をあちこちとてらしていましたが、天井のすみに、ひどくクモの巣のはっている場所を見つけました。

「あれかもしれない。クモの巣でかくしてあるのかもしれません。そのへんに、竹ぎれかなにかありませんか。」

それを聞くと、ひとりの刑事が、どこからか一本の竹ぎれをさがしだしてきました。明智はそれをうけとって、天井のすみのクモの巣をはらいのけますと、あんのじょう、そこに小さなマイクロフォンが、とりつけてあったではありませんか。

「これですっかり、秘密がとけました。高橋さんの庭の物置き小屋に、電話機をすえつけたのと同じやりかたです。怪人団には、電気のことを、よく知っているやつがいるらしいですね。」

「ああ、なんということでしょう。高橋さんは、カブトムシの中に怪人がいるとおもいこんで、しんけんになって、ラウドスピーカーと話をしていたのです。それじゃあ、わたしに一千万円もってこいといったのが、むだになりますね。怪人団は、さいしょから、金をとる気がなかったのでしょうか。これがどうもふにおちませんね。」

134

高橋さんが、首をかしげていうのでした。
「いや、むろん、金はほしかったのです。しかし、ゆうべ、あなたと電話で話したとき、そばに中村警部がいることを感づきましたね。それで用心をしたのですよ。金に目がくれて、つかまってしまっては、なんにもなりません。そこで、こんなことを考えついたのです。あなたが、ひとりで来て、札たばのふろしきづつみをおいていったら、あとから、とりにくるつもりだったのでしょう。そして、なんのじゃまもなく金が手にはいったら、そのときはじめて、ほんとうの賢二君をかえすつもりだったのかもしれません。
　また、もし刑事が、地下室へのりこんでくるようなことがあったら、札たばはそのままにして、ほんものの賢二君をどこかへつれさり、あなたや中村警部に、ざまをみろとでもいいしらせる計画だったのです。二つに一つ、どちらにしても損はしないという、じつにうまい考えですよ。」
　それを聞くと、人びとは、怪人のおくそこしれぬ悪知恵に、あきれかえってしまいました。しかし、明智探偵の知恵は、さすがにそれよりも、もういちだんすぐれていました。
　怪人の悪だくみを見やぶったばかりか、小林少年にさしずをして、怪人の本拠をつきとめようとさえしているのです。

ふしぎな尾行(びこう)

　原っぱのすみの、暗闇(くらやみ)の中に、ヘッドライトもルームランプも消した、一台の大型(おおがた)自動(じどう)車(しゃ)がとまっていました。それからすこしはなれた、深(ふか)い草むらの中に、ひとりのこじき少年がはらばいになって、じっと自動車のほうを見つめていました。

　このこじき少年は、いうまでもなく明智探偵(あけちたんてい)の助手(じょしゅ)の小林君(こばやしくん)です。どこまでも、怪人団(かいじんだん)の自動車を尾行(びこう)して、その行くさきをつきとめるのが小林少年(こばやししょうねん)の任務(にんむ)でした。しかし、尾行するといっても、こちらは自動車を持っていないのです。あいての自動車のどこかへもぐりこんで、かくれているほかありません。

　小林君は、それにはなれていました。いつかも、怪人の自動車の後部(こうぶ)のトランクへ身をひそめて、賢二君(けんじくん)をとりもどしたことがあります。今夜(こんや)も、あの手をもちいるつもりでした。

　小林君は、そっと怪人の自動車のうしろへはいりよりました。まっ暗ですし、草がボウボウとはえているのですから、あいてに気づかれる心配(しんぱい)はありません。

　車体にたどりついて、後部のトランクのふたを持ちあげてさぐってみますと、中には怪(かい)

人団のカバンなどがはいっているばかりで、じゅうぶんすきまがありますのようなすばやさで、その自動車のにもつ入れの中へすべりこみました。そして、カバンなどを前のほうへおしやり、いちばんおくのすみによこたわりました。大型の自動車ですから、足をちぢめればらくによこになれるのです。

この自動車は、どこまで行くかわかりません。どんなにながいあいだ、そこにかくれていなければならないかもわかりません。そこで、小林君は、いろいろのものを用意していました。黒いきれでつくった大きな袋を、だいじそうにかかえていたのです。その中には、探偵七つ道具や、水をいっぱいいれた旅行用のウイスキーびんや、かたパンの紙袋や、着がえの服まではいっているのです。そのほかに、なんだかえたいのしれない、大きなまるいブリキかんや、こまごましたものが、いっぱいはいっていました。

小林君はその袋の中から、針金をみょうなかたちにまげた、二センチぐらいの大きさのものを、二つとりだしました。そして、それを自動車のにもつ入れの、ふたの両方のはしにはさんで、そっと、そのふたをしめました。すると、針金がじゃまになって、ふたはピッタリしまらないで、ほそいすきまがあいているのです。にもつ入れの中の空気がごれて、息がつまってはたいへんですから、そのすきまから、空気がとおるようにしておくためです。さすがに小林少年は、そんなこまかいことまで、まえもって用意していたので

つぎには、袋の中から、大きな、黒いふろしきのようなものを取りだしました。そしてそれで、自分の頭から足のさきまで、すっぽりとつつんでしまったのです。これは、もし怪人団のやつが、自動車のにもつ入れのふたを、ひらくようなことがあっても、すぐには見つからないためです。

そうして、じっとしていますと、しばらくしてエンジンの音が聞こえ、いきなり自動車が走りだしました。だんだん速力がくわわって、おそろしい速さで走っているのです。

その行くさきは、いったいどこなのでしょう。自動車の中には、手足をしばられ、さるぐつわをはめられた賢二少年が、ふたりの男にはさまってこしかけています。怪人たちは、賢二君をどこへつれていくのでしょう。

一時間、二時間、いつまでたっても、自動車はとまるようすがありません。ますます、速力が速くなるばかりです。きゅうくつなにもつ入れの中に身をちぢめていた小林君には、そのあいだが、どんなにながく感じられたことでしょう。肩や腰が、いたくなってきました。せまい箱の中ですから、すわることも、寝がえりをすることもできません。

三時間、四時間、自動車はまだ走りつづけています。だんだん道が悪くなってきたとみえて、ガタガタとはげしくゆれるのです。おなかもへってきました。小林君は例の袋の中

138

から、かたパンをとりだしてかじり、ウイスキーびんの水を飲みました。
ああ、このふしぎな自動車旅行は、いったい、どこまでつづくのでしょう。

そびえる鉄塔

途中で、一度やすみました。自動車にガソリンを入れたのです。そして、しばらくやすむと、また走りだしました。しばらくすると、のぼり坂にさしかかったらしく、速力がにぶくなりました。おそろしいでこぼこ道です。小林君は、泣きだしたくなるほどの苦しみでした。
もう、からだがしびれてしまって、気がとおくなりそうでした。それでも、自動車は、とまるようすがありません。それからまた、ながいながい時間、ゆれにゆれたうえ、やっと目的地にたっしたらしく、ぴたりととまったまま動かなくなりました。
小林君のかくれている、にもつ入れのふたのすきまから、うっすら光がさしています。夜が明けたのです。
自動車をおりた怪人団の男たちの話し声が、かすかに聞こえてきました。そっと、にもつ入れのふたをひらいてみますと、そこは、大きな森の中でした。自動車からおりた人たちは、森の大木のあいだのほそい道を、むこうのほうへのぼっていくようすです。ああ、

わかりました。ここからさきは、もう自動車がとおらないので歩くほかないのです。歩いて山をのぼるのです。ここは、深い山の中にちがいありません。

小林君は、大いそぎでかくれ場所からとびだしました。そして、自動車のよこにまわって、そっと中をのぞいてみましたが、車の中には、だれものこっていないことがわかりました。怪人団のやつらは賢二君をつれて、森の中へはいっていったのです。小林君は、例の黒いきれの大袋を肩にかついで、そのあとを追いました。

見あげるような大木がたちならび、空も見えないほどの深い森です。その中に、ほそい道がついています。道といっても、めったに人の通らないところらしく、クマザサのしげった中をガサガサと、かきわけて進むのです。

音をたてて、あいてに気づかれてはたいへんですから、よほど注意して歩かなければなりません。といって、足もとに気をとられていると、あいてを見うしないそうになります。

小林少年の苦労は、なみたいていではありません。

それはじつに長い道のりでした。一時間いじょうも、歩きづめに歩いたのです。すっかりつかれはてて、今にもたおれそうになったとき、やっと目的地につきました。とつぜん、目のまえが、パッと明るくひらけたのです。

といっても、森を出はなれたのではありません。森のまん中の広い空き地に、たどりつ

いたのです。怪人団の男たちは、どんどんその空き地へ出ていきましたが、小林君は見つかったらたいへんですから、森を出ることができません。一本の太い木の幹にからだをかくして、空き地をながめたのです。

そこには、びっくりするような、ふしぎなものがありました。空き地のむこうのほうに、大きな黒いお城がたっていたのです。日本のお城ではなくて、西洋のお城です。一方のはしに、五十メートルもあるような、高い塔がそびえています。水道の鉄管を、何百倍にしたような、なんのかざりもない、まるい塔です。それがヌーッと、空にそびえているありさまは、じつに異様な感じでした。

その塔には、あつい鉄板がはりつめてあるように見えました。ところどころに小さな窓がひらいています。塔のよこには、やっぱり鉄でできた高いへいが、ずっとつづいていて、その中にいろいろな建物があるらしく、きみょうなかたちの屋根が、いくつも見えているのです。へいの中ほどに、いかめしい鉄の門があって、その鉄のとびらは、ピッタリとしまっていました。

いつか、ふしぎなじいさんの、のぞきカラクリで見た、あの鉄塔と同じです。ですから、ここが怪人団の鉄塔王国にちがいありません。いよいよ敵の本拠にのりこんだのです。

小林少年は、そんなことを考えながら胸をドキドキさせて、大木の幹のかげからのぞい

ていますと、怪人団の男四人と、そのうちのふたりに両方から手をとられて、よろめきながら歩いている、かわいそうな賢二少年の姿が、だんだんむこうへ遠ざかっていくのが見えました。

やがて、彼らが、いかめしい鉄の城門に近づきますと、鉄のへいの上の見はりの窓から人の顔があらわれ、上と下とでなにか問答をくりかえしていましたが、すぐに人の顔がひっこみ、鉄門のとびらがしずかにひらかれて、やっと人ひとり通れるすきまができました。用心のためでしょう、それいじょうはひらかないのです。賢二少年をつれた四人の男は、そのわずかのすきまから、ひとりずつ、門の中へ吸いこまれるように姿を消していきました。

男たちを吸いこむと、とびらはふたたびしずかにしまって、あたりはシーンとしずまりかえってしまいました。深山のふかい森にかこまれて、いかめしくそびえる鉄の城。その中には、いったい、どんなおそろしいものがすんでいるのでしょうか。死の城、妖魔の城です。小林君はふと、その鉄の城門のむこうがわに、ウジャウジャとうごめいている、巨大なカブトムシのむれを想像して、ゾーッと背すじがつめたくなる思いでした。

やっと、ここまで尾行はしたものの、このあと、どうすればよいのか、まるで、けんとうもつきません。うっかり森を出て城に近づけば、どこかから怪人団のやつが見はっていな

142

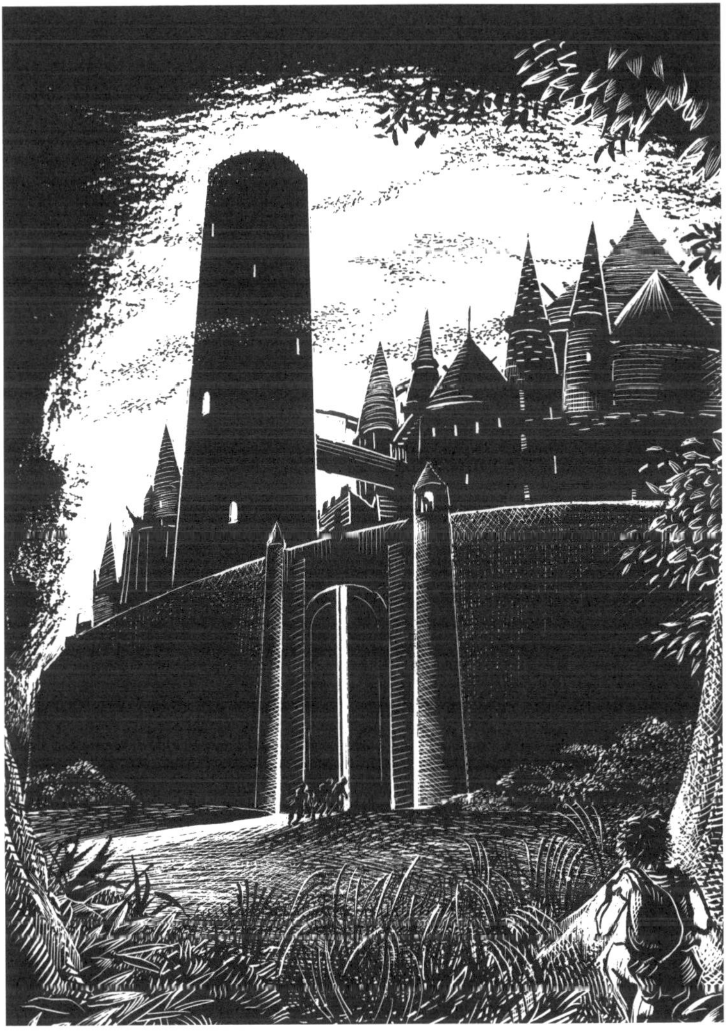

て、たちまち、とらえられてしまうでしょう。それに、厳重な鉄の門をひらくてだては、まったくありませんし、あの高い鉄のへいをよじのぼるなんて、思いもよらないことです。小林君は道のない森の中を大まわりして、ながい時間かかって、城のよこからうしろのほうへまわってみました。しかし、よこにもうしろにも、同じような高い鉄のへいがはりめぐらされ、しのびこむすきまなど、まったくないことがわかりました。

小林君は考えこんでしまいました。いったい、どうすればいいのでしょう。しんぼうづよく見はっていて、ふたたび城門がひらくのを待ち、なんとかくふうしてしのびこむか。しかし、どれほど待てばいいのか、けんとうもつきません。それに、一日いじょうは食糧がつづかないのです。

「あっ、いいことがあるぞ！」

小林君は、じつにうまいことを思いつきました。怪人団の自動車は、森の入り口に、のりすてたままになっています。あすこまでひっかえして、自分であの自動車を運転して、どこか近くの町に出て、東京の明智先生に電話をかければよい。そうすれば、先生じしんでここへのりこんでこられるか、そうでなければ、なにかよい知恵を、さずけてくださるにちがいない。小林君は、自動車のところまでひきかえす決心をしました。自動車の運転には自信があります。明智先生にすすめられて、運転をならっておいたのが、今こそ役に

144

たつのです。

それから、また一時間あまり、例の大袋をかついで、つかれた足をひきずりながら森の中を歩きました。くるときにふみつけたクマザサを目じるしに、道らしい道もないところを、かきわけて通るのですから、ときどき道にまよって、とんでもない方角へまよいこむこともあり、その苦労はなみたいていではありません。

でも、やっとのことで、自動車のおいてあるところまで、たどりつくことができました。小林君は、よろこびいさんで自動車の運転台にとびのり、出発しようとしましたが、そのとき、ふと、あることに気づいてギョッとしました。胸をドキドキさせながら、ガソリンのメーターをしらべました。

ああ、やっぱりそうでした。怪人たちがのんきらしく自動車をすてておいたのには、わけがあったのです。

ガソリンがなくなっていたのです。この分量では、二キロも走れば動かなくなってしまいます。

こんな山の中に、ガソリンスタンドがあるはずはなく、ガソリンが手にはいらなければ、自動車は動かないのです。こんなところへほうりだしておいても、ぬすまれる心配はすこしもなかったのです。怪人たちが、つぎに出発するときには、城の中からガソリンをはこ

んでくるのでしょう。

小林君はガッカリして、運転台にすわりこんだまま、しばらくは、からだを動かす気にもなれませんでした。

山小屋の主

それから、小林少年は自動車をおりて、そこにぼんやりとつっ立ったまま、あたりをながめていましたが、ふと気がつくと、遠くのほうにモヤモヤと動いているものがあるのです。おやっとおもって、よく見ますと、それは白いひとすじの煙でした。むこうの森の中から煙がたちのぼっているのです。

煙が出ているからには、あのへんに人が住んでいるのかもしれない。そう考えると小林君は、にわかに元気づいて、そのほうへ歩きはじめました。やっぱり、道もない森の中を、クマザサをかきわけて歩くのです。煙のあがっているところは、すぐそばのように見えていたのに、森の中へはいっていくと、方角がわからなくなって、なかなかその場所が見つかりませんでしたが、ずいぶん歩きまわったすえ、やっと小さな山小屋を見つけました。

それは、丸太を組んでつくった、七～十平方メートルのほったて小屋ですが、近よっ

て、のぞいてみると、中に人がいるようすなので、入り口に立って声をかけてみました。

すると、「オー」とこたえて、小屋のあるじが出てきました。顔じゅうひげにうずまった、おそろしげな男です。彼は小林君のこじき姿をジロジロながめていましたが、ふしぎそうに、

「おめえのような子どもが、いまじぶん、どうしてこんな山おくへやってきただ。」
とたずねます。

「道にまよったのです。おじさん、ぼくをとめてください。つかれてしまって、おなかがペコペコで、もう歩けません。」

小林君は、あわれっぽくもちかけました。

「ふーん、道にまよったといって、こんな人も通らぬ山おくへまよってくるなんて、おめえ、よっぽどどうかしているぞ。だが、まあいい、こっちへはいるがいい。めしぐれえ、くわしてやるだ。」

こわい顔ににあわぬ、しんせつな男でした。小林君は、例の大袋を持ったまま、小屋の中にはいって、いろりのそばに腰をおろしました。

やがて男は、いろりにかけてあるなべの中から、ぞうすいのようなものをちゃわんによ

147

そって、小林君にたべさせてくれました。小林君は、それをすすりながら、
「おじさんは、こんなところで、なにをしているの？」
と、たずねてみました。
「おれか、おらあ猟師だよ。この山にゃ、いろんな鳥やけだものがいるからな。それをとってふもとの村へ売りにいくだ。それがおれのしょうべえさ。アハハハ……」
と、大きな口をあいて笑いました。顔じゅうひげだらけでまっ黒ですから、ひらいた口の中が、おそろしく赤いように見えました。
「ぼく、道にまよってね、このへんの山ん中を歩きまわったんだよ。そうすると、このむこうのほうに大きな鉄のお城があったよ。おじさん知ってる？」
「知ってるとも。」
「あれ、だれのお城なの？ だれが住んでいるの？」
「ばけものが住んでいるさ。」
「えっ、ばけものだって？」
「カブトムシのばけものだ。この山ん中に、イノシシほどもあるカブトムシのばけものが、ウジャウジャすんでるだ。ふもとの村でもそれを知ってるから、だれもこの山へのぼらねえ。おれたちのなかまの猟師も木こりも、みんな逃げだしてしまった。おれはごうじょう

もんだからな。逃げれえ。いまじゃ、この山ん中に住んでるのは、おれひとりになっちまった。ワハハハ……」

男はまた、大きなまっ赤な口をひらいて、笑いとばすのでした。

「おじさん、そのカブトムシに、であったことあるの？」

「なんどもあるよ。だが、おらあ、カブトムシのばけものだけはうたねえ。たたりがおっかねえからな。カブトムシがあらわれたら、こっちで逃げだすのよ。」

「そのカブトムシが、あの鉄の城にすんでるの？」

「そうだ。城の中にゃ、カブトムシの王さまがいるだ。ほかのカブトムシは、みんなその王さまのけらいだっていうことだ。」

「鉄の門がピッタリしまっているの？」

「おらあ、ひらいているのを、見たことがねえ。あの門がひらくことがあるぞ。いつでもピッタリしまってるんだ。おれは、いっぺん、おっかねえのをがまんして、城の中が見たいとおもってね。それで、おら、あの鉄のへいのまわりを、グルグルまわってみたが、どこにもすきまがねえ。城の中の音でも聞いてやろうとおもったゞ。すると、なあ、小僧、鉄の門に耳をおっつけて、中の音でも聞いてやろうとおもった。するとな、なあ、小僧、おっかねえ音が聞こえただ。何百という、何千人の人が、ないしょ話をしているような、いやあな音だった。

おら、ゾーッとして、いちもくさんに、逃げだしただ。それからというもの、いくら命しらずのおらでも、気味がわるくて、あの城にゃ近よる気がしねえ。遠くからチラッとあの鉄の塔のてっぺんが見えても、おら、おじけをふるって、逃げだすだよ。」
山小屋の主の大男は、目を異様にひからせてあたりを見まわしながら、さもこわそうにいうのでした。

ハトと縄ばしご

それから、小林君は、山男のような猟師から、いろいろのことを聞きだしました。そして、ここが木曾山脈にぞくする、あの高山の山つづきであること、東京からここへ来るのには、どういう道を通るかということなどをたしかめました。
その夜八時ごろ、小林君は、山男が眠ってしまったのを見すまして、例の黒い大きな袋をさげて、そっと山小屋をぬけだし、うらの空き地に出ました。そして、袋の中から、茶つぼを大きくしたようなブリキかんを取りだして、そのふたをひらきました。すると、中からクークーという、みょうな声が聞こえます。小林君は、
「よし、よし、さぞきゅうくつだったろうね。だが、いよいよ、おまえの働くときがきた

んだよ。しっかりやっておくれ。」
といいながら、かんの中に手を入れて、一羽のハトをひきだし、自分のポケットにいれていた、なにか小さなものを取りだして、それをハトの足にくくりつけました。
「さあ、しっかり飛ぶんだよ。そら……」
手をはなしますと、ハトは、しばらく考えているようすでしたが、やがて、大きな羽をひろげて、パッと飛びたちました。そして、見るまに、森の高い木の上に、姿をけしてしまいました。まっ暗な夜中のことですから、ハトのゆくてを見さだめることはできません。ただ、その羽音で、ぶじに大空へまいあがったことを察するばかりです。
「これでよしと。……さあ、いよいよ大冒険だぞ。」
小林君は、力づよくひとりごとをいって、身じたくに取りかかるのでした。例の大きな袋の中から、黒いシャツ、黒いズボン、黒い手ぶくろ、黒い地下たびを取りだし、今まで着ていた、こじきのボロ服をぬいで、それと着かえ、頭から足のさきまで、ピッタリ身についた、黒ずくめの姿とかわりました。黒ずきんは、顔ぜんたいをつつむようになっていて、目のところに、二つのほそい穴があいているばかりです。小林君は袋の中から、黒ビロードの、はばのひろいバンドのようなものを取りだし、それをしっかりと腰にまきつけました。このバンドの内側には、たくさんのリッ

クがついていて、探偵七つ道具がはいっているのです。

そしてぬぎすてたこじきの服を、小さくたたんで袋にいれ、それをそこの木の枝にかけておいて、いよいよ、大冒険の第一歩をふみだすことになったのです。

目ざすのは、いうまでもなく、怪人の住む鉄の城です。小林君は腰のバンドから、小型の懐中電灯を取りだして、ときどきパッとあたりをてらしながら進むのですが、道もないまっ暗な森の中ですから、いくども方向をまちがえ、やっと鉄塔の見えるところへ出るのに、三十分もかかってしまいました。

そこは森にかこまれた、ひろい空き地ですから、闇といっても、空のほのあかりで黒い巨人のような鉄の城のかたちが、クッキリとうきあがって見えるのです。

その空き地へ出ると、小林君は懐中電灯をけして、城のほうへ近づいていきました。こちらは、頭から足のさきまで、ピッタリ身についたまっ黒な姿ですから、たとえ城の中から、敵がのぞいていたとしても、気づかれる心配はありません。

城の鉄のへいのそばに近よると、小林君は、腰のバンドから、例の絹ひもの縄ばしごを取りだしました。はしごといっても、これは黒い絹糸をたくさんよりあわせた、細いけれども、じょうぶな一本のひもなのです。それに、四十センチぐらいのかんかくで、大きなむすび玉ができています。そこへ足の指をかけてのぼるのです。また、この絹ひものはじ

には、鉄でできた、ふしぎなかぎのようなものがついていて、どんなところへでも、ひっかかるようになっています。
　小林君は、その絹ひもをのばし、鉄のかぎに近いところを右手に持って、高い城のへいを見あげました。へいの高さは五メートルもあるのです。その頂上をめがけてねらいをつけ、ヤッとばかりに、鉄のかぎをなげあげました。すると、かぎがへいのうらの出っぱりに、カチッとひっかかり、いくらひっぱっても、はずれないようになったのです。
　小林君のまっ黒なこびとのような姿は、その絹ひもをつたわって、スルスルと鉄のへいをのぼり、たちまち頂上にたどりつきました。そして、かぎをかけかえ絹ひもをへいの内側にたらし、また、それをつたって城内の地面におりたち、たくみにひもをあやつって、へいの上のかぎをはずすと、それを手もとにたぐりよせ、小さくまるめて、腰のバンドの中へおしこみました。十メートルもある絹ひもですが、まるめると、ひとにぎりになってしまうのです。
　城の中はまっ暗で、シーンとしずまりかえっています。しばらくあたりを見まわしていますと、ずっとむこうのほうに、ぼんやりと四角な赤っぽい光が見えました。建物の窓の中に、あかりがついているらしいのです。小林君は足音をしのばせて、そのほうに近づいていきました。

カブトムシ大王

　城の中には、大きな建物が、まっ黒な怪物のようにそびえていましたが、近よってみると、それは大きな石をつみかさねてつくった石の建物でした。

　光のさしていた窓の戸は、ひらいたままです。城のまわりに、あんな高い鉄のへいがめぐらしてあるので、中の建物は、しまりをする必要もないのでしょう。

　小林君はその窓わくにとびついて、両手でからだをささえながら、そっと、窓の中をのぞいてみますと、そこは大広間とでもいうような、ガランとした広い部屋で、むこうの壁の柱に石油ランプがつりさげてあって、その赤ちゃけた光が、部屋の中を、ぼんやりとてらしているのでした。

　しばらく待っても、だれもはいってくるようすがないので、小林君は、そのまま窓をのりこえて、部屋の中にはいりこみました。

　部屋のむこうがわのドアのところへ行って、おしてみると、これもなんなくひらきましたので、そのまま暗い廊下を、奥のほうへたどっていきました。

　長い廊下は、右に左にいくどもまがって、ずっと奥のほうへつづいていました。その両

側にはたくさんのドアがしまっていて、その中には、人が寝ているようすでした。かぎのかかっていないドアを、そっとほそめにひらいて、中をのぞいてみましたが、まっ暗で、なにも見えませんけれども、たしかに、人が寝ているらしく感じられたのです。

そうして、廊下を奥のほうへはいっていきますと、そのつきあたりに、たてにスーッと、糸のようなほそい光が見えました。ドアがピッタリしまらないで、そのすきまから、部屋の中のあかりが、もれているのです。

小林君は、しのび足でそこへ近より、ドアのすきまに目をあてて、中をのぞいてみました。

それは、りっぱな広い部屋でした。部屋のかざりつけが、みんな金色にピカピカひかっているのです。てんじょうからは、宝石をちりばめたような、ガラス玉のかざりのある、シャンデリアがさがって、それに、十数本のろうそくがもえています。その光が、無数のガラス玉を通して、キラキラかがやいているのです。

部屋のまんなかには、まっ赤なビロードをはった、でっかい安楽イスがすえてあって、そこに、ふしぎな人物がこしかけていました。それは、見おぼえのある「のぞきじいさん」でした。このお話のはじめに、小林君にのぞきカラクリで、鉄塔王国のけしきを見せてくれた、あの魔法つかいのようなじいさんでした。頭の毛はまっ白で、胸までたれたフ

サフサとした白ひげのあるあのじいさんが、やっぱり、はでなはなしまの洋服を着て、そのりっぱないスにこしかけていたのです。

イスのまえの、まっ赤なじゅうたんの上に、二ひきの巨大なカブトムシが、よこたわっていました。一ぴきは、人間のおとなより大きいやつで、それはグッタリと、寝そべっているように見えました。中には人間がはいっていないで、ただビニールのカブトムシのぬけがらだけが、そこにおいてあるらしいのです。

もう一ぴきのカブトムシはもっと小さくて、中には人間の子どもでもはいっているらしくおもわれましたが、このほうは、モゾモゾ動いているのです。ほんとうに子どもがはいっているのかもしれません。

「ワハハハハ……」

とつぜん、安楽イスにかけているじいさんが、大きな口をあけて、白ひげをふるわせて、びっくりするような声で笑いました。

「おい、どうだ、くたびれたかね。おまえにいっておくが、おまえは、きょうから鉄塔王国の兵隊だ。カブトムシ軍の新兵だ。わかったか。きょうは、その訓練の第一日だ。これから毎日、はげしい訓練をうける。そして、だんだん、えらい兵隊になるのだ。兵隊を卒業すると、*将校になる。将校になると、わしの事業の手助けをさせる。東京へも、大阪へ

＊軍隊で、少尉以上の武官

156

も、いや、もっと遠くまで、わしといっしょに遠征するのだ。そしてカブトムシ軍隊の力を、世間のやつに見せてやるのだ。わかったかね。

わしは、この鉄塔王国のカブトムシの威力を日本じゅうに、見せつけてやりたいのだ。

わしは鉄塔王国の国王だ。カブトムシ大王さまだ。わかったか。おまえのおやじは、わしの命令にしたがわなかった。軍用金を出さなかった。その罰として、おまえをわしの国のカブトムシ軍の兵隊にしたのだ。わしの命令にしたがわぬやつへの見せしめにするのだ。

カブトムシ軍隊の訓練は、はげしいぞ。わしは新兵が入隊した第一日に、こうして訓示をあたえ、それから、わしみずから、カブトムシの動きかたを、やってみせることにしている。今夜はすこしおそくなった。もう九時半だ。しかし、いちおう、やってみせることにする。こういうものを着て、虫のように走ったり、とんだりするんだから、なかなかむずかしい。この鉄塔王国の将校のうちにも、わしだけの働きのできるやつは、ひとりもいないのだ。さあ、よく見ておくがいい。」

白ひげのじいさんは、そういって立ちあがると、赤いじゅうたんの上においてあった、ビニールの大カブトムシのからをひっくりかえして、腹のほうの出入り口をひらき、服を着たまま、足のほうからその腹のさけめへ、はいりこんでいくのです。そして、頭まですっかりはいってしまって、中から腹のさけめをとじると、あおむけになっていたのを、

クルッとひっくりかえり、ガサガサとはいだすのでした。

それから、じつにおそろしいカブトムシの運動がはじまりました。

頭にはえたおそろしい一本のツノ、ギクシャクした長いあし、まっ黒な背中に白いどくろもようのある、巨大なカブトムシは、おそろしい速さで、部屋の中をかけまわりました。

かけるにつれて、あしのかんせつがギシギシとなり、ヌーッとのびたまっ黒な長いツノが、なにかをつき落とすように、クイクイと、あがったりさがったりするのでした。

カブトムシのかけまわる速さは、ますますくわわってきました。今はじゅうたんの上を走るだけでなくて、安楽イスや、そこにあるテーブルの上にかけあがり、かけおりるのです。ちょうどいつかの夜、銀座の大通りで、自動車の車体をのりこして進んだのと、同じいきおいでした。

やがて、もっとおそろしいことが、おこりました。カブトムシは、部屋の壁を、よじのぼりはじめたのです。ほんとうのカブトムシは、壁でも天井でも、自由にはいまわります。

この人間カブトムシも、それと同じことをやろうというのです。

巨大な、まっ黒なからだが、ガリガリとおそろしい音をたてて、壁ぎわのたなを足場にのぼりはじめました。いくども失敗して中途からころがり落ちたすえ、とうとう天井まではいあがりました。そしてそこから、パッとじゅうたんの上へ落ちるのです。ほんとうの

158

カブトムシが、木の枝から落ちるように、まっさかさまに落ちてくるのです。それを、いくどもくりかえすのです。

天井から、おそろしい音をたてて落ちるときには、たいてい、背中を下に腹を上にして、モガモガやっているうちに、ピョイと、まともな姿勢になるのです。これも、よほど練習しなければ、できないわざにちがいありません。

二十分ばかり思うぞんぶんにとびまわったあとで、カブトムシはやっと運動をやめてあおむけになったかとおもうと、例の腹のさけめから、ぬっと白ひげのじいさんの顔があらわれました。見ると、その顔は汗でビッショリです。

じいさんは、カブトムシのからだからすっかりぬけだすと、もとの安楽イスにこしかけました。そして、そこへ、うずくまって、じっとしていた子どもカブトムシに話しかけました。

「どうだ、わかったか。カブトムシはこんなぐあいに動くのだ。おまえには、まだとてもできないが、あすから、ほかの兵隊たちといっしょに訓練をしてやる。わしがむちをふるって、ピシリ、ピシリと、背中をたたきつけながら訓練してやる。

では、もう部屋へひきとって、寝るがいい。十二号室だ。わかっているだろうな。さあ行きなさい。」

そういわれると、かわいそうな子どもカブトムシは、モソモソ動きはじめました。そして、ドアのほうにむかって、はってくるのです。ドアのすきまから、むちゅうになってのぞいていた小林君は、はっとしてとびのき、廊下の闇の中に身をかくしました。

ドアがひらいたかとおもうと、すぐにピッタリとしまりました。

暗闇といっても、どこか遠くのほうのあかりが、そのへんをうす明るくしているので、やっと物のかたちを見わけることができます。

しばらくすると、壁に身をつけて、かくれている小林君の前を、黒いカブトムシが、ゴソゴソとはっていくのが見えました。さっきの子どもカブトムシです。闇の中にほんのりと、背中のどくろのもようがういて見えます。まっ暗な中を、同じように黒い巨大な妖虫が、モゾモゾとはっていきます。ハッキリ見えないだけに、それはなんともいえない気味わるさでした。

小林君は、闇の中にうごめく、この妖虫のあとをおって、壁ぎわをすこしずつ歩きだしました。

なぜでしょう。

読者諸君は、とっくにおわかりですね。その子どもカブトムシの中には、怪人団にさらわれた、あの高橋賢二少年がとじこめられていたからなのです。

160

むちのひびき

小林少年は、子どもカブトムシのあとをつけて、十二号室にはいりました。それから、その部屋の中で、どんなことがあったかは略します。なぜなら、それは、まもなくわかるときがくるからです。

お話は、そのあくる朝、同じ石の建物の中の、大広間でおこったできごとにうつります。

その朝、大広間には、ピシッ、ピシッと、むちの音がひびいていました。

その広間の中を、十数ひきの大カブトムシが、ゾロゾロと行列をつくってはいまわっていました。その輪になった行列のまんなかに、はでな、しまの洋服を着た、白ひげのじいさんが手に長いむちを持って立っているのです。

それは、いつか賢二少年が、にいさんの壮一君といっしょに、おうちのそばの町かどで、のぞきカラクリをのぞいたときの光景とそっくりでした。そして、あののぞきカラクリを見せてくれたじいさんこそ、いま、この部屋のまんなかに、むちを手にして立っているじいさんと同じ人だったのです。

「そら、しっかりあるくんだ。おい、十一号、むきがちがうぞ。列をはなれてはいるな

ピシリーッ。おそろしいむちが、十一号とよばれたカブトムシの背中にとびました。
「こんどは走るんだぞ。おくれたやつはむちのおみまいだ。そら、いいかかけあしっ……」
号令とともに、むちが空中でピシッ、ピシッとなりました。
十数ひきの巨大なカブトムシたちは、むちをおそれてかけだしました。いくつともしれぬあしの床をこする音が、ザーッというような、異様なひびきをたてるのです。巨大な妖虫どもが、大きな輪をかいてグルグル、グルグル、広間の中をかけまわるありさまは、じつに、なんともいえないへんてこな、うす気味のわるい光景でした。とつぜん、
そして、かけあしで、三度ほどまわったときでした。
「とまれっ……」
じいさんが、はげしい声で号令をかけました。
「おい、十二号、こちらへこい。」
そして、十二号の背中に、ピシリッとむちがあたりました。
「おかしいぞ。おまえ、いつのまに、そんなにうまくなった。きのうはいったばかりの兵隊が、そんなに走れるはずがない。おかしいぞ。おい、あおむきになれ。そして、顔を出してみろ。」

また、むちがとびました。しかし、列をはなれた十二号のカブトムシは、じっとしたまま、身動きもしません。
「いよいよおかしいぞ。きさま、だれかにかわってもらったな。だれだ、この子どもの身がわりになったやつは。さあ、出てこい。顔を見せろ。出ないと……」
ピシリーッ、二度三度、むちが背中にとびました。それでも、十二号は、ごうじょうにだまりかえっています。そこにうずくまったまま、てこでも動かないというかっこうです。
そのときです。部屋の外の廊下のほうから、ただならぬもの音が近づいてきました。
「さあ、こっちへこい。きさま、けしからんやつだ。ベッドの下なんかにかくれて、訓練をなまけやがって、……閣下、きのうはいった十二号の新兵が、ベッドの下にかくれているのを見つけて、ひっぱってきました。」
賢二少年が、ふたりのあらくれ男に両手をとられて、部屋の入り口にあらわれました。じいさんのおもだった子分なのでしょう。ジャンパーを着た、人相のわるいやつです。これがこの王国の『将校』なのかもしれません。
「うーん、やっぱりそうだったか。するとここにいる十二号はなに者だ。おい、おまえたち、こいつをひんむいてくれ。」
じいさんは、白いひげをふるわせてどなりました。ふたりの男は、その命令を聞くと、

賢二少年をじいさんにわたしておいて、いきなり、十二号のカブトムシにとびかかっていきました。そして、カブトムシをとらえて、しばらくもつれあっていましたが、やがて、ふたりの男の口から、おどろきのさけび声がほとばしりました。

「やっ、きさま、だれだ。どこから、やって来たのだっ。」

十二号のカブトムシの、腹の中からあらわれたのは、ほかならぬ小林少年でした。小林君は賢二少年をかわいそうにおもって、身がわりをつとめてやったのですが、十二号の身のこなしが、かよわい賢二君にしてはあまりうますぎたので、替え玉がバレてしまったのです。そのうえ、かくれていた賢二少年まで見つかっては、もうどうすることもできません。

老魔術師の正体

「ワハハハ……、おおかた、そんなことだろうとおもっていた。きさま、手の小林だな。チンピラのくせに、だいたんなやつだ。よくここへしのびこんだ。うん、わかったぞ。きさま、いつもの手をつかったな。わしらの自動車のトランクの中へかくれて、ついてきたんだな。

だが、こうして見つけられたら、もうだめだ。かわいそうだが、鉄塔王国のおきてにしたがって、厳罰にしょする。わしの国には死刑はない。血を見るのがきらいだ。だから、この国の兵隊は、鉄砲やピストルや剣は持たないのだ。そのかわりに、カブトムシの妖術を武器にしているのだ。しかし、この国の厳罰というのは死刑よりもおそろしいのだ。死刑ではないが、やっぱり命がけの罰だ。さあ、このふたりの子どもをひっくくって、さるぐつわをかませろ！」

怪老人は、はげしい声で命令をくだしました。ふたりのあらくれ男が、用意していた縄をとりだして、小林少年と賢二君に近づいてきました。

そのときです。うっかりしていた怪老人のからだへ、黒いものがパッとぶつかっていました。黒いふくめんはとられていましたが、首から下は足のさきまで黒ずくめの小林少年が、怪老人にとびついていったのです。そして、あっというまに、老人の長い白ひげとしらが頭を、ひきちぎってしまいました。それは、つけひげとカツラだったのです。その下からあらわれたのは、まだ若わかしい男の顔でした。

小林少年の目にもとまらぬはやわざに、さすがの悪人も「あっ」とさけんで、おもわず両手で顔をおさえましたが、もう、まにあいません。こんどは、小林君のほうが笑うばんでした。

「アハハハ……、カブトムシ大王っていうのは、きみのことだったのか。それにしても、まずい変装だね。変装の名人にも、にあわないじゃないか」

「なに、変装の名人だと？」

老人にばけていた首領は、なぜか、ギョッとしたように聞きかえしました。

「明智先生には、はじめからわかっていたんだよ。ただ、いわなかっただけさ……」

「なんだと……」

小林少年は、また、さもゆかいそうに笑いました。そして、あいての顔を、まっ正面から指さしながら、

「怪人二十面相！　それとも、四十面相とよんだほうが、お気にめすのかい。……こんなおかしなまねをして、世間をさわがせるやつが、二十面相のほかにあるものか。いくら変装したって、そのやりくちで、すぐにわかっちゃうよ。ハハハ……、こんどもきみのまけだったね。きみのねらいは、いつも明智先生だ。世間をさわがせておいて、明智先生がどうすることもできないのを見て、手をたたいて笑いたいのだ。明智先生をまかしたいのがきみの念願なのだ。ところが、こんどもだめだったねえ。こうして、ちゃんと見やぶられてしまったじゃないか。

しかし、悪人たちが、小林君に、いつまでもかってなことをしゃべらせておくはずがあ

166

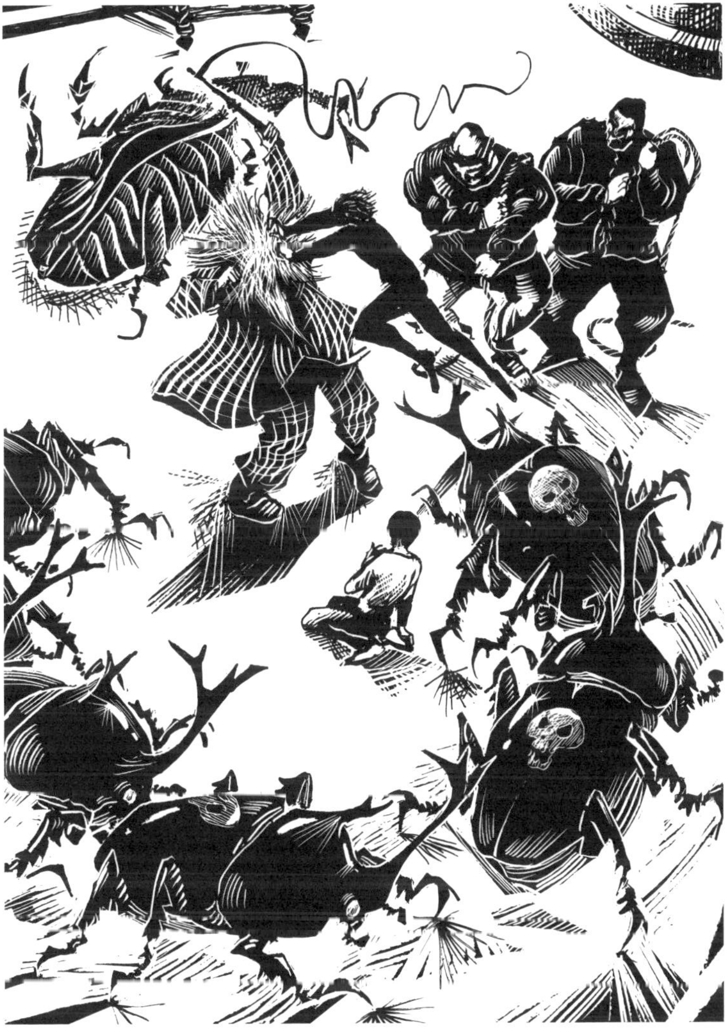

りません。そのとき、ふたりのあらくれ男が、両方から小林君をだきすくめ、グルグルと縄をかけてしまいました。
　老人にばけていた二十面相は、それを見るとさもここちよさそうに、また大笑いしました。
「ワハハハ……、こんどは、おれの笑うばんだよ。かわいそうに。りこうらしく見えても、やっぱり子どもだねえ。敵の城の中へ、たったひとりでとびこんできて、おれの正体をあばこうという勇気にはかんしんするが、さて、そうしてしばられてしまったら、もうおしまいじゃないか。やいて食おうとにて食おうと、こっちの思うままだぜ。ハハハ……、きのどくだねえ。いよいよ、おれの国の、いちばんおもい刑罰にしょせられるのだ。……おい、このふたりのチンピラを、鉄塔の頂上へ、おいあげてしまえっ。」
　二十面相は、そこでおそろしい表情になって、はげしい声で命令しました。
　そのときには、賢二君も、小林少年と同じようにしばられていました。そして、ふたりのあらくれ男が、二少年の縄じりをとって、大広間の外へ引っぱっていくのです。二十面相も、ニタニタ笑いながら、そのあとからついていきます。
　ああ、二少年は、これからどんなおそろしいめにあうのでしょう。二十面相がいったとおり、小林君はすこし知恵がたりなかったのではないでしょうか。いくら敵の正体をあば

いても、ふたたび生きて帰れないようになっては、せっかくの苦心も水のあわではありませんか。

ワシのえじき

石の壁の長い廊下をいくつもまがって、行きついたのはまるい鉄の部屋でした。鉄塔の一階らしいのです。壁には黒い鉄板がはりつめてあり、きゅうな鉄のはしごがついています。

「さあ、これをのぼるんだ。」

二十面相のさしずで、ふたりのあらくれ男は二少年をおいたてて、そのはしごをのぼりました。二階、三階、四階、みんなまるい鉄の部屋です。そして、五つめのはしごをのぼると、パッとあたりが明るくなって、鉄塔の屋上に出ました。

まるい床には、いらめんに鉄板がはりつめてあり、それをとりまいて、ひくい鉄のてすりのようなものがついています。

「下をのぞかしてやれ。」

二十面相のことばに、男たちはふたりの少年を屋上のはじへつれていって、てすりにか

らだをおしつけ、下をのぞかせました。

　小林少年は、それほどでもありませんが、賢二君は、まっさおになってしまいました。鉄塔の壁が、まっ縦にはるか下のほうまでつづいていて、まるで、高い高い断崖のはじに、立っているような気持ちです。おしりのへんがくすぐったくなって、足がブルブルふるえてきました。

「どうだ、わかったか。きさまたちは、ぜったいにここから逃げだすことはできないのだ。ここは空中のろうやだ。鉄格子もなにもないあけっぱなしだが、こんな厳重なろうやはない。逃げようとすれば、命がなくなるだけだ。まあ、ここでゆっくりやすんでいるがいい。アハハ……、それじゃああばよ。いまはそれほどでもないが、そのうちにだんだん、このろうやのおそろしさがわかってくるよ。」

　二十面相は、ふたりの男をさきにおりさせ、自分はあとから、鉄ばしごをおりました。そして、屋上への出入り口についている鉄のふたを両手でおろし、そのすきまから顔だけを出して、にやにや笑いながらいいました。

「おい、小林君、ねんのためにいっておくが、この山にはワシがいるんだよ。きみたちはその大ワシと、たたかわなければならないのだ。死にものぐるいにたたかって、きみたちの力がつきたときが、最期だよ。ワシのえじきになってしまうのだ。」

そして、バタンとはしごの上の鉄のふたがしまり、カチカチとかぎのかかる音がしました。

ふたりの少年は、こうして、鉄塔の屋上にとじこめられてしまったのです。

「小林さん、どうすればいいの？　ぼくこわいよ。」

賢二君は、泣きだしそうな顔で、小林少年にとりすがりました。

「だいじょうぶだよ。ぼくたちはまだ、まけたんじゃない。きっと、二十面相をやっつけてみせるよ。しばらく、がまんしているんだ。」

小林少年の自信ありげなことばに、賢二君もいくらか元気をとりもどしましたが、それにしても小林君は、いったいどうして、二十面相をやっつけることができるのでしょう。

小林君は、例の絹ひもの縄ばしごをつかって、鉄塔をおりるつもりでしょうか。とてもそんなことはできません。絹ひもの長さは十メートルしかないのに、鉄塔は数十メートルの高さです。

「小林さん、ぼくたち、どうして、ここを逃げるの？」

「待つんだよ。」

「え、待つって？」

「今晩か、おそくとも、あすの朝までに、おもしろいことがおこるんだ。それまでのしん

171

「ぼうだよ。……ごらん、空がまっさおによく晴れているじゃないか。歌でもうたおうよ。」

小林君は、のんきなことをいって、なにか歌をうたいはじめました。

それから、日がくれるまで、じつに長い長い一日でした。歌をうたったり、なぞなぞあてっこをしたり、しまいには、賢二君の学科のおさらいまでして、気をひきたてようとしましたが、そのうちに、ふたりとも、おなかがへってきました。そして、日のくれるじぶんには、ものをいう元気もなくなって、鉄のてすりによりかかり、足をなげだしたまま、グッタリとなっていました。

もう、あたりはまっ暗です。遠くのほうから、もののきしるような音、うなり声のようなものが聞こえてきます。山にすんでいる鳥やけだもののなき声です。

小林君は、てすりにもたれながら、からだをねじまげるようにして、まっ暗な森の中を、あちらこちらと、注意ぶかく見まわしていましたが、なにか、こころ待ちにしているようすです。

そうしてまた何時間かがすぎさりました。ふたりともつかれているので、ときどきうとうと眠りますが、すぐにはっと目をさまします。寝てしまっては、たいへんだとおもうからです。

もう、真夜中を、とっくにすぎていました。つめたい風が吹いてきました。耳をすます

と、まっ暗な下界からは、けだものの　うなり声らしい音が、だんだん近づいてくるようにおもわれます。

とつぜん、小林少年が「あっ」と、小さくさけびました。闇の中をすかして見ると、ずっとむこうにホタルのような小さな光が、パッパッと、ついたり消えたりしていたのです。

小林君は、大いそぎで立ちあがると、バンドの七つ道具の中から、懐中電灯をとりだしました。そして、それを高くささげながら、パッパッと、つけたり消したりするのでした。賢二君も、これを見ると、びっくりして立ちました。そして、小林少年のそばによってたずねるのです。

「小林さん、どうしたの？　なにをしているの？」
「電灯の光で、モールス信号＊をやっているんだよ。ほら、よくごらん、むこうでも、ずっとむこうのほうに、ホタルのような光が見えるだろう。あれは懐中電灯だよ。むこうでも、信号を知っているんだ。」
「えっ、じゃあ、あすこに人がいるんだね。いったい、あれはだれなの？」
「みかたjust だよ。待ちに待った明智先生さ。」
「えっ、明智先生？」

＊アメリカのサミュエル・モースが考案した通信符号。長短二つの組み合わせによって文字をあらわす。トン・ツーともいう

173

「賢二君、ぼくはね、ここへくるときに、明智先生の事務所でかっている伝書バトをつれてきたんだよ。そのハトのあしに、この鉄の城のある場所を、くわしく書いた通信をくくりつけて、ゆうべ、はなしてやったのさ。その通信がとどいて、明智先生が助けにきてくださったのだよ。先生ひとりじゃない。長野県の警察から、おおぜいの警官隊もきているんだって。いまの懐中電灯の信号で、それがわかったんだよ。もうだいじょうぶだ。賢二君、ぼくたちはたすかったよ。」

「わあ、すてき。伝書バトを飛ばすなんて、やっぱり小林さんは、えらいねえ。」

賢二少年も、にわかに元気になってきました。

通信がすむと、むこうのホタルのような光は、パッタリ消えたまま、ふたたびあらわれませんでした。闇の中を警官の一隊が、明智探偵をせんとうにたてて、鉄の城のまわりへ、ヒシヒシとせめよせているのでしょう。

今にも、そのさわぎがおこるかとおもうと、小林君は胸をドキドキさせながら、耳をすませてようすをうかがっていましたが、いつまでたっても、下の城の中の建物は、シーンとしずまりかえっているばかりです。

これはいったい、どうしたことでしょう。もう、さっきから一時間以上たちました。東の空のほうが、うっすら明るくなってきました。夜明けにまもないのです。

174

しかし、そのとき、明智探偵と警官隊とは、やっぱり、縄ばしごによって、つぎつぎに鉄のへいをのりこえ、城の中へしのびこんでいたのです。そして怪人団のゆだんを見すまして、悪人たちをひとりのこらずとらえようと、ひそかに計画をめぐらしていたのです。

そうとは知らないものですから、塔の上の小林君は、ひとりでもどかしがっていました。

が、するとそのとき、空のかなたから、ブーンというぶきみな音がひびいてきました。

「なんだろう」と、ふしぎにおもって、その方角を見つめていますと、うす明るくなった空の一方に、異様なかたちの黒い怪物があらわれて、それがだんだんこちらへ、近づいてくるのが、かすかに見えました。なんだか、大きな鳥のようなかたちです。ああ、もしかしたら、これが二十面相のいった、あのおそろしい人食いワシではないのでしょうか。

大ワシのような怪物は、この塔の上をめがけて、とんでくるらしいのです。その黒い影が、大きくなってきます。ブルン・ブルンと風を切る羽の音が、ものすごいひびきです。ふたりの運命は、どうなるのでしょう。

ああ、それは、はたして大ワシだったのでしょうか。

妖虫の最期

鉄の城の建物という建物は、数十人の警官隊にとりかこまれ、カブトムシ王国はじまっていらいの大混乱がおこっていました。さらわれてきた少年たちの兵隊は、だれも手むかいなどしません。みんな警官のみかたになって、怪人団のおとなたちの部屋の、あんない役をつとめました。

怪人団の悪人どもは、さすがにがんこにてむかいをしました。深夜の大戦争でした。城の中には、秘密の地下道だとか、いろいろなしかけがあって、二十数人の悪人どもをすっかり捕らえるには、二時間あまりもかかったほどで、警官隊に数人のけが人もでました。

そうして、すっかりしばりあげてしまって、少年たちに、もうほかに悪人はいないかとたずねますと、かんじんの鉄塔王国の首領がいないという答えでした。つまり、怪人二十面相だけが、どこかへ姿をくらましてしまったのです。いや、姿の見えないのは、二十面相ばかりではありません。名探偵明智小五郎も、どこかへくもがくれしてしまって、いくらさがしてみても、見つからないのでした。

そのとき、明智探偵は、怪人二十面相と一騎うちの勝負をしていたのです。二十面相は、

すきを見て、ただひとり鉄塔のほうへ逃げていきました。明智ははやくも、それを見つけて追跡したのです。おわれていると気づいた二十面相は、とある小部屋へ逃げこんで、中からドアにかぎをかけてしまいました。明智は、からだごとそのドアにぶつかって、とうとうそれをやぶりましたが、たった二、三分のあいだに、どこへ逃げたのか、部屋の中には、だれもいなくなっていました。出入り口は、今やぶったドアのほかにはありません。

明智は四方の壁をたたきまわって、秘密の通路でもあるのではないかとしらべましたが、べつにあやしいところもないのです。

そのとき、天井のほうに、みょうな音がしました。「さては」とおもって、懐中電灯でてらしますと、天井から、ドシンとおそろしい音をたてて、一ぴきの巨大なカブトムシが、目の前に落ちてきました。

二十面相は、明智がドアをやぶっているわずかのひまに、その部屋においてあったカブトムシのからを身につけて、とくいのわざで、壁をはいあがってかくれたのでしたが、いつまでも壁をはっていくことはできません。やがて力がつきて、床の上に落ちたのです。

それから、巨大なカブトムシと明智探偵との、おっかけっこがはじまりました。カブトムシはスルリと身をかわして廊下に出ると、鉄塔のほうへ、おそろしい速さで走っていくのです。

177

カブトムシは鉄塔の一階にかけこむと、例の鉄のはしごをのぼりはじめました。二階、三階、四階、つぎは屋上です。その屋上への鉄ばしごにとりついたカブトムシは、明智探偵を見おろして、おそろしい笑い声をたてました。
「ワハハハ……、明智先生、おれをおいつめたとおもって、とくいになっているね。だがおれのほうには、武器があるんだ。きみを、あっといわせる武器があるんだ。おい、明智先生、この上の屋上には、だれがいるとおもう。きみのだいじな弟子の小林と、それから賢二が、空中のろうやにとじこめてあるんだ。ふたりの子どもが人質だ。きさまが、おれをとらえようとすれば、このふたりを塔の上からつき落としてしまう。さすがの明智先生も、こうなっては、手だしもできまい。ワハハハ……、例によって、これがおれのおくの手だよ。あがっていきましたが、二十面相のカブトムシは、そこの鉄のふたをかぎでひらき、屋上へはいいのこして、
　ワハハハ……」
あがっていきましたが、二十面相のカブトムシは、そこの鉄のふたをかぎでひらき、屋上へはいあがっていきましたが、「あっ」と、おどろきのさけび声をたてました。
　そのころ、夜は白々とあけて、鉄塔の屋上は、もう明るくなっていました。そのひと目で見える屋上に、小林少年と賢二少年の姿が、どこにも見あたらなかったのです。二十面相のカブトムシは、あわてふためいて、屋上をかこむ鉄のてすりを、おそろしい速さでさ

がしまわりました。しかし、てすりの外に、身をかくしているようすもありません。
まったく、ありえないことがおこったのです。屋上のただひとつの出入り口には、ちゃんとかぎがかかっていました。塔からとびおりるはずはありません。そんなことをすれば命がないのです。ではどこへかくれたのか。いや、かくれる場所なんて、ぜったいにありません。ああ、ふたりの少年は、魔法をつかって煙となって、空へまいのぼってしまったのでしょうか。

そう考えて思わず空を見あげたとき、その空のかなたから、ブーンという異様な音がひびいてきました。そして、一羽の巨大な鳥が、こちらへ近づいてくるのです。いや鳥ではありません。もう夜があけたので、その姿がはっきり見わけられます。それは一台のヘリコプターでした。

ヘリコプターは、みるみる鉄塔の真上にきて、透明な乗員席がよく見えるほどの近さにありました。それを見ると、二十面相のカブトムシはふたたび、「あっ」と、さけび声をたてないではいられませんでした。その透明な乗員席には、操縦士のほかに、小林少年と賢二少年がのりこんで、にこにこしながら塔上の怪物を見おろしていたからです。

さっき、二少年をめがけて飛んできたのは、大ワシではなくて、このヘリコプターだったのです。むろん明智探偵のはからいで、塔上の二少年をすくうために、長野県警察の手

で、近くの町からの電話連絡によって、松本市の新聞社からよびよせたものでした。そして、ヘリコプターから、縄ばしごをおろして、ふたりをすくいあげたのです。

　そうこうするうちに、明智探偵をさがしていた警官たちが鉄塔に気づいて、塔の一階にかけつけ、鉄ばしごをふみながら、屋上へおしよせてきました。屋上はもう警官でいっぱいです。

　二十面相は、もうどうすることもできません。警官たちにつかまってしまうばかりです。塔上に進退きわまった巨大な妖虫は、ジリジリとあとじさりをして、一方のすみの鉄のてすりに、からだをくっつけてしまいました。

　つぎの瞬間には、おそろしいことがおこりました。カブトムシは、てすりをのりこえたのです。明智探偵も、おおぜいの警官たちも、おもわず、「あっ」と、声をたてました。しかし、もうおそかったのです。

　巨大なカブトムシは、てすりの外側にしばらくしがみついていましたが、やがてスーッと、目もくらむ数十メートルの地上へと、矢のように落ちていきました。そのとき、かすかに、「あばよ！」という声が聞こえたようにおもわれました。

　これが、日本じゅうをさわがせたカブトムシ大王、怪人二十面相の、あわれな最期だったのです。

180

解説

のぞきカラクリの世界

戸川　安宣（編集者）

あなたが、たとえば本書の後半の舞台となる木曾山中のような山奥の、満天の星空の下に友だちといっしょにいると思ってください。都会では見られないような数々の星が空いっぱいにきらきらと輝いています。

そのとき、友だちがやおら天体望遠鏡をとりだし、星空にむかってレンズをのぞきこみました。そして「うわーっ！」と感嘆の声をあげました。

肉眼で見てもすばらしい星空です。理科の教科書や図鑑でしか見たことのない天の川もはっきりと見ることができます。

その星空を天体望遠鏡でのぞけば、いったいどんな世界が見えてくるというのでしょうか。もう、早くのぞきたくてたまりません。

「ねえねえ早く、ぼくにも見せてよ」

もうじっとしていられない……そういう感じ、わかりますよ、ね。

望遠鏡で見る世界——それがこんなにわくわくさせられるのは、なぜでしょう？　……そう、たしかにそれも望遠鏡は遠くのものが近くに、小さなものが大きく見える。……そう、たしかにそれもありますが、もうひとつ忘れていけないのは、レンズの穴で切りとられた丸い空間、それはのぞいている自分しか見ることのできない世界だということなのです。そしてそのレンズのなかには、肉眼では見ることのできない世界が開けているのです。

本書のはじまりのところで、のぞきカラクリをひく奇妙なおじいさんが登場します。おなじみ少年探偵団の団長で明智探偵の助手、小林芳雄少年が興味をひかれてのぞいてみると、そこにはなんともいえない恐ろしい情景が展開されていたのです。どことも知れぬ山奥に、お城のような建物が建っています。そしてそのまわりに、カブトムシがうじゃじゃとうごめいているのです……。

なんとも恐ろしい、そして魅力的な物語のはじまりではないでしょうか。

しかも、そののぞきカラクリでのぞいたけしきとうりふたつのことが、物語の後半で実際に起こるのです。ああ、ぞくぞくするではありませんか！

この物語は「少年」という雑誌に、昭和二十九年の一月から十二月まで連載されました。

そのときのタイトルは『鉄塔の怪人』というものでした。『怪人二十面相』から数えると、長い少年探偵もののお話としては十番目にあたります。

この作品には、シリーズのほかのものとちょっと違ういくつかの点があります。

まずひとつは、鉄塔王国の者だと名のる悪人が、一千万円を寄付してほしい、そうでなければ息子の賢二くんを連れていく、とおどすのです。これまで登場した悪人はどれも、高価な宝石や美術品をねらうけれども、お金には関心がない、という者ばかりでした。それがここでは、息子を連れていかれたくなかったら大金を支払えと要求するのです。

第二に、カブトムシのおばけを手下のようにつかう悪人たちは、この日本のどこかに鉄塔王国という別世界がある、という信じられないような話をいたします。そこで「たちのよい子どもたちを集めて、みっちりしこんで、りっぱな兵隊にする」というのです。お金を出すのがいやなら賢二くんを連れていく、とおどすのです。これまで登場した悪党たちはほとんど、値打ちのある美術品を集めることが目的だったことを考えると、ずいぶん変わ

東京の路面電車（昭和27年当時）

183

作品が映画化された。撮影現場で乱歩先生とともに。

った考えをもった連中であることがわかります。

やがて、まんまと賢二くんを連れさった悪人たちのあとをたくみに追う小林少年は、木曾山中に世にもおそろしい鉄塔王国を発見します。それは、この物語のはじめで小林くんが不思議なおじいさんののぞきカラクリのなかに見た、あの奇妙なけしきとそっくりだったのです。

こうしてお話はみごとに発端とむすびつきます。そこでは、子どもたちがカブトムシのぬいぐるみのなかに入れられ、動きまわる訓練をさせられていたのです。

さあ、そのあとどうなるか、読んでのお楽しみ、ですが、ともあれ全編ハラハラドキドキの、手に汗にぎるサスペンスの連続です。そして、手品のトリックのように考え抜かれた数々のしかけがあります。それを、明智探偵や小林少年がみごとに解決していきます。悪人と名探偵の知恵と知恵とのたたかいを、たっぷりとお楽しみください。

このお話は、作者の江戸川乱歩先生がおとなのために書いた『妖虫』という作品を、少

年読者のために書きあらためたものです。もし将来、『妖虫』を読む機会がありましたら、そのときは、どこをどう変えているのか、ようく読み比べてみてください。きっと、乱歩先生の工夫がわかって、二重に楽しめることでしょう。そして、いかに先生が少年読者の読み物のために、あれこれと知恵をしぼっていたかがわかって、びっくりされるに違いありません。

編集方針について

一　第二次世界大戦前の作品については、旧仮名づかいを現代仮名づかいに改めました。
二　漢字の中で、少年少女の読者にむずかしいと思われるものは、ひらがなに改めました。
三　少年少女の読者には理解しにくい事柄や単語については、各ページの欄外に注（説明文）をつけました。
四　原作を重んじて編集しましたが、身体障害や職業にかかわる不適切な表現については、一部表現を変えたり、けずったりしたところがあります。
五　『少年探偵・江戸川乱歩全集』（ポプラ社刊）をもとに、作品が掲載された雑誌の文章とも照らし合わせて、できるだけ発表当時の作品が理解できるように心がけました。

以上の事柄は、著作権継承者である平井隆太郎氏のご了承を得ました。

　　　　　　　　　　　　　　　　　　ポプラ社編集部

編集委員・平井隆太郎　砂田弘　秋山憲司

本書は1998年11月ポプラ社から刊行
された作品を文庫版にしたものです。

文庫版　少年探偵・江戸川乱歩　第10巻

鉄塔王国の恐怖
発行　2005年2月　第1刷
　　　2021年10月　第16刷
作家　江戸川乱歩
装丁　藤田新策
画家　佐竹美保
発行者　千葉 均
発行所　株式会社ポプラ社
東京都千代田区麹町4-2-6　8・9F　〒102-8519
ホームページ　www.poplar.co.jp
印刷・製本　図書印刷株式会社

落丁、乱丁本はお取り替えいたします。
電話（0120-666-553）または、ホームページ（www.poplar.co.jp）
のお問い合わせ一覧よりご連絡ください。
※電話の受付時間は、月～金曜日10時～17時です（祝日・休日は除く）。
読者の皆様からのお便りをお待ちしております。
いただいたお便りは著者にお渡しいたします。
本書のコピー、スキャン、デジタル化等の無断複製は
著作権法上での例外を除き禁じられています。
本書を代行業者等の第三者に依頼してスキャンやデジタル化することは、
たとえ個人や家庭内での利用であっても著作権法上認められておりません。
N.D.C.913　186p　18cm　ISBN978-4-591-08421-2
Printed in Japan　ⓒ　藤田新策　佐竹美保　2005

P8005010

文庫版 少年探偵・江戸川乱歩 全26巻

怪人二十面相と名探偵明智小五郎、少年探偵団との息づまる推理対決！

1. 怪人二十面相
2. 少年探偵団
3. 妖怪博士
4. 大金塊
5. 青銅の魔人
6. 地底の魔術王
7. 透明怪人
8. 怪奇四十面相
9. 宇宙怪人
10. 鉄塔王国の恐怖
11. 灰色の巨人
12. 海底の魔術師
13. 黄金豹
14. 魔法博士
15. サーカスの怪人
16. 魔人ゴング
17. 魔法人形
18. 奇面城の秘密
19. 夜光人間
20. 塔上の奇術師
21. 鉄人Q
22. 仮面の恐怖王
23. 電人M
24. 二十面相の呪い
25. 空飛ぶ二十面相
26. 黄金の怪獣

少年探偵　18
奇面城の秘密
江戸川乱歩

もくじ

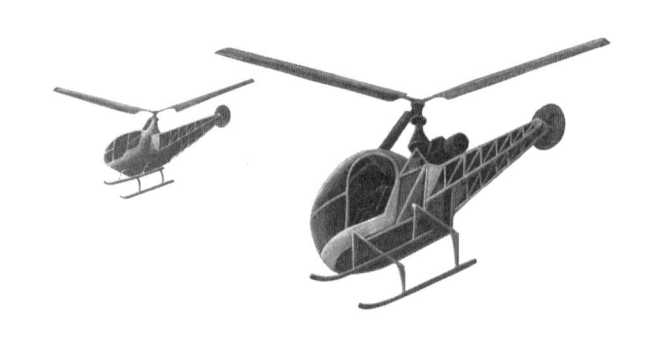

怪人四十面相 ……… 6
アドニスの像 ……… 12
屋根の上 ……… 19
水ぜめ ……… 27
空からの怪音 ……… 33
第二のヘリコプター ……… 38
操縦士の正体 ……… 42
暗号の光 ……… 47
すりの源公 ……… 52
ポケット小僧 ……… 59
ふしぎな変装 ……… 63
警視総監 ……… 71
まぼろし警官隊 ……… 76
カバンの中 ……… 83

四十面相の美術館	90
巨人の顔	95
恐ろしい番人	103
ポケット小僧の冒険	110
秘密会議	117
替え玉ふたり	121
敵のただ中へ	126
黒い小僧	131
いもむしごろごろ	138
巨人の目	144
最後の手段	150
警察官の勝利	157
最後の切りふだ	163
解説　新保博久	170

| 装丁・さし絵 | 藤田新策 |

少年探偵 奇面城の秘密 江戸川乱歩

怪人四十面相

ある日麹町高級アパートの明智探偵事務所へ、ひとりのりっぱな紳士がたずねてきました。それは東京の港区に住んでいる神山正夫という実業家で、たくさんの会社の重役をしている人でした。その神山さんが、明智探偵としたしい友だちの実業家の紹介状を持って、たずねてきたのです。

明智は、神山さんを応接室にとおして、どういうご用かと聞きますと、神山さんは、心配そうな顔で、

「じつは、明智さん。わたしは怪人四十面相に、脅迫されているのです。」

と、恐ろしいことをいうのでした。

「エッ、怪人四十面相？ そいつのもとの名は怪人二十面相ですね。しかし、そいつは、三月ばかりまえに、『サーカスの怪人』の事件で、わたしがとらえて、いまは、刑務所にはいっているはずですが……」

明智探偵は、いぶかしそうにいいました。

「ところが、やつは、とっくに牢やぶりをしていたのです。」

＊シリーズ第15巻

「それはおかしい。あいつが牢やぶりをすれば、すぐにわたしの耳にはいるはずです。また、新聞にものるはずです。わたしは、まったく、そういうことを聞いておりません。」

「いや、それが、いまさっきわかったのです。わたしは、この事件を警察に知らせました。警察でも、あなたとおなじようにふしぎに思って、刑務所をしらべたのです。すると、どうでしょう。四十面相はいつのまにか、まったくべつの人間といれかわっていたのです。よく四十面相によくにた男が、身がわりになって刑務所の独房にはいっていたのです。いつ、どうして、この替え玉といれかわったかは、いくらしらべても、わからないのです。四十面相の替え玉になったやつは、ばかみたいな男で、なにをたずねても、エヘラ、エヘラ、笑っているばかりで、どうすることもできないのだそうです。」

それを聞くと、明智探偵の顔が、ぐっとひきしまりました。一刻も、すてておけない大事件です。

「ちょっと、お待ちください。」

明智はそういって、イスから立つと、部屋のすみのデスクの上の電話機をとりました。

そして、しばらく話していましたが、もとのイスにもどって、

「いま、警視庁の中村警部にたずねてみましたが、おっしゃるとおりです。四十面相は

ずっと前から、刑務所をぬけだしていたらしいのです。……ところで、その四十面相が、あなたを脅迫したというのは？」

「まず、さいしょは、十日ばかり前に、とつぜん、へんな声の電話がかかってきたのです。きみの悪い、しわがれ声でした。

その声が、近いうちに、レンブラントのＳ夫人像をちょうだいにいくから、用心するがいいと、恐ろしいことをいって、ぷっつり電話をきってしまいました。

レンブラントのＳ夫人像というのは、昨年わたしがフランスで手にいれてきたもので、数千万円のねうちの油絵です。これは、わたしが持ちかえったときに新聞にものりましたから、ごぞんじのことと思います。」

「知っています。あれは、日本人の持っている洋画のうちで、最高のものでしょう。その油絵は、どこにおいてあるのですか。」

「わたしのうちの洋館の二階の美術室にかけてあります。その部屋には、いろいろな西洋画がならべてあるのですが、みなレンブラントの足もとにもおよばないものばかりです。

四十面相がレンブラントだけをねらったのは、さすがに目が高いというものです。」

神山さんは、そういって、にが笑いをするのでした。

「で、まだ、ぬすまれたわけではないのですね？」

＊ 十七世紀のオランダの画家

「まだです。しかし、ここ四、五日があぶないと思います。じつは、きのうの朝、寝室で目をさましますと、バッドのそばの机に、こんな手紙がのせてありました。うちのものをしらべても、だれも知らないといいます。どこから、どうしてはいってきたか、まったくわからないのです。」

神山さんは、ポケットから西洋封筒をとりだし、中の手紙を明智にわたしました。それには、こんな恐ろしい文句が書いてあったのです。

　レンブラントのS夫人像は、きょうから五日のあいだに、かならずちょうだいする。じゅうぶん警戒するがよろしい。きみの屋敷を、警官隊にとりまかせても、おれはへいきだ。おれは魔法使いだからね。では、きみのだいじなレンブラントに、わかれをつげておきたまえ。
　　　　　　　　　四十面相より

「この手紙で、はじめて、相手が四十面相とわかったのです。ひょっとしたら、だれかのいたずらじゃないかと思いましたが、ねんのために警察にとどけると、警察では刑務所をしらべ、さっきもお話ししたように、四十面相が脱獄していることがわかったのです。
警察では、けさから、十人の警官をわたしのうちへよこして、警戒にあたらせてくれま

した。夜昼交替で、いつも十人の見はりがついているのです。それに、わたしのうちには大学にかよっているむすこもいますし、書生もふたりいるほかに、わたしが社長をしている会社の若い社員に、三人ほどとまりにきてもらっているので、美術室のまわりはむろん、屋敷のまわりにも、ぐるっと見はりがついているわけです。

警察では、いくら四十面相でも、これだけ警戒すればだいじょうぶだろうというのですが、なにしろ四十面相というやつは、魔法使いですからね。わたしは、どうも安心ができないのです。

そこで、これまで、たびたび四十面相を手がけていらっしゃる明智さんに、ご相談するほかないと考えたわけです。ひとつ、お力をおかしねがえないでしょうか。」

明智探偵はそれを聞くと、深くうなずきながら、

「しょうちしました。できるだけやってみましょう。いまの電話で、中村警部も、わたしに手をかしてくれとたのんでいました。

それに四十面相は、二十面相と名のっていたころから、わたしにとっては、きってもきれない関係のあるやつですからね。こいつがあらわれたと聞いては、わたしも、うしろを見せるわけにはいきませんよ。」

と、にっこり笑ってみせるのでした。神山さんは、たのもしげに明智の顔を見て、

＊ 他人の家のせわになって、家事を手つだい勉強する人

「それをうかがって、わたしも安心しました。わたしのためばかりではありません。四十面相をのばなしにしておいたなら、どんな恐ろしいことをはじめるかしれません。世間のためですよ。どうか、お力をおかしください。」

「よくわかりました。では、これからごいっしょにいって、おたくを拝見することにしましょう。ことに美術室は、よく見ておかなければなりません。それには、わたしひとりでなく、少年助手の小林をつれていきたいのですが、かまいませんでしょうね。小林は、よく頭のはたらく、すばしっこい少年で、たいへん手だすけになるのです。」

「かまいませんとも。小林少年のことは、わたしもよく知っていますよ。わたしのすえの男の子どもが、小学校六年生ですが、これが小林君の大ファンなのですよ。小林君が来てくださったら、大よろこびでしょう。」

「ハハハハ……、小林は、少年諸君に、すっかり有名になってしまいましたからね。小林が町を歩いていると、小学生の男の子や女の子が集まってきて、サインをもとめるのですよ。そんなとき、小林ははずかしがって、顔をまっ赤にしていますがね。」

「そうでしょう。うちの子どもなんかも、小林少年に夢中ですからね。」

そこで明智がベルをおしますと、じきにドアがひらいて、りんごのようなほおをした小林少年の顔がのぞきました。

アドニスの像

＊ 第8巻『怪奇四十面相』での事件

明智探偵と小林少年は神山邸につくと、見はりをつとめている警官とも話しあい、屋敷

「小林君、四十面相が脱獄したんだ。そして、この神山さんのおうちにあるレンブラントの油絵を、ぬすみだすという予告をしたんだ。いつものやりくちだよ。で、いまから神山さんのおたくへいくのだが、きみもいっしょにきてくれないか。」
「ええ、つれてってください。でも、四十面相のやつ、どうして脱獄したのですか。」
「それは、車の中でゆっくり話す。替え玉をつかったんだよ。」
「あ、それじゃあ、いつかの手ですね。」
「うん、あいつのとくいのやりくちだ。……どうだ、小林君、むしゃぶるいが出ないかね。こんどは、きみに大役をつとめてもらうつもりだよ。」
「ええ、ぼく、なんでもやります。あいつには、ずいぶん、ひどいめにあっているのですからね。かたきうちです。」

そして、三人は階段をおり、アパートの入り口に待たせてあった神山さんの自動車に乗って、港区の神山邸へといそぐのでした。

の内外をくまなく見てまわり、ことにレンブラントの油絵のかかっている美術室は、ねんいりにしらべました。そしてある計画をたてたのです。それがどんな計画だったかは、やがて、わかるときがくるでしょう。

それから四日のあいだは、なにごともなくすぎさりましたが、警官隊の見はりは、昼も夜も厳重につづけられ、いかに四十面相でも、これでは、しのびこむすきもないように見えました。

そのあいだにひとつだけ、ちょっと、へんなできごとがありました。つぎの朝のことです。神山さんが美術室へはいってみると、はじめて神山邸をしらべた、部屋のすみに立ててあったアドニスの石膏像が、まっぷたつにわれて、ころがっていたのです。

そのまわりには、こなごなにわれた石膏のかけらがとびちり、そばに、明智と小林少年が、ころがっていました。外の原っぱで野球をしていたボールが、ひらいた窓からとびこんで、石膏像の腹にあたったらしいのです。

美術室の窓は、いつもしめきって、かけがねがかけてあるのですが、お手つだいさんがそうじをするときには、窓をあけますから、窓をあけておいて、お手つだいさんが、ちょっと部屋を出たすきに、ボールがとびこんだのかもしれません。

アドニスというのは、大むかしのギリシア神話の中に出てくる美しい青年で、そのはだかの像を有名な彫刻家がいくつもつくったのですが、いまのこっているのは、ごくわずかです。ほんものは大理石にほったものですが、フランスの美術商が、それとそっくりの石膏像をこしらえて売りだしたのを、神山さんが買って帰ったもので、青年アドニスがはだかで立っている、おとなよりも大きな美しい石膏像です。それが野球のボールで、まっぷたつにわれてしまったのです。

この石膏像は、大きくても、たいしてねうちのあるものではありませんが、神山さんが、はるばるフランスから買ってきたものですから、そのままにしておくわけにはいきません。

さっそく、ハヤノ商会という石膏像専門の店に電話をかけて、もとどおりにつがせることにしました。

すると、ハヤノ商会の人がやってきて、この場でなおすことはできないからというので、われた石膏像をトラックにつんで、工場へ持ちかえりましたが、それが四日めに、もとのとおりにつぎあわされて、もどってきました。ハヤノ商会の四人の社員が、それを二階の美術室にかつぎあげて、もとの場所においてかえりました。

警察では、この社員たちのうちに、四十面相の手下がまぎれこんでいたらたいへんだというので、石膏像をはこびだしたときにも、持ちこんだときにも、厳重に見はっていまし

たが、べつにあやしいこともなかったのです。

レンブラントのS夫人像は、もとのところにかかったままです。銀行の大金庫の中へ、でもあずけたら、という意見も出ましたが、持ちはこびなんかしたら、その道があぶないというので、美術室から動かさないことにしたのです。

さて、石膏像が持ちこまれた日は、ちょうど四十面相の手紙にあった、五日めにあたっていました。五日以内に、かならずぬすみだしてみせるというのですから、きょうの夜中までが期限です。それをすぎれば、四十面相は負けたことになります。

いまは午後の三時です。夜中までは、もう九時間しかありません。警戒は、いよいよ厳重になりました。警官と書生や社員などをあわせて十数名の強そうな男たちが、屋敷のあらゆる場所に見はりをつづけているのです。

神山邸の洋室の書斎には、主人の神山さんと、明智小五郎と、警視庁の中村警部とが、テーブルをかこんで、ひそひそと話しあっていました。

「明智君、きみはなにか考えがあるようだが、だいじょうぶだろうね。今夜がいちばんあぶないのだ。どうだろう、われわれ三人で、夜あかしをして、美術室にがんばっていることにしたら？」

中村警部が、心配そうな顔で、そんなことをいいだすのでした。

15

「それもいいが、ぽくに考えがある。美術室は、からっぽにしておくほうがいいのだよ。ちゃんと、ぬすまれないような手だてがしてあるから、安心したまえ。

四十面相は、これまでにも、たびたび、こういう予告をした。そして、ちゃんと予告どおりにやってみせた。ぽくたちは、いつもあいつに出しぬかれている。いくら厳重に見はっていても、あいつにかかっては、なんにもならない。

だから、こんどは、がらっとやりかたをかえて、美術室はからっぽにしておこうと思うのだ。むろん、ドアや窓には、かぎをかけてあるがね。

つまり、さそいのすきを見せるのだよ。そして、あいつをおびきよせておいて、つかまえようというわけさ。」

明智探偵は、自信ありげにいうのでした。

「しかし、屋敷のまわりの見はりは、やっぱりつづけたほうがいいでしょうね。いくら四十面相でも、鳥のようにとんでくるわけではないでしょうから、見はりさえしておれば、美術室へはいることができないのですからね。」

神山さんが、心配そうに口をはさみました。

「いや、それも、ほんとはどうでもいいのです。いくら見はっていても、あいつはちゃんとやってきますよ。しかし、いざというときに手だすけになりますから、見はりは、やっ

ぱり、つづけたほうがいいでしょうね。」

　明智は、屋敷のまわりの見はりも、必要がないというのです。そのうえ、美術室をからっぽにしておくのですから、神山さんや中村警部には、なんだか、あぶなっかしいように思われるのです。

　やがて、夜になりました。

　美術室の窓には、中からかけがねをかけ、ドアには外からかぎをかけ、その外の廊下にイスをおいて、見はりをしていました。

　十人の警官は、家のまわりをかこんで、すこしのゆだんもなく、警戒についていました。

　中村警部は、たえず、そのへんを歩きまわって、見はりの人々のかんとくをしていました。

　明智探偵は、日のくれるころどこかへ立ち去ったまま、まだ帰ってきません。このかんじんのときに、名探偵は、いったい、なにをしているのでしょう。

　だんだん夜がふけていきました。

　どこかで、時計が十時をうつのが聞こえました。

　そのとき、二階の美術室の中に、ふしぎなことがおこったのです。

　美術室は、小さな電灯ひとつだけをのこして、ぜんぶの電灯が消してありました。その

うす暗い中で、パチッ、パチッと、なにか、もののはぜるような音がしています。ネズミがなにかかじっている音でしょうか。いや、このりっぱな美術室にネズミなんか出るはずがありません。

ああ、ごらんなさい。あのアドニスの巨大な像が、かすかにゆれているではありませんか。石膏像が生きて動きだしたのでしょうか。

やがて、もっとふしぎなことがおこりました。

パチッ、パチッと、石膏像がひびわれはじめたのです。そして白い石膏の表に、こまかいすじがいくつもできて、そのすじが、みるみるひろがっていくではありませんか。

パラパラッと、石膏のかけらが床に落ちました。それが、だんだん大きくなってくるのです。

石膏のひびわれは、いよいよ大きくなり、そのあいだから、なにか黒いものがあらわれてきました。

床には、じゅうたんがしいてあるので、その音は、ドアの外まで聞こえません。

やがて、右の足がひざのへんからはなれて、その中から、べつの黒い足がニュッと出てきました。つぎに、左の足におなじことがおこり、ひざから上に石膏をかぶった黒い二本の足が、台座からじゅうたんの上におりてきました。

18

右左の手が、肩のところからすっぽりとぬけて床に落ち、その下から、べつの黒い手があらわれました。

それから二本の黒い手が、いそがしくはたらいて、からだをおおっていた石膏を、ぜんぶとりのけてしまいました。

それは、まっ黒なシャツを着た、ひとりの人間だったのです。頭にも黒い覆面をかぶっています。目のところだけくりぬいてあるのです。アドニスの像の中には、生きた人間がかくれていたのです。

屋根の上

いうまでもなく、この男が四十面相でした。彼はアドニスの石膏像が修繕に出されたとき、ハヤノ商会という石膏商とつうじて、その像を持ちだし、自分をその中にとじこめてもらって、四人の部下に神山邸へはこばせたのです。部下はハヤノ商会の店員にばけて、うまくそのアドニス像を、美術室にもどしておいたのです。

二階の美術室には、うす暗い電灯がひとつだけつけてありました。見はりの書生がふたり、ドアの外の廊下にいるばかりで、室内にはだれもおりません。明智探偵が、わざとそ

石膏をやぶってあらわれた黒シャツの四十面相は、あたりを見まわしてだれもいないことをたしかめると、壁にかけてあるレンブラントのS夫人像のところへいって、それを壁からおろし、がくぶちをはずして、木のわくにとりつけてあるカンバスを、ていねいにぎとりました。そして、それを、くるくると棒のようにまいてしまったのです。わくのまま持ちだしてはかさばりますので、油絵のカンバスだけをまるめて、持ちやすくしたのです。

それから、腰にまきつけていた大きな黒いふろしきをはずすと、まるめたカンバスをつつみ、それをななめに背中にしょって、ふろしきの両方のはしを、胸の前でむすびました。こうしておけば、逃げだすときに両手が自由で、身がるに動けるからです。

四十面相は、その仕事を、すこしも物音をたてないようにやってのけました。さっき石膏像をやぶったときにも、音がしないように注意しましたし、床にあついじゅうたんがしいてあるので、いくらか音がしても、外までは聞こえなかったのです。

ですから、廊下に見はっていたふたりの書生は、四十面相が美術室の中でレンブラントの油絵をぬすんでしまったなどとは、すこしも知りませんでした。ふたりは、四十面相が外からやってくるとばかり思っていたのです。

うしておいたのです。

四十面相は、美術室のガラス窓を、音のしないようにひらくと、ひょいと窓わくの上にとびあがり、その外にとりつけてある樋をつたって、サルのように身がるに、大屋根にのぼっていきました。

彼は大屋根なんかにのぼって、いったい、どうするつもりなのでしょう。神山さんの西洋館は、広い庭のまん中にたっているので、となりの家の屋根へとびうつって逃げだすというようなことは、思いもよらないのです。

西洋館のまわりをとりかこんでいる警官たちも、四十面相が屋根へ逃げるなんて、すこしも考えていなかったので、だれも上のほうは注意していません。四十面相は、外からはいってくるとばかり思っていたのです。

しかし、その中で、たったひとり、なんだかへんだなと気づいた警官がありました。その警官も、屋根のほうを見ていたわけではありませんが、なにげなくふと顔を上にあげたとき、大屋根にとびついた四十面相の二本の足だけが、目のすみにうつったのです。

その足は、すぐに、大屋根の上に見えなくなってしまいましたが、一瞬間、灰色のコンクリートの壁のてっぺんのところに、ぶらんとさがっている、二本の黒い棒のようなものが見えたのです。

警官は、それが人間の足だとは、思いもよりませんでした。まっ暗な中ですから、はっ

きり見えたわけではなく、なんだか、そんな気がしたのです。
その警官は、大屋根の上を、じっと見つめました。屋根の上はいっそう暗いので、なにも見えませんが、気のせいか、赤いかわらの上を、まっ黒なやつがじりじりとはいあがっていくような感じがしました。

たとえ気のせいでも、いちおう中村警部に報告したほうがいいと思いました。そこで、その警官は、やはり庭に立っている中村警部をさがしだして、このことを知らせたのです。
中村警部のそばには、明智探偵と小林少年が、どこからかもどってきて立っていました。
明智はいまの報告を聞くと、
「うん、やっぱりそうだ。もう絵はぬすまれたかもしれない。ぬすんだとすれば、警官にかこまれている庭へ、おりてくることはできないから、屋根にのぼるしかないわけだね。」
と、なにもかも知っているようなことをいいました。
「エッ、もうぬすまれたって？ どうして、それがきみにわかるんだ。四十面相は、いったい、どこからしのびこむことができたのだろう。きみはそれを知っていて、なぜふせがなかったのだ。」
中村警部が、明智をせめるようにどなりました。
「いや、知っていたわけじゃない。あいつのことだから、魔法使いのようにどこからかし

「なんだって？　それじゃ、きみにもあいつのしのびこむのを、ふせぐことができなかったというのか。」

「いや、ちゃんとふせいである。これには、ちょっとわけがあるんだ。くわしいことはあとで話すがね。ともかく、美術室をしらべてみよう。もし油絵がぬすまれていたら、あいつが屋根へ逃げたというのは、ほんとうにちがいない。」

「うん、すぐにいってみよう。」

中村警部も、美術室をしらべてみるのがだいいちだと思いましたので、明智のことばに賛成して、もうそのほうへ、かけだしていました。明智探偵と小林少年も、それにつづきます。

二階の美術室へはいって、かぎでドアをひらくと、中村警部は、「アッ」と叫んで、立ちすくんでしまいました。

そこには、アドニスの石膏像が、ばらばらにくだけて、とびちっていたからです。

「これはどうしたことだ。きょう修繕して、持ってきたばかりじゃないか。それをまた、こんなにこわしてしまった。こんな夜ふけに、野球をやっているやつがあるんだろうか。」

警部が、あっけにとられてつぶやきました。

「こんどは、ボールがあたってこわれたのじゃないよ。中からこわしたやつがあるんだ。」

明智が、みょうなことをいいました。

「エ、中からだって？ それは、どういう意味だ。」

「この石膏像の中に、四十面相がかくれていたのさ。」

「エ、あいつが？ かくれていた？ おい、明智君、きみはそれを知っていたのか？」

「いや、いや、知っていたわけじゃないよ。いまここへきて、やっと気がついたのだ。このわれかたでわかったのだ。ぼくも、うかつだった。あいつのやりそうな手だからね。それを考えなかったのはぼくの手ぬかりだった。」

明智は、残念そうにいいました。

そのとき、中村警部は、またしても、「アッ」という叫び声をたてたのです。

「アッ、ぬすまれたッ。見たまえ、レンブラントのがくぶちがおろしてある。中はからっぽだッ。」

「うん、ぼくの思ったとおりだ。あいつは、やっぱりぬすんでいった。しかしね、中村君、これは心配しないでもいい。ぼくが、きっととりかえしてみせるよ。」

明智は、自信ありげに、きっぱりといいきるのでした。

24

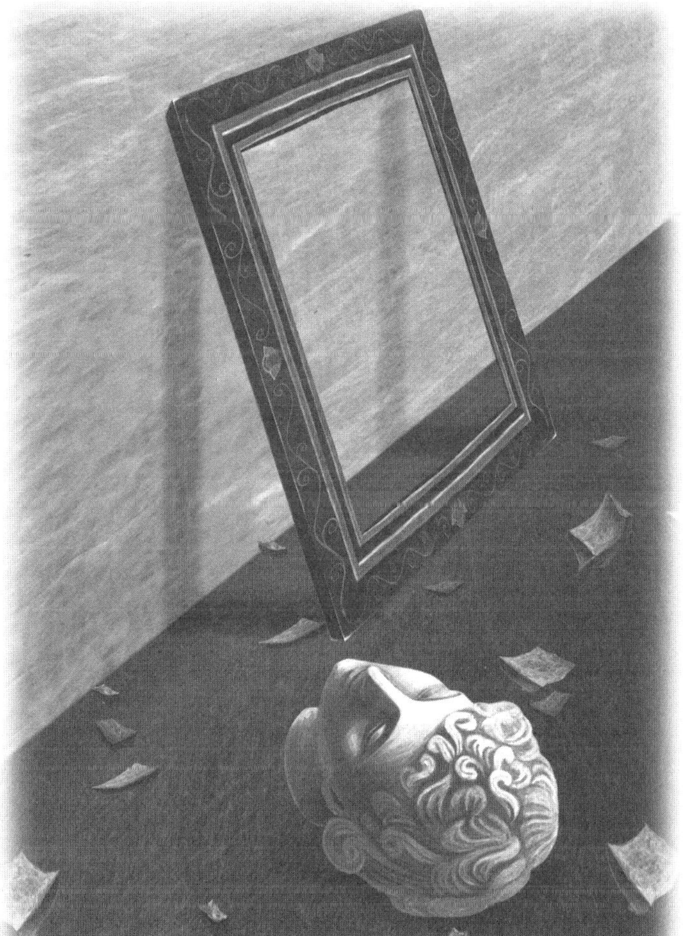

「それじゃあ、あいつは、レンブラントのカンバスだけをとりはずして、それを持って屋根の上へ逃げたというのだね。」

「うん、そうにちがいない。屋根のほかに逃げる場所はないからね。」

「四方をかこまれているんだから、屋根へのぼったって、逃げられるわけはない。いったい、あいつは、どうするつもりなんだろう。」

中村警部が、ふしぎそうにいいます。

「相手は魔法使いだ。どんな手があるかもしれない。ともかく、屋根の上を見はる必要があるね。それには、ふつうの電灯なんかでは、暗くてよく見えないだろう。消防自動車をよぶんだね。そうすれば、＊探照灯もあるし、長い自動ばしごもある。それがいちばんいいよ。」

「うん、それがよさそうだね。じゃ、ぼくが消防署へ電話をかけることにしよう。」

中村警部はそういって、あたふたと階下へおりていきました。

いっぽう、庭のほうでは、警官たちが、階下の部屋の電灯にコードをつぎたして、庭から大屋根を照らし、みんなで、そこをながめていました。

「アッ、黒いものが動いた。たしかに、あいつだよ。」

「うん、屋根の上にひらべったくなっているけれども、ボーッと黒く見えるね。あれが四

＊夜間、遠くまで照らしだすようにした照明装置。サーチライト

十面相にちがいない。警部さんに報告しよう。」

そういって、ひとりの警官が、西洋館へとびこんでいくのでした。

水ぜめ

しばらくすると、赤い消防自動車がかけつけ、門から庭へはいってきました。中村警部のさしずで、探照灯が点じられ、白い棒のような強い光が、西洋館の人屋根を照らしました。

やっぱりそうです。黒いシャツを着た男が、ぴったりと、屋根にからだをくっつけて、はらばいになっています。そのすがたが、はっきりと照らしだされたのです。

四十面相は、顔をふりむけて、まぶしそうにこちらを見ました。そして、いきなり逃げだしたのです。逃げだすといっても屋根の外へは出られません。とびおりたりなんかすれば、死んでしまうばかりです。

彼は、屋根をはって、頂上の棟がわらまでたどりつくと、ひょいとそれをまたいで、むこう側に、すがたを消してしまいました。

探照灯の光は、棟がわらのむこうまでは、とどきませんから、四十面相を見うしなわな

いためには、自動車を、むこう側にまわして、そこから、探照灯をあてるほかはありません。

消防車の運転手は車を動かして、裏へまわろうとしました。それを見た中村警部は、

「いや、そのままでいい。あっちへまわったら、あいつはこっち側の屋根へ逃げるだろう。そうすれば、また、ここへもどってこなければならない。あいつが棟がわらを、こえるのはすぐだけれども、自動ばしごをのばしなさい。そうして、大屋根までとどかせてくれれば、ぼくの部下がのぼっていって、あいつをつかまえるよ。」

と、さしずをしました。

すると、ガラガラッとモーターがまわって、自動ばしごが、上へ上へとのびはじめました。そして、みるまに、大屋根の高さになったのです。

そういうことになれた中村警部の部下のふたりの警官が、靴をぬぎ、上着をぬぎ、身がるないでたちになって、空にむかって、まっすぐに立っている自動ばしごを勇敢にのぼっていきます。

警官隊のうち、裏側に三人ばかりのこして、みんな消防自動車のまわりに集まっています。主人の神山さんも、書生たちも、その中にまじっています。明智探偵と小林少年だ

け、どこにも、すがたが見えないのでした。

四十面相が屋根に逃げるすこし前にも、ふたりは、どこかへ、すがたをくらましていましたが、このかんじんなときに、またもや、ゆくえがわからなくなってしまったのです。

いったい、どこへいったのでしょうか。

ふたりの警官は、もう自動ばしごの三分の二ほどを、のぼっていました。あと二メートルで、大屋根にとどきます。

そのとき、棟がわらのむこう側から、四十面相の頭が、ひょいとこちらをのぞきました。

そして、警官たちが、はしごをのぼってくるのに気づいたようすです。

ふたりの強そうな警官が、屋根へあがってきたら、もうおしまいです。彼らは、手錠やとり縄を持っています。腰のサックには、たまをこめたピストルまで用意しているのです。

四十面相がいくら強くても、とてもかなうものではありません。

四十面相は、どうするつもりでしょう。とうとう、つかまってしまうのでしょうか。

見ていると、彼は、棟がわらをのりこして、こちら側の屋根へ出てきました。そして、だんだん、屋根のはしのほうへおりてくるのです。いったいなにをしようというのでしょう。

「オヤッ、やつは、とびおりるかもしれないぞ。救命具を用意したまえ。」

中村警部の声に、消防士たちは、車にそなえつけてある、まるいズックの救命具をとりだして、五人でそれをひろげ、屋根の下へ近づきました。とびおりてくる四十面相のからだを、そのまるいズックの上に、うけとめようというのです。

しかし、四十面相は、とびおりるけはいはありません。彼は、屋根のとっぱなまでくると、そこにかかっていた自動ばしごに両手をかけて、力まかせに、ゆさぶりはじめたではありませんか。

そのために、いまにも屋根に手をかけようとしていた警官が、ふいをつかれて、ずるずるッとはしごをすべり落ちました。

「アッ、あぶないッ。」

そのまま、下まで落ちてくるのではないかと、手に汗をにぎりましたが、三段ほどすべり落ちただけで、はしごの横木につかまって、やっとのことでふみとどまりました。あとからのぼっているもうひとりの警官は、まだずっと下のほうにいたので、ふたりが、ぶつつかりあうこともなかったのです。もし、ぶっつかれば、ふたりとも命はないところでした。

さきの警官はこれに屈せず、またはしごをのぼって、屋根に手をかけようとしましたが、四十面相は、それを待ちうけていて、また、はしごを、ゆさゆさとゆさぶるのです。

こんどは、用心をしていたので、すべり落ちないですみましたけれど、こんなにゆさぶられては、とても屋根にのぼることはできません。

しかたがないので、警官は、腰のサックからピストルをとりだしました。

「こらッ、てむかいするとぶっぱなすぞッ。命がないぞッ。」

そうどなっておいて、空にむかって、一発、だあんと発射しました。

「ワハハハ……」

四十面相は、さもおかしそうに笑いだすのでした。

「ワハハハ……、そんなおどかしは、おれにはきかないよ。おれは、なんにも武器を持っていないのだ。武器を持たない相手を、殺すことはできないはずだね。いくらおどかしの空砲をうったって、おれはびくともしないよ。ワハハハ……、ざまあみろ。」

こんな相手にかかっては、どうすることもできません。四十面相のからだをうつことはできないのを、ちゃんと知っているのです。警官はあきらめて、ピストルを腰のサックにもどしてしまいました。

そして、また、いくども屋根にとりつこうとしましたが、そのたびに、四十面相がはしごをゆさぶるので、落ちないようにしがみついているのがやっとでした。とても犯人をつかまえることなどできるものではありません。

下では、中村警部たちが、相談していました。

「水ぜめにしたらどうだろう。ホースで、あいつに水をぶっかけるんだよ。そうすれば、すべって落ちてくる。それを、救命具でうけとめればいい。」

中村警部がいいますと、主任の消防士も賛成しました。

「やってみましょうか。消火栓をひらいてホースをつなげばいいのです。ホースの水は、ひじょうな力ですから、あいつはきっと、すべりますよ。」

「うん。それをやるほかはないと思うね。だが、うまくうけとめられるかな。やりそこなったら、あいつは死んでしまうからね。あいつを殺してはいけないのだ。なかなか、むずかしい仕事だよ。」

中村警部は、心配そうに首をかしげました。

こんなとき、明智探偵がいたら、もっといい知恵を出してくれるのでしょうが、明智も小林少年も、どこへいったのか、まだすがたを見せないのです。

「よしッ、やってみよう。しかし、注意しておくがね、ほんとうに、すべり落ちるまでやらないで、ただ、あいつをびっくりさせればいいのだ。いまにも、すべり落ちそうになれば、いくらあいつだって、手をあげるにちがいない。そのとき、はしごをのぼっていて、ひっくくってしまえばいいのだからね。」

中村警部は、とうとう決心をして、命令をくだしました。

そこで、ホースがのばされ、消火栓につながれました。地面をはっている白いホースが、へびのようにのたうって、ふくらんできました。

ふたりの消防士が、ホースの筒先をにぎっています。

ホースのふくらみがツウッとのびて、筒先にたっしました。そして、音をたてて水がほとばしりはじめました。

水は一本の白い棒になって、外に吹きあげています。筒先はすこしずつむきをかえ、大屋根のとっぱなにむけられました。

四十面相は、頭から夕立ちのような水をかぶり、あわてて屋根にはらばいになりました。水のいきおいは、刻々、はげしくなるばかりです。

空からの怪音

怪人は、いまにも水の力でおしながされ、屋根からすべり落ちそうです。

下では五人の消防士が、ズックの救命具をひろげて、怪人が落ちてくるのを、待ちかまえていました。

ああ、もうぜったいぜつめいです。怪人は死にものぐるいで、屋根のかわらにしがみついていますが、いつまでがんばれるものではありません。やがて力がつきて、水におしながされ、屋根からすべり落ちるにきまっているのです。

さすがの怪人四十面相も、とうとう、つかまってしまうのでしょうか。どんなおくの手を用意していないともかぎりません。しかし、あいつは魔法使いみたいなやつです。

そのとき、どこからか、ぶるるるるる……という、へんな音が聞こえてきました。消防自動車のモーターの音ではありません。ホースからほとばしる水の音でもありません。それらとはちがったへんな物音が、まっ暗な空のむこうから、ひびいてくるのです。

そのふしぎな音は、刻一刻と高くなってきました。

ぶるるるん。

ぶるるるん、ぶるるるん。

飛行機がとんでいるのでしょうか。いや、飛行機の音とも、どこかちがっています。

「アッ、星がとんでいる。流星かな？ 流星にしては、いやにゆっくりとんでいる。おい、あれを見たまえ。へんな星みたいなものがとんでくるよ。」

ひとりの警官が、そばに立っている警官に、そのほうを指さしてみせました。

「うん、とんでくるね。だが星じゃない。アッ、あれはヘリコプターだぜ。さっきからの

へんな音は、プロペラの音だよ。」

そういっているうちに、夜空にもくっきりと、ヘリコプターのすがたが浮きだしてきました。

プロペラの音は、話し声も聞こえないほど大きくなり、空からは、あやしい風が吹きつけてきました。

「アッ、屋根の真上にとまった。ヘリコプターが、四十面相を助けだしにきたんだッ！」

そうです。ヘリコプターは、洋館の二階の屋根の真上にとまっています。プロペラをゆっくりまわして、ちょうしをとりながら、そこの空中に、じっと浮かんでいるのです。ガラスのようなプラスチックでかこまれた操縦室のドアが、サッとひらくのが見えました。

操縦室には、ふたりの人間のすがたが小さく見えています。そのうちのひとりが、ひらいたドアのところから、なにか長いものを、下へ落とすのが見えました。

「アッ、縄ばしごだッ。四十面相を縄ばしごで、ヘリコプターの中へひきあげるつもりだッ。」

地上の人々の口から、ワアッという、どよめきがおこりました。しかし、どうすること

もできません。
　縄ばしごは、屋根の棟のむこう側にあり、四十面相は、そのほうへはいよっていくのです。
　ホースの水は、あいかわらず怪人の頭の上からふりそそいでいますが、彼をすべらせることはできません。四十面相は、かわらにしがみついて、すこしずつ屋根の棟に近づき、とうとう棟をのりこして、むこう側へすがたを消してしまいました。
「アッ、のぼっていく。のぼっていく。四十面相が、縄ばしごをのぼっていく……」
　くやしそうな叫び声がおこりました。やっぱりヘリコプターは四十面相の味方だったのです。空から怪人をすくいだしにきたのです。
「おい、水をぶっかけろ。そして、あいつを、縄ばしごから落としてしまえ。」
　中村警部が、やっきとなってどなりました。しかし、残念ながら、ホースの水は縄ばしごごまで、とどかないのです。
　四十面相の黒いすがたは、ヘリコプターの操縦室のすぐ下まで、のぼりつきました。彼は、左手で縄ばしごを持ち、右手をはなして、地上の人たちをあざけるように、その手を空中にひらひらさせています。
「ワハハハハ……。諸君、ごくろうさま。レンブラントの名画は、たしかにちょうだい

したよ。それじゃあ、あばよ！」

そのことばは、地上までとどきませんでしたが、人をばかにした大笑いの声は、みんなの耳にはいりました。四十面相は、レンブラントの名画のカンバスを、わくからはがして、ほそくまるめ、ふろしきにつつんで背中にせおっているのです。

警官たちは、じだんだをふんでくやしがりましたが、どうすることもできません。ピストルをうとうにも、とてもあの高い空までとどかないのです。

「しかたがない。警視庁に連絡して、こちらもヘリコプターをとばそう。そしてあいつを追っかけるんだ。」

中村警部は、歯ぎしりしながら、そんなことをつぶやきました。警視庁には、こんなときのために、二台のヘリコプターが、いつでもとべるように用意されているのでした。

中村警部は、ひとりの警官をよんで、警視庁に電話することを命じようとしましたが、

そのとき、ふと、みょうなことに気がつきました。

「オヤッ、あのヘリコプターには、見おぼえがあるぞ。あれは警視庁のヘリコプターじゃないか。はてな、これはいったいどうしたことだ。」

まちがいありません。たしかに目じるしがあるのです。それにしても、警視庁のヘリコプターが、怪人四十面相を助けにくるなんて、そんなばかなことが、あっていいもので

37

しょうか。

ひょっとしたら、怪人の部下が、警視庁のヘリコプターをぬすみだして、首領を助けにきたのかもしれません。

中村警部はなにがなんだかわけがわからなくなり、ただもう、ぼんやりと空を見あげて、その場につっ立っているばかりでした。

第二のヘリコプター

怪人四十面相は、縄ばしごをのぼりきって、操縦室の入り口に両手をかけると、鉄棒のしりあがりで、ひょいと中へはいりました。

「松下か?」

怪人が声をかけますと、操縦席にいた男は、縄ばしごをたぐりあげながら、

「はい!」

と答えました。

「もうひとりは、だれだ?」

「新米の、あっしの助手ですよ。」

松下とよばれた男は、みょうにかすれた声でいいました。彼は、鳥打ち帽を深くかぶり、洋服のえりを立てて、なぜか、顔をかくすようにしています。
「ふうん、こんな助手がいたのかい。子どもみたいに、ちっちゃいやつじゃないか。」
　いかにも、その助手は、子どものように背のひくい、へんな男でした。やっぱり鳥打ち帽を深くかぶり、だぶだぶの服を着ています。子どもが、おとなの服を着ているようなかっこうです。
　四十面相は、ちょっとふしぎそうな顔をしましたが、いまは、そんなことを考えているばあいではありません。一刻もはやく、この場を逃げださなければならないのです。
　松下という部下は、操縦席について、きゅうにヘリコプターを上昇させ、そのまま東のほうへ進めました。
　ヘリコプターの前方には、自動車のヘッドライトのようなものがついていますが、操縦室の中は、うす暗いのです。電灯も、操縦機のところを照らしているばかりで、おたがいの顔も、はっきり見えないほどでした。
「松下、いくさきはわかっているな。」
　四十面相が、ねんをおすようにいいました。
「どちらにしましょう。」

松下が、うつむいたまま、やっぱりかすれた声で聞きかえします。

「どちらだって？　ばかッ、きまってるじゃないか。きめんじょうだ。」

「きめんじょうですか。」

「うん、きめんじょうだよ。きみはなにをぼんやりしているんだ。へんだぞ。どうかしたのかッ。」

「いや、なんでもないんです。ちょっと、ほかのことを考えていたので……」

「なにッ、ほかのことを？　おいおい、しっかりしてくれ。操縦しながら、ほかのことなんか考えるやつがあるか。ここは空の上だよ。落ちたら命がないんだぜ。」

「すみません。」

松下は、かすれた声で、しおらしくわびをいいました。

空は雲がかかってまっ暗ですが、目の下には東京の町のあかりが、美しくかがやいています。まるで宝石をばらまいたようです。

「おいッ、松下。きみは、きょうはよっぽど、どうかしているな。方角がちがうじゃないか。さっきのままでいいんだ。どうして、もとのほうへひっかえすんだ。」

東のほうへ進んでいたヘリコプターが、いつのまにか、ぐるッとむきをかえて、西にむかってとんでいるのです。

40

「かしら、だまっていてください。ヘリコプターのことは、あっしにまかしといてくださいよ。気流が悪いんです。ちょっと、まわり道をするだけです。」

やっぱり、へんてこなかすれ声です。

「きみ、その声はどうしたんだ。かぜでもひいたのか。」

「ええ、ちょっとね。なに、たいしたことあありませんよ。」

四十面相はさっきから、松下のいうことがどうもよくわかりません。ひょっとしたら、こいつにせ顔をかくすようにして、下ばかりむいているのもへんです。ものじゃないのかな、と、恐ろしいうたがいが心をかすめました。

そのときです。右手のほうの空に、ひとつの光がとんでいるのに気がつきました。星ではありません。

とすると、空をとぶ光といえば、飛行機かヘリコプターのほかには、ないはずです。

飛行機ではありません。どうも、こちらとおなじような、ヘリコプターらしいのです。

やっぱりヘリコプターでした。こっちへ近づいてくるようです。まるい、すきとおった操縦室が見えてきました。その中にいる人間のすがたまで、ありありと見えてきました。

そのヘリコプターはぐんぐん近づいてきます。五十メートル、三十メートル、やがて十メートルまで接近しました。

そして、こちらとおなじ方向へならんでとんでいます。もう、操縦士の顔がぼんやりと見えるほどです。

オヤッ、あそこにいるのは、松下じゃないか。

四十面相は、ギョッとしたように、こちらの松下の横顔を見つめました。ちがう、ちがう。こいつは、おれの部下の松下じゃない。あやういところを助けてくれたので、部下とばかり思っていた。部下のうちで、ヘリコプターを操縦できるやつは、松下のほかにないのだから、こいつを松下だと思いこんでいた。

だが、ちがう。こいつは松下じゃない。むこうのヘリコプターにいるのが松下だ。すると、こいつはいったい、何者だろう？

「おいッ、きみは松下じゃないんだなッ。」

四十面相は、操縦士のわきばらをこづきながら、おしころしたような声できめつけました。

操縦士の正体

松下とよばれていた男は、はじめて顔を上にむけ、正面から四十面相をにらみつけまし

「松下でないとすると、だれだと思うね。」
「なにッ、さては、きさまッ。」
「おっと、身動きしちゃいけない。ぼくの手がくるったら、みんなおだぶつだからね。それに、きみの背中にかたいものがあたっているのが、わかるかね。ピストルの筒先だよ。きみのうしろに、ぼくの助手の小男がうずくまって、ピストルをつきつけているんだよ。手むかいをすれば、きみの命はないんだぜ。」
「ちきしょうッ！　きさま、いったい何者だッ？　敵か味方か。まさか味方じゃあないだろう。すると、さっき、屋根の上から、おれを助けてくれたのは、どういうわけだ。」
「助けたんじゃあない。つかまえたんだよ。そして、いまきみを警視庁へつれていくところさ。」
「それじゃあ、きさま、警視庁のやろうかッ。」
「そうでもないよ。おい、四十面相、ぼくをわすれたのかね。」
　操縦士はそういって、ポケットから、あぶらをしませたてぬぐいをだすと、それで自分の顔を、ぐるぐるとなでまわしました。変装のけしょうをふきとったのです。
「アッ、きさま、明智小五郎だなッ。」

「ウフフフフ……、やっとわかったかね。そして、きみのうしろからピストルをつきつけているのは、ぼくの少年助手の小林だよ。おとなの服を着て、小男にばけていたのさ」
　読者諸君、ちょっと、思いだしてください。四十面相が神山邸の洋館の屋根にのぼったとき、屋敷をとりまく警官隊の中に、明智探偵と小林少年のすがたが見えなかったことは、前の章に書いてあります。あれを思いだしてください。ふたりは、そのとき、警視庁のヘリコプターをかりだして、神山邸へとんできたのです。
　明智探偵は、自動車はもちろん、飛行機でも、ヘリコプターでも、操縦できる腕まえを持っていました。名探偵というものは、万能選手でなければなりません。明智は青年時代から、あらゆるスポーツでからだをきたえてきました。そして、飛行機の操縦までも、じゅうぶん練習していたのです。
「おい、四十面相。きみは、せっかく苦心をして、牢やぶりをしたかとおもうと、もうかまってしまったね。こんなにはやくつかまるなんて、いつものきみにも、にあわないことじゃないか。
　ハハハハハ。きみがヘリコプターを持っていることは、ちゃんとわかっていた。だから、きみが、あの西洋館の高い屋根へ逃げのぼったとき、ぼくは、すぐにヘリコプターを思いだした。そのほかに、四方をかこまれたあの屋根から、逃げる方法はないのだからね。

きみは部下とうちあわせておいて、ちょうどいい時分に、ヘリコプターがあそこへとんでくるようにしておいた。そして、自分のヘリコプターに乗って、逃げだすつもりだった。

ぼくはそれがわかったので、小林君をつれて、警視庁にかけつけ、ふたりとも変装をして、このヘリコプターに乗りこんだ。そして、きみの部下のヘリコプターがやってくる前に、先をこして、あの屋根の上にあらわれたのだ。

よく見れば、きみのヘリコプターと、これとは形がちがっているのだが、水ぜめにあって、めんくらっていたきみには、その見わけがつかなかった。助けだしにきたからには、自分のヘリコプターだと思いこんでしまったのだ。そして、まんまと、ぼくのわなにかかったというわけだよ。

あそこにとんでいるのが、きみの部下の松下という男だろう。ひとあしおくれて首領をさらわれ、びっくりして追っかけてきたのだ。だが、まさか、こっちのヘリコプターを、射撃するわけにもいくまい。首領のきみが、乗っているんだからね。

あの男は、どうしていいかわからなくなって、ただぼくたちを、つけているのだ。いまに、自分もつかまってしまうのも知らないでね。ハハハハハ……。

それじゃあ、きみをつかまえたことを警視庁に知らせて、よろこばせることにしよう。きみも聞いていたまえ。」
　明智はそういって、操縦席の前にある無線電話の送話器をよびだすのでした。
「こちらは空中警邏機第二号＊。報告します。ただいま警視庁にむかって飛行中。いまから、約十分のゝち、神山邸洋館屋上で、怪人四十面相を逮捕の予定。着陸地点に数名の警官を配置してください。」
　明智は送話器にむかって、おなじことを二度くりかえしました。すると、むこうから、
「警視庁りょうかい。」
という返事が、はっきり聞こえてきました。
「四十面相、もうひとつきみに知らせておくことがある。きみはレンブラントの名画をぬすみだして、背中にしょっているつもりだろうが、それはとんだ思いちがいだよ。そのふろしきづつみをといて、よくしらべてみるがいい。」
　明智にそういわれて、四十面相は、びっくりしたような顔をしました。そこで、のろのろと、ふろしきづつみをおろし、中のカンバスを出してひらきました。そして、ひと目その画面を見ると、思わず、「アッ！」と声をたてないではいられませんでした。

＊パトロール機

46

ごらんなさい。それは、いつのまにか、レンブラントとはにてもにつかない、へたくそな風景画にかわっていたではありませんか。

四十面相のあっけにとられた顔を見ると、明智探偵は、さも、こきみよさそうに、笑いだすのでした。

「ハハハハ……。おい、四十面相君。こんどはなにからなにまで、きみの負けだね。ぬすみだした絵は、まるでちがったにせものだった。助けだされたと思ったヘリコプターは、警視庁の警邏機だった。そして、それに乗っていたのは、きみがこの世で、いちばん恐れている明智小五郎だったとは。ハハハハ……」

暗号の光

「ワハハハハ……」

四十面相も明智に負けないで笑いだしました。こういう悪人になると、それくらいのことでは、なかなかへこたれないのです。

「ワハハハハ……、明智君、さすがは名探偵だねえ。うまくやられたよ。

だが、レンブラントの絵が、いつのまに、こんなつまらない風景画にかわったのか、お

れはすこしも気がつかなかった。わくからはがしたときには、たしかにあの名画だったんだがなあ。明智君、ひとつこの手品の種あかしをしてくれないかね」

それを聞くと、明智も笑いだして、

「きみは魔法使いのくせに、あれがわからなかったのかい？　きみの背中にピストルをあてているのは、おとなのオーバーを着ているけれども、じつは、ぼくの少年助手の小林なんだよ。この小林がその風景画のカンバスのまるめたのを持って、神山さんの美術室にかくれていたのさ。本棚のうしろにね。そして、きみが石膏像をやぶってあらわれ、レンブラントの絵をわくからはがして、棒のようにまるめて、ちょっと床においたときに、本棚のかげから、手をのばしてすりかえてしまったのだよ。小林君も、なかなか手品はうまいからね。ハハハハ……」

「ふうん、そうだったのか。これはいちばん、やられたね。きみのチンピラ助手も、すみにおけないよ……。ところできみは、これから、おれをどうしようというのだね」

「わかっているじゃないか。さっき警視庁と無電で話したとおりだよ。日比谷公園の広っぱに、おおぜいの警官が待ちかまえている。その中へ、このヘリコプターを着陸させて、きみをひきわたすのさ。」

そんな話をしているとき、四十面相は左の手で、みょうなことをやっていました。

そッと、ポケットから小型の懐中電灯をとりだし、それを、プラスチックの操縦席の横にむけて、明智探偵たちに気づかれないように、ピカッ、ピカッ、ピカッと、つけたり消したりしていたのです。

そのむこうには、四十面相の部下のヘリコプターが、こちらのヘリコプターとならんでとんでいます。もしかしたら、四十面相は、そうして味方のヘリコプターへ、懐中電灯の暗号通信をしていたのではないでしょうか。

「ワハハハ……、こうなると、四十面相も、あわれなもんだね。また刑務所へくらいこむのか。だが、明智君、おれはやっぱり魔法使いなんだぜ。きみのほうが手品をつかえば、おれのほうは魔術をつかうのさ。こうして、つかまったように見えていても、ほんとうは、つかまってやしないんだぜ。ウフフフフ、まあ、いまにわかるよ。」

四十面相は負けおしみのようなことを、くどくどとしゃべっています。懐中電灯の通信をごまかすためかもしれません。

まもなく、いままでならんでとんでいた、むこうのヘリコプターが、だんだん遠ざかっていき、やがて、うしろのほうへとびさってしまいました。

それからしばらくすると、こちらのヘリコプターは、日比谷公園の上に近づいていました。

広っぱには、高いはしらの上に照明灯がつけられ、その光の中に、十数名の制服のおまわりさんが、大きな円をえがいて立ちならんでいました。

そのうしろにむらがっている背広服の人たちは、きっと新聞記者なのでしょう。写真機をさげている人もまじっています。警視庁づめの記者たちが、四十面相がつかまったと聞いて、おまわりさんのあとから、かけつけてきたのでしょう。

明智の操縦するヘリコプターは、その広っぱの真上までくると、しずかに下へおりはじめました。地面に近づくにしたがって、広っぱのようすがはっきり見えてきました。むらがっているのは新聞記者ばかりではないようです。もう十二時をすぎた夜ふけですが、どこからともなく、野次馬が集まってきて、そのかずが、だんだんふえてくるのでした。

おまわりさんは、ヘリコプター着陸のための、広い場所をあけておかなければなりませんので、まん中へ出てこようとする人たちをとめるのに、やっきとなっているようです。なかなかヘリコプターを着陸させることができません。広っぱの上空で五分ほども手間どってしまいました。

やがて、明智探偵は、ヘリコプターをゆっくり下降させました。地面に近づくと、あらしのようなプロペラの風が吹きまくり、恐ろしい砂ぼこりがたちます。むらがっている

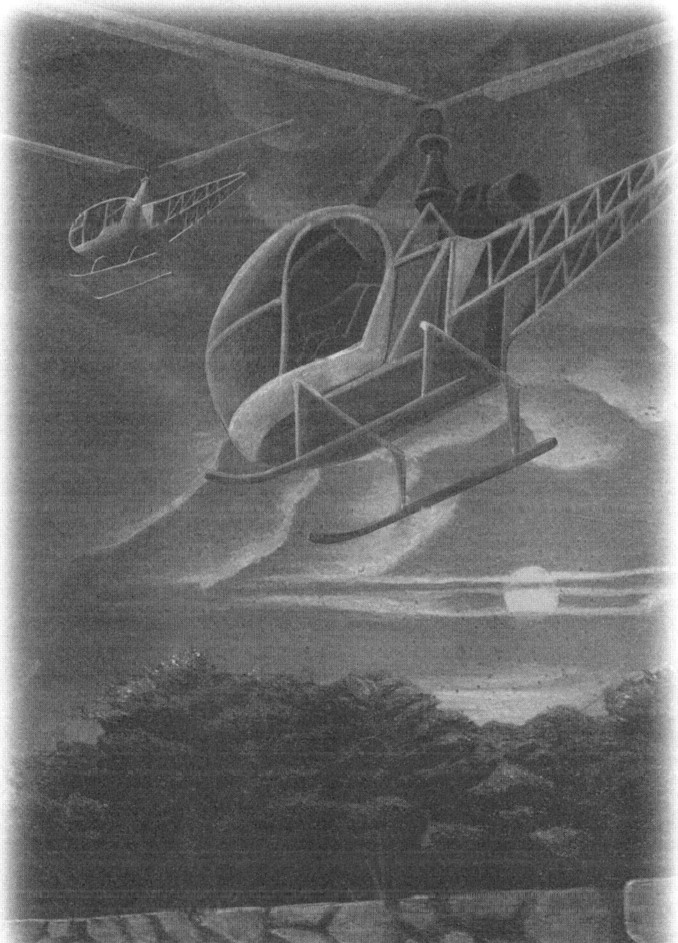

人々は、目をおさえて、広っぱのすみのほうへ逃げだしました。
それで、やっと地面が広くなったので、明智はヘリコプターを着陸させることができましたが、すると、逃げだしていた野次馬が、新聞記者たちといっしょに、ドッとおしよせてきて、たちまち操縦席のまわりは、黒山の人だかりになってしまいました。

すりの源公

ヘリコプターの操縦席のドアがひらかれ、待ちかまえていたおまわりさんが、そこへ近づくと、いきなり四十面相の手をとって、外へひきずりおろしました。そのときまでおとなしくしていた四十面相が、恐ろしいいきおいで、おまわりさんの手をふりきって、いきなり、パッとうしろの群衆の中へおどりこんだではありませんか。

「アッ!」とおどろいた警官たちが、そのほうへ、とびかかっていきました。

さいわい、四十面相がとびこんだのは、新聞記者たちの中でした。

「ちくしょう。逃がすものか。おまわりさん、ここにいますよ。はやくつかまえてください。」

記者たちが、口々にわめきながら、黒シャツすがたの四十面相を、前のほうへおしだし

手錠を持った警官が、それにとびついていって、かちんと両手にはめてしまいました。
　もうこんどは、逃げられません。十数名の警官にとりまかれて、四十面相はおとなしく、すぐむこうの警視庁のほうへ、ひったてられていくのでした。
　まもなく四十面相は、警視庁の地下のしらべ室へ、つれこまれていました。正面には、捜査一課の係長のひとりである中村警部が、厳然とイスにかけています。
　中村警部は四十面相のために、たびたびだしぬかれているので、うらみかさなる相手です。
　こんどこそは、もう逃がさないぞと、恐ろしい目でにらみつけていました。
　その横に、明智探偵と小林少年がひかえていました。四十面相は、ふたりの警官にまもられて、その前にしょんぼりと立っているのです。
「おい、四十面相、本名は遠藤平吉だな。きみは、せっかく脱獄したかとおもったら、もううつかまってしまったじゃないか。すこし、おいぼれたようだな。」
　中村警部が、きみよさそうにいいました。
「エッ、四十面相？……遠藤平吉？」
　なんだかへんです。小林少年は、はやくもそれに気づいて、明智探偵のひざをつっつき

ました。そして、
「あいつ、どっか、顔がちがいますよ。ヘリコプターに乗っていたやつと、顔がちがってますよ。」
とささやくのでした。
中村警部は、いまはじめて、近くで顔を見るのですから、そこまでは気がつきません。
「おい、遠藤、はっきり返事をしないか。きみは四十面相と名のる男だね。」
はげしくどなりつけますと、男は、きょとんとして、
「エッ、とんでもない。あっしゃ、そんなものじゃありませんよ。ひどいめにあったんです。日比谷の林の中で、三人の男につかまって、こんなものを着せられちまったんです。そして、むりやり広っぱの人ごみの中へつれこまれ、おまわりさんの前へ、つきだされたんです。なにがなんだか、さっぱりわけがわかりませんや。」
黒シャツの男は、不平らしく、つぶやくのでした。
なんだか、ようすがおかしいのです。口のききかたも、四十面相とはまるでちがっています。
「そんなことをいってごまかそうとしたって、その手にはのらないぞ。きさまが四十面相

54

「アッ、そうだ。これを見ておくんなさい。その三人のやつが、しらべ室へいったら、これを見せるがいいといって、こんなものを……」

男はそういって、黒シャツのポケットから、一枚の紙きれをとりだして、中村警部の前にさしだします。

うけとってみますと、その紙きれには、えんぴつで、こんなことが書いてありました。

　　こいつはすりの源公です。四十面相の身がわりには、すこしやすっぽいけれども、ともかく、すりをひとりつかまえてあげたんだから、まあ、がまんしてください。それじゃ、あばよ。
　　　　　　　　　　四十面相より
　警視庁どの

中村警部はそれを読むと、恐ろしい顔になって、黒シャツの男をにらみつけました。

「おまえ、源公っていうのかッ。」

「へえ、あっしゃ、源公ですよ。」

男はへいきな顔で、すましています。

中村警部は、そばにいた警官に、なにか耳うちしました。すると、警官はすぐに、部屋

の外へ出ていきましたが、まもなくひとりの背広の人をつれてかえってきました。それは、すり係りの刑事だったのです。

刑事は、部屋にはいって、黒シャツの男をひとめ見ると、

「アッ、おまえ、源公だなッ。またやったのか。いったい、なんど、くらいこめばいいのだ。」

と、しかるようにいいました。そして、中村警部のほうにむきなおり、

「係長、こいつは前科七犯の有名なやつです。源公にちがいありません。」

と、きっぱりいいきるのでした。

ああ、四十面相は、やっぱり魔法使いでした。ヘリコプターの中にいたのは、まちがいのない四十面相でしたが、それがいつのまに、こんなすりに、いれかわってしまったのでしょう。

明智探偵は、ちょっと、首をかしげて考えていましたが、すぐに魔法の種に気づきました。

「中村君、わかったよ。さっき四十面相が、ヘリコプターからひきずりおろされたとき、警官の手をふりきって、新聞記者のかたまっている中へ逃げこんだ。すると、記者の人たちが、こいつをとらえて、つきだしてくれたんだが、その瞬間に、人間のいれかえがおこ

つまり、あの新聞記者たちはにせもので、四十面相の部下がばけていたんだ。そして、まえもってこの源公というすりをつかまえておいて、四十面相の身がわりにたてていたのだ。なにしろ、四十面相とおなじ黒シャツがただ着ておいて、あのさわぎの中だから、警官たちも気づかなかったのだよ。この源公に黒シャツを着せておいて、とっさに、人間のすりかえをやったのだからね。

それにしても、四十面相の部下は、ヘリコプターが日比谷公園につくことを、どうして知っていたのでしょう。明智探偵はそこまでは気づきませんでしたが、読者諸君はごぞんじです。それは、空をとんでいるとき、四十面相の部下のヘリコプターが、こちらとならんでとんでいました。それにむかって、四十面相は懐中電灯の信号をおくったのです。たぶん、モールス信号だったのでしょう。

四十面相の部下の ヘリコプターは、その通信をうけると、すぐにどこかへ着陸して、電話でなかまにこのことを知らせ、日比谷へさきまわりしているように、はからったのにちがいありません。

明智は、さらに説明をつけくわえました。

「あの黒山の人だかりだから、ほんものの四十面相は、どこかへ身をかくしてしまったにちが

＊ アメリカのサミュエル・モースが考案した通信符号。長短二つの組み合わせによって文字をあらわす。トン・ツーともいう

57

だ。記者にばけた部下たちが、オーバーかマントを用意していて、四十面相の黒シャツの上から着せてしまえば、夜のことだから、もうわかりっこないのだからね。」

「アッ、そうかッ。おい、新聞記者をよんできたまえ。みんなよんでくるんだ。」

中村警部がどなりました。ひとりの警官がとびだしていったかとおもうと、ぞろぞろとおおぜいの新聞記者が、しらべ室へはいってきました。

「公園のヘリコプターのそばで、この男をつきだしてくれた人はいませんか。」

警部がたずねますと、記者たちは、たがいに顔を見あわせていましたが、その中のひとりが答えました。

「いや、あれは新聞社のものじゃありませんよ。だれだかわからないが、ぼくたちのあいだに、六、七人、へんなやつがまじっていたのです。その連中が、こいつをつきだしたのです。」

「ふうん、ちゃんと用意をしていたんだな。それで、ほんものの四十面相が、どこへ逃げたか、きみたち気づきませんでしたか。」

警部が聞きますと、記者たちはびっくりして、

「エッ、じゃあ、こいつは四十面相じゃないのですか。」

「うん、すっかり黒星でもうしわけないが、やられたんだ。あいつらは、この源公というすりに、黒シャツを着せて、上からオーバーかなにかはおらせて、あそこへつれてきていたんだね。そして、とっさに人間のすりかえをやったんだ。」

中村警部は、すこし、めんぼくないような顔で説明しました。

なるほど、警視庁としては、大失策にちがいありません。しかし、明智探偵と小林少年は、それほど失望しているようにも見えないのはなぜでしょう……。ふたりは、まだあきらめていなかったからです。四十面相のほうにおくの手があれば、ちゃんと、もうひとつおくの手が用意してあったからです。

ポケット小僧

お話は、すこし前にもどって、ヘリコプターが、日比谷公園の広っぱに着陸したところからはじまります。

ヘリコプターのまわりに集まっている新聞記者や、野次馬の中に、二人の小さな子どもがまじっていました。

三人とも、*浮浪少年のような、きたないなりをしていましたが、その中に、まるで幼稚

＊ 定まった住所や仕事がなく、方々をうろついている少年

園の生徒のような、小さい少年がいました。

この三人は、小林少年の命令でここへやってきた、チンピラ隊の少年たちでした。いちばん小さい少年は、ポケット小僧とよばれているチンピラ隊員です。

この三少年は、ばらばらにはなれて、おおぜいのおとなのあいだを、リスのようにくぐりぬけて、ぬけめなく見はりをしていました。小林団長から、四十面相を見はっていて、なにかあやしいことがあったら知らせるようにと、いいつけられていたのです。

四十面相をとらえたら、日比谷公園の広っぱまでつれてくることは、ヘリコプターに乗る前からきまっていたので、小林君は、あらかじめチンピラ隊に連絡して、はやくから公園へきているようにさしずしておきました。チンピラたちは、ひまなからだですから、いくら長く待っていても、へいきなのです。

三人のチンピラの中でも、いちばんすばしっこくて、頭のはたらくのはポケット小僧です。彼はからだが小さいので、おとなのあいだを、くぐって歩くことができます。

「おや、だれだッ、ぼくのまたのあいだをくぐったやつは？」

びっくりして見まわしても、ポケット小僧は、もうとっくに人ごみの中へすがたをかくしているのです。

そうして、あちこちとくぐり歩いているうちに、ポケット小僧は、へんな男を見つけま

60

した。
その男は鳥打ち帽をまぶかにかぶり、大きなオーバーを着て、四、五人の新聞記者のような人たちにとりかこまれていましたが、ポケット小僧は、その人のまたのあいだをくぐったときに、へんなことを見てしまったのです。
その男はズボンをはかないで、ぴったり足にくっついた、まっ黒なズボン下のようなものをはいていました。まるでサーカスの曲芸師のようです。
「へんなやつがいるな。」
と思ったので、ポケット小僧は、その男のそばをはなれないようにして、気をつけていましたが、すると、ヘリコプターから四十面相がひきおろされ、あのさわぎがはじまったのです。
黒シャツの四十面相は、警官の手をふりきって、こちらの人ごみの中へ、とびこんできました。
それから、じつにふしぎなことが、はじまったのです。
新聞記者らしい四、五人の男が、かけこんでくる四十面相の手をとって、あのあやしいオーバーの男のそばへひきよせました。そして、手ばやくオーバーをぬがせると、それを四十面相に着せてしまいました。鳥打ち帽もとって、四十面相にかぶせたのです。

オーバーと、鳥打ち帽をとられた男は、四十面相とそっくりのすがたをしていました。
黒シャツに黒ズボンでした。顔もどこかにていているのです。
新聞記者のような人たちは、そのへんな男を、人ごみの前のほうへつきだしながら、口々に叫ぶのでした。
「こいつだ、こいつだ。こいつが、いま、人ごみの中へ、かくれようとしたんだ。」
そして、その男を、警官たちにひきわたしたのです。
顔もにているし、服装がまったくおなじなので、警官たちは、替え玉とは気づかず、その男に手錠をはめて、むこうへつれていってしまいました。
四十面相がつれていかれたので、新聞記者や、ものずきな野次馬は、あとから、ぞろぞろついていきましたが、大部分はそのまま、公園の外へひきあげていき、あたりは、すっかりさびしくなってきました。
オーバーに鳥打ち帽の四十面相は、すばやく公園のすみのほうへ走っていって、こんもりとしげった林の中へ、すがたをかくしました。
ポケット小僧は、見うしなってはたいへんだと、こっそり、そのあとをつけました。小さな子どもですから、べつにあやしまれることもありません。そのうえ、小僧は尾行の名人ですから、まだそのへんにいたおとなたちに、さとられるようなへまはやりません。

62

このことを明智先生や小林少年に知らせたいのですが、そのひまはなかったのです。四十面相はヘリコプターの反対のほうへ逃げたので、あとにもどって知らせていたら、見うしなってしまうかもしれないのです。仲間のチンピラがそばにいたら、知らせてくれるようにたのむこともできたでしょうが、ふたりのチンピラは、どこへいったのか、すがたが見えません。

ふしぎな変装

四十面相がかくれたしげみの中には、大きな四角なカバンがかくしてありました。部下に命じて、そこへ持ってこさせておいた変装用のカバンなのです。

四十面相は懐中電灯をつけて、そのカバンをひらきました。洋服やシャツなどが、いっぱいつまっています。彼は、カバンのふたの裏についているポケットに手をいれて、小さな鏡と箱をとりだしました。その箱の中は、顔をかえる絵の具や、つけひげや、いろいろなものがはいっているのです。

彼は、カバンのふたをしめ、その上に鏡を立てて、懐中電灯で自分の顔を照らしながら、変装のおけしょうをはじめました。

そこは深い木のしげみにかこまれていて、懐中電灯の光が外へもれる心配はありません。

もう、夜の十二時をすぎています。さっきまで広っぱに集まっていた、野次馬たちも帰ってしまって、公園の中には、人っ子ひとりいなくなってしまいました。新聞記者にばけていた四十面相の部下たちも、どこへいったのかすがたが見えません。

四十面相は、ゆうゆうとして変装をやっています。じつに落ちつきはらったものです。

それにしても、彼はなぜこんな公園の中などで、変装をはじめたのでしょうか。オーバーの下から黒いズボン下のあらわれているこのままのすがたで町に出れば、いくら夜中でも人にあやしまれますが、それなら部下に自動車を用意させて、それに乗って逃げてしまえばいいのです。

そうしないで、こんなふじゆうな場所で変装をはじめたのには、なにかわけがあるのかもしれません。

四十面相は、だれも見ていないと安心していましたが、じつは、ひとりの小さな少年が、しげみのむこう側にはいって、木の葉のすきまから、じっと中をのぞいていたのです。

この少年は、少年探偵団の仲間のチンピラ隊にぞくするポケット小僧なのです。からだがひどく小さくて、ポケットにでもはいるくらいだというので、そんなあだ名がついてい

ましたが、すばしっこくて、たいへんりこうな少年でした。

前に書いたとおり、このポケット小僧は、四十面相がにせものといれかわったのを気づいて、ほんもののほうのあとをつけて、このしげみへやってきたのです。

ポケット小僧は、しげみの外に寝そべって、相手に気づかれぬように、じっと中のようすをうかがっていました。

いくえにもかさなりあった木の葉のすきまからのぞいているのですから、よくは見えません。それでも、四十面相が懐中電灯の光で、顔に絵の具をぬっていることはわかりました。

なにしろ、四十の顔を持つといわれる変装の大名人です。その手ばやいこと……。たちまち顔をしあげて、こんどはカバンの中から黒い服をとりだすと、それを黒シャツの上から着こみ、バンドをしめ、肩からなにかさげて、帽子をかぶり、靴をはきました。変装がおわると、いままで着ていたオーバーをカバンにいれ、ふたをしめて、そのカバンを手にさげ、木のしげみから出てきました。

ポケット小僧は相手に見つからぬよう、すばやくしげみの反対側にかくれましたが、見ると、そこにあらわれたのは、ひとりの警官でした。四十面相は警官にばけたのです。

ああ、なんといううまい変装でしょう。警官の制服に制帽、肩から革ひもで、ピストル

のサックをさげているようすは、だれが見てもほんもののおまわりさんです。ポケット小僧はその顔を見て、びっくりしてしまいました。さっきまでの四十面相と、まるでちがっていたからです。四十面相が変装したのではなくて、ほんとうのおまわりさんが、どこからかやってきたとしか思われません。

四十面相が、四十の顔を持つといわれるほどの変装の名人だということは、聞いていましたが、これほどの名人とは知りませんでした。ほんとうに魔法使いです。

カバンをさげた四十面相のおまわりさんは、しゃんと胸をはって大またに歩いていきました。

ポケット小僧はさとられないように気をつけながら、ちょこちょことあとをつけていきます。

おまわりさんは、公園を出ると、すぐそばにある警視庁のほうへ進んでいきました。警視庁といえば、四十面相にとっては、いちばん恐ろしいところです。その恐ろしいところへ、へいきで近づいていくのです。

やがて、警視庁の入り口のところまできました。入り口の広い石段に、警官が立っています。その前には警察用の自動車がたくさんならんでいて、夜中でも、警官たちがいったりきたりしています。

66

四十面相のにせ警官は、その石段の前までいくと、なにを思ったのか、石段をのぼりはじめました。ああ、四十面相はどうかしたのでしょうか。「さあ、つかまえてください」といわぬばかりに、警視庁の中へはいっていこうとしているのです。

ポケット小僧は、あきれかえって、そのうしろすがたをながめていました。どろぼうが警官にばけて、警視庁へはいっていくのです。こんなばかなことがあるものでしょうか。

にせ警官は、石段に立っている警官に、片手をあげてあいさつすると、そのまま玄関の中へはいっていきます。

ほんものの警官は、すこしもあやしまず、おなじように手をあげてあいさつをかえしました。

警視庁へは、一日に何千という警官が出入りするのですから、みんながおなじみというわけではありません。制服さえ着ていれば、自分たちの仲間だと思うのもむりはないのです。

にせ警官は、大カバンをさげていましたが、犯罪事件の証拠品として、そういうものを持ってくる警官はよくあるのですから、これもうたがわれる心配はありません。にせ警官のすがたが玄関の中へ見えなくなってしまったとき、ポケット小僧は、大いそぎで石段をかけあがり、そこに立っている警官によびかけました。

「おまわりさん、いまのやつをつかまえて。大きなカバンをさげていたやつだよ。あれは四十面相だよ。おれ、あいつが変装するところを見ちゃったんだ。はやくあいつをつかまえなけりゃ……」

警官はびっくりしてこちらを見ましたが、きたないふうをした浮浪児のような子どもなので、手をふりながら、あっちへいけというあいずをするばかりで、いっこうにとりあってくれません。

「おまわりさん、ほんとうだよ。はやくしないと、あいつ、逃げちゃうじゃないか。おじさんは四十面相知らないのかい？　おっそろしい大どろぼうだぜ」

ポケット小僧は、警官の手にすがりついて、いっしょうけんめいに叫びました。

「こら、あっちへいくんだ。ここは、おまえたちのくるところじゃない。チンピラのくせに、警官をからかうなんて、けしからんやつだ」

警官が、つかまれている手をいきおいよくふりきったものですから、ポケット小僧は、石段の上に、ころがってしまいました。

「アッ、いたい。おじさん、なにをするんだい！」

やっとおきあがって、おしりをさすりながら、

「子どもだと思って、ばかにしてるんだな。そうじゃないよ。からかってるんじゃないよ。

ほんとうだよ。あいつ四十面相だよ。はやく……はやくしないと、逃げちゃうよ。」

「くどいやつだな。あっちへいけというのに。」

警官は、横をむいて、知らぬふりをしようとしました。

「アーッ、そうだ。ここに明智先生がきているだろう。名探偵の明智小五郎先生だよ。おれ、あの先生の弟子なんだよ。そうすれば、おれがうそをいっていないことが、わかるんだから。」

そこへ、玄関のほうから、警部補の制服を着た警官がおりてきましたが、ポケット小僧のわめき声を聞くと、そばによってきて、「どうしたんだ」とたずねました。

ポケット小僧は、このひとなら話がわかるかもしれないと思ったので、さっきからいっていることを、もう一度くりかえしました。

「明智さんなら、しらべ室におられるはずだ。知らせてあげるほうがいいね。この子どものいうことが、もしほんとうだったら、たいへんだからね。きみ、しらべ室をさがしてみたまえ。捜査一課の中村係長さんといっしょのはずだよ。」

上役に命令されたので、警官はしかたなく石段をかけあがって、玄関へはいっていきました。

しばらくすると、警官は小林少年をつれてもどってきました。小林君は、明智探偵と

いっしょにしらべ室にいたのです。
「アッ、小林さん！」
「アッ、ポケット小僧！」
顔を見あわせると、ふたりがいっしょに叫びました。
「これは探偵の仕事を手つだってくれるチンピラ隊の子どもです。りこうな子ですから、この子のいうことは、まちがいありません。」
小林少年は、明智探偵の助手として、警視庁でもよく知られていました。その小林君がそういうのですから、もうすててはおけません。
そこへ、明智探偵や中村警部もかけつけてきて、ポケット小僧からことのしだいを聞きとると、にわかに警視庁内の大捜索がはじまりました。
警視庁には何百という部屋があるのですが、夜中につめている警官の数も多いのでたいへんです。
まもなく、ぜんぶの部屋の捜索がおわりました。しかし、あやしい警官は、どこにもいないのです。
とっくに、裏口から逃げさったのかもしれません。それなら、はじめから警視庁へはいらないで、逃げてしまえばよさそうなものではありませんか。

よ、わけがわからなくなってきました。

警視総監

　その夜は、四十面相がつかまって、ヘリコプターではこばれてくるというので、捜査一課の堀口警視も、課長室につめていましたが、庁内の捜索がおわってしばらくすると、ひとりの警官が課長室へはいってきて、挙手の礼をしました。
「課長、総監がおよびです。」
「え、総監が？　総監室にきておられるのか。」
「四十面相のことを聞かれて、いま公舎からおいでになったところです。」
「そうか。すぐいく。」
「課長、それから、中村係長もいっしょにくるようにとのことでした。よんでまいりましょうか。」
「うん、よんでくれたまえ。ぼくはさきにいっているから。」
　堀口捜査一課長が、警視総監の部屋へはいると、まもなく中村係長もそこへやってさま

総監室は、りっぱな広い部屋です。まん中に大きな机がおいてあって、そのむこうに背広すがたの山本警視総監が、ゆったりと、こしかけていました。夜中のことですから、秘書官もつれていないのです。

「や、ごくろうですね。四十面相のさわぎを聞いて、心配だから、わたしもちょっときてみました。くわしいことは、まだ聞いていないが、このさわぎは、どうしたことだね。」

総監にたずねられたので、堀口課長は、今夜のできごとを、かいつまんで報告しました。

「ふうん、すると、また、あいつにしてやられたわけだね。明智君が、ヘリコプターでつれてきたまではおおできだが、それからあとがいけない。いくら変装の名人だからといって、にせものをつかまされたり、警官にばけて庁内にはいりこまれたりしたのでは、警視庁の名おれだ。しっかりしてくれなくちゃこまりますね。これはいったい、だれの責任なんだね。」

堀口課長が、もうしわけなさそうに答えました。

「わたしの責任です。わたしの部下が、あやまちをしでかしたのですから。」

「いや、責任はわたしにあります。わたしが、この事件の係りなのですから。」

中村係長も、青ざめた顔でおわびをいって、うなだれてしまいました。

72

「たったひとりの四十面相が、警視庁の手におえないとあっては、都民にもうしわけがない。これからは、しっかりやってくれたまえ。それにしても、四十面相というやつは恐ろしい怪物だね。われわれは、やつのおもちゃにされているようなもんだ。

ところで、わたしは、さっき、この事件について、ひとつの案を思いついたのだがね。じつは、その案をわたすために、こうして出かけてきたのだ。これだ。ここにわたしの案というのを書きつけておいたから、あとで読んでくれたまえ。」

山本総監はそういって、ポケットから封筒をとりだし、机ごしに堀口課長に手わたしした。その封筒の中に総監の案を書いた紙がはいっているのです。

「今夜、よく読んでくれたまえ。その案についての諸君の意見は、あすの朝聞くことにしよう。では、わたしは、これで帰るから。」

総監はイスから立ちあがって、ゆったりとドアのほうへ歩いていきます。堀口課長と中村係長は、それを見おくるために、あとにしたがいました。

廊下に出てしばらくいきますと、むこうから、あわただしくかけてくるすがたがありました。明智小五郎と小林少年です。

明智は警視総監の前までくると、とおせんぼうをするように、立ちはだかりました。

「アッ、明智君！」

総監は、おどろいて立ちどまります。

「総監、ちょっとお話があります。」

「え、わたしにかね。」

「そうです。きゅうにお話ししなければならないことができたのです。」

「長い話なら、部屋にもどるが……」

「いや、ここでけっこうです。総監、ふしぎなことがおこりました。警視総監がふたりになったのです。」

「え、なんだって？　きみがなにをいっているのか、わたしにはよくわからないが……」

「ぼくにも、さっぱりわかりません。じつは、いま総監の公舎へ電話をかけて、たずねたのです。すると、山本総監は、公舎の寝室でよく眠っておられるということでした。いったい、これはどうしたわけでしょうか。」

「そ、そんなばかなことが……」

「いや、ぼくは、それだけでは信用できないので、総監をおこしてもらって、電話口に出てもらいました。ぼくは、いま総監と話してきたばかりです。」

「ば、ばかなッ。でたらめもいいかげんにしたまえ！」

　山本総監は、まっ赤な顔になってどなりつけました。

「でたらめではありません。あなたにはおわかりになっているはずです。」

「わたしに、なにがわかっているというのだ。」

「ふたりの総監のうちひとりは、にせものだということがです。」

「にせものだって？」

「そうです。あなたが、にせものなのです。ぼくは、さっきから四十面相が、なぜ、警官にばけて警視庁にはいりこんだかということを考えていました。すると、あなたが、この真夜中に、ひょっこり総監室にあらわれて、堀口課長や中村係長をよびつけました。ぼくは、こいつはおかしいぞと思ったのです。四十面相というやつは、とっぴなことをやって、世間をアッとおどろかすのが、だいすきです。自分の力を見せびらかしたい、物をぬすむのにも、いついつの何時にぬすむという予告をして、じゅうぶん用心させておいてぬすむのがすきです。これも世間をアッといわせたいからです。それに、警視庁は、四十面相にとってはにくいかたきです。そのかたきをアッといわせてやったら、どんなにゆかいでしょう。四十面相はきっと、そう考えたと思います。

四十面相が警官にばけただけでも、世間はアッといいます。それが、警視総監にばけるなんて、じつにすばらしい思いつきではありませんか。」

明智はそこまでいって、じっと相手の顔を見つめました。

「それじゃ、きみ、わたしが四十面相だというのか。」

「そうだ。きみは四十面相だッ！ついちかごろ、警視総監の背広が一着ぬすまれている。それはきみが、部下にぬすませたのだ。そして、その背広を警官の服といっしょに、あの大カバンにいれさせておいたのだ。きみは警官にばけてここへやってきた。そして、どこかのあき部屋で、その背広と着かえ、総監になりすまして、総監室へはいったのだ。」

ああ、なんということでしょう。世間に知れわたっている警視総監と、そっくりの顔にばけるなんて、四十の顔を持つ、変装の大名人でなくてはできないことです。

それにしても、明智に見やぶられた四十面相は、ここで、どんな手をうつのでしょうか。

まぼろし警官隊

総監にばけた四十面相は、おどろいて逃げだしたでしょうか？　いや、逃げようとしても逃げられるものではありません。ここは警視庁の建物のまん中なのです。彼は、ふてぶてしく笑いました。

「さすがは名探偵、よく見やぶった。だが、おれが四十面相だったら、どうしようというのだね。」

と落ちつきはらっています。
「むろん、ひっとらえるのさ。手をあげろ！」
　明智のことばといっしょに、横にいた中村警部が、サッとピストルをかまえました。警部は背広を着ていましたが、まんいちの用意に、ポケットにピストルをしのばせていたのです。
　捜査一課長は、いよ出てきたばかりの総監室へ電話をかけました。四十面相をとらえるために、警官隊をよこすように命じたのです。四十面相は両手をあげて、立ちおうじょうをしています。さすがの怪盗も、ピストルをつきつけられてはどうすることもできません。そのとき、廊下のむこうからどやどやと、おおぜいの制服警官がかけつけてきました。十人あまりの人数です。そして、四十面相のまわりをかこんで、ねじふせようとしました。
　警官がとりかこんだので、中村警部はピストルがうてなくなりました。うてば、味方の警官をきずつけるからです。
　それがいけなかったのです。そのすきを見て、四十面相は、すばやく自分のピストルをポケットからとりだし、いきなり天井にむけてうちました。
　がらがらとガラスのわれる音。たまは天井の電灯にあたって、ガラスがわれ、電灯は消

えてしまいました。でも廊下にはいくつも電灯がついていますから、まだまっ暗ではありません。

それから、恐ろしいたたかいがはじまりました。相手がピストルをうったので、警官たちもみなピストルを手にしました。

ばん、ばん、ばんと、つづけざまのピストルの音。四十面相がうったのか、警官たちがうったのか、よくわかりません。しかし、音がするたびに、廊下の電灯がつぎつぎとうちこわされ、あたりはまっ暗になってしまいました。

「うぬッ、つかまえたぞッ。おい、手をかしてくれ。手錠だ、手錠だッ！」

「なにを、これでもかッ！」

ばしッとなぐりつける音。二、三人のからだが廊下にころがって、くんずほぐれつ、とっくみあう音。

「アッ、逃げたぞッ。追っかけろ！」

「ちくしょう、逃がすものか。つかまえたぞッ。ここだ、ここだ。」

警官たちは、四十面相ともつれあって、だんだん廊下のむこうへ遠ざかっていきます。

捜査一課長と中村警部は、物音をたよりに、それを追っていきましたが、廊下の電灯がみんな消えてしまっているので、なにがなんだかまるでようすがわかりません。

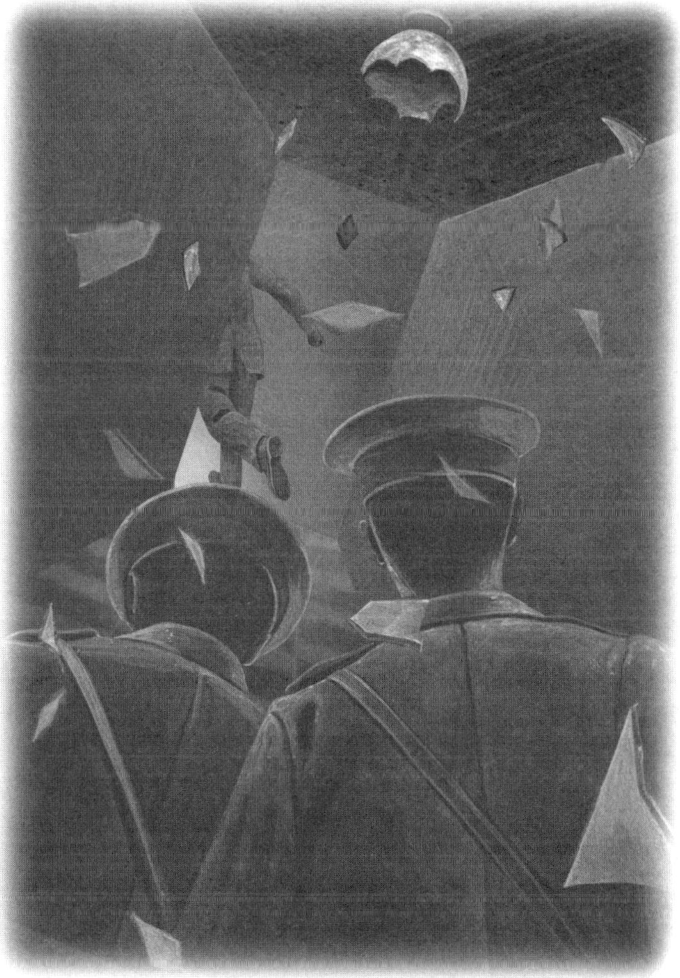

やっと、廊下のまがりかどまでたどりつきましたが、そこからさきの廊下もまっ暗です。たちどまって耳をすますと、ふしぎなことに、あたりはしいんとしずまりかえっています。いままであんなにさわいでいた警官たちは、どこへいったのか、そのへんには人のけはいもないのです。

そこへ、小林少年が懐中電灯を持ってかけつけてきました。その電灯で、廊下のさきのほうを照らしてみましたが、そこには、だれもいないことがわかりました。十余人の警官隊は、四十面相といっしょに、まぼろしのように消えうせてしまったのです。

まがった廊下は一本道で、ほかにいくことはできません。どこかの部屋にはいったのかと、そのへんのドアをひとつひとつあけて、懐中電灯でしらべてみましたが、どの部屋も、まったくからっぽなのです。

「アッ、しまった！」

闇の中から、明智探偵の声が聞こえたかとおもうと、明智らしい人影が、廊下のむこうへ、とぶように走っていくではありませんか。

捜査一課長や中村警部には、なにがしまったのか、なぜ、明智探偵が走っていったのか、わけがわかりません。しかし、そこにつっ立っているわけにもいきませんので、明智のあ

80

とを追って、廊下のむこうへ歩いていきました。
また、廊下をひとまがりしますと、むこうに電灯がついているので、あたりが見わけられるようになりました。
見ると、明智探偵が、こちらへ歩いてきます。
「明智君、どうしたんだ？」
中村警部がたずねますと、名探偵はがっかりしたような声で答えました。
「またやられた。あいつが、そこまで用意していようとは思わなかった。」
「エッ、すると、いよの警官たちは？」
「うん、みんな四十面相の部下だったのさ。新聞記者にばけたやつらが、警官の服を着たどこかにかくれていたのかもしれない。いずれにしても、四十面相をつかまえるように見せかけて、じつは、助けだしてしまったのだ。廊下の電灯がわれたのも、それだまでではなくて、暗くするために、かたっぱしから電灯をねらいうちにしたのだよ。」
その廊下のはずれは、警視庁の裏門のところへ出ていました。彼らは、裏門からまっ暗な道路へ逃げだしてしまったのにちがいありません。

「ぼくは、裏口にいた警官たちにすぐ手配をして、追っかけるようにたのんでおいたが、あいつらは、門を出たら、ばらばらにわかれて、四方にちらばってしまっただろうから、とてもつかまるまい。ことに四十面相は、あんな変装の名人だから、またたくまにべつの人間にばけてしまったかもしれない。」

ああ、なんということでしょう。大どろぼうが警視総監にばけたばかりか、その部下たちも警官にばけて、にせ総監をすくいだすなんて、じつに思いもよらないはなれわざです。さすがの明智探偵も、そこまでは考えていませんでした。

四人が、ぼんやり顔を見あわせていますと、うしろのほうから、おおぜいの靴音がして、八、九人の警官がぞろぞろあらわれました。

課長の電話で、総監室の前にかけつけた警官たちです。彼らがかけつけたときには、にせ警官隊は、廊下をまがってしまったあとだったのです。なにがなんだかわけがわからず、まごまごしているうちに時間電灯が消えているので、なにがなんだかわけがわからず、まごまごしているうちに時間がたって、やっといまごろ、ここへやってきたのです。

中村警部は、自分たちも失敗したのですから、部下をしかるわけにもいかず、ともかくも、にせ総監のあとを追っかけるように命令するのでした。

カバンの中

お話は、すこし前にもどります。

明智探偵が総監の公舎へ電話をかけ、警視庁にあらわれた総監が、にせものだということをたしかめるまでは、明智のそばに、小林少年とポケット小僧がついていましたが、それから明智と小林少年とが、総監室へいそいでいくのを見おくって、ポケット小僧だけは、べつのほうへ歩きだしました。ポケット小僧は、こんなふうに考えたのです。

「四十面相が警視総監にばけたとすると、その変装用の服は、あのカバンの中にはいっていたにちがいない。あいつは、どこかのあき部屋にかくれて、あのカバンの中から、総監の服を出して着かえ、顔をかえてから総監室へあらわれたのだ。

それなら、あのカバンが、どこかにおいてあるにちがいない。そのまますてていくかもしれないが、ひょっとしたら、あれを四十面相のすみ家へ持ってかえるかもしれない。

カバンの中のものをみんなとりだせば、からだの小さいおれは、あの中へかくれられる。

そして、四十面相のすみ家をつきとめることができるじゃないか。

よし、やってみよう。見つかったときのことだ。まさか、殺されやしない

だろう。」

ポケット小僧は、かしこくもそう考えると、あき部屋からあき部屋へと、カバンをさがして歩きました。

そして、十いくつめの部屋で、とうとうそれを見つけたのです。

「待てよ。このままカバンの中にはいって、ふたをしめたら、息がつまってしまう。カバンの革に、小さな穴をたくさんあけておかなけりゃあ。」

そこで、ポケット小僧は、べつの部屋から、紙をとじるきりをさがしだしてきて、それを持ってカバンのある部屋にはいり、ぴったりドアをしめて、仕事にかかりました。

まず、カバンの中のものをすっかりとりだして、その部屋の戸棚の中にかくし、それから、カバンの革の目だたない場所へ、きりをさして五十ほどの穴をあけました。

その仕事は、十分ほどでおわりましたので、すぐにからだをまるくして、カバンの中に横になり、自分でふたをしめました。すると、ふたについているばねじかけの金具が、ぱちんとしまって、もう中からはひらかぬようになってしまいました。

ポケット小僧は、もと浮浪少年のチンピラ隊員ですから、苦しいことにはなれています。からだをまるめて、長いあいだ、じっとしていることなんか、へいきなのです。また、その穴から、外の物音も聞こえるの穴をあけたおかげで、息はらくにできます。

で、たいへんべんりです。

すると、まもなく、しずかにドアのひらく音がして、何者かが、しのび足で部屋の中へはいってきました。

そして、かすかな足音が、すぐそばに近づいたかとおもうと、ポケット小僧のからだが、ぐらっとひっくりかえりました。カバンを持ちあげたのです。

「おっそろしく、重いカバンだな。」

そんなひとりごとが聞こえました。ポケット小僧は、うたがわれやしないかと、びくびくしていましたが、それは四十面相の部下のものらしく、カバンの中に、なにがはいっているかもよく知らないのでしょう。べつにうたがいもせず、そのまま、えっちら、おっちら、カバンをどこかへはこんでいきます。

やがて、建物の外へ出たようです。五十いくつのきりの穴から、つめたい風がはいってきました。

そして、また五分ほども歩いたと思うころ、

「おい、持ってきたよ。あけてくんな。」

というささやき声がして、なにかドアのひらくような音が聞こえ、カバンは、ふわッと宙に浮いて、どっかりと下におろされました。

85

「ああ、わかったぞ。ここは自動車の中だな。ふふん、うまくいったわい。この自動車は、きっと四十面相のすみ家へいくにちがいない。」

ポケット小僧は、まるでからだのいたみもわすれて、にやりと笑うのでした。すぐに出発するのかと思うと、そうではなくて、自動車はすこしも動きません。そのまま、三十分ほどもすぎました。その三十分が、ポケット小僧には、二、三時間にも思われたほどです。

彼は知りませんでしたが、ちょうどそのころ、にせ警官隊が、にせ総監の四十面相をとりかこんで大さわぎをやっていたのです。そして、うまく警視庁の裏門から逃げだしたのです。

やがて、自動車のドアの音がして、だれかふたりほど中へはいってきたようです。

「出発！　フルスピードだ！」

強い声が聞こえました。

「かしら、うまくいったようですね。で、ゆくさきは？」

「きめんじょうだ。」

「きめんじょうだ。」

いきなり、自動車が走りだしました。それからは、もうだれも、ものをいいません。きめんじょうというところへいくらしいのですが、ポケット小僧には、その意味がわか

らないのです。きめんじょうなんてへんな名の町は、聞いたこともありません。
高級の自動車らしく、エンジンの音は、ごくわずかです。しかし、いくら高級車でも、道が悪いので、ときどき恐ろしくゆれます。やがて三十分も走りつづけると、車のゆれかたが、きゅうにはげしくなってきました。アスファルトのしいてない、いなか道にさしかかったのでしょう。
「おやおや、ずいぶん遠くまでいくんだな。」
ポケット小僧は、心の中でおどろいています。だんだんからだのいたみがひどくなってきました。いいかげんにおろしてくれないと、がまんができなくなるかもしれないと思いました。
およそ一時間も走ったころ、やっと車がとまりました。やれやれ助かったと思っていますと、カバンは、一度車からおろされたのですが、こんどはまた、べつの乗りものにつみこまれたらしいのです。
「おや、こんどは貨物列車かもしれないぞ。汽車で十時間もはこばれるのだったら、たいへんだ。からだがいたいだけじゃない。だいいち腹がへって、がまんができないかもしれないぞ。」
ポケット小僧は、うんざりしてため息をつきました。

すると、そのとき、ぶるるん、ぶるるるる……という音が、かすかに聞こえ、スウッとからだが浮きあがるような気がしました。エレベーターに乗っているような感じです。

「アッ、わかった。ヘリコプターだ。四十面相はヘリコプターを持っているそうだから、きっとそのヘリコプターだ。だが、ヘリコプターで、いったいどこへいくんだろう。」

ポケット小僧は、なんだかこころぼそくなってきました。

「先生、ゆくさきはきめんじょうですね。」

「うん、警視庁と明智のやつを、アッといわせてやったから、一週間ばかりやすむつもりだ。きめんじょうは、いいからな。」

「きめんじょうのかくれ家は、世間はまだちっとも知らないのですね。」

「うん、知るはずがない。だが、おれは、きめんじょうということばを、すこしばらまいてやろうかと思うんだ。いかにも恐ろしげな名前だからね。世間のやつはきみ悪がるだろうて。名前だけわかって、それがどこにあるかは、ぜったいにわからない神秘の謎というやつだよ。ウフフフフ……」

ことばのようすでは、四十面相とその部下が話しているように思われます。

ポケット小僧は漢字をすこししか知りませんので、きめんじょうと聞いてもなんのこと

88

だかわかりませんが、もっと漢字を知っている人なら、すぐに想像できるはずです。

きめんじょう……鬼面城。あてはまる字といっては、まずこのふたつです。

どちらにしても、恐ろしい名前です。いったい、その鬼面城、または奇面城というのは、どこにあるのでしょう。そして、それはどんなに奇怪なお城なのでしょう。

ポケット小僧には、そこまではわかりませんでしたが、いまの話の「恐ろしげな名前」ということばで、いよいよきみが悪くなってきました。きめんじょうへつれていかれて、どんなめにあわされるのかと思うと、さすが大胆なポケット小僧も、からだが、ゾウッと寒くなってくるのでした。

ヘリコプターは一時間ちかくもとんで、やっとどこかへ着陸しました。

ドアのひらく音。人のおりるけはい。そして、カバンは持ちあげられ、どこかへはこんでいかれます。

どうも、ひどくさびしい場所のようです。空気がつめたいらしく、カバンの中にいても、恐ろしく寒いのです。

それから、長いあいだぐるぐるまわり歩いているようでしたが、やがてカバンは、どこかへおろされました。

どうも、ふつうの家の中へ持ちこまれたような感じがしません。といって、空気がすこ

しも動かないのをみると、原っぱでもありません。なんだか、ひどくうすきみの悪い場所です。

いまにもカバンのふたをあけられるかと、びくびくしていましたが、部下の男はカバンをおくと、そのままどこかへ立ちさったらしく、あたりは、墓場のようにしずかになってしまいました。

しばらくがまんしていましたが、いくら待ってもだれも近づいてくるようすがないので、ポケット小僧は、ポケットからナイフをとりだして、カバンの革をきりひらき、そこから手をだしてとめがねをはずし、そっとふたをひらいてみました。まっ暗です。地獄のようにまっ暗で、しんとしずまりかえった、ひえびえとしたつめたい場所です。いったいここはどこなのでしょう。

四十面相の美術館

ポケット小僧は、いつもポケットに、万年筆型の懐中電灯を持っていますので、それをつけてあたりを照らしてみました。

コンクリートの壁にかこまれた、物置き部屋のようなところです。すみずみに、木箱だ

とか、イスやテーブルのこわれたのなどが、つみあげてあります。いっぽうの壁に、ドアがついていることがわかりましたので、そのドアに耳をあててみましたが、なんの音も聞こえません。とってをまわすと、ドアはスウッとひらきました。

首を出してのぞいてみると、そこはコンクリート壁の廊下のような場所でした。小さな電灯が天井についていて、ぼんやりとあたりを照らしています。コンクリートをぬったまま、なんのかざりもない、まるでトンネルみたいな廊下です。

ポケット小僧は、その廊下づたいに右のほうへ歩いていきました。なにしろ、ポケットにはいるくらい小さいといわれているのですから、うす暗い廊下を壁づたいに、こそこそ歩いていますと、まるで目につきません。

もしむこうから人がきても、壁にひらべったくからだをつけてしまえば、気づかれる心配もないほどです。

トンネルのようなうす暗い廊下をひとつまがって、十五メートルほどいきますと、道がふさがってしまいました。

大きな岩が、とおせんぼうをするように、廊下のまん中に立っているのです。

ふと気がつくと、どこか遠いところから、ごうごうという水の流れているような音が聞こえてきます。

岩の両側に二十センチぐらいのすきまがありましたので、そこからのぞいてみますと、岩のすぐむこうに、底も知れないまっ暗な穴がありました。さっきのへんな音は、その穴の底から聞こえてくるようです。

つめたい風が、サアッと顔をかすめました。

「ああ、わかった。この下に川が流れているんだ。」

何メートルとも知れない深い谷底に、川が流れているのです。ですから、そこは穴ではなくて、廊下と十文字になった谷なのです。

深い谷が廊下を横ぎっていて、その底を水が流れているのです。

「ここは、いったいどこだろう。建物の廊下のまん中に、こんな深い谷があるなんて聞いたこともない。へんな家だなあ。」

ポケット小僧は、こわくなってきました。ぶるぶるッと身ぶるいして、うしろのほうへひきかえしました。

もとの物置き部屋の前をとおりすぎて、もっとおくへ歩いていきますと、また、廊下がまがっていて、そこには大きなドアがしまっていました。

その中には、明るい電灯がついているとみえて、ドアのかぎ穴から光がもれています。

耳をすますと、その部屋の中でだれかが話をしているようです。

ポケット小僧は、かぎ穴へ目をあてて、中をのぞいてみました。

それは、アッとおどろくような、りっぱな部屋でした。きらきらひかるガラスばりの陳列棚のようなものが、いっぱいならんでいて、そのガラスの中には、黄金の仏像や、美しいもようのある大きなつぼや、いろいろな彫刻や、宝石をちりばめた王冠や、首かざりなどが、目もまばゆいばかりにかざってあるのです。

天井からは、何百という水晶の玉でかこまれたシャンデリアがさがり、その明るい光が、かぞえきれない美術品を照らしているのです。

シャンデリアの下に、りっぱな彫刻のあるまるいテーブルがおかれ、金色の四つのイスが、それをとりかこんでいて、そこにふたりの男が、こしかけていました。

ひとりは、警視総監にばけたままの四十面相。もうひとりは、制服警官にばけたままの部下でした。きっと、こいつが、ポケット小僧のかくれているカバンをはこんだのでしょう。

「いつ見てもいい気持ちだな。どうだ、このおれの美術館は……、東京の博物館だって、こんなに美しくはないだろう。

ハハハハ……。世間のやつらは、こんな山の中に、四十面相の美術館があるなんて夢にも知るまい。明智探偵だって、警視庁のやつらだって、おれの奇面城がどこにあるか、

すこしも知らないのだ。

おれは、いままでたびたび明智につかまったが、ここだけは知らせてやればよかったのだ。このほうぼうにすみ家を持っているからな。そのどれかを知らせてやればよかったのだ。この美術館のある奇面城だけは、ぜったいに知らせることはできない。」

四十面相が、ほこらしげにいいますと、警官すがたの部下が、ごきげんをとるようにあいづちをうちました。

「そうですとも。まさかこんな山の中の樹海のまん中の、あの人間の顔とそっくりの大岩の下に、こんな美術館があろうなんて、だれが想像するでしょう。

かしらは、じつにいい場所をおえらびになりましたよ。

そのうえ、あの恐ろしい番人がいれば、たとえ、人間が奇面城に近づいてきても、あの番人を見たら、まっ青になって逃げだしますよ。われわれにたいしては、ネコのようにおとなしいやつですがね。ハハハハ……」

それを聞いて、ポケット小僧は、いよいよ恐ろしくなってきました。

「それじゃここは、山の深い森のまん中なんだな。そこに、人間の顔のような大岩があって……、おれはいまその中にいるんだな。

だが、恐ろしい番人って、なんだろう？　自分たちにはネコのようにおとなしいといっ

たが、そいつは、いったいどんなやつなんだろう。人間じゃないかもしれないぞ。」

それから、部屋の中のふたりは、まだしばらく話をしていましたが、ぽつぽつ寝室へひきあげそうになりましたので、おどろいてドアをはなれ、もとの物置き部屋へひきかえしました。

まず、ドアの内側に長い板ぎれを立てかけて、だれかがドアをひらけば、それがたおれて音がするようにしました。その音で、目をさますためです。

それから、こわれたイスを三つならべて、その上にごろりと横になると、大胆不敵なポケット小僧は、まもなく、ぐっすりと眠りこんでしまいました。

巨人の顔

ポケット小僧が、ふと目をさましますと、まだ部屋の中は、まっ暗でした。そんなはずはない。ぐっすり寝たんだから、もう夜があけているはずだと、ふしぎそうにあたりを見まわしていましたが、

「ああ、そうだ。この部屋には、窓がないのだ。」

と、やっとそこへ気がつきました。

ドアのほうを見ると、ゆうべ立てかけておいた板ぎれは、そのままになっています。だれもこなかった証拠です。

それにしても、おなかがぺこぺこです。ここにだって台所はあるだろうと思ったので、こっそり、なにかたべるものをさがすつもりで部屋を出ました。

廊下も、ゆうべとおなじ暗い電灯がついているだけで、すこしも日の光はさしておりません。

奇面城というのは、岩でできているらしいから、ここは岩の中の洞窟なんだと思いました。

ゆうべの美術館のドアをとおりこして、もっとおくへ進んでいきますと、どこからかおいしそうなにおいがしてきました。

「ははあ、肉をやいているな。きっと、こっちに台所があるにちがいないぞ。」

鼻をぴくぴくさせながら、においのほうへ歩いていきますと、ドアがひらいていて、そこから、かすかに白いゆげのようなものが、ただよいだしています。

ああ、ここだなと思って、そっとのぞいてみますと、やっぱりそこが台所でした。白いコック帽をかぶった男が、しきりにビーフステーキをつくっているのです。

ジュウジュウと肉のやける音、油っこいうまそうなにおい、はらぺこのポケット小僧は、

よだれがたれてきそうでした。

小僧は、ドアのかげにかくれて、しんぼうづよく、コックがどこかへ出ていくのを待っていました。

すると、二十分ほどたって、ビーフステーキをこしらえてしまうと、コックは、いそぎ足でドアのほうへやってきました。手洗いへでもいくのでしょう。

小僧はびっくりして、いっそう深くドアのかげに身をかくしましたが、なにしろポケット小僧といわれるほどからだが小さいので、こういうときにはべんりです。ドアのうしろで、ひらべったくなっていると、そこには人がかくれているなんて、すこしもわからないのです。

コックがいってしまうと、小僧はすばやく台所の中へはいって、できたてのビーフステーキひときれと、じゃがいもとパンを、そこにあったナプキンにつつみ、リスのように、すばしっこく逃げだしました。

廊下を物置き部屋のほうへいそいでいきますと、むこうにチラッと人影が見えました。コックではありません。えびちゃ色のセーターを着た大きな男です。四十面相の部下でしょう。

ポケット小僧は、いきなり台所のほうへかけもどって、また、もとのドアのうしろへ身

をかくしました。
　大男はそれとも知らず台所の中へはいって、しきりにコックをよんでいました。まもなくコックが帰ってきたのを見て、こんなことをいうのです。
「おい、はやく朝めしをださないか。もう九時だよ。おかしらの散歩の時間がおくれるぞ。おかしらは、朝めしのあとで、山の中を歩きまわるくせがあることを知らないのか！」
「そうがみがみいうもんじゃねえ。もうできたんだよ。すぐ持っていくって、おかしらにそういっといてくんな。」
「よし、はやくするんだぞ。」
　そうして、大男は立ちさり、すこしたってコックが、大きなぼんの上にごちそうをのせて出ていきました。
　小僧はコックが帰ってくるまでじっとがまんしていて、コックが台所へはいるのを待って、こっそりと、もとの物置き部屋へ帰りました。
　そして、木箱の上にナプキンをひろげると、まだゆげのたっているビーフステーキにかじりつき、パンをむしゃむしゃとやりました。そのうまかったこと。ポケット小僧は生まれてから、こんなうまいものをたべたことがないと思いました。
　すっかりたべてしまうと、また廊下に出て、こっそりドアのかぎ穴をのぞいてまわりま

ゆうべの美術館はからっぽでした。四十面相の部下が五、六人も集まって、食事をしている部屋もありました。まっ暗で、なにも見えない部屋もありました。ある部屋では、まるで発電所のように、大きなかまの中で石炭がもえ、発電機がまわっていました。

「ああ、そうだ。こんな山の中に電灯線がきているはずはない。じゃあ、ここでつかっている電気は、みんな自分でおこしているんだな。さっきビーフステーキをやいていたのも、電熱器のようだったぞ。わああ、おったまげた。」

四十面相のやつ、自分で電気をおこしていやあがる。」

ポケット小僧は、その大じかけに、びっくりしてしまったのです。

なおもまわり歩いているうちに、とうとう、四十面相のいる部屋を見つけました。かぎ穴からのぞくと、その部屋も、恐ろしくりっぱにかざりつけてありました。イスも、テーブルも、壁も、カーテンも、すっかり金ぴかなのです。ほんとうの金かどうかはわかりませんが、まるで、仏壇の中のように、金色にかがやいているのです。

四十面相は、まっ黒なビロードの服を着ていました。その肩や胸に、ちかちかひかる金色のもようがついているのです。まるで、どこかの国の将軍のようです。

四十面相は、いまビーフステーキの食事を、おわったところでした。テーブルの上には、

グラスがいくつもならび、いろいろな洋酒のびんが立っていました。
四十面相のそばに、美しい女の人が立っています。まっ白な、ふわふわした洋服を着て、首には真珠の首かざりがかがやいているのです。
「じゃあ、おでかけになりますか。」
女の人が、やさしい声でいいました。
「うん、朝の散歩をかかすわけにはいかん。森の中を歩きまわるのは、いい気持ちだからな。きょうは、おまえも、いっしょにいこう。」
四十面相は、そういって立ちあがりました。
ポケット小僧は、それを聞くと大いそぎでドアの前をはなれ、壁のいちばん暗いところに、ぴったり身をつけて、そっとドアのほうを見ていました。
ドアがひらいて、四十面相と女の人が廊下に出ました。そして、またドアがしまりました。
ふたりは、なかよくむこうへ歩いていきます。
さいわいポケット小僧に気がつかなかったようです。
小僧は壁づたいに、ふたりのあとを追って、ずん歩いていきます。
「へんだなあ。こっちへいったら、あの大岩で、いきどまりになっているのに。」

100

ポケット小僧は、ふしぎに思いながらついていきます。

ふたりは、あの大岩のところへくると、四十面相が手をのばして、右手の壁のすこしくぼんだところを、ぐっとおしました。すると、あの大岩が、ギイイッと音をたてて、むこうへたおれていくではありませんか。

こちらから見ていると、大岩のてっぺんには二本のがんじょうなくさりがついていて、たぶん電気じかけでしょう、そのくさりがのびるにつれて、大岩がむこうへたおれていくのです。

むかしのお城のつり橋と、おなじしかけでした。とうとう大岩は横だおしになり、あの深い谷の上に横たわったのです。

四十面相と女の人は、その岩の橋をわたってむこうへ歩いていきます。見ると、そこからむこうは、コンクリートのぬってない岩のトンネルです。そして、そのトンネルの入口が、すぐむこうにまぶしくひかっていました。トンネルの外には、太陽が照りかがやいているのです。ふたりがトンネルを出てから、しばらくのあいだ待って、ポケット小僧はその岩の橋をわたり、すばやくトンネルの入り口まで走っていって、そっと外をのぞいてみました。

ふたりは遠くへいってしまったとみえて、そのへんには人のすがたもありません。

トンネルの外は、岩と土のまじった広っぱです。そのまわりを、見とおしもきかぬ深い森が、とりまいています。

ポケット小僧はトンネルからとびだして、広っぱのまん中にある大きな岩のかげに、うずくまって、トンネルの上を見あげました。もし、だれかに見つかってはたいへんだと思ったからです。そこにうずくまって、トンネルの上を見あげました。

ポケット小僧の顔が、まっ青さおになり、目がとびだしそうに見ひらかれました。なにがそんなに、小僧をおびえさせたのでしょう。

ああ、ごらんなさい。トンネルの上には、五十メートル四方しほうもあるような、巨大きょだいな岩山が、そびえていたではありませんか。しかも、それはただの岩山ではありません。その巨大な岩山ぜんたいが、人間の顔の形をしていたのです。

奈良ならの大仏だいぶつのからだの何倍なんばいもあるような、想像そうぞうもできないほどの、大きな大きな顔なのです。

ああ、その顔……。なんという恐おそろしい顔でしょう。悪魔あくまが笑わらっているのです。さしわたし十メートルもあるような巨大な目で、じっと、こちらをにらみつけています。そして、

彫刻ちょうこくではありません。岩山は、しぜんにそういう形をしていたうえに、いくらか人間が手をくわえたもののように思われます。

102

するどい牙のある三十メートルの口で、何百人の人間でも、ひとのみしようと待ちかまえているようです。

恐ろしい番人

その巨人の顔の前は広っぱになっていて、いっぽうのすみにヘリコプターがおいてあります。ポケット小僧はヘリコプターのそばへいき、操縦席にのぼりついて、その中をしらべてみました。

しかけのうしろに、ズックでつつんだ四角なかごがおいてあります。中をのぞいてみると、キャベツのきれはしが、ころがっていました。

このかごは、どこかの町で食料品を仕入れて、ここへはこぶときにつかうのでしょう。

ポケット小僧は、その大きなかごを見て、にやりと笑いました。うまい考えが浮かんだからです。

「行きはカバンの中、帰りはかごの中、ウフフフ……。おれもなかなか知恵があるなあ。」

そんなひとりごとをつぶやいて、ヘリコプターをおりましたが、そのとき、どこからか、みょうな叫び声が聞こえてきました。

103

「ギャアッ、ギャアッ!」

というようなへんな声です。鳥がないているのでしょうか。深い山の中ですから、どんな恐ろしい鳥がいるかわかりません。

ポケット小僧はびっくりして、声のするほうを見ました。広っぱには、なんにもおりません。そのむこうの森の中から聞こえてくるのです。

おずおずと、そのほうへ近づいていきました。森には何百年もたったような大きな木が、見とおしがきかないほど、しげっていました。それらの木の幹にはツタがまといつき、はいあがり、映画で見たジャングルのようなありさまです。どこかから、ターザン*の「ヤッホー……」という叫び声が聞こえてきそうなけしきです。

「ギャアッ、ギャアッ!」

そのとき、ついまぢかで、あのみょうななき声がしました。

ポケット小僧は、おもわず逃げごしになりながら、木のあいだをすかして見ますと、五、六メートルむこうの暗い森の中に、なんだか黄色いようなものが、ぶらんぶらんと、ぶらさがっているのが見えました。

鳥ではありません。ネコのような動物です。そいつが、あと足をつたにまかれて、木の上からぶらさがっているのです。

* アフリカのジャングルの王者としてかつやくする青年。小説や映画で有名

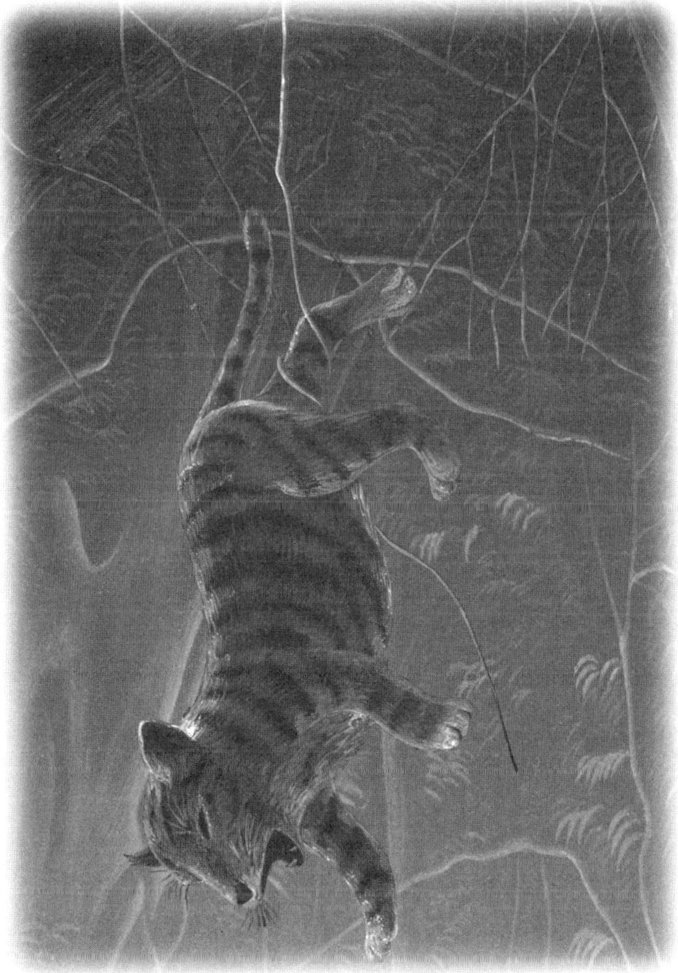

まきついたツタをとこうとして、いろいろに身をくねらせるのですが、どうしてもとけません。ブランコのように、さかさまにぶらさがったまま、あのみょうな声をたてて、助けをもとめているのです。

ポケット小僧はそれを見て、「ネコならなんでもないや」と思いながら、もっとそばまで近づきました。

足をツタにしめつけられ、ギャアギャアいって苦しんでいます。かわいそうになってきました。

「よし、いま、おれがはずしてやるからな。待ってろよ。」

背のびをして、宙でもがいているネコをだきとり、足にからまっているツタをといてやりました。

ネコは、ポケット小僧の胸に顔をすりつけて、じっとしています。助けてもらったのをよろこんであまえているのです。

その頭をなでてやりながらよく見ますと、どうもようすがおかしいのです。ネコにしてはすごい顔をしています。三毛ネコのように見えますが、黄色と黒のしまがもっとはっきりして、なんだか虎のような感じです。ひょっとしたら、これは、虎の子ではないでしょうか。

そう思うと、ポケット小僧はこわくなってきました。じっとこちらを見ている青くひかる目が、だんだんものすごくなってくるのです。

そのときです。

「ごうッ……」

という恐ろしいうなり声が聞こえました。だいているネコではなくて、もっとむこうのほうから、ひびいてきたのです。

びっくりして、そのほうを見ますと、木の幹のあいだを、ちらっと黄色いものが横ぎりました。黄色に太い黒のしまのある動物です。

「アッ、虎だッ！」

と思うと、ポケット小僧は、もう身動きができなくなってしまいました。

そいつは、ヌウッと大きなものすごい顔をあらわし、のそりのそり、こちらへ近づいてきます。大きな虎です。いま助けてやった虎の子の親かもしれません。

ああ、わかりました。四十面相の部下が、「恐ろしい番人」といったのは、こいつのことだったのです。

四十面相は、イヌのかわりに、この大きな虎を飼って、奇面城の番をさせているのでしょう。

ポケット小僧は、いまにもこの虎に食われてしまうのかと、生きたここちもありません。といって、逃げだそうにも、足が動かないのです。らんらんとかがやく大きな目で、じいっとにらまれると、電気にでもかかったように、身がすくんでしまうのです。

虎はもう、すぐ目の前にきていました。はっはっと、くさい息がこちらの顔にかかるほどです。

すると、ポケット小僧にだかれていた虎の子が、腕からとびだして、大虎のそばへかけよって、じゃれつくのでした。

大虎は、虎の子のからだをなめてやりながら、さもかわいくてしかたがないというように、目をほそくしています。

そのようすでこの大虎は、父親ではなくて、母親のように思われました。

しばらくすると大虎は、また、「ごうッ……！」とうなって、ポケット小僧のほうを見ました。しかし、べつに危害をくわえるようすもありません。なんだか、「ぼうやを助けてくださって、ありがとう」と、お礼をいっているように見えました。

ポケット小僧は、からだは小さくても、大胆な子どもですから、それを見ると、すっかり安心して、そっと手を出して、大虎の頭をなでてみました。

ガッと食いついてくるかと思うと、そうではなくて、目をほそめて、おとなしくしてい

108

ます。恩人のポケット小僧に、すっかりなついてしまっているのです。
「きみは、恐ろしい顔をしているが、心はやさしいんだね。よしよし、じゃあ、いつかまた、きみのやっかいになるときがあるかもしれないよ。」
 ポケット小僧は、人間に話しかけるようにそんなことをいって、しばらく虎の頭や首をなでていましたが、四十面相が朝の散歩から帰ってきて、見つかるとたいへんですから、いそいで奇面城の洞窟のほうへ、ひきかえすのでした。
 親子の虎は、それを見おくって、のそのそついてきます。
 そして、洞窟の前までできたとき、またしても、どこからか、「ごうッ……！」という恐ろしいうなり声がひびいてきました。
 うしろからついてくる、二ひきの虎ではありません。どこかの、そのほら穴の中から、ひびいてきたようです。洞窟の入り口にならんで、いくつも小さなほら穴があるのですが、いまの声は、そのほら穴の中から、ひびいてきたようです。
 それじゃ、まだほかに虎がいるのかと、びっくりして立ちどまっていますと、そのほら穴のひとつから、ヌウッと大きな虎がすがたをあらわしました。こいつは、さっきの虎の子の父親かもしれません。
「ごうッ……！」
 そいつは、ほら穴から全身をあらわして、もう一度うなり声をたてました。

すると、うしろにいた母親らしい虎が、そこへ歩いていって、顔をつきあわせて、なにか知らせているようでした。

「あの子を、助けてくださったのよ」といっているのかもしれません。

二ひきの大虎は、顔をそろえて、ポケット小僧のほうを見ました。やさしい目をしています。

「ありがとう。」

と、お礼をいっているのでしょう。

ポケット小僧は、恐ろしい猛獣がそんなにやさしくしてくれるので、すっかりうれしくなってしまいました。親子三びきの虎と、もうすこし遊んでいたいと思いましたが、四十面相や部下のものに見つかってはたいへんですから、いそいで三びきの虎のほうへ手をふって、わかれをつげると、そのまま洞窟の中へはいっていきました。

ポケット小僧の冒険

ポケット小僧が奇面城の洞窟に帰ると、まもなく、四十面相と美しい女の人が、散歩かたもどってきました。

それからまる二日のあいだ、ポケット小僧は、洞窟の中に足をひそめていたのです。夜は、あの物置き部屋で眠り、昼は、見つからぬように気をくばりながら、ほうぼうの部屋をのぞきまわり、四十面相のすみ家のようすをしらべました。

さいわい、洞窟の廊下はうす暗いので、四十面相の部下たちに出あっても、すばやく身をかくせば、相手にさとられないですむのです。食事は、ときどき台所からぬすみだせばいいのですから、おなかがへるようなこともありません。

そうして、しらべたところによりますと、洞窟の中に住んでいるのは、四十面相からコックまでくわえて、十一人にすぎないことがわかりました。

四十面相の部下は、もっとたくさんいるのでしょうが、いまここには十一人だけなのです。しかし、十一人がごはんをたべているのですから、どこからか食料をはこばなければなりません。電気をおこす石炭もいるでしょうし、そのほか、いろいろなものを持ってこなければなりません。

自動車のとおれない山の中です。そういうものをはこぶには、人間が背中にしょって山道をのぼってくるか、ヘリコプターをつかうほかはないのです。あのヘリコプターは、たびたびここからとびたって、そういうものを、はこんでいるのにちがいありません。

ポケット小僧は、それを待っていたのです。東京へ帰るのには、そのおりを待って、う

111

まくやるほかはないと考えていたのです。

すると、さいわいにも三日めの夜、そのおりがきました。四十面相が、ふたりの部下に、ヘリコプターでどこかの町へいって、食料品をつんでくるように命令しているのを、立ち聞きしたのです。

そこで、ふたりの部下が身じたくをして、洞窟を出ていくあとを、そっとついていきました。

夜のことですから、外に出るとまっ暗です。ふたりの部下は懐中電灯をつけて、足もとを照らしながら、ヘリコプターのほうへ近づいていきます。昼間のうちに、いつでもとべるように準備がしてあったのです。

ポケット小僧は、ふたりがヘリコプターに乗りこまないさきに、あの操縦席のイスのうしろにある、ズックをかぶせたかごの中へ、もぐりこむつもりでした。

しかし、いくら闇夜といっても、ふたりを追いこしたら、すぐに見つかってしまいます。なにか計略をもちいなければなりません。

ポケット小僧はりこうな少年ですから、それもちゃんと考えてありました。そして、いきなり、ふたりの部下のそばをはなれて、横手の森の中へかけこみました。彼は、ふた

「キャーッ、助けてくれェッ……」

と叫んだのです。
おどろいたのは、ふたりです。だれもいるはずのない森の中から、ひめいが聞こえてきたので、すててておくわけにはいきません。
おおいそぎで森の中へかけこんで、そのへんをさがしまわりました。
しかし、ふたりがそこへはいってきたころには、もうポケット小僧は森の中を走って、ヘリコプターのほうへ近づいていました。
そして、部下たちがさしつかっていて、森の外へ出たときには、とっくに、あの操縦席のかごの中へ身をひそめていたのです。
かごにはズックがかぶせてあるので、中からその口をしめれば、大きなふろしきづつみのようになり、もう見つかる心配はありません。
「たしかに、人間の声だったな。」
「うん、おれもそう思った。だが、鳥がないたのかもしれない。この山には、人間みたいななき声をだすおばけ鳥がいるからね。聞きちがいだよ。こんなところへ人間がくるはずがないからね。」
ふたりの部下は、ぶつぶつそんなことをつぶやきながら、操縦席へ乗りこんできました。
やがて、プロペラがまわりはじめます。

ぶるるん、ぶるるん、ぶるるん。
　そして、機体がスウッと浮きあがったかとおもうと、どこともしれずとんでいくのです。
　一時間もとんだでしょうか。だんだん速度がにぶくなり、機体がさがっていって、どこかへ着陸しました。
　ポケット小僧はズックにつつまれているので、それがどんな場所だか、すこしもわかりません。
「おい、あすこに自動車が待っているぜ。さあ、かごをおろすんだ。」
　ズックにつつまれたかごを、操縦席の入り口のところまでひっぱっておいて、地面におりたふたりが、それをひきずりおろすのです。
　かごは、グッとひかれ、どしんと地面にたたきつけられました。
　そのひょうしに、中にいるポケット小僧は、頭や肩や腰をひどくかごにぶっつけましたが、歯をくいしばってがまんしていました。
　いくらいたくても、声をたてることもできません。なにしろ、ポケットにはいるといわれているほどの小さな少年ですから、めかたもかるく、ふたりの部下は、まさか、かごの中に人間がはいっているなんて夢にも知りませんので、いつもよりすこし重くても、うたがってみようともしないのでした。

かごを地面におくと、ふたりは、むこうの自動車のほうへ歩いていったようすです。そのすきにポケット小僧は、そっとズックの口をひらいて、外をのぞいてみました。家などどこにも見えません。町から遠くはなれた広い原っぱのようなところです。

二十メートルほどむこうに、ヘッドライトを消した自動車の黒い影が見え、ふたりの部下はそのそばに立って、なにか話をしています。

「いまだッ！」

と思いました。ズックの口をじゅうぶんひらいて外へ出ると、もとのとおりにズックをしめ、そのままはうようにして、ヘリコプターから遠ざかっていきました。

部下たちは、なにも知りません。自動車の運転をしていた男にも手つだわせて、車の中から、箱にはいったもの、紙につつんだものなどを、かごのところへはこんでいます。肉、かんづめ、やさいなどの食料品でしょう。

ポケット小僧は原っぱのくさむらの中に寝そべって、遠くからそのようすを見ていました。

しばらくすると、ズックでつつんだかごをヘリコプターにのせ、ふたりの部下も運転手にわかれをつげて、操縦席に乗りこみました。

そして、ぶるるん、ぶるるんと、ヘリコプターは空へ、自動車もヘッドライトをつけて、むこうの大きな道へと、遠ざかっていきました。

彼らは、とうとう気がつかなかったのです。

しかし、これからが大仕事です。ポケット小僧は助かったのです。東京に帰って明智探偵や小林少年にこのことを報告し、おおぜいの警官隊といっしょに奇面城を攻撃して、怪人四十面相をとらえなければなりません。

まる二日、洞窟の中をしらべ、悪人たちの話を立ち聞きしたおかげで、ポケット小僧には、奇面城がどのへんの山の中にあるかということも、だいたいわかっていました。いよいよ、奇面城の総攻撃がはじまるのです。名探偵明智小五郎は、どんな計略を考えだすでしょうか。また、四十面相は、どのような手だてで、これをふせぐのでしょうか。

千変万化の知恵と力のたたかいが、やがてはじまろうとしているのです。

ポケット小僧は、それを考えると胸がわくわくしてきました。怪人四十面相のほんとうのすみ家、あの恐ろしい奇面城が、どこにあるかを知っているのは、世界じゅうにおれひとりだと思うと、うれしくてしかたがないのです。

ヘリコプターも自動車も、影が見えなくなってしまったので、ポケット小僧は安心して立ちあがりました。そして、原っぱを横ぎり、国道らしい大きな道に出ると、さっきの自

動車がいった方角へ、暗闇の中をてくてくと歩きだすのでした。

秘密会議

チンピラ隊のポケット小僧は、まっ暗な街道を、一時間あまりもてくてく歩いて、やっと大きな町にたどりつきました。それは埼玉県のT町だったのです。

ポケット小僧は、T町の駅の長イスの上で一夜をあかし、あくる朝の汽車で東京に帰りました。三百円ほど持っていたので、やっと汽車のきっぷが買えたのです。

東京に着くと、すぐに明智探偵事務所へいって、明智先生と小林団長にあい、くわしく報告しました。

「わあ、えらいぞ、ポケット小僧。たいへんな手がらをたてたねえ。」

小林少年が、思わず歓声をあげました。

明智探偵も、ポケット小僧の頭をなでながら、

「どんなおとなもおよばない大手がらだよ。四十面相のほんとうのかくれ家、奇面城なんて、長いあいだだれも知らなかった。ぼくも、まったく気づかないでいた。それをきみが、ひとりの力で発見したんだからね。きっと警視総監からごほうびが出るよ。

* 現在の約三千円

「よし、これからすぐに警視庁へいこう。そして、総監にこのことを報告して、どうして奇面城をせめるか、その方法を相談しよう。」

明智探偵はそういって、卓上電話の受話器をとると、警視庁の中村警部をよびだし、総監にこのことをつたえてくれるようにたのみました。すると、総監も捜査課長も待っているからという返事があったので、そのまま自動車をよんで、ポケット小僧をつれて、警視庁へいそぎました。

それから二十分ほどして、警視庁の総監室には、大机の正面に山本警視総監、その前に明智小五郎、堀口捜査一課長、中村警部が席につき、ポケット小僧も、明智探偵のとなりの大きなイスに、ちょこんとこしかけて、しかつめらしい顔をしていました。

山本総監は、四十面相が自分にばけて、警視庁をばかにしたことを、ひじょうにおこっていましたので、この事件にかぎって、総監室で秘密会議をひらくことにしたのです。

「きみがポケット小僧か。よくやってくれた。あとで、どっさりほうびをあげるよ。で、きみは、その奇面城がどこにあるのか、わかっているんだろうね。」

総監が、ポケット小僧にたずねました。

「はい、それは奇面城にかくされているあいだに、四十面相の部下たちの話を立ち聞きしてわかりました。それはこぶし岳という山です。その山の北側の深い森の中に、あの恐ろし

118

い顔の岩があるのです。」

それをひきとって、明智探偵が説明しました。

「甲武信岳というのは、埼玉県と長野県の境にそびえている山です。そこから食料などを仕入れるのにいちばん近い町は、埼玉県のＴ町です。奇面城からＴ町へは、二日か三日に一度、四十面相のヘリコプターが、かよっているらしいのです。ポケット小僧は、そのヘリコプターにかくれて逃げだしてきたのです。」

すると、堀口捜査課長が、こともなげにいうのでした。

「武装した警官を一小隊ほどやって奇面城をかこませるんですな。奇面城の中には、四十面相もいれて十一人しかいないというから、武装警官一小隊でじゅうぶんでしょう。自動車のいけるところまでいって、それからは歩いてのぼるんですな。」

それを聞くと、明智探偵はかぶりをふって、

「いや、それはあぶないですよ。奇面城のまわりには、見はりのものがいるにちがいない。警官隊が山をのぼっていったら、すぐに気づいて、じゅうぶん用意をする。あいつらはピストルや銃を持っているでしょうし、そのほか、どんな武器があるかわからない。それと正面からたたかっては、こちらにもけが人をだします。正面しょうとつは、さけたほうがいいと思います。」

と反対をとなえました。
「ふん、なにか計略をもちいるというんだね。明智君、きみには、うまい計略があるのだろうね。」
山本総監がたずねました。
すると明智探偵は、イスを前にのりだし、大机にひじをついて、ひくい声で話しはじめるのでした。
「じつは、こういう計略を考えたのです。四十面相のヘリコプターが、たえずT町へやってくる。それをうまく利用するのですよ……」
明智探偵は、そこでいっそう声をひくくしましたので、総監をはじめ、捜査課長も中村警部も、ぐっと顔を前に出し、四人が頭をくっつけるようにして明智のないしょ話を聞きとりました。
「うん、おもしろい。明智君らしいやりかただ。ひじょうにむずかしいけれども、きみならできるかもしれない。やってみるだけのねうちはあるね。」
総監は明智の話を聞いて、にこにこしながら賛成しました。
「それについて、中村君、きみの部下の三浦刑事をかしてもらいたいんだがね。あの男は、警視庁第一の変装の名人だからね。」

明智が中村警部にたのみますと、警部はこころよく承知しました。
「いいとも、三浦はたしかに変装がうまい。四十面相までいかなくても、十面相くらいの腕まえはあるよ。あの男が役にたつあいだは、どうかつかってくれたまえ。」
それから三十分ほど、こまかいうちあわせをしたあとで、この総監室の秘密会議はおわりました。山本警視総監はイスから立って、
「では明智君、きみからのよい知らせを待つことにします。よろしくたのみますよ。」
といって、明智探偵の手をにぎるのでした。

替え玉ふたり

ポケット小僧が奇面城を逃げだしてから二日めの夜のことです。もう十時をすぎていました。
埼玉県T町郊外のあのさびしい原っぱに、いつかの晩とそっくりの自動車が、ヘッドライトを消してとまっていました。
その自動車に乗っているふたりの男は、じっと星空を見あげて、なにかを待っているようすです。

しばらくすると、はるかむこうの空から、ぶるるるる……という音が聞こえ、それが、だんだん大きくなってきました。ヘリコプターです。

やがて、ヘリコプターは恐ろしい風をまきおこして、すぐむこうに着陸しました。そして、操縦席からふたりの男がおりて、こちらへ歩いてくるのが、星の光でかすかに見えます。

ふたりの男は、ズックでおおった大きなかごを、両方からさげていました。

「ひゅう、ひゅう。ひゅう？……」

こちらの自動車の中のひとりが、口笛で、ある歌のふしを吹きました。すると、

「ひゅう、ひゅう、ひゅう……」

むこうから歩いてくる男のひとりも、おなじふしの口笛を吹くのです。これがあいずの暗号なのでしょう。

ふたりの男は、自動車のそばに、かごをおろして立ちどまりました。自動車のドアがひらいて、中から箱にいれたもの、紙袋にいれたものなど、いろいろの食料品を、つぎつぎとさしだします。外のふたりは、それをうけとっては、かごの中にいれるのです。

五分もたたないうちに、かごがいっぱいになりました。

「じゃ、こんどは十四日の晩だよ。時間はいつものとおり。これが品書きだ。それじゃあ、

あばよ。」
　このつぎまでに、買いいれておくものを書きつけた紙をわたし、ふたりの男は重くなったかごをさげて、え、ちら、おっちら、ヘリコプターのほうへ帰っていきます。
　それを見おくって自動車は出発し、広い街道をむこうへ遠ざかっていきます。ところが、そのとき、みょうなことがおこりました。
　走りさった自動車のあとへ、いまとそっくりの大型自動車が、どこからかスウッとやってきて、ぴたりととまったのです。
「ひゅう、ひゅう、ひゅう……」
　自動車の窓から、するどい口笛がなりひびきました。さっきの暗号とおなじ歌のふしです。
　ヘリコプターに、かごをつみこんでいたふたりの男が、こちらをふりむきました。ふたりは、ずっとむこうをむいていたので、自動車がいれかわっていることに気がつかないようです。
「おい、よんでるぜ。なんか聞きわすれたことでもあるのかな。めんどうだけれど、いってみよう。」
「うん、そうしよう。ひゅう、ひゅう、ひゅう……」

と、こちらもおなじ口笛を吹いて、自動車のほうへ近づいていきます。
ふたりが、自動車の横までいきますと、ドアがひらいて、自動車のふたりも、外へ出てきました。そして、ヘリコプターのふたりと、むかいあって立ちました。

「アッ。」

ヘリコプターのふたりが、びっくりしたように叫んで、両手を上にあげました。自動車のふたりが、てんでにピストルをかまえていたからです。
自動車の運転手のとなりに小さな子どもがいて、窓の中からじっと、こちらを見ていました。それはポケット小僧でした。

「さあ、そのピストルはぼくが持つ。こいつらの服をぬがせてから、縄をかけてくれたまえ。」

自動車の男のひとりがそういって、もうひとりからピストルをうけとり、二丁のピストルを両手にかまえました。

それを見ると、車の中にいたポケット小僧もとびだしてきました。もうひとりの男は、ポケット小僧に手つだわせて、ヘリコプターのふたりの服をつぎつぎとぬがせたうえ、手足をしばり、さるぐつわをはめました。

「よし、それじゃあ、このふたりを自動車の中へいれるんだ。」

124

ピストルをかまえていた男も、それを地面において手つだいました。

それから変装です。変装用のけしょう箱をとりだし、懐中電灯でヘリコプターの男たちの顔をしらべながら、それににせて自分の顔をいろどるのです。

自動車に乗ってきた男は、ふたりとも変装のくろうとらしく、顔をつくることが、じつにじょうずでした。またたくまに、ヘリコプターの男たちとそっくりの顔になってしまいました。

それがすむと、ぬいだ背広は車の中にほうりこみ、運転台の男に声をかけました。

「さあ、出発してよろしい。このふたりの男を本署へつれていってください。ふたりのあつかいについては、署長さんがよくごぞんじですからね。」

それを聞くと運転台の男は、うなずいて車を出発させました。

いまの話のようすでは、この自動車はＴ町警察署のもので、運転手はおなじ署の警官なのでしょう。

ヘリコプターの男になりすましたふたりは、そのまま、ポケット小僧といっしょにヘリコプターに乗りこみ、ひとりが操縦席について出発しました。この男はヘリコプターになれているらしく、その操縦ぶりはじつにみごとなものでした。

125

敵のただ中へ

それから一時間ほどのち、四十面相の部下のにせものと、ポケット小僧を乗せたヘリコプターは、奇面城の前の広っぱに着陸していました。

四十面相の部下のヘリコプター係りは、ジャッキーとよばれている男で、その助手のもうひとりの男は、五郎という名でした。ポケット小僧がそれを、ちゃんとおぼえていたのです。

ジャッキーと五郎になりすましたふたりは、食料をつめたかごをヘリコプターからおろし、それをはこんで、奇面城へはいろうとしました。

そのとき、「ごうッ……」という恐ろしいうなり声が、どこからかひびいてきたのです。

「アッ、いけない、虎だ。虎がやってくる……」

ポケット小僧が、とんきょうな声をたてました。

「エッ、虎だって？」

ジャッキーと五郎が、口をそろえて叫びました。ふたりも、虎の番人がいることは聞いていましたが、四十面相の部下に変装してしまえば、だいじょうぶだと思いこんでいたの

ところが虎は、おけしょうや服装なんかではごまかされません。においです。虎の鼻は人間よりもずっとするどいので、人間のひとりひとりのにおいが、ちゃんとわかるのです。

いま、ヘリコプターからおりたふたりは、これまでかいだこともないような、においを持っている。

こいつはあやしいぞと、虎は考えたのでしょう。

星あかりですかして見ると、虎は考えたのでしょう、もう十メートルほどむこうまで近づいていました。

にせジャッキーとにせ五郎は、ピストルを持っていましたから、うまくうてば、それで虎を殺すことができるかもしれません。

しかし、そんなことをすれば、たちまちあやしまれて、せっかくここまでのりこんできた苦心が、水のあわになってしまいます。逃げるほかはありません。うまく木の上にでものぼれば、難をのがれられるかもしれないのです。

そこでふたりは、虎と反対のほうへ、いちもくさんにかけだしたのです。

「アッ、走っちゃいけないッ」

ポケット小僧があわてて叫びましたが、もうおそい。そのときは、もう、虎もかけだしていたのです。

猛獣にであったときは、じっとしていなければいけない、ということを、ふたりのおとなはわすれてしまったのです。

じっとしていれば、虎のほうでもにらんでいるばかりですが、走りだしたら、虎はいっぺんにとびかかってきます。虎とかけっこしたって、とても勝てるものではありません。このままほうっておいたら、ふたりは、虎に食われてしまう運命です。

ポケット小僧は、とっさに考えました。

「二ひきの虎は、ぼくのことをおぼえていないかしら。このあいだ虎の子を助けてやったときには、あんなによろこんでいたんだから、まだおぼえているかもしれない。よしッ、いちかばちか、やってみよう。」

そう決心すると、ポケット小僧は大手をひろげて、いまジャッキーと五郎にとびかかろうとする、二ひきの虎の前に立ちふさがりました。

ああ、あぶない。ポケット小僧は、ふみつぶされてしまうかもしれません。

立ちふさがっているポケット小僧の目の前に、二ひきの虎の恐ろしい顔が、グウッと近よってきました。

「アッ、もうだめだ。」
と思いました。そして、目をつぶってしまいました。
ポケット小僧はいまにもふみつぶされるか、いまにもかみつかれるかと、かくごしていましたが、なにごともおこりません。
顔に、あつい息が、ふうっ、ふうっとかかりました。そしてあたたかい毛皮のようなものが、からだにこすりついてくるのです。

ポケット小僧は、へんだなと思いながら目をひらきました。

すると、一ぴきの虎は、むこうに立ちどまってじっとこちらを見ています。もう一ぴきの虎は、ポケット小僧にからだをすりつけてあまえているではありませんか。やっぱり子どもを助けられた恩を、わすれないでいたのです。からだをすりつけているのは、母親の虎にちがいありません。むこうに立って、それを見ているのは、父親のほうでしょう。

ジャッキーと五郎は、それを見てびっくりしてしまいました。
「ポケット君、きみは虎をだまらせる力があるのか。おどろいたねえ。」
ジャッキーが、つくづく感心したようにいうのでした。
「そうじゃありません。この虎はぼくに恩がえしをしているのです。」

ポケット小僧は、このあいだ虎の子を助けてやったことを話しました。
「おお、そうだったか。虎もえらいが、きみもえらいぞ、やさしい心というものは、どんな動物にだって通じるのだねえ。」
ジャッキーは、思わずポケット小僧の頭をなでて、ほめたたえるのでした。
「ジャッキーさん、あれが奇面城ですよ。」
ポケット小僧は、てれかくしのように、星空にそそり立つまっ黒な岩山を指さしました。
「なるほど、恐ろしい形をしているねえ。
……それじゃあ、奇面城の中へはいろうか。虎には見やぶられるが、虎ほどの鼻のきかない人間には、見やぶられる心配はないからね。」
そこで、三人は、食料品のかごをはこんで、巨人の顔の下の洞窟へはいっていきました。
あの岩の橋をおろすかくしボタンは、入り口のほうにもあります。ポケット小僧は、そのボタンのありかを、ちゃんと知っていたのです。
そのボタンをおして、大きな岩の橋をおろし、三人はいよいよ、四十面相のすみ家へはいっていきました。

130

黒い小僧

それから、三人は奇面城の洞窟の中にはいり、ジャッキーと五郎は、四十面相の部屋へいって、
「いま、帰りました。」
とあいさつしました、四十面相は、ふたりがにせものであることに、すこしも気づかないのでした。

ジャッキーと五郎は、それでいいのですが、ポケット小僧が、もしだれかに見つかったらたいへんです。奇面城には、そんな小さな子どもは、ひとりもいないからです。

そこでポケット小僧は、東京から用意してきたまっ黒なシャツ、頭からかぶる黒覆面、黒いてぶくろ、黒い靴下を身につけて、全身まっ黒なすがたになって、敵の目をくらますことにしました。

ポケットにはいるくらい小さいというので、「ポケット小僧」とあだ名がついているのですから、そのちびすけがまっ黒になったら、こんどは黒い小僧です。

黒い小僧は、前とおなじように、夜は、がらくたのほうりこんである物置き部屋のすみ

で寝ました。たべものは、前のようにすいじ場からぬすみださなくても、にせのジャッキーと五郎がわけてくれますから、心配はありません。

黒い小僧は、恐ろしく小さいうえに、頭から足のさきまでまっ黒なのですから、洞窟の廊下で四十面相の部下に出あっても、けっして見つかりません。廊下はうす暗いし、黒い小僧はとてもすばやいので、うまく相手の目をくらましてしまうからです。

それから二週間ほどたちました。四十面相は奇面城におちついたまま、どこへも出ていくようすがありません。

にせものののジャッキーと五郎は、そのあいだに、五度もヘリコプターに乗って、ふもとの町へいきました。それは、食料品やそのほかのものをはこぶためでもありましたが、もっとほかに目的があったのです。

ヘリコプターが、ふもとの町から帰るときには、ひとりずつあたらしい味方の人間を、こっそり乗せていたのです。一度にひとりずつですから、五度では五人の人間が、奇面城につれこまれたことになります。

それでいて、奇面城に住んでいる人数は、やっぱり十一人なのです。黒い小僧はべつです。おとなが十一人です。そして、それらの人は、みんな四十面相の部下なのです。あとらしくやってきた五人の男も、それぞれ部下のだれかにばけて、なにくわぬ顔で仕事をし

ていますから、だれもうたがうものはありません。その五人は、ジャッキーや五郎におとらぬ変装の名人でした。

しかし、ふしぎなことがあります。ヘリコプターがふもとの町へいくときには、ジャッキーと五郎だけで、四十面相の部下を乗せているわけではありません。そして、帰りにひとりずつつれてくるのですから、いまでは、奇面城の中の人数は十一人たす五人の、十六人になっていなければなりません。それがやっぱり十一人のままなのですから、どうもへんなのです。

あたらしくきた五人のにせ部下のかわりに、ほんとうの部下が五人、どこかへかくされてしまったのです。むろん、にせのジャッキーと五郎がやったことにちがいありませんが、その五人の部下は、いったいどこへかくされているのでしょうか。

ところで、二週間ほどたったある日のこと、黒い小僧が、たいへんな失敗をやってしまいました。

黒い小僧は、忍術使いのようなまっ黒なからだで、洞窟の中のあちこちを、毎日しらべまわっていました。そして秘密の通路や秘密のしかけなどを、いろいろ見つけだして、にせジャッキーに報告しているのでした。

洞窟の廊下や部屋の中を、ネズミのようにチョロチョロと歩きまわっても、すこしも気

133

づかれないので、つい、ゆだんをしましたのです。そして、とうとう四十面相の部下に見つかっ

そのとき、ポケット小僧は、廊下を歩いていました。はじめのうちは、前にもうしろにも、ゆだんなく気をくばっていたのですが、このごろは、歩くときには前つい、うしろのことをなんか考えないで歩いていることがあるのです。

そのときも、うしろのことをわすれていたのですが、のっぽの初公という四十面相の部下が、ポケット小僧のうしろから歩いてきました。「のっぽ」といわれるほどあって、恐ろしく背の高いやつです。

のっぽの初公は、目の前を、頭から足のさきまでまっ黒なちびすけが、ヒョコヒョコ歩いているので、びっくりしました。おばけではないかと思いました。

そのちっぽけな、まっ黒なのっぺらぼうなやつは、ヒョイとうしろをむくと、赤い舌をぺろっと出して、顔に目がひとつしかない一つ目小僧かもしれない。そして、初公はゾウッとしました。

こんにちは……」というのかもしれないと思うと、初公はゾウッとしました。

しかし、怪人四十面相の部下になるほどのやつですから、そのまま逃げだすほど、おくびょうではありません。初公は、しばらく、黒い小僧のあとをつけてから、

「こらッ、ちびすけ待てッ。」

とどなりつけて、いきなりポケット小僧につかみかかりました。

ポケット小僧は、「しまった」と思いましたか、リスのようにすばしっこく、パッと身をかわして逃げだしました。

のっぽの初公は、身をかわされて、よたよたと前にのめりそうになりましたが、かけっことなれば、ちびすけなんかに負けるものではありません。ちょこちょこと走る黒い小僧のあとから、初公の長い足が、のっしのっしと追っかけます。

のっぽとちびすけのかけっこですから、すぐにつかまってしまいそうですが、初公がほんきで走ったら、たちまちいきすぎてしまいますし、ポケット小僧は追っつかれても、長い足のあいだをくぐって、チョコチョコと逃げまわるので、なかなかつかまるものではありません。そのうちにポケット小僧は、岩の廊下にひらいているひとつのドアの中へ逃げこみました。

のっぽの初公も、すぐにその部屋にとびこみましたが、ちびすけは、どこへかくれたのか、いくらさがしても見つかりません。

そこは四十面相が着がえをする部屋で、いっぽうの押し入れのようなところには、いろいろな服が、いっぱいかけてあるのです。

その押し入れの中もさがしましたが、ちびすけのすがたはありません。

135

初公は、部屋のまん中につっ立って腕組みをして、すっかり考えこんでしまいました。
　みなさん、ポケット小僧は、いったいどこへかくれたと思いますか。じつに、ポケット小僧の名にふさわしいところへかくれたのです。
　といいますのは、押し入れの中に、ずらっとかけならべてある服の中の、いちばん大きい外套のポケットの中へかくれたのです。
　むろん、いくらポケット小僧が小さくても、ポケットの中へからだをかくすことはできません。外套にのぼりついて、大きなポケットに足をいれたまま、宙にぶらさがっていたのです。
　黒い外套に黒いちびすけですから、うす暗い光では見わけがつきません。
　それに初公は、押し入れの中の床ばかりさがしていたので、上のほうで宙づりをしているポケット小僧は、どうしても見つからなかったのです。
「へんだぞ。あいつ、やっぱりばけものだったかな。」
　のっぽの初公は、腕組みをしたままひとりごとをいいました。
「いや、そんなはずはない。きっと、どっかにかくれている。待てよ。どうしても、あの押し入れの中があやしいわい。」
　そういって、もう一度押し入れをしらべました。こんどは、さがっている服をひとつひ

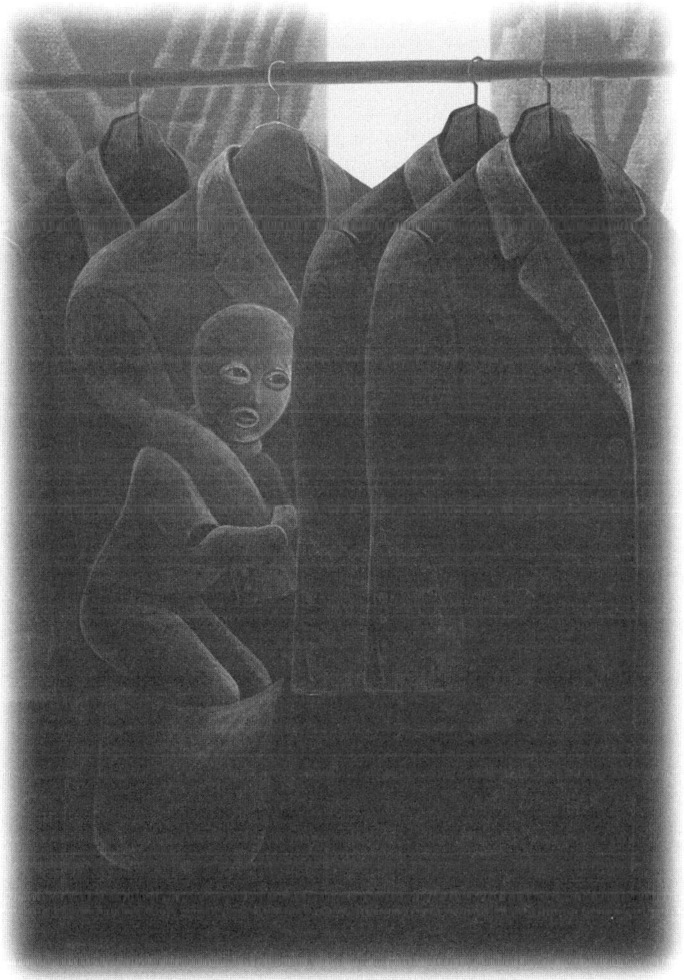

とつ、手でさわってみるのです。
ポケット小僧は、もう運のつきだと思いました。

いもむしごろごろ

ポケット小僧は、大外套のポケットに両足をいれ、外套にとりすがって息をころしていました。のっぽの初公は、押し入れのすみのほうから、ひとつひとつ服にさわりながら、こちらへ近づいてきます。

もう三つめまできました。もう二つめです。ああ、もうとなりまできました。こんどは外套の番です。

初公の長い手が、外套のえりのへんから、だんだん下へおりてきました。その手が、ポケット小僧の頭にさわりました。

まだ気がつきません。

長い手が、ポケット小僧の顔をなで、首から胸にさがってきました。

「ウッ」という、おしころした声が聞こえました。

とうとう気がついたようです。

ポケット小僧は、外套のポケットから足をぬきだして、ヒョイと、押し入れの床にとびおりました。

「うぬッ！　こんなとこにかくれていやがったなッ。」

初公は、両手をひろげてつかみかかってきます。

ポケット小僧は、その手のあいだをすりぬけて、あちこちと逃げまわる。それを、のっぽの初公が、息をきらせて追っかける。じつにふしぎな鬼ごっこです。

しかしポケット小僧は、もう逃げられません。相手は、自分の四倍もあるような大男です。いつかはつかまってしまうにきまっています。

つかまってしまったら、四十面相の前にひったてられ、いろいろと聞かれることでしょう。拷問されることでしょう。

拷問の苦しさに、このあいだからのことを、すっかり白状してしまうかもしれません。そうすれば、せっかく明智先生のたてられた計略が、まったくむだになってしまうのです。

それを思うと、ポケット小僧は、泣きだしたくなりました。カバンの中にかくれて、この奇面城へしのびこんでから、きょうまでの苦労が、すっかり水のあわになってしまうのです。

「ちくしょう、とうとうつかまえたぞッ！」

初公のうれしそうな声がひびきました。初公の長い手が、小僧の肩をがっしりつかんでしまったのです。ああ、いよいよ運のつきです。

ところがそのとき、思いもよらぬことがおこりました。がっしりとつかんでいる初公の手が、スウッと、ポケット小僧の肩から、はなれていったではありませんか。

ポケット小僧は、「オヤッ」と思って、初公の顔を見あげました。

すると、初公の口に、白いものがおしつけられているのが見えました。そのハンカチをまるめたような白いものを、初公の口におしつけているのは、べつの手でした。初公の手でなくて、ほかの人の手でした。初公の両手は、てむかいしようとはせず、だらんとさがっています。そのうちに、初公のからだぜんたいが、白いものを口におしつけている男は、初公をだいたまま床にひざをつき、初公も床にすわった形になりました。

そのとき、はじめてうしろの男の顔が見えたのです。それはジャッキーでした。

「アッ、先生！」

ポケット小僧は、おもわず叫んで、ハッとしたように口をおさえました。「先生！」などとよんだら、ジャッキーにばけている人の正体がわかってしまうからです。

「あぶないところだったね。ぼくは、きみがここへ逃げこむのを、むこうから見たので、

いそいで麻酔薬をしませたハンカチを持ってきて、こいつを眠らせたのだ。もうだいじょうぶだよ。」

「すみません。おれ、ゆだんしちゃって、すみません。」

ポケット小僧は、いかにももうしわけなさそうに、ピョコン、ピョコンと、二度おじぎをしました。

「いいんだよ。きみがこれまでにたてた手がらのことを思えば、なんでもないよ。それにしてもポケット小僧が、ほんとうにポケットの中へはいったのは、これがはじめてだろうね。はははは……」

ジャッキーはそういって、おかしそうに笑いましたが、すぐにまじめな顔になって、

「しかし、こいつは、このままにしてはおけない。眠りからさめて、四十面相にこのことをしゃべったら、たいへんだからね。やっぱり、あそこへほうりこんでしまわなければ。」といいました。あそことは、いったいどこなのでしょう。

もしかしたら、あの岩の橋をあげおろしする底も知れない谷間のことではないでしょうか。

そんなところへほうりこんだら、むろん命はありません。明智探偵や警察の人たちが、そんなむごたらしいことをするはずがありません。

では、いったい、どこへほうりこむのでしょうか。

ポケット小僧は、その場所をよく知っていました。というのは、ポケット小僧自身だったからです。

最初奇面城へしのびこんだとき、洞窟の中を歩きまわっていて、ふと、そこへまよいこんだのです。

そのとき小僧は、廊下のはずれにある、しぜんにできた岩のわれめのようなへもぐりこんでいました。もぐりこむと、穴はだんだん広くなり、十メートルほどいくと、そこに畳にして四畳半ほどもある、広い洞窟ができていました。懐中電灯で、あたりを照らしてみると、そこへはだれもはいったことがないらしいのです。入り口があまりせまいので、四十面相の部下たちは、この洞窟に気がつかなかったのでしょう。

ポケット小僧は、ジャッキーや五郎に、そのことを話しましたので、この洞窟をこんどの計略につかうことになり、夜中に、ソッと入り口の岩をけずって広くしたり、その穴にドアのかわりに岩のふたをつくって、外から見えぬようにしたり、いろいろ工夫をこらしたのです。

ジャッキーは廊下に出て、あたりにだれもいないことをたしかめてから、ぐったりとなった初公をせおって、その秘密の洞窟へといそぎました。ポケット小僧も、あとからつ

いていきます。

さいわい、だれにも見とがめられず、洞窟の入り口につきました。

まず、ジャッキーが岩のわれめから中へはいこんで、ドアがわりの石のふたをのけ、中から両手を出して、初公のからだを、ひきずりこむのでした。

中は広くなっているのですから、入り口さえとおってしまえば、あとはらくです。初公のからだを、ぐんぐんひきずって、おくの広い洞窟にきました。ポケット小僧は用意の懐中電灯を出して、そのへんを照らしています。

ああ、ごらんなさい。洞窟の中には、五人の男が、いもむしのように、ごろごろころがっているではありませんか。みんなさるぐつわをはめられているのです。ジャッキーは、初公にもおなじようにさるぐつわをはめ、手足をしばりました。五ひきのいもむしが、六ぴきにふえました。

ヘリコプターで五人の味方がはこばれ、四十面相の部下にばけているこの洞窟にほうりこまれていたのでしました。そのかわりに、ほんものの五人の部下が、この洞窟にほうりこまれていたのです。

この計略は、みんな明智探偵が考えだしたものです。警視庁はそれを助けて、刑事のうちの変装の名人たちを、奇面城におくったのです。

巨人の目

いま奇面城には、四十面相と美しい女の人のほかに、十人の部下がいるばかりです。そのうちの七人まで入れかわってしまったのですから、ほんものの部下はたった三人です。どんなことがあっても負ける心配はありません。

いよいよ、総攻撃のときがきたのです。

ジャッキーと五郎は、またヘリコプターをとばして、ふもとの町へいき、そこでT警察の人たちと、うちあわせをしました。

奇面城総攻撃は、あすの早朝ときまりました。東京の警視庁から中村警部がひきつれてきた九人の警官と、土地の警官隊四十人、あわせて五十人の警官隊が、山のふもとの四方から、奇面城めがけてのぼっていくことになったのです。

そんなおおげさなことをしなくても、ジャッキーと五郎と、五人のにせものの部下が、四十面相をとらえてしまえばよさそうに思われますが、相手は、なにしろ魔術師のような怪物ですから、どんなおくの手を用意しているかわかりません。奇面城の洞窟の中に、どんなしかけがしてあるかわかりません。それで、万にひとつも敵をとりにがさないように、

五十人の警官隊で、奇面城をとりかこむことにしたのです。ジャッキーをはじめ七人のにせものが、内部からこれにおうじてはたらくことはいうまでもありません。

さて、総攻撃の朝がきました。

洞窟のおくのりっぱな寝室で眠っていた四十面相は、ハッとしてベッドからとびだし、ちばやく金モールのかざりのついたビロードの服を着ると、となりの美術室にかけこんで、この黄金のイスにこしかけました。そして、ベルをならして、部下をよぶのでした。

入り口のドアをひらいて、ジャッキーがはいってきました。

「およびですか。」

「うん、非常ベルがなったのだ。ふもとに配置してある見はり番からの知らせだ。なにか一大事がおこったらしい。ひょっとしたら、警察の手がまわったかもしれない。いまに、ふもとから知らせにかけつけてくるだろうが、その前に、巨人の目からのぞいてみよう。きみもいっしょにくるがいい。」

四十面相はそういって、どんどん部屋を出ていきます。ジャッキーも、そのあとを追いましたが、にせもののかなしさに、巨人の目とはなんのことだか、それがどこにあるのか、さっぱりわかりません。

＊ 金の糸で作った組みひも。帽子や肩章などにつかう

145

金ぴかのビロードの服を着た四十面相は、洞窟のおくの小さなドアを、かぎでひらいて、中にはいりました。

ジャッキーの知らない部屋でした。いつもかぎがかかっているので、まだ、はいったことがないのです。

そこは一坪ほどのせまい部屋で、いっぽうの岩壁に、鉄ばしごがとりつけてありました。

四十面相は、それをかけのぼっていきます。ジャッキーも、あとからつづきました。四メートルほどのぼると、岩のおどり場があって、そこからまた鉄ばしごがつづいています。はしごのまわりは、だんだんせまくなり、しまいには、人間ひとりやっととおれるほどの岩のすきまになりましたが、鉄ばしごは、そこをまだまだ上のほうへ、つづいているのです。

ジャッキーは、四、五十メートルものぼったように感じました。すると、やっといきどまりました。そこは、一坪もないようなせまい岩の部屋で、いっぽうに大きなまるい窓がひらいて、明るい光がさしこんでいました。

その窓の横の岩の棚の上に、大きな双眼鏡がのっています。四十面相は、それをとって目にあてると、まるい窓の外をながめました。

146

ジャッキーも、その窓からのぞいてみましたが、あまりの高さに、ぐらぐらッとめまいがしました。奇面城のまわりの森が、はるか遠くのほうへつづいています。すぐ下を見ると、広っぱにとまっているヘリコプターが、おもちゃのように小さく見えるのです。窓といっても、べつにガラス戸がはまっているわけではありません。ただ、さしわたし一メートルほどのまるい穴が、ぽっかりとひらいているだけなのです。うっかりすると、そこから下へ落ちそうです。目もくらむような高さですから、ここから落ちたら、むろん命はありません。

ああ、わかりました。このまるい窓は、奇面城の巨人のひとみだったのです。秘密のところだけ穴があいていて、遠方を見はらす物見の窓になっていたのです。

「あ、あすこへやってきた。三番見はり小屋の三吉だな。なにか重大な知らせを持ってきたのにちがいない。」

四十面相がそういって、いままでのぞいていた双眼鏡を、ジャッキーにわたしました。

ジャッキーはそれを目にあてて、三吉という男が、森の中の細道をかけあがってくるのを見ました。

警官のすがたは見えないかと、ほうぼうさがしましたが、まだ味方は、近くまできていないようです。

147

三吉(さんきち)は、こちらを見あげて、手をふりました。

ジャッキーは、三吉の立場になって、この巨人(きょじん)の目からのぞいているすがたを、見つけたのでしょう。

想像(そうぞう)してみました。

巨大(きょだい)な岩の顔(かお)の、巨大な目のひとみの中に、双眼鏡(そうがんきょう)を手にした四十面相(めんそう)の上半身(じょうはんしん)が見えるのです。金ぴかのビロードの服(ふく)を着た、どこかの国の王さまのような四十面相が見えるのです。なんというふしぎな光景(こうけい)でしょう。

「よしッ、下へおりて、三吉の話を聞こう。」

四十面相はそういって、鉄(てつ)ばしごをおりはじめました。まっすぐに立ったはしごですから、おりるほうがむずかしいのです。

ふたりが、やっと下までおりたとき、そこへ三吉がかけつけてきました。

「かしら、たいへんだ。警官隊(けいかんたい)が、四方(しほう)からのぼってきます。ほかの見(み)はり小屋(ごや)からも、知らせがありました。ぜんたいでは五、六十人、ひょっとすると百人もいるかもしれません。」

三吉は、息(いき)をきらせて報告(ほうこく)しました。

「やっぱり、そうだったか。よしッ、おまえたちは、みんな警官隊とたたかうのだ。ピス

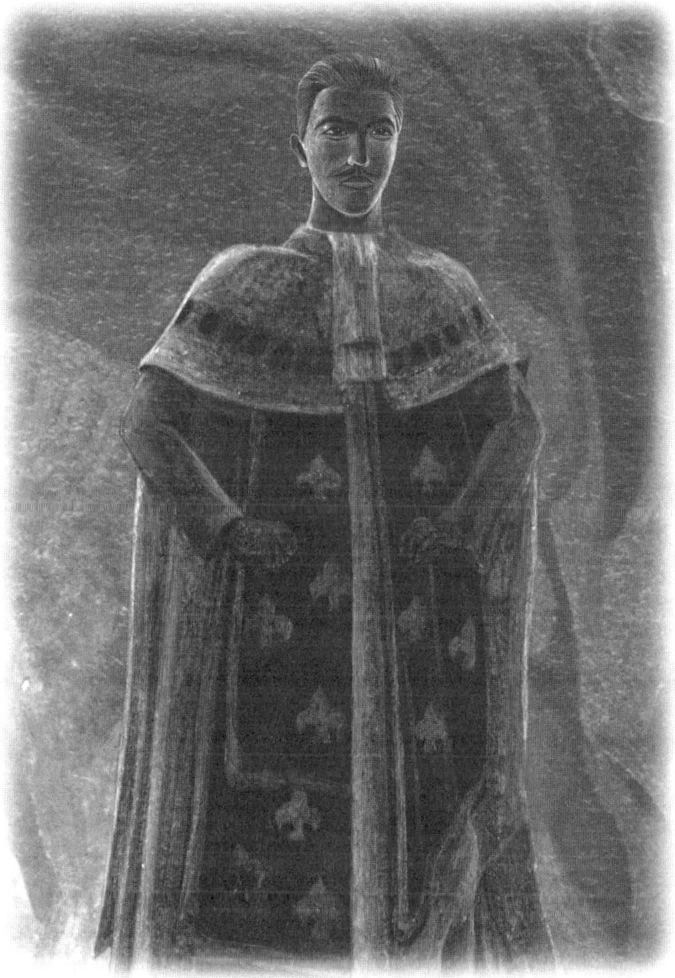

トルは空にむけてうて。人を殺しちゃいけない。わかったか。おまえたち、一番から六番までの見はり小屋の人数をあわせると、三十人はいるはずだ。山のことは、おまえたちのほうがよく知っている。相手は、ふなれな町のやつらだ。うまく知恵をはたらかせて、くいとめるんだ。」

四十面相は、そう命令して三吉を帰しました。

「さあ、ジャッキー、ヘリコプターだ。あれに乗って、もっと山おくへかくれるんだ。しっかりやってくれッ。」

四十面相とジャッキーは、洞窟の廊下をかけだして、あの深い谷にかかっている大岩のつり橋をわたり、巨人の顔の前の広っぱに出ました。ヘリコプターは、すぐむこうに見えています。

最後の手段

四十面相とジャッキーとは、ヘリコプターの操縦室へ乗りこみました。このヘリコプターは、いつでも出発の用意ができているのです。

ジャッキーは、スターターのクラッチをいれました。ぶるんぶるんぶるん。エンジンが

動き、プロペラがまわりはじめました。

しかし、なんだかへんです。エンジンの音が、いつもとちがっています。プロペラのまわりかたも、みょうにいきおいがないのです。

ジャッキーは機械にとりついて、いっしょうけんめいにやっていましたが、やがて、あきらめたように、エンジンをとめてしまいました。

「かしら、だめです。」

「エッ、こしょうだって。どこがこしょうか、わかっているのか。」

「わかっていますが、きゅうにはなおりません。」

「どのくらいかかるんだ。」

「三時間はかかりますね。」

「ちくしょうッ。しかたがない。おりよう。そして、べつの手だてを考えるんだ。」

四十面相は、ヘリコプターからとびおりて、巨人の顔のほうへいそぎました。ジャッキーも、あとからついていきます。

巨人の顔の首のところに、いくつも岩穴がならんでいますが、そのひとつが、奇面城の門番の、三びきの虎の部屋になっているのです。

べつに鉄棒がはめくあるわけではありません。四十面相や部下のものには、よくなれて

いるので、はなし飼いにしてあるのです。
　その虎の岩穴へはいってみますと、二ひきの大虎は、ぐったりと寝そべったまま、四十面相が声をかけても、知らん顔をしています。
　いつかポケット小僧が助けてやった、あのかわいらしい子どもの虎だけが、かなしそうに、鼻をくんくんならしながら、二ひきの大虎のまわりを、ぐるぐるまわっているのです。
「眠っているのかな。いや、なんだかへんだぞ。」
　四十面相は、ふしぎそうにつぶやいて、大虎のそばに近づくと、そのからだにさわってみました。
「アッ、つめたくなっている。死んでいるんだ。いったいどうして……」
　いそいで、もう一ぴきのほうをしらべましたが、これもつめたくなっています。
「病気ではない。病気で二ひきとも、いっぺんに死ぬなんてことは考えられない。鉄砲で前に、息がたえたらしいのです。
　四十面相は、しゃがんで、一ぴきの虎の口をしらべました。
「アッ、やっぱりそうだ。血だッ。血をはいている。毒をのまされたのにちがいない。」
　二ひきとも、口と鼻から血をたらしていました。たしかに毒殺されたのです。

152

四十面相は、そこにつっ立ったまま、じっと腕組みをして考えていましたが、ハッとしたように目をひからせました。
「いったい、これはどうしたわけだ。だれかが虎を毒殺した。だが、おれの部下のほかに、ここへ近づいたものはないはずだ。ジャッキー、なんだか、きみの悪いことがおこったぞ。ゆだんはできない。いよいよ、最後の手段をとるほかはないようだ。」
　四十面相がそういって、岩穴の外へ出たとき、遠くのほうでピストルをうちあう音がとどろきました。警官隊と、四十面相の部下の見はり人たちのたたかいが、はじまっているのです。
「ワアッ。ワアッ。」
という、おおぜいの声が聞こえてきます。そして、それが、だんだんこちらへ近づいてくるのです。どうも四十面相の部下たちの旗色が悪いようです。
　そのとき四十面相が、「アッ」といって、広っぱのむこうの森のほうを見つめました。警官です。そこへ、ぽっつりと、制服警官のすがたがあらわれたのです。
「ワアッ……」
という声がしたかと思うと、四十面相の部下らしい男が、うしろからとびだして警官にくみつきました。

警官は、パッと腰を落とし首をさげて、その男を、ドウッと前へなげつけました。

そして、ねじあっているうちに、ふたりいっしょにたおれ、くんずほぐれつの格闘になりました。

男はすぐにおきあがって、こんどは前からくみついてきます。

森の中からもうひとり、制服の警官がとびだしてきたのです。そして、くみあっているころがっている四十面相の部下の上に、のしかかっていきました。

とうとう、四十面相の部下は、ふたりの警官におさえられ、ぽかぽかと、なぐられています。

四十面相が、おもわず叫びました。
「アッ、いけない。あたらしい敵があらわれたぞ。」

それを見ると、こちらの四十面相は、ヒョイとしゃがんで、そこに落ちていた石ころを、いくつか拾ったかとおもうと、自分の部下の上に馬乗りになっている警官にむかって、はっしとばかりなげつけました。

石は警官の肩にあたり、「アッ」と叫んで、たおれそうになります。つづいて第二弾。ピュウッとうなって、もうひとりの警官の腕に命中しました。

警官たちは、やっと、こちらの敵に気がつきました。見ると、金モールのかざりのある

154

王さまのような服を着ています。
「さては、あいつが四十面相だな。」
と、さとったらしく、ふたりとも、恐ろしいいきおいで、こちらへかけだしてきました。
「いけないッ、たいきゃくだッ」
四十面相は、手にのこっていた石ころを、警官の正面にたたきつけておいて、そのまま洞窟の入り口へかけだしました。
「ジャッキー、はやく逃げるんだッ。そして、橋を落としてしまえッ。」
ジャッキーもかけだしました。洞窟にかけこんで、岩の橋をわたりました。
「さあ、この橋を落としてしまえッ」
四十面相が叫びました。しかし、にせもののジャッキーは、どうすれば橋が落ちるのかわかりません。うろうろしていると、四十面相がたまりかねて、どこかのかくしボタンをおしました。
ダダダダダダダダ……ン。
耳もろうするばかりの大音響をたてて、あの大きな岩の橋が、谷底へ落ちていったのです。
いざというときには、くさりがはずれて、大岩が谷底へ落ちるしかけになっていたので

155

しょう。

谷は何十メートルとも知れない深さです。そのはるか下に川が流れているらしく、ごうごうという水音が聞こえています。

谷の幅は三メートル。走り幅とびの選手ならとびこせるかもしれませんが、ふつうの人には、とてもとべるものではありません。ちょっとでもまちがえば、深い谷底に落ちて、命をうしなうことがわかっているのですから、選手だって、ここをとぶ気にはなれないかもしれません。

四十面相は、とうとう最後の手段をとりました。洞窟の中と外との連絡を、まったくたちきってしまったのです。

こうすれば、外からせめこむことは、ぜったいにできませんから、いちおう安心ですが、そのかわり、四十面相と、あの美しい女の人と十人の部下は、洞窟の中にとじこめられて、いつまでも外へ出ることができないのです。そのうちに、食糧がなくなってくるでしょう。

しかし、どこからも、食糧をはこぶ道はありません。ひと月もしないうちに、みんな、うえ死にをしてしまうかもしれないのです。

にせのジャッキーや、五郎や、五人のにせものの部下や、ポケット小僧までも、四十面相と運命をともにして、うえ死にしなければならないのでしょうか。

警察官の勝利

警官隊は、いくてにもわかれて、四十面相の部下たちとたたかいながら、奇面城めがけて進んできました。

総指揮官は警視庁の中村警部です。そのそばには、三名の警官がついていましたが、もうひとり、学生服の少年のすがたが見えます。明智探偵の助手の小林少年です。小林君は、すばしっこくとびまわって、中村警部の命令を、警官たちにつたえるやくめをひきうけているようでした。

「みんな、木の幹に、ひっくくってしまえ。」

中村警部から命令が出ました。警官たちが大声で、つぎからつぎへとそれをつたえます。警官のほうが、倍にちかい人数ですから、ふたりでひとりをやっつければいいのです。

四十面相の部下を、ひとりずつとらえて、用意の細引きで、つぎからつぎと、てごろの木の幹にしばりつけていくのです。

そして、一時間ほどたたかっているうちに、とうとう四十面相の三十人の部下ぜんぶを、森の中の幹にしばりつけてしまいました。警官隊の勝利です。

＊麻で作ったじょうぶで編い縄

五十人の警官たちは、どっと奇面城の前におしよせました。中には負傷したものも数名ありましたが、そういう人たちは、友だちの警官が、肩にかつぐようにして、つれてきたのです。

　巨人の顔の下の入り口に近づいていきますと、中からふたりの警官がとびだしてきました。さいしょ四十面相を追っかけて、石をなげつけられた警官たちです。

「だめです。敵は橋を落としてしまいました。底も見えない深い谷にかかっている石の橋です。それを落としてしまったのです。われわれは奇面城のおくへはいることができません。」

　とびだしてきた警官のひとりが、報告しました。

　中村警部は、数名の警官をつれて、橋の落ちたところまで、はいってみました。いかにも、恐ろしく深い谷です。幅は三メートルぐらいですが、のぞいてみると、下はまっ暗で、はるか底のほうから、ごうごうという水音が聞こえてきます。谷底には川が流れているのです。

　中村警部は、しばらく考えていましたが、やがて、決心したようにうなずきました。

「よしッ、橋をかけるんだ。森の中のてごろの杉の木を二本きりたおして、枝をはらってここへ持ってくるんだ。長さはこの谷の幅の倍くらいあるほうがいい。六メートルぐらい

「この命令が、洞窟の外につたえられ、警官隊の中の十人あまりが、木をきりたおすために、森のほうへかけだしていきました。

洞窟のおくには、四十面相が九人の部下にかこまれて、入り口のほうを見ていました。あの美しい女の人は、どこかの部屋にかくれているのでしょう。ここにはすがたが見えません。

谷のところから十メートルもおくにいるのですが、中村警部の命令する声が、よく聞こえてきました。

「杉の丸太で、あそこへ、橋をかけるつもりらしいですね。」

ジャッキーが、かしらの顔を見ていいました。

「うん、こっちは、それをふせぐんだ。物置きに、まさかりがあったはずだ。あれを持ってきて、橋をかけようとしたら、たたき落としてしまえ。」

四十面相が命令しました。五郎がいそいで物置きへ走っていって、大きなまさかりをか

つぎだしてきました。

　三十分もすると、警官たちは六メートルほどの杉の木を二本たおして、枝をきりはらい、おおぜいでそれをかついで洞窟の中へやってきました。

「五、六人で、根もとのほうをしっかり持って、むこう側へたおすんだ。二本わたせば、その上をはってとおることができる。」

　中村警部のさしずで、一本の木に六人ずつの警官がとりついて、かけ声いさましく、谷のむこう側へわたそうとしました。

　こちらは四十面相。いまにも二本の杉丸太がわたされそうになったので、いそいで命令をくだしました。

「さあ、いまだ。谷の岸までいって、まさかりで杉の木をたたき落とすのだッ。」

　ところが、それを聞いても、まさかりを持った五郎は、にやにや笑っているばかりで、動くようすがありません。

「おいッ、五郎、どうしたんだ。おまえ、警官のピストルがこわいのかッ」。

　四十面相は、やっきとなって、どなりつけました。しかし、五郎は、あいかわらず、に

「それじゃ、ジャッキー、おまえがやれ。五郎、そのまさかりをジャッキーにわたすんだッ。」

ジャッキーもへんじをしません。やっぱり、にやにや笑っているのです。

「ええ、いくじのないやつらだ。それじゃあ、おれがたたき落としてやる。さあ、まさかりをこっちへよこせ。」

四十面相が、五郎のほうへ近よろうとしますと、その前へジャッキーが立ちふさがって、とおせんぼうをしました。

「こら、なにをするんだ。ジャッキー、おまえはまさか……」

「そうです。なにをするのです。」

ジャッキーが腕組みをして、四十面相をぐっとにらみつけました。

「エ、なんだと。おれのじゃまをするというのかッ。きさま、おれの部下じゃないか。なんという口をきくのだ。」

ジャッキーは、なにも答えないで、じっとこちらをにらみつけているのです。

四十面相は、ふしぎそうにジャッキーの顔を見つめていましたが、なにを思ったのか、サッと顔色がかわりました。

161

「やっ、きさま、ジャッキーではないのだな。だれだッ。……もしや、もしや……」
「ハハハハ……、やっと気がついたね。そうだよ。ぼくは明智小五郎だ。四十面相、とう、ほんとうのかくれ家を見つけられてしまったねえ。」
「おいッ。そのほかのやつらも、なにをぼんやりしているのだ。こいつは明智小五郎だぞ。なぜ、つかまえないのだッ。」
四十面相は、まわりに立っている部下たちを、どなりつけました。
「ハハハハ……。きみのほんとうの部下は、この中にふたりしかいやしないよ。あとはみんな警視庁の刑事諸君だ。変装のうまい刑事をよりすぐって、きみの部下といれかわってしまったのだよ。」
明智が説明しました。
「アッ、それじゃあ、五郎もにせものだなッ。きさまと五郎とで、ヘリコプターをとばして、ふもとの町から、替え玉をつれてきたんだなッ。」
「そのとおり。きょう、ヘリコプターをとべないようにしておいたのもぼくだし、二ひきの虎を眠らせたのもぼくだよ。そうして、きみをつかまえる用意がすっかりできていたのだ。……おお、見たまえ。警官隊が橋をかけて、こちらへわたってきた。四十面相！　きみはもう、どうすることもできないのだッ。」

162

明智が、とどめをさすように叫びました。

最後の切りふだ

あの深い谷にわたされた二本の杉の木の上を、よつんばいになって、警官たちがつぎつぎとこちらへわたってきます。さきに立つ十人ほどは、もう谷のこちら側に立って、ピストルをかまえながらしずかに近づいてくるのです。

「ちくしょう。よくも、おれをだましたな。だが、ほんとうのおれの部下はどこにいるんだ。おれの味方は、どこにいるんだ。」

「ハハハ……。ぼくたち、にせものは七人。ほんものは、たったふたりしかのこっていないのだ。とてもかないっこないと、そこのすみで、ぶるぶるふるえているよ。」

明智が指さしたすみっこに、四十面相のコックともうひとりの若い男が、青い顔をして、しょんぼりと立っていました。

「よしッ、いよいよ、おれの最後がきたようだな。おれは、血を見るのがきらいだが、こうなったらしかたがない。かくごしろッ。みな殺しだぞッ。」

四十面相は、いきなり右と左のズボンのポケットから、一丁ずつピストルをとりだし、

「さあ、ぶっぱなすぞッ……」

両手でそれをかまえました。

カチッ、カチッと、両方のピストルの引き金をひきました。どうしたわけか、たまがとびだしません。また、カチッ、カチッ……カチッ、カチッ、カチッ……だめです。カチッ、カチッというばかりです。

「ハハハハ……。その二丁のピストルには、たまは一発もはいっていないよ。ぼくが、ピストルのたまをぬくのをわすれているはずじゃないか。うかつだと思うのかね。きみは、いつものぼくのやりくちをよく知っているはずじゃないか。ハハハハ……」

それを聞くと、四十面相の顔が、むらさき色になりました。

「ちくしょう。いよいよ、おれの力を見せるときがきたなッ。さあ、つかまえるならつかまえてみろッ。」

彼はそう叫ぶと、二丁のピストルをなげつけておいて、パッと走りだしました。恐ろしい速さです。

ジャッキーも五郎も、そのほかのにせの部下たちも、それから谷をわたってきた制服の警官たちも、四十面相のあとを追ってかけだしました。

四十面相は、まず自分の部屋にとびこむと、あの美しい女の人の手をひいて、べつのド

アからかけだし、おくへおくへと走っていきます。女の人は白いスカートのすそをみだして、いまにもたおれそうに見えます。

廊下が枝道になって、岩の階段が下へおりていきます。四十面相と女の人は、そこをかけおりました。岩のトンネルのようなところをとおって、八畳ぐらいの洞窟に出ました。

明智探偵たちは、四十面相につづいて、その洞窟にはいりましたが、ここには電灯がついていないので、まっ暗です。みんなが懐中電灯をつけようかと思っていますと、洞窟の中が、パッと明るくなりました。

空中にたいまつがもえているのです。赤いほのおがめらめらとのぼって、洞窟の天井をなめています。それは、四十面相が、一本のたいまつに火をつけて、高くささげているのでした。白衣の女の人は、四十面相の左手にかかえられて、やっと立っているように見えます。

「明智先生、それから警視庁の先生たち、みんなそこへやってきたね。ワハハハハ……。いいか、よく見ろ。ここにたるが三つならんでいる。ほら、大きなたるが三つだ。この中に、なにがはいっていると思う。……火薬だよ。このたいまつをなげこめば、いちどに爆発するんだ。

この部屋は、おれの美術室の真下なんだ。あそこにかざってある何億円の美術品が、

こっぱみじんになるのだ。いや、そればかりではない。この岩の天井が落ちて、きみたちは、ひとりのこらず死んでしまうのだ。ワハハハ……。ゆかい、ゆかい。どうだ、おれの最後の切りふだがわかったかッ｡」

四十面相は、勝ちほこったように笑いながら、手に持ったたいまつを、火薬のたるの上で、むちゃくちゃにふりまわしているのです。

火の粉がたるの中へ落ちたら、たちまち爆発がおこるでしょう。そして洞窟そのものが、こっぱみじんになり、人間はみんな死んでしまうのです。

そのときです。

闇の中から、四十面相とはちがう、みょうな笑い声がひびいてきました。

「ワハハハハ……。ワハハハ……」

それを聞くと、四十面相は、ぎょっとしたように、キョロキョロとあたりを見まわしました。

「やい、そこで笑っているのは、だれだッ？　なにがおかしいのだッ」

「ぼくだよ、明智だよ。きみのいきごみがあんまりおおげさなので、ついおかしくなったのさ。おい、ポケット君、もういいから、出てきたまえ｡」

明智がよびますと、三つならんだたるのうしろから、まっ黒な小さい男がチョコチョコ

166

とかけだしてきました。

明智は、その小さい男をだくようにして、

「おお、ポケット小僧君。きみはあの三つのたるに、どういうことをしたか、いってごらん。」

「先生、もう明智先生といってもいいのですね。ぼくは先生の命令で、バケツに水をいっぱいいれて、なんどもここへはこびました。そしてその水を、いっぱいになるまで、二つのたるにいれました。」

ポケット小僧のことばに、四十面相はハッとして、ふたのとってある三つのたるに、つぎつぎに手をいれてみました。どのたるも、火薬の上まで、水がいっぱいです。

「ワハハハ……。どうだね、火薬がこう水びたしになってしまっては、いくらたいまつをなげこんでも、パチッともいやしないぜ、気のどくだが、きみの運のつきだよ。最後の切りふだがだめになってしまったのだから、あとは手錠をはめられるばかりだね。」

明智のことばが、おわるかおわらぬうちに、もえさかるたいまつが、パッととんできました。明智がとっさに体をかわしたので、たいまつはうしろの岩壁にあたって、火花をちらしました。

たいまつのつぎにとびついてきたのは、人間のからだでした。四十面相が、うらみかさ

なる明智探偵にくみついてきたのです。

ふいをつかれて明智はたおれ、四十面相は、その上に馬乗りになりました。

しかし、四十面相の味方は、かよわい女の人ひとり。明智のほうには、たくさんの警官がついています。四十面相は、一度は馬乗りになったものの、すぐおしたおされて、手錠をはめられてしまいました。

手錠をはめたのは、警官たちのうしろから出てきた中村警部でした。そして、そのそばには、学生服の小林少年が、にこにこしながらつきそっていました。

「おお、中村君、小林もよくきてくれた。とうとう、四十面相をとらえることができたよ。」

明智探偵は、中村警部と小林少年に両手をのばして、あくしゅしました。

「小林さん、ぼくここにいるよ。」

黒いシャツ、黒いてぶくろ、黒い靴下、すっぽりかぶる黒い覆面、全身まっ黒な小さい男が、つかつかと小林少年の前に進んで、その手をにぎりました。

「おお、ポケット小僧、きみはえらいねえ。この奇面城を発見したのも、火薬に水をかけて四十面相をこうさんさせたのも、みんなきみの手がらだからねえ。」

小林少年はポケット小僧の手をにぎりかえして、さもなつかしそうにいうのでした。

168

「おれ、うれしくってたまらないよ。明智先生が四十面相に勝ったんだ。そして、四十面相がつかまってしまったんだ。」

ポケット小僧は、そこまでいうと、感きわまったように両手をあげました。

「明智先生、ばんざあい。小林団長、ばんざあい……」

すると、小林少年も、目に涙を浮かべながら、これにこたえて叫ぶのでした。

「少年探偵団、チンピラ隊、ばんざあい！」

解説

人気シリーズは子孫を生む

新保博久（ミステリー評論家）

みなさんは『鬼平犯科帳』のことを聞いたことがあるでしょう。池波正太郎の原作は読んでいなくとも、テレビなどでおなじみですね。ところで、もし今から百十年以上も前（一八八七年）、英国でコナン・ドイルがシャーロック・ホームズを創造しなかったら、この『鬼平犯科帳』も存在しなかっただろうと言うと、ふしぎに思いますか？ 捕物帳という江戸探偵物語のスタイルを考えついた作家は岡本綺堂ですが、大正六（一九一七）年、その『半七捕物帳』を書きはじめたのは、当時三冊まで出ていたシャーロック・ホームズの短編集を英語で読んで、自分でも似たようなものを作りたくなったからだといいます。それから十年ほど書き続けて、もう打ち切りにしようと中断させたところへ、野村胡堂が銭形平次を誕生させました（昭和六＝一九三一年）。

先輩の綺堂がホームズをお手本にしたので、もっと陽気なキャラクターにしたいと、銭形平次は怪盗アルセーヌ・ルパンを善人にしたものをと考えたのだそうです。これは「オール讀物」に毎月、読み切りで連載されて、半七以上の人気を博し、四百編近くも書かれました。

銭形平次が退場してから十年、新たにそれに代わるような人気シリーズを育てたいという、「オール讀物」編集部の期待にこたえて登場したのが『鬼平犯科帳』の長谷川平蔵です。しょっちゅう罪人を見のがしてやる「仏の銭形」に対して、「鬼の平蔵」というところでしょう。

このように、すぐれたシリーズは、その影響で別な作家にまた新たなシリーズを書かせ、さらに別なシリーズに受け継がれてゆくものなのです。ものまねから始まる場合も、わざと先人とは逆のコースをとろうとするのも、先輩作品を意識していることには変わりありません。どちらにしても、やがて前例からの影響を脱して、その作者独特の持ち味を生かせたものだけが、人気作品として読み継がれてゆくのです。

作品が書かれたころの日比谷公園（昭和33年）

怪人二十面相も、最初はフランスのモーリス・ルブランが生んだ怪盗ルパンをお手本にしたことは言うまでもありません。本書『奇面城の秘密』という題名も、ルパンものの名作『奇巌城』（一九〇九年）を連想させます。「少年探偵」シリーズには『虎の牙』という、ルブラン作品（一九二一年）と同名の一巻がすでにありますが、この全集では混乱しないよう『地底の魔術王』と改題されています。

『奇面城の秘密』と『奇巌城』ではストーリーはまったく違いますが、奇面城が怪人四十面相の隠れ家であるように、奇巌城もルパンが盗んだ美術品を集めて、結婚生活を送るつもりでいた場所でした。珍しく四十面相に連れ添う女性が登場するのも、それを意識したのかもしれません。

『奇巌城』でルパンを追いつめるのは、宿敵ガニマール警部よりも、コナン・ドイルの名探偵を借りてきたホームズよりも（むしろホームズは大失態を演じます）、ルパン・シリーズでこの一作だけに登場する天才高校生でした。

『奇面城の秘密』でも後半、チンピラ別働隊のポケット小僧が、明智小五郎や小林団長以

奇面城があったという甲武信岳

上に大活躍します。『奇面城の秘密』は一九五八年の一年間、「少年クラブ」に連載されましたが、その前年「少女クラブ」に連載された『魔法人形』でポケット小僧が初登場したときは、探偵団の少女団員マユミを補佐する役どころにすぎませんでした。

「少年探偵」シリーズのフランチャイズだった雑誌「少年」では、いつも小林少年が立て役者だったので、他の雑誌に連載する場合は、ほかの団員のほうを活躍させて、変化をつけようとしたのかもしれません。こういう細かな工夫も、シリーズを読み続けて飽きさせないものにしているのでしょう。しかしポケット小僧は、小林少年ほど頭は切れませんが、あだ名のとおり、どこにでももぐりこめる小柄さと機敏さで、「少年」連載をふくめてシリーズ後期の作品に欠かせないキャラクターに育ちました。

ところで、さっき、すぐれたシリーズはまた新しいシリーズを生むと申しました。しかし「少年探偵」シリーズだけは、多くの作家が似たようなものを書きましたが、どれも本家（け）に対抗できるほどには至（いた）らなかったのです。それだけこのシリーズがすばらしかったからであり、また、やがて読者は卒業して、おとな向きの小説を読むようになっていき、代わりになるものが必要なかったからでしょう。その下の子どもたちにも、「少年探偵」があればじゅうぶんだったのです。だから、こうして現在も読（よ）み継（つ）がれているわけです。

編集方針について

一　第二次世界大戦前の作品については、旧仮名づかいを現代仮名づかいに改めました。

二　漢字の中で、少年少女の読者にむずかしいと思われるものは、ひらがなに改めました。

三　少年少女の読者には理解しにくい事柄や単語については、各ページの欄外に注（説明文）をつけました。

四　原作を重んじて編集しましたが、身体障害や職業にかかわる不適切な表現については、一部表現を変えたり、けずったりしたところがあります。

五　『少年探偵・江戸川乱歩全集』（ポプラ社刊）をもとに、作品が掲載された雑誌の文章とも照らし合わせて、できるだけ発表当時の作品が理解できるように心がけました。

以上の事柄は、著作権継承者である平井隆太郎氏のご了承を得ました。

ポプラ社編集部

編集委員・平井隆太郎　砂田弘　秋山憲司

本書は1999年2月ポプラ社から刊行
された作品を文庫版にしたものです。

文庫版 少年探偵・江戸川乱歩　第18巻

奇面城の秘密
きめんじょう　ひみつ

発行　2005年2月　第1刷
　　　2021年10月　第11刷
作家　江戸川乱歩
えどがわらんぽ
装丁・画家　藤田新策
ふじたしんさく
発行者　千葉均
発行所　株式会社ポプラ社
東京都千代田区麹町4-2-6　8・9F　〒102-8519
ホームページ　www.poplar.co.jp
印刷・製本　図書印刷株式会社

落丁、乱丁本はお取り替えいたします。
電話（0120-666-553）または、ホームページ（www.poplar.co.jp）
のお問い合わせ一覧よりご連絡ください。
※電話の受付時間は、月〜金曜日10時〜17時です（祝日・休日は除く）。
読者の皆様からのお便りをお待ちしております。
いただいたお便りは著者にお渡しいたします。
本書のコピー、スキャン、デジタル化等の無断複製は
著作権法上での例外を除き禁じられています。
本書を代行業者等の第三者に依頼してスキャンやデジタル化することは、
たとえ個人や家庭内での利用であっても著作権法上認められておりません。

N.D.C.913　174p　18cm　ISBN978-4-591-08429-8
Printed in Japan　ⓒ　藤田新策　2005

P8005018

文庫版 少年探偵・江戸川乱歩 全26巻

怪人二十面相と名探偵明智小五郎、少年探偵団との息づまる推理対決！

1. 怪人二十面相
2. 少年探偵団
3. 妖怪博士
4. 大金塊
5. 青銅の魔人
6. 地底の魔術王
7. 透明怪人
8. 怪奇四十面相
9. 宇宙怪人
10. 鉄塔王国の恐怖
11. 灰色の巨人
12. 海底の魔術師
13. 黄金豹
14. 魔法博士
15. サーカスの怪人
16. 魔人ゴング
17. 魔法人形
18. 奇面城の秘密
19. 夜光人間
20. 搭上の奇術師
21. 鉄人Q
22. 仮面の恐怖王
23. 電人M
24. 二十面相の呪い
25. 空飛ぶ二十面相
26. 黄金の怪獣